Wakefield Press

•

Forever Shores

In 1990, with his wife, Mariann, Peter McNamara steered his genre magazine *Aphelion Publications* (1985–1987) towards book publishing. As a specialty genre publisher, Aphelion went on to produce fourteen trade paperbacks, including the highly successful anthology *Alien Shores*. Through his steerage as the Convenor of the Aurealis Awards, Peter has brought Australian authors in the science fiction, fantasy and horror genres to national as well as international acclaim. The Mac Award honours his outstanding contributions to the genre in Australia. He lives, with Mariann, on the edge of Adelaide's CBD.

Margaret Winch lives in the Adelaide Hills. She earned her literary stripes lecturing and tutoring engineering and technology students in Literature and Society at South Australia's Institute of Technology, after completing a History honours thesis in the same field. Margaret writes and reads extensively across mainstream and many more isolated genres, and Peter looks to her for advice and direction. Their friendship goes back more than 30 years, during which time they have exchanged (not always agreeably) a great variety of literary advice and opinion.

Forever Shores

Edited by

PETER McNAMARA
and MARGARET WINCH

Wakefield
Press

Wakefield Press in association with Aphelion Publications
1 The Parade West
Kent Town
South Australia 5067
www.wakefieldpress.com.au

First published 2003
Copyright in this collection © Peter McNamara and Margaret Winch, 2003
Copyright in the stories remains with their authors

Edited by Gina Inverarity
Cover painting by Conny Valentine
Cover designed by Liz Nicholson, design BITE
Designed and typeset by Clinton Ellicott, Wakefield Press
Printed and bound by Hyde Park Press

National Library of Australia
Cataloguing-in-publication entry

Forever shores: fiction of the fantastic.
ISBN 1 86254 622 3.
1. Science fiction, Australian. 2. Fantasy fiction, Australian.
I. McNamara, Peter, 1947–   . II. Winch, Margaret, 1945–   .

A823.087608

for Jack

*who carried a brightly burning torch
to the New Land*

and in memory of George

*whose unstinting professionalism
and great generosity
prepared the way.*

*My special thanks go to my wife, Mariann, and son, Patrick,
my extraordinary family, whose vitality and resolve got me through
the difficulties of assembling this anthology*

*... and to my co-editor, Margaret, whose clear and precise
assessments covered for my own tardiness and inadequacy.*
Peter McNamara

Contents

•

Acknowledgements

•

'Rain Season' by Leanne Frahm was first published in *Eidolon #27* (Eidolon Publications 1998); 'The Boy Who Didn't Yearn' by Margo Lanagan was first published in *White Time* (Allen & Unwin 2000); 'The Sword of God' by Russell Blackford was first published in *Dreamweavers* (Penguin 1996); 'Stone Gift' by Robert N. Stephenson was first published in *Tessellations* (eds Kain Masson and Jason Blechley 2000); 'The Phoenix' by Isobelle Carmody was first published in *Green Monkey Dreams* (Penguin/Viking 1996).

Thanks go to Russell Blackford, Van Ikin and Sean McMullen, editors of *Strange Constellations* (Greenwood Press 1999); Paul Collins, Steven Paulsen and Sean McMullen, editors of the *MUP Encyclopedia of Science Fiction and Fantasy* (Melbourne University Press 1998); and Dirk Strasser, Stephen Higgins and Keith Stevenson, editors of *Aurealis*, for the use of biographical and archival detail.

Introduction

•

Margaret Winch

Fantasy *1. imagination unrestrained by reality. 2. Psychol. a sequence of more or less pleasant mental images, usually fulfilling a need not gratified in the real world.*

Reality is what we humans as social animals have agreed (through conditioning, osmosis and social control) to call reality; it is the world-taken-for-granted (Berger 1969). Different societies/cultures adopt a consensual stance on different realities and therefore display different fantasies. Fantasy has always been with us, its nature remains the same, but its specific examples change over time and place, as the definition of reality changes. To identify the themes of popular fantasy is to reveal the underbelly of a social culture, its deepest hopes and darkest fears.

Western reality, since the Age of the Enlightenment, has relied on rationalism and scientific 'fact'. Reality in this definition is what is able to be tested by methods appropriate to the dominant scientific paradigm – observable, replicable and therefore suscep-tible to consensus. What is not available to such testing is fantasy (other than real). Fantasy is the body of beliefs, ideas, experiences, images that cannot be explained or accounted for by science or logic. It is not 'evidence based' in the sense that science requires. It posits a different world entirely.

1

The twentieth century mined deep veins of fantasy that revealed the extent of disillusionment with the dominant reality – here we can acknowledge the great dystopian fantasies, among them *Brave New World* and *Animal Farm*. But the Age of Aquarius saw a different response, an escape from the horrors and complexities of the twentieth century and a return to simpler heroic values and magic. The release of *The Lord of the Rings* in the 1960s coincided with the flowering of the hippie movement, flower power, and 'drop out, turn on, tune in!' This was a sea change in popular fantasy and brought about a host of imitations during the last three decades of the century. For those of us old enough to remember, the question 'Where were you when you first read *The Lord of the Rings*?' has almost the same capacity to call up the sense of a life-changing event, a fulcrum, as the question 'Where were you when you heard JFK had been assassinated?' (Or, for those who are younger, we could perhaps say it was like 'Where were you when you heard about September 11?')

In the present collection, Alexander James in his story *A Spell at the end of the World* cleverly picks up on this, when he conceives of a popular work of heroic fantasy (surely *The Lord of the Rings*) as having been engineered by the London Supernatural Council (a kind of Guild of Sorcerers) with the express purpose of providing cover for the work of sorcerers in the age to come. How? 'It will cement the sorcerer's art as fantasy, enter culture and divert ordinary people from our reality.' In James's hands, what is presented as fantasy is the real reality.

So, could it be that the worlds created by some of the fantasy writers of the past thirty years are somehow more real than the grubby and increasingly frightening everyday life we share? Fantasy is criticised by some as escapist drivel, pulp fiction, unworthy of serious interest. Much of fantasy has escapist appeal, indeed, but it is not coincidence that many of its themes are linked to and tap into the pressing social concerns of our time – the environmental movement, for instance, the increasing popular obsession with natural healing and alternative medicine, the interest in witchcraft and other esoteric religions. Could it be that, while reflecting the sense of alienation that many of us feel with our world, fantasy also – in expressing our deep yearning for reconnection with the natural world, with spirituality, with what we would like our selves to be – provides us with a basis on which to build a better reality?

Then, of course, there are the popular fantasies described as 'paranoid' by those who cling to the 'realities' of scientific, economic, social and political progress. There are many horrific fictional examples of 'science gone wrong' but, interestingly, two of the most prevalent recent fantasy themes have been those of alien abduction and government conspiracy, expressions of a dark and fearful questioning of the 'accepted' reality. Here, we have only to look at the extraordinary success of *The X Files*, the statistics on those (particularly in the United States) who believe that they have seen UFOs or been abducted by aliens and subjected to bizarre scientific/medical experiments, the continuing interest in the Rothwell Incident, the Bermuda Triangle. Recent terrorist activity in the real, everyday world may prove to have diverted attention from alien enemies, but it's a reasonably sure bet that political conspiracy will fuel fantasies for some time to come. And the fact that our previously unquestioned realities have been shown to be vulnerable will doubtless provide new, richer material for fantasy writers.

For those of us who first fell to fantasy in a serious way on the publication of *The Lord of the Rings*, and those who have been acquainted with it through the recent successful films adapted and directed by Peter Jackson, the main attraction is likely to have been the wizardry involved in constructing an entire world, different from our own but connected to us too by means of values to which we can aspire. This is something appropriately worked through in vast volumes – trilogies or longer – the most common form of fantasy during the last thirty years. Think of David Eddings, David Gemmell, Stephen Donaldson, Terry Goodkind. But also more recently, Marion Zimmer Bradley, Robin Hobb, Juliet Marillier, Holly Lisle, Sara Douglass and Fiona McIntosh.

Much more long fantasy is being published by women than ever before. Might this be because the New Age fantasy values conform more readily to what have traditionally been seen as 'women's values'? So while David Gemmell, for example, has had success with his popular *Chronicles of the Jerusalem Man*, a combination of swords and sorcery and Western shoot 'em up adventure, we are increasingly seeing fictions that concern themselves with spirituality, healing, nurturing, interaction with the natural world, and a desire to preserve rather than master.

What of short fantasy? It seems that in recent times this has so far been much less frequently published. Among other restrictions, the short form obviously lends itself far less to the creation of comprehensive worlds and the exploration of large themes and narratives. So in putting this anthology together, there have been some surprises. Foremost was the huge variety of stories submitted. This posed a dilemma: how were we to define 'fantasy' in a short story form? At first, one of us got hung up on the selection criteria while the other growled, 'Fantasy is whatever I say it is!' In the final selection, fantasy has been whatever we agreed it was. Out of the range of submissions, we agreed on those of excellence that *could* be designated fantasy. We rejected those that, though excellent, we agreed were mainstream or science fiction. While not every reader will agree with us, we are confident that the result is a collection that ranges from conventional to modern, and expands the definition of the genre.

For many readers, fantasy has always had to do with the magical, the different from the here-and-now everyday pedestrian world – an escape to a better world, perhaps. But these stories push the envelope in all directions – some horrific, some humorous, some ironic, some New Age, some just weird – in a variety of different styles and contexts. We hope there will be something for everyone who reads fantasy here, and also for those readers who haven't tried it before.

Introduction

•

Peter McNamara

I've only a couple of personal notes to add.

Both notes concern my belief that genre writing and publishing in this country doesn't work hard enough at building or reinforcing its own mythology.

Something for me to note *positively* was the pleasure I received when I found that the assembly of this anthology was coincident with Terry Dowling's return to the *Rynosseros* cycle. An even greater pleasure was to recently receive from Terry a package of these stories to read: the three short pieces, 'Coyote Struck By Lightning', 'Coming Down' and 'Sewing Whole Cloth', that assemble to form 'Rynemonn'. Tom Tyson is the nearest we have to an icon of Oz genre writing (whatever became of Chandler's Grimes?) – we all want to see him complete his personal journey, but none of us want to lose him. Like the red desert he inhabits, he's part of us.

But as one icon shifts ground, a replacement emerges – so that another coincident pleasure was the arrival – only in short story form at this stage – of Alexander James's urban sorcerer, Barker Moon (though I believe 'A Spell at the End of the World' features one of Barker's ancestors).

At once, I was both struck by lightning and under a spell. Why not, I asked myself, centre the anthology around this rare crossover of characters and worlds? Why not take the opportunity to offer this resonant Tom story to all those who have waited so long for it (sorry, Terry, but you've hardly been rushing it), and push young Alexander (another unhurried writer) along by thrusting his alter ego out into the public glare?

I feel as if I'm right in the middle of one of those very rare moments in genre history. There's electricity involved. I want to hold the moment, but, of course, everything is transitory, and I know I can't.

But other anthologists can come back to it. Though the Blue Captain's destiny now presents itself, Tom has far from run his course (this moment will need to be revisited) – while Barker is just striding onto the stage. We haven't got a feel for him yet.

To personal note number two, an accounting for my tastes.

The line between science fiction and fantasy is often blurred beyond distinction. Stories readily slide across the boundary, and are defined only by the reader's personal tastes and intuition, and perhaps, if one can pick it, the author's intent.

The Aurealis Awards, which splits into divisions of science fiction, fantasy, horror, young adult and children's genre literature, regularly points up this difficulty in categorisation. Recently, Terry Dowling's 'The Lagan Fishers', Jack Dann's 'The Diamond Pit' and Lucy Sussex's 'Merlusine' turned up in short-lists on both sides of the fantasy/science fiction dividing line. My instincts and reading of intent told me they were *all* fantasy stories, but in a couple of cases, even the authors disagreed with me. It seems they had intended quite the opposite.

One author pressed on me the fact that their tale was set some considerable period into the future, and that automatically made it science fiction. I disagreed. Setting, for me, has little or nothing to do with it. Tone and architecture are the defining characteristics.

Which brings me to something a bit more detailed about my view of why we chose these stories. Storyline is probably the first thing *I* try to pick up on – and that doesn't necessarily mean a steady progression from beginning to middle to end (not that there's anything wrong with that!) but some 'journey' has to be involved. And the storyline has to rise out of the plot. That's fundamental.

There's not much room in a short story to develop character, but I still like to get a *feel* for the characters – more than height and hair or eye colour. Style, tone and voice are all aspects that lift a story (and are vital in sketching the characters), but what I look for most eagerly is good architecture – at its most basic, the way form complements content. As I see it, the storyline is the 'telling' of the tale, but the architecture is its true 'expression'.

Short stories are a contained force, and many writers find them more difficult to execute than the less urgent, often-rambling novel form, but, when well constructed, they take on an elegance to which novels simply can't aspire. We should all be reading more anthologies.

While I'm confident that everything in this anthology is classi-fiable as fantasy, some stories would look equally at home in other categories. 'Rynemonn', 'Players', 'Glimmer', 'Heaven', 'Waste' and 'A Room for . . .' would not be out of place in a science fiction collection, while 'Spell' and the gruesome 'Charlottes' could find a home in anything with the word 'dark' addressing it. The leanings of the others split between pure fantasy and mainstream.

Though everything is really mainstream, isn't it? We just like to think we're different.

The Phoenix

•

Isobelle Carmody

'Princess Ragnar?'

Ragnar turned to William and tried to smile, but her hatred was so great that it would allow no other emotion. She did not feel it as heat but as a bitter burning cold flowing through her, freezing her to ice, to stone. Driven by such a rage, a princess might unleash her armies and destroy an entire city to the last person. She might command the end of a world.

'Princess? Are you cold?'

She barely heard William's words, but when she shook her head, before he turned away to keep watch for Torvald, she saw in his pale-green eyes the same blaze of devotion that had flared three summers past when he had pledged himself to her.

Her mind threw up an image of him making that pledge, the words as formal as the words from an old Bible.

'Princess, I, William, am sent by the Gods to serve and guard you in this strange shadowland, until we are shown the way home by such signs and portents as I am trained to recognise. I pledge my life to you.'

Twelve years old, with one slightly turned eye, a broken front tooth, ripped shorts and a too large cast-off T-shirt advising the world to 'Be happy', and here he was pledging his life to her.

He had a collection of T-shirts abandoned by the drug addicts and drunks who came to stay at Goodhaven to dry out. The weird thing was that those T-shirts always seemed to have something pertinent to say about what was happening when he wore them, and in the end, she came to see them as signs, just as William saw as signs a certain bird flying overhead, or a particular rock resting against another.

Hearing his absurd pledge, she had experienced a fleeting instinct to laugh out of nervousness or incredulity. That would have changed everything. Life could be like that sometimes – hinging on one tiny little thing or other. But she hadn't laughed because underneath the urchin dirt and crazy talk, she had seen a reflection of her own aching loneliness.

'Are you sure you have the right person?' she had said, instead of, 'Are you crazy?' But it was close. They even started with the same words.

'You are Princess Ragnar,' he had said.

Those words sent a shiver up her spine, even after so much time. Because she had never seen him before. Then there was how he said her name – as if he was handling something infinitely precious. No one had said it like that before in her whole life except maybe her mother, though perhaps that was just a memory born of wishful thinking.

'How do you know my name?' she had demanded.

He had grinned, flashing the chipped tooth that she later learned had been broken when he'd happened on a drying-out drunk who had managed to drink a whole cupboard-full of cough medicine. The Goodhaven people stocked up on everything because they thought the world was going to end any day now and they wanted to be prepared. Though how a hundred tins of baked beans and a cupboard-full of cough medicine was supposed to help you survive the end of the world was beyond Ragnar. The drunk's back-handed slap had left William with the chip in his tooth that his aunt called God's will. In fact, that was what William had told her when she'd asked what had happened to his front tooth.

'It was God's will.' As if God had slapped him one.

•

The chip was wide enough to make him talk with a lisp, but since he could still use his teeth, fixing it would have been cosmetic and his aunt and uncle eschewed worldly vanity, believing it to be one of the things that brought most of the human debris they called Poor Lost Souls to Goodhaven in the first place.

Besides that, William was simple and it would hardly matter to the poor addled child that he had a chipped tooth when his brain was all but cracked clear through.

Those words came to her in William's mimicked version of his aunt's high-pitched folksy voice. That was how she explained him away to occasional government visitors and fund-raising groups concerned about a child being exposed to the sort of people who came to Goodhaven.

'Oh, he has seen much worse than anything he could ever see here,' William had mimicked his aunt. 'Why, his brain cracked under the pressure of seeing his mother and father murdered before his very eyes. He was there all alone a good two years before some-one found him wandering around mad as a hatter.'

William had been looked after by the same people who had murdered his parents, though no one could figure out why they would bother. Maybe it was because he was so young. He was four when his relatives had agreed to take him on.

He was no simpleton. Ragnar had seen that right off, but he was sure as heck one strange piece of toast, and no wonder. Seeing your parents murdered would be enough to make anyone a little crazy.

Of course, she had known nothing at all about that the first time they'd met.

She had been swimming and had come out of the water wearing nothing but her long red hair. There was never anyone around during the week and she had been pretending to be the mermaid; trying to make up her mind whether the love of a prince would be worth the loss of her voice and the feeling that she was standing on knives every time she took a step. Especially when her father said love did not last, or else why had her mother run off and left them?

She was trying to figure out where she had left her clothes

when William walked out carrying them. He had his eyes on her face and he did not once let them drop. He just held out her clothes and she snatched them up and pulled on jeans and a sloppy paint-stained windcheater, her face flaming.

Then he had suddenly fallen to his knees.

Her embarrassment evaporated since she was clothed now and anyway the boy clearly had no prurient interest in her nakedness.

She put her hands on her hips. 'Who the heck are you?'

'The gods have seen that you are lonely, Ragnar, and so I was sent to be your companion.'

Anything she would have said was obliterated by astonishment. For she was lonely beyond imagining. Her father had forbidden her to let anyone at her school know they were living illegally in the boathouse, which made it easier to have no friends than to make up believable lies. They had been squatting since the owner had moved to America, having told her father he could use the boathouse for his dinghy if he kept an eye on it. Her father took the dinghy out maybe three times a year and she was always convinced he would drown because he never took any of the things you were supposed to take like flares or lifejackets. He didn't have to fish since his Sickness Benefit paid for food and cask wine. He worried her sick when he went out, and she could never understand why he did it. It wasn't even as if he ever caught anything big enough to be legal or good eating.

Once, while they were keeping vigil for his return, William told Ragnar matter-of-factly that her father fished because he remembered when he had been a real fisherman.

'He was never a real fisherman,' Ragnar snorted. 'He was some sort of mechanic.'

'In his past life he was a fisherman and he slept with one of the goddesses. She took you away with her, but because you were part human, the gods made her send you here. As a punishment to her because she broke the rules.'

'Seems to me the gods and goddesses do nothing but break rules. Look at Prometheus and Pandora.'

'They are lesser gods,' William had said with a lofty kind of pride. 'My princess comes from an older and greater race of gods. And if he was not a fisherman once, then why does your father fish?'

As usual his habit of suddenly circling and darting back on an argument left her gasping like a fish out of water. The thing was she did not know why her father had brought them here to this spit of flat sand between an industrial wasteland and a whole lot of salt pans and wetlands. Nor why he fished.

Ragnar had known no other life. Not really. She sometimes remembered a mother who did not seem to have much to do with the mother her father muttered and cursed about. William had an answer for that as well. He thought that she was remembering not her mother in this life, but the goddess mother of her other life.

'Then how come my father remembers me being born?'

'The gods can make anyone remember or forget. They made your father remember his wife having a child – and maybe she did have a baby.' His eyes flashed as he warmed to this theme. 'Maybe she took their real child with her and the gods just stepped in and put you here, so he would think she left his baby. So he would take care of you and keep you out of the eye of the world.'

William was as worried about the eye of the world as her father. William, because of his uncle and aunt's fear of negative publicity that might affect Goodhaven's funding sources, and her father because he did not want to be thrown out of the boathouse, or have Social Security people poking around. Sending her to school worried him because if he didn't They would be after him – They being the Government – but if he did, people would find out where they were living. He had solved the problem by sending her to school, but telling her that if anyone figured out where she lived, she would be taken away to an orphanage and locked up. That had frightened her so much she said so little at school that people thought there was something wrong with her. Fortunately integration policies, and her own consistently normal marks, kept them from trying to send Ragnar to a special school of the sort William told such horror stories about. His relatives had tried a whole lot of schools before he had managed to convince them he was too far gone for school.

'I like people thinking I'm crazy. It's easier and I know what I am inside so what they think doesn't matter.'

Of course as she grew older, Ragnar's fear of the authorities was diluted to wary caution, but her father sealed her silence. He said they would never allow her to take Greedy away with them.

Greedy was a crippled seagull William had rescued and given to her as a gift, saying that in the realm of the gods, the seagull was her personal hawk. It was so devoted, William told her solemnly, that it had followed her to this world, but in order to come to her the gods offered the proud hawk only the form of a lowly scavenger. He told her the hawk's real name was Thorn, but secretly she nicknamed it Greedy, because it was.

'Thorn is hungry because in his previous life he was starved by the gods to try to make him forswear his allegiance to you,' William had told her reproachfully the one time he heard her calling the bird Greedy.

William had an answer for everything. Truth was, he was a lot smarter than most of the kids and the teachers at school, at least in ways that mattered. He did not read, but he could tell stories better than any book, and he had built around the two of them a fantasy that was far more wonderful than life could ever offer. In the years since they had first met, he had been her companion and everything else she had wanted – slave, brother, confidant, friend. He had shed blood to seal his pledge though she had not wanted or asked for it, and he had promised to serve and obey, honour and protect her – with his own life if necessary.

He had watched her for a long time to make sure she was truly the one, he told her earnestly one time as they were baking mussels in a battered tin pot of salty water on a small fire. The water had to be salty or the crustaceans tasted vile.

'But how did you know in the end?'

He shrugged. 'I found a sign and I knew – a ring of dead jelly-fish on the beach in the shape of a crown.'

It was easier to obey William's odd instructions than to try to understand why he thought a toilet brush in seaweed was a warning that you were being discussed, or how walking a certain way round an overturned shell could avert an accident. It was very rare that he wanted her to do anything troublesome, though once when he said they must walk along the railway lines for so many paces, she worried a lot because, if they were caught, they would end up in the children's court. But they had done it and William claimed that was what had stopped a council van coming down to Cheetham Point to check out rumours of people living there.

Did he manipulate events as he claimed? Mostly, Ragnar figured not, but it never hurt to take out insurance. Because there were many times when William knew things he could not know. Sometimes she would be going to catch the train and he would tell her that she would miss it, so he would wait for her in their secret place. And the train mysteriously would not come. Other times he would tell her it was going to rain when she was dressed lightly and, sure enough, by the end of the day, it would be pelting down.

Coincidence? Maybe. Ragnar did not believe she was a princess in exile. Not really. Though she did feel as if she had been born for more than this bit of barren land. One part of her looked at her father when he was drunk with his mouth open, a thin ribbon of drool falling from his lips, and knew she had been born of nobler blood. Sometimes when she was sitting in class, knowing the answers, but never speaking out because being too smart could bring you into the Public Eye even more than being too dumb, a little voice would whisper to her that she was special and destined for greatness, just as William said.

Sometimes when she and William sat at the very end of the land watching the sun fall in a haze of gold into the ocean, he would ask her if she felt the magic, and she would nod, lifting her chin and holding back her shoulders as regally as a princess, proud even in exile. Greedy would shiver on her lap, as if for a moment remembering his life as a mighty hawk hunter, bane of mice and small birds and even of cats.

It had been through such a sunset of molten gold that Torvald came to them. The day was uncommonly still and a sea-mist was shot with bloody gold and red lights as the sun fell. Ragnar saw something shimmer and all at once could see a young man with golden hair flying in the wind, and a proud handsome face, coming on his boat out of the mist, and her lips had parted in breathless wonder. Then she heard the whining stutter of the speedboat engine and realised he was coming across the water to Cheetham Point from the Ridhurst Grammar School jetty.

She felt foolish the way she always did when she entered a little too deeply into William's world of myth and magic. Just the same, sitting in the back of the boat with one hand lightly on the tiller, long pale hair about his face, there was no denying he looked marvellous. She wished she could see what colour his eyes were, for her daydreams, but of course he would turn back before he reached the Point because of the shallows.

Only he did not turn. For a moment she thought he had miraculously managed to sail over the sandbar even with the tide out, but then he had come suddenly to a grinding halt, beached until the tide rose again. After making some useless attempts to get the boat off the sandbar, he looked back, obviously concluding it was too far to swim. Then he turned to face the Point.

I will always see him that way, Ragnar thought. Him turning that first time to face them, so tall and handsome, the sky all gold and glorious behind him.

'We must help him, Princess,' William had announced.

Ragnar had been shocked, because one of the rules was that they should never seek out the Public Eye or any other eye. During the holidays when boat people came, they stayed away from the Point during the day, mostly within Goodhaven grounds. And they always stayed away from the rich spoiled Ridhurst students who would do anything for a dare, including tormenting a small boy.

'He's from Ridhurst,' Ragnar hissed, remembering how William had shivered when he told her how a group of students had ridden around and around him in ever smaller circles on their roaring motorbikes.

•

'He is one of us,' William had announced, though he looked paler than usual.

Ragnar stared at him incredulously. 'One of us?'

'Aye, Princess. He is the golden-haired voyager from over the sea whom you are destined to wed. His coming is a sign that the way will open soon for us to return. We must save him because there will only be one chance for all of us to cross.'

'William, he is not from over the sea. He came from Ridhurst . . .'

But he was running across the sand and shouting to the young man to wait and that they would help him. The handsome stranger waved back, and sat on the edge of the boat.

'We'll get the Longboat,' William cried out over his shoulder.

The Longboat was a slim wooden boat to which its owner hitched his larger boat when he came to the Point each Christmas. It was bolted to a post outside the shed that housed his bigger boat, but William discovered that with a bit of wriggling you could get the chain off in spite of the lock. They often used the Longboat to fish or to go for short jaunts, but never in broad daylight.

'William, stop, I . . . order you to stop!' She only used her Royal prerogative to stop William from his most dangerous schemes, because it did not seem fair to take advantage of his illusions that way. But on this occasion he seemed not to hear her. He was wriggling the chain out from its bolt and dragging it towards the water, straining his skinny arms.

'Oh, for heaven's sake!' Ragnar muttered, then bent and helped him. The sooner they got this over with the better. They rowed out to the sandbar and up close Torvald was as handsome as he had been from the distance. His teeth were perfectly straight and white and his eyes as blue as the sweetest summer sky. He was a picture-book prince, which may have explained what happened next.

'Hi,' he said, smiling right into her eyes. 'Thanks for the rescue. No one warned me about the sandbar.'

Ragnar had melted at the sound of his voice, deep and soft, with just a touch of an accent. But she managed to say, 'It wasn't me . . . I mean, William got the boat.'

'I meant thanks to you both. William, is it?' He held his hand out but William bowed.

'I am William and I am the pledged protector of Princess Ragnar in her exile.'

Ragnar could have died. Her face felt as if it had third-degree burns.

'Really? Well, I am Torvald the Curious from over the seas,' the stranger answered and bowed low to William and then to Ragnar. 'I am pleased to make the acquaintance of the beauteous Princess Ragnar.'

William gave Ragnar an 'I told you so' look as Torvald the Curious stood up and smiled at them both.

'Come aboard our humble craft, my Lord Torvald, and we will bear you to shore and give you what humble sustenance we can offer in this place of exile until the waters allow you to depart,' William said.

Torvald's smile deepened and without further ado, he gave their boat a push to free it from the sandbar, and climbed in. William rowed them back and Ragnar looked steadfastly towards the shore, refusing to look at Torvald whom she could see staring at her out of the corner of her eye.

The humble sustenance turned out to be her leftover school lunch and a rather shrivelled looking trio of apples that was William's offering. Torvald lowered himself to sit in the sand, stretching his long legs out in front of him, and when William solemnly offered him their picnic, he smiled a little and chose one of the apples.

'It looks as if you were expecting me. And this . . .' He held up the apple. 'This seems appropriate, somehow.'

'Truly,' William agreed. 'Eve offered the apple of knowledge to Adam, and Aphrodite offered an apple to Paris.'

'Ah, but he should have taken the apple from the Goddess of Wisdom, shouldn't he?'

'Perhaps,' William said. 'But some things are cast in the stars and love is one of them. It will have its way, no matter what tragedy it calls in its wake.'

Torvald's smile faded properly for the first time then. Perhaps that was the moment he realised this was no game to William. His eyes shifted to Ragnar questioningly, and she forced herself to meet his gaze with no expression, because to show what she felt would be to betray William, and to act as if she believed what William believed would be to betray herself. Also if she started talking, this golden-haired young man would begin to ask questions.

Torvald's expression of puzzlement grew more intense. 'So . . . you are both in exile?' he said at last.

'Truly your name fits you,' William said.

Torvald looked confused until he remembered the name he had announced himself with. 'I am afraid I am curious to the point of rudeness. My father said I will never make a politician unless I learn to tell lies sweetly.'

'No,' William said. 'You will not be a politician.'

Torvald frowned at him. 'You think not?'

William shook his head. 'Politicians cannot afford to be curious. You will always be a seeker of the only true beauty which is truth.'

Torvald blinked, much as Ragnar thought she must have done the first time she encountered William the Sage. That, he told her, had been his role before he was sent to her. He had been a seer of things to come. A Merlin.

'You are a strange boy,' Torvald said. 'Do you live here?'

Ragnar plunged in hurriedly. 'No. We just came down for the day. We live over in Calway.' That ought to put him off since it was a Housing Commission area.

'That is a long way. Did you walk?'

'We came around the beach.' She pointed vaguely to the route she walked after catching the train from town on school days.

'Past Ridhurst?'

She nodded. 'You go there, don't you?' Better to turn the talk back on him. She found that a useful way of dealing with curiosity.

But he just nodded and said, 'You are brother and sister?'

'I am the servant and protector of Princess Ragnar,' William said calmly.

Ragnar wanted to strangle him. 'We're friends,' she said.

'I have that honour also,' William agreed.

Torvald looked from one of them to the other.

'Your father is a politician?' Ragnar asked, somewhat desperately.

'He is a politician of sorts. A diplomat.' His eyes crinkled deliciously into a smile again. 'He lies for his country rather than for a political party.' Now his eyes were on William and they were serious. 'But why did you say I will not be a politician? It is what my father wishes and I am not averse to the idea. He sent me here so that I will make important connections for the future. The sons and daughters of many influential people come to Ridhurst but it seems to me they worry about cricket and parties and the right clothes more than important matters. But perhaps I misjudge them as trivial and shallow because I arrived only last week. When I know them better, things might be different.'

'Maybe,' Ragnar said, thinking of the young women in their pale uniforms lifting their brows at her high school uniform when she got off the bus at their stop. The trouble was it was the closest stop to home, and even then it took a good half hour to walk round the beach to Cheetham Point.

Somehow, she had managed to get him talking about his father the diplomat and his appointment to Australia. His father was in Canberra but he had decided to send Torvald to the highly recommended Ridhurst as a boarder, at least until his mother, a doctor, followed a year later.

Ragnar was relieved when William announced suddenly that they must go back out or the Ridhurst boat would float free of the sandbank without him.

The trip back was conducted in relative silence, but as Torvald climbed out of the boat, he smiled at them both. 'I thank you again for saving me from sitting like a fool in the boat until now. No doubt that is what was intended by the students who suggested I might enjoy a boat ride across to Cheetham Point.'

'It was our pleasure to help you thwart your tormentors, Lord Torvald. Farewell.'

'Perhaps we will meet again?' Torvald's eyes shifted to Ragnar and she felt the blood surge in her cheeks.

'I don't think so,' she said. 'Come on, William.'

'As you will, my princess.'

Ragnar cringed.

She thought that would be the end of that, but Torvald proved true to his name. He waited on the path a number of days and even wandered around Calway in the hope of bumping into his two off-beat rescuers. She, having some inkling perhaps, had gone a roundabout way through the wetlands to avoid the walk by the school, but one afternoon came home to see Torvald and William deep in conversation in the dunes near the boathouses.

Her heart lurched in sick fear.

'Princess Ragnar,' Torvald said, getting to his feet.

Ragnar's fright was swamped with rage at the thought he was mocking William.

'What are you doing here?' she snarled.

William looked worried. 'It is well, Princess. Truly. He will bring you no harm. He is your . . .'

'What do you want?' Ragnar demanded, cutting off whatever William would have said for fear he would start talking about future weddings.

'I am Torvald the Curious.'

Ragnar did not know what to say in the face of that, especially with William sitting there beside her looking stricken. She calmed herself because maybe he had not said anything to this Ridhurst student about where they lived. Though it must look queer for them to come down here again like this.

'My father owns a boathouse and we were planning to camp out for the night, but it's not allowed. I'm sorry if I snapped at you.'

'William is right. I mean no harm to you, Princess Ragnar.'

'Don't call me that!'

'Being noble-born you may address the princess by her name if she is willing,' William interpreted.

Ragnar sat down, speechless.

'Then I shall call you Ragnar and you will call me Torvald, or Tor. I prefer the latter.'

'Thor . . .' William muttered.

Oh great, Ragnar thought. She glared at Torvald and asked William to leave them alone for a moment.

He rose at once, saying he would look for Thorn.

'Thorn?' Torvald asked.

'A crippled seagull that William thinks is a reincarnated hawk. Just like he thinks I'm a princess and you're some sort of lord,' she said angrily. 'What are you doing here sucking up to him and pretending to believe what he says? Are you going to write a paper for Ridhurst on the local feral kid?'

'William is a very interesting boy. I think he can see into the future sometimes. It's often the way with those society deems to be mad or simple. They see what most people do not. You are angry because you fear I will harm him, but I am not a student with a motorcycle and no brains or compassion.' Torvald's voice was mild and serious.

'He told you about that?'

'He told me many things, and he was right when he said I will not harm either of you.'

Ragnar was frightened again. 'What did he tell you about me?'

'Nothing that I would ever use to harm you. I swear it on the honour of Torvald the Curious.'

'Don't mock him!'

'I do not mock. You mistake me. I have honour and I have sworn by it. And who is to say that William is not right?'

'What?'

'He says we are destined for one another, and that my soul was the soul of a god who loved you, and has followed you into exile.'

Ragnar's face was burning. 'You don't love me.'

He did not answer for a long moment, but only let his eyes hold hers. Then he said, 'How do you know I did not fall in love with you the first moment I saw you coming towards me in that little boat, your red hair gleaming like molten copper and your face as fair as any goddess's? How do you know that the moment I saw you all the hungers and longings of my life were not answered?'

Oh, his words were as beautiful as his face, and they had gone through her defences like a hot knife through butter. And in those months that followed she had come to love him body and soul; she had come to believe that William saw a different reality and in it, she was truly a princess and Tor her destined love.

And then two nights past, she was on the train dozing, catching the late train home from school because she was rehearsing for a school play in which she was one of the King of Siam's lesser wives. She woke out of a deep sleep to hear Tor's beloved voice, and for a moment she revelled in the sweetness of it, until she realised she was not dreaming and his words were anything but sweet.

'I am telling you, Rosco, you or any of your friends mess this up for me and I will throttle you. I have a sweet set-up for myself and that red-haired peach is ripe and ready to drop into my hands. I gave her romance with a capital R and she ate it up along with her ferrety little friend.'

'Should've run right over the gruesome little creep, cursing us, and two days later I broke my arm and Tristam fell over and slipped a disc.'

'Yes, well, I think William the Wacko loves me enough to kill for me. He thinks I am some sort of king which means he has class even if his brains are scrambled.'

'Just so long as you're not getting soft on them. If it wasn't for you playing the girl out, I would've reported the soak of a father for living in the sheds weeks back.'

'Idiot.' Tor's voice held a serrated edge of scorn Ragnar had never heard before. 'I said the girl pleased me. I did not say I would introduce her to my parents or bring her to a school dance. She is a pig, but I prefer her in her shack where I can get at her – until I am bored. After that you may have what revenge you want on the boy.'

'After you finish shacking up with the Pig Princess, eh? Ha ha ha.'

Torvald had laughed too. Hard cruel laughter from a Torvald she had been too blind to see. Ragnar sat there in her corner as the train pulled up, praying they would not spot her. She stayed on until the East Potter stop, and then walked the seven kilometres back along the highway to the Cheetham Point turn-off, driven by the viciousness of her self reproaches and taunting echoes of William's words.

'I loved you the first moment I saw you . . .'

'She is a pig but I prefer her in her shack where I can get at her . . .'

'I will never harm you . . .'

'I would not introduce her to my parents . . .'

She might not have told William, but he was waiting for her in a T-shirt that said 'Shit Happens'. It does, she thought, savage and half-mad with despair. She let William encircle her with his thin hard arms, and told him everything. And when there were no more tears, and the ice had begun to form over her emotions, she looked up into his face and found his pale eyes curiously blank.

'He proved too weak to withstand the darkness of this world and we should leave him to it. That would be the greatest torment for such as he,' William said distantly. 'Yet he is one of us and he must be punished for a betrayal that must make the gods weep when they learn of it. As they will when we return.'

'Return?'

William nodded. 'It is time. Two nights from now when the sun sets, a way will open to the realm of the old gods by their grace. This once and once only. I have dreamed it and I have read the signs. If we turn from it, we will be trapped here forever in this land of cruelty and darkness.'

Ragnar had been too distraught to really listen. All she understood was that William had a plan that would punish Torvald for his seduction and betrayal.

'What do you want me to do?'

William asked her to send Torvald a message to come over the water to them on Sunday afternoon. It was Friday and normally he would not come on weekends for fear he would be spotted and followed by Ridhurst students who might discover the truth. Or so he had told her, she thought bitterly. William told her to write that the tide would be high enough for him to negotiate the sandbar in the Ridhurst dinghy.

Coldly Ragnar wrote the note and slipped it into the internal mail box in Ridhurst after dark while her father snored in his bed. She had not known what William planned then or now. She didn't care as long as Torvald suffered.

'He comes,' William breathed.

Ragnar squinted through a rising sea-mist and saw Torvald launch the heavy school boat. She sat, stiff-backed and still as a statue as the boat came over the water and William ran to meet him and bring him back to where a picnic feast was laid out.

'Ragnar, my love,' Tor said and bowed as he always did. But now Ragnar saw the gallant gesture for the mockery it had always been and her hatred weighed in her stomach, heavy as a stone.

'Tor.' She forced her lips to shape a smile but there must have been something wrong in it, because instead of smiling back, Torvald frowned questioningly at her. He would not ask aloud what was wrong though, because of William. He would wait as always until William withdrew and they could speak freely.

Ragnar bent her head to hide the rage bubbling within her and stroked Greedy with fingers that trembled. He would not settle – no doubt he sensed the turmoil in her.

'Now we shall drink a toast, my lord, for this very night the way opens to the realm of the gods from whence we all came,' William said, and passed a chipped enamel mug to Torvald.

'What?' Torvald asked.

'Drink,' William said and handed a plastic mug to Ragnar, who was staring at Torvald with such longing and loathing that her soul felt as if it were curdling in her breast.

'Tonight we drink to the joy of William the Sage, who returns to the realm of the gods where he is an honoured Merlin.' William drank and, like an automaton, so did Ragnar. Torvald shrugged and drank.

William spoke again with an almost hypnotic solemnity, holding up his own jam jar as if it were a jewelled goblet. 'Tonight we drink to Thorn the mighty hunter as he returns to his airy realms . . .' He drank again and so did Ragnar and Torvald.

'Tonight the Princess in Exile returns to claim her kingdom . . .'

Ragnar drank her father's cheap red wine, and found her head spinning because she had barely eaten for the last two days. But Torvald had not taken another drink.

'You are leaving?' he asked worriedly. 'Would you go without me?'

'I am not finished, my lord,' William said sternly. 'We drink the bitter dregs to you for a betrayal that will sunder you forever from the princess. We might have let that be torment enough, were you a creature of this dark world. But you are of the golden realms and so your treachery is too deep for us to let you live – even here in this shadow world.'

'What?' Torvald asked, but his words slurred so badly they could barely understand. 'Princess Ragnar?'

Ragnar's confusion over William's words dissolved in a boiling lava of bitter despair. 'Don't you mean Pig, Tor? Don't you mean Ragnar the Pig whom you would never introduce to your parents or bring to a dance?'

His eyes widened in shock. 'But, Ragnar . . .' His eyes clouded and he fell forward, catching himself on one hand. He stared at the spilled wine seeping into the pale sand. 'The . . . drink?'

'Not poison but enough tranquilliser from the Goodhaven store to kill a horse, or a lord who betrayed his true land and his deepest love,' William said sadly.

Fear flowed over the handsome features, then acceptance. 'William . . . I do not blame you for this.' He looked at Ragnar. 'I was trying to divert Roscoe and his friends from reporting your father when I spoke . . . as I did on the train. They would . . . never be held back by compassion or . . . honour, so there was no point in speaking of such things to them . . . had . . . had to . . . to play their game.' He coughed and fell forward onto his elbow, twisting his head so that he could look into Ragnar's horrified eyes.

'Had to play . . . a cruel game they could understand and sympathise with. Even admire. I . . . did not want to tell you the truth until I had thought of a . . . solution. You see, in a way, I did betray you. They . . . they followed me, you see . . .'

'Torvald!' Ragnar screamed and gathered him into her arms, her terror too deep for words. Surely William had been joking. Surely he had only been trying to frighten Torvald.

'I should have told you the truth sooner . . . my love. Shouldn't have tried . . . being a hero . . .'

His eyes fell closed. Ragnar shook him and knelt to press her head to his chest. She could find no heartbeat nor breath in him. She tried mouth to mouth resuscitation, letting herself think of nothing but the rhythm of breathing and pushing on his chest. How long she tried she could not have said but when William's hand fell on her shoulder and she sat up, her head spun.

'Bring him to the boat, Princess. They will be able to revive him perhaps in the sunlit realm of the old gods where all things are possible.'

Ragnar stared at him hopelessly, thinking that she had let one of the two people she loved in all the world kill the other. It was not poor battered William's fault, for he had never known any sort of normality. It was her fault Tor was dead, her fault William was a murderer.

'I have made you a murderer . . .' she whispered, stricken.

But William's eyes met hers steadily. 'Tor's is not the first death at my hand in this dark world.'

'What?' Ragnar whispered.

'I killed my father. He was trying to scalp my mother when I woke. So I took the gun he had thrown down and I killed him.'

All the horror of the night coalesced around the bleak dreadful image of a small boy forced to shoot his father, and Ragnar's heart swelled with pity.

'Ah, William . . .' she whispered, blinded by tears. 'What are we going to do?'

He reached out and took her hand in a surprisingly strong grip.

'I have never lied to you, Princess. We belong to a world where there is hope and this is a world where there is none. Only come now, and help me get Lord Torvald's body into the longboat.'

Ragnar stumbled to her feet and took Torvald's feet as William instructed. She did not know or care what he wanted to do. She had brought him to murder. Now she supposed they would dispose of the body.

The body. They half dragged Tor over to the side of the Longboat which was anchored close to the water and, straining and pushing, heaved him over the edge. Ragnar felt sick at the thumping sound his body made as it landed in the bottom of the boat. She climbed in beside him, gagging at a queer acrid smell as she lifted Torvald's golden head onto her knees.

'Thorn!' William called and Ragnar looked up in time to see the seagull stagger hippity-hop over the sand to his feet with a creaking caw of delight. He scooped the bird up and put it in the boat then pushed it off into the water and climbed in beside them. Ragnar stared up at him as he lifted a plastic bottle from the bottom of the boat and tipped what looked like water over Torvald's unconscious form. Greedy squawked as he was drenched, and the smell was intensified as William sprinkled it over Ragnar's legs and dress.

'What is it?'

'It is the test,' William said, emptying the last of the liquid over himself and the boat.

Ragnar watched him throw the bottle into the water and rummage in his pockets, before withdrawing something. 'A test?' she asked dully.

William lit a match that flamed the colour of the clouds on the horizon all shot through with the bloody brightness of the sun's death, and smiled at her.

'Do not be afraid, Princess. It is the last test of courage required by the gods – know that we are worthy to dwell in their realm.'

'William ...' The clouds in Ragnar's brain dissolved as the match fell onto Torvald's body. Flame made a feast of him, but he did not move because he was beyond pain.

She watched the flames play over him and William came to sit beside her. He took her hand, sticky with tears and petrol, in his own thin strong fingers and kissed it reverently.

'What comes will be a moment of pain before the gods pluck us from the crucible.' He looked down at Torvald. 'Love was first born where we journey, Princess. Hold fast to that, for all love in this world is but the palest shadow of it. Where we go, love has magical properties and there may be a way to bring him back.'

'We will die . . .'

'No. It only seems so, else there would be no testing. But hold fast, Ragnar, for you are a princess and the gods are watching.'

Ragnar wondered if she was mad but as the flames tasted the petrol on her dress and licked along the hem almost teasingly, she felt a surge of hope, for it seemed to her she could hear the brassy call of a horn, peeling out an eldritch welcome for a long-lost princess.

She stroked Torvald's face as flame licked flesh, and steeled herself not to scream, for she was a princess among the gods, and she was bringing her beloved home.

As flame rose around them like a winding sheet, Thorn the hunter lifted himself on crippled wings and flew.

Players in the
Game of Worlds

●

Damien Broderick

There's a world I know where the women are a head taller than the men, and file their ferocious teeth to points. The men are fierce little guys.

A different world, but the same, another earth, has luminous rings spread brilliantly across the whole sky, bright as a full moon. Those rings are all that remained of the moon when it fell chaotically too close to the world and got torn apart by tidal forces. There are no people there, only about twenty million different kinds of dinosaurs in a range of sizes and colours. Lots of them are meat-eaters, with shockingly bad breath.

On a third world, the people are lean and lightly furred. The pale pupils of their eyes are slitted vertically. I believe their remote ancestors, maybe fifteen million years ago, were the great Ice Age cats now extinct in our world. All the apes and humans are extinct in theirs. Has any of them managed the trick of slipping here through the mirrored cracks between the worlds? If so, perhaps they gave rise to legends of vampires or werewolves. I don't think any of them came here, though. They love the taste of simian blood, which is why the apes and humans are extinct in their earth. We'd have noticed them, trust me.

On a fourth, the humans are gone, but machines are

everywhere. Evolution by other means. Same old, same old, but different. Always different.

I don't suppose I have the appearance of a Player in the Game of Worlds. You wouldn't think it, to look at me. Well, that's not true, of course, since that's *exactly* how I look – but if you knew about us you'd probably expect a Player to resemble premium Bruce Willis, all bruised muscles and weary but romantic hard-bitten sarcasm. Or maybe you'd think we look like those macho but insanely hand-some Hollywood guys with ponytails who spend most of the day working up their lats and pecs and biceps, and fine-tuning their flashy karate kicks.

Nah – I'm just this Aussie walking down the street, booting a loose plastic bottle top into the gutter, hands in my pockets, hair in my eyes, looking a bit wary. Just another graduate student dressed in black, in fashion uniform.

It's the first uniform I've worn in a decade, since I got marched into the principal's office for turning up at school in jeans, high-tops and sweat shirt.

'Mr Seebeck,' the principal started frostily.

'Ms Thieu, that's pronounced "Zay-bek",' I said quietly, standing in front of her desk with my hands joined behind my back. Maybe my hands were a little sweaty. It was easy being nervous around adults when I was a kid.

She blinked. '"Zaybek", eh? August, what do they call you for short? Gus? Auggie?'

'August,' I said.

She blinked again. After a moment she went on smoothly, 'Where are your family from, August?'

'Australia,' I told her. Good grief. 'Fourth generation. My great-great-grandfather was Estonian.' I paused, and just as she started to say something else, I added, 'On my father's side.'

The principal coughed behind her hand. 'Yes, obviously, Mr Seebeck. It's deeply sexist, but society has always preserved the parental name only through the male ancestors.' Actually, that's not so obvious once you know about the other worlds, where they do things differently. As a nearly pubescent kid, though, I didn't know about them, and Ms Thieu certainly didn't. She just straightened up in her leather chair, considering me with a serious look. 'However, young man, I haven't requested you to join me in order to discuss your family history. I want to know why you aren't in school uniform.'

'I don't like uniforms,' twelve-year-old-me said. I wasn't rude, but I didn't budge or apologise.

'One of the features of living in a civilised society,' Ms Thieu informed me, fingers pressed together in a steeple, 'is that some-times – often, in fact – we must do things we don't like.'

I said nothing.

'You do see what I'm getting at, August?'

'Not really,' I said. 'School uniforms suck. They just make us instit –, instut –' I broke off, the word blocked on my tongue.

The principal looked surprised. 'Institutionalised? That's a big word for a . . .' She shuffled the papers on her desk, found my records, 'a twelve-year-old boy. And an inappropriate one, luckily. We are not trying to break your spirit, Mr Seebeck. We don't wish to turn you into a faceless robot. Far from it. This school's policy demands that all students wear the same clothes precisely to *protect* your individuality.'

I gazed at her in frank disbelief.

'Think about it, August. If everyone could wear anything they liked, the place would turn into a squabbling barn yard. Wealthy children might choose to wear expensive designer outfits. That would make the less privileged feel uncomfortable.'

Right. And that doesn't happen already? I said nothing, just looked at the floor, waiting for her to finish and let me return to class.

It went on for a while, and instead of going back to the class room I was sent home early with a note to my parents, asking them to ensure that I wore appropriate uniform items in future. I talked it over with Mum and Dad that night, and they agreed with me: it was my decision. Next day I went back in jeans and polished leather shoes and neatly ironed school shirt. Mr Browning, the arithmetic teacher, was in charge of assembly. When he saw the jeans, he freaked, sent me back to the principal's office.

Yack yack, blah blah, yada yada. I just waited it out. I ended up missing three weeks of school, studying happily at home, and Dad and Mum met the school board on five separate occasions. An article appeared in the *Advertiser* that embarrassed the school, and eventually they just dropped the issue. I wore whatever I wanted after that.

James Davenport, the class clown, turned up a week later in a taffeta tutu and dancing shoes with pink pompoms, and said it was against the equal rights laws to forbid his free choice of garb. Everyone laughed a lot, and the teachers choked with rage but Ms Thieu decided to let it ride without a word, and three of the fourteen-year-old tough kids tried to beat Davers up and called him a gayboy, but the rest of us stood up for him, to his surprise, and all he copped was a bruised arm. His sister's dress got mangled. He didn't wear it again, not that he wanted to, because he'd made his point, and so had I, and school life went on as usual.

I didn't know about the different probability worlds back then. I didn't know about the Tree Yggdrasil. But I did know I was different, not quite like the other guys, not even mad Davers who probably really did have a screw loose. Over the next few years I did my homework and went to class and sailed through most of the material in English and Mathematics and Social Studies and Geography and the dreary rest of it, and watched a lot of TV, and learned to play electric guitar and sang fairly badly in our band *Pillar of Salt* with three other dudes from the neighbourhood.

When my parents were killed in a plane crash in Thailand, everything went white and empty for a long time.

I started back at a different school, in the adjacent state of Victoria, when Mum's older sister Aunt Miriam became my legal guardian. She lived in Melbourne, nearly a thousand kilometres away from Adelaide.

I had to go through the whole uniform thing again, but I guess there must have been a note about that sorry history tucked into the file of records sent across from the previous school. The head of my new centre for involuntary servitude finally shrugged and agreed that dress code was a matter best left to the individual conscience.

I liked that. Mr Wheeler was a decent guy, and a good football coach. I played a little with the school team, but never really got the hang of it. Guess I'm pretty much a loner, outside of my special buds. That's okay, too.

Aunt Miriam fell in love with a violinist, the second chair in the National Orchestra, when I was sixteen and in my second-last year of school. He lived across town in upmarket South Yarra, and I went to live with them for six months in his pleasant but rather cramped apartment, took the long train ride every day to school, but none of us really enjoyed the arrangement. I think I cramped their style, even though I spent most of my time either at the gym, practising with the band, at the library or in my own room. When Itzhak had the chance to go to Tel Aviv for a year, naturally Miriam went with him. They agonised over taking me too, but decided that I'd had enough trauma and moving from place to place in the last few years. Would have been cool with me. Whatever.

So I ended up for six months in the care of Great-Aunt Tansy, Miriam's and Mum's aged aunt, who still lived in a ramshackle old house near the top of a hill in Thornbury, the next suburb over from the one where I'd first stayed with Miriam. That meant I didn't need to shift schools again – in fact, it was closer.

Saying that I ended up in her care is misleading; more accurately, Great-Aunt Tansy ended up in my care. That makes it sound as if she were senile. Nothing like that. She was a fine person, Tansy, and I had always been fond of her. It's just that strange things tended to happen around her.

Now I know why, of course. But I didn't then, and for a long time it creeped me the hell out.

Itzhak was invited to first chair in Chicago at the end of that year, and he and Miriam rented a large place of their own just outside the central business district. I went across the Pacific crammed into economy class for a holiday and stayed for a year, finishing high school. That was the year Kennedy was elected President – John, I mean, son of the war hero Jack, not his Uncle Robert, who had greeted the returning Apollo astronauts although it had been his disgraced nemesis Richard Nixon who'd launched the Moon project. There were plenty of mutters from the Republicans that year at what they denounced as the disgraceful nepotistic sight of one Kennedy all but following another into the White House. Me, I was apolitical, didn't care for those games. I had enough trouble being taken seriously when I told the kids in my new school that the Australian president had once been a TV quiz champion. But the Honourable Barry Jones seemed to me a good choice for head of state; he knew a damned sight more about science and technology, not to mention cinema and art and history and all the rest, than most of the lawyers and political insiders who jostle for the reins of power in both my own nation and the USA.

Being the first Aussie that most of my new high school class mates had ever seen in person, I was a novelty item, subject to the sort of attention usually reserved for rock stars or sports heroes. Celebrity life had its merits. I happily abandoned my virginity in the back seat of Tammy Nelson's fire-engine red Mustang convertible, something I'd never quite managed back home. Somehow, between carousing at senior parties and learning the rules of American football, I managed to graduate with honours, and flew home to kill some time before starting a medical degree at Melbourne University. Great-Aunt Tansy welcomed me back, gave me my old room, then waved me off a week later as I headed for the outback to do a little jackarooing, which is tending huge herds of beef cattle that roam across dry grassland spreads the size of small European nations. It's not done on horseback these days, not much. Helicopters and four-wheel drives are the preferred method. I learned to round up a few thousand head of cattle at a time from the back of a bounding Suzuki motorbike, and on a blazing 41 degree Celsius Christmas Day I ate ritual damper and rum cake with the other jackaroos and two hotly pursued jillaroos, drinking Bundy rum and Coke and singing western laments. American West, that is. Nothing is more unnerving that hearing three Aboriginal stockmen whose ancestors had dwelled in that part of the country for upward of 50,000 years singing 'The Streets of Laredo' in totally unselfconscious American hillbilly accents. That's how they heard it on the radio, that's the way they sang it.

I drove home in the old four-wheel-drive Pajero I'd won on a lucky hand of poker, with a swag of tax-free cash in each of my high-top R.M. Williams boots, and at a drive-through booze shop bought a bottle of Bundy for myself, for old times' sake, and a bottle of premium sherry for Aunt Tansy. Dugald O'Brien, her old golden Labrador, met me joyously at the gate, tail wagging. I don't know how he does it; somehow he knows when I'll be arriving, and welcomes me with his simple, blessed affection.

'Do Good, my man,' I told him, 'likewise,' and scratched his ears, then crouched to give him a proper hug, dropping my swag. The poor chap was growing old, and he limped a little as he followed me into the hallway.

The comforting smells of Tansy's home welcomed me in like a warm memory of childhood. It made me embarrassed: I was grimy, and I'm sure I stank like a horse. I found her in the enormous kitchen, gave her a kiss, deferring the hug for later, and told her I was headed upstairs for the shower. She lifted the remote and flipped off her TV set.

'I'm sorry, dear, you can't.'

'Huh?' I paused halfway up. I'd driven 1500 kilometres with not much more than fuel and food breaks; I was numb with fatigue, starting to see double.

Great-Aunt Tansy was cutting her pastry mixture with a metal template shaped like a heart. She looked up at me, eyes wide and watery blue and honest. 'This is Saturday night.'

'What there is left of it. I know should phone around, catch up with people, Tansy, but I'm bone tired. After I've have a good soak, I think I'll just slip into – '

'No, darling, that's what I'm saying. You can't have a shower upstairs. Every Saturday night, there's a corpse in that bathroom.'

I choked, came all the way down the stairs again rather carefully, not clattering, and poured a cup of coffee, waiting. Tansy did her magic with strawberry jam, popped the tray into the hot oven, began blending a fresh mix for date scones. She made the best jam tarts since Queen of Hearts, which I guess made me the Knave, since I'd pilfered plenty of them over the years. She sat perched on a three-legged stool beside the heavy oak kitchen table, rolling an amorphous lump of putty in flour with an old-fashioned rolling pin. As ever, no conscious effort went into the expert motions of her hands: it was a tantra, as graceful and automatic as I was trying to make my martial arts kata. Absent-minded as an old hen, Great-Aunt Tansy, and twice as industrious.

After a time, I raised my eyebrows. 'And that's why I can't have a bath tonight? Because you have a dead man in the bath.' If anyone else had made that comment, I'd have laughed, or said something scathing. But it was Aunt Tansy's testimony, and she was in her eighties, as fragile as expensive glassware.

'You can use mine, dear, downstairs. In fact, I think you should, and the sooner the better.' Her white bun of ancient silky hair bobbed. 'The fact of the matter is, you stink like a polecat.' I watched her press down on the white, datey dough, and the clean round shapes of the scones came out of that putty and sat snugly on the tray she had waiting for them. I felt the sleepy contentment of that large old eccentric nineteenth-century house closing around me again, and my mind drifted away from her absurd statement. It was easy to forget at Aunt Tansy's. I yanked myself out of the sleepy mood, and thought of a corpse in a bathroom.

'Always the same corpse, is it?' I affected nonchalance, draining the last of my cool coffee.

'Heavens no, child, don't be absurd. There's a fresh one every week.' She took the scones over to the oven, slid them in above the tarts. The tray rattled. 'All shapes and sizes. Last week it was a nice looking young fellow in a tweed suit.' She came back to the table and held out her cup; I poured more coffee. The poor thing was trembling, and it wasn't the caffeine; she was scared stiff. My amusement turned to dismay. They kept promising an imminent cure for Alzheimer's, but as far as I knew no effective treatments had come out of the pharmaceutical labs just yet. Firm kindness seemed to be the only available prescription. Tansy had done a lot for me.

'What do you do with these bodies?' Pretty difficult, humouring people's delusions without making it obvious. And Tansy was sharp. But she took it straight.

'They're always gone in the morning. Sometimes a bit of blood, you know, but I wash the bath out with citric cleanser and you'd never know there's been a body there.'

Her cup clattered faintly on its saucer. I was getting scared myself.

'How long's this been going on?'

'It started just after you left for the bush. Let's see – six of them so far. And another one tonight, I expect.'

I had seen some strange things in two countries, not the least of them mad Davers running about an Adelaide football field in cleated boots and his sister's frilly dress, pursued by jocks, but so help me I'd never seen anything so weird or blood-curdling as quiet little Great-Aunt Tansy talking about corpses in her upstairs bath.

'You've told the police, I suppose?'

She gave me a scornful look.

'Think I want to get locked up? August, they'd have me committed to an insane asylum.' Her trembling worsened. I was ashamed, because I was trying to work out how to find appropriate psychiatric help. You didn't just drive your aged relative to the local clinic and ask them to run some tests on her sanity. Or did you? I was starting to think that I'd need to call Miriam and Itzhak in on this, and did some calculations. No, it was still only about six in the morning in Chicago. Let it ride, see what we work can out right here and now. Besides, incredibly enough, some part of me was beginning to trust her report – or rather, to assume that *something* strange was happening in the old house, something she'd misinterpreted rather unfortunately. I'd never known Aunt Tansy to be entirely wrong about anything important.

'I'll just go up and have a quick look,' I said, and took our cups to the sink.

'You be careful, August,' she told me. To my immense surprise, she reached down and held out an old cricket bat that had been leaning against one table leg on her side. 'Take this. Give the buggers a good whack for me.'

Instead of going upstairs immediately, I packed Great-Aunt Tansy off to bed early in her slightly sour old-lady-scented ground floor bedroom at the front of the house. Then she insisted on a final cup of cocoa for both of us, so I rolled my eyes to heaven and gave in.

I opened the bathroom door and gazed carefully around. Tiled walls, pale green, pleasantly pastel. It struck me as odd, peering about the large room, that for years I'd bathed here and made stinks without ever really looking at it. You take the familiar for granted. Two large windows, dark as night now, gave on to trimmed grass two full storeys below, and the fruit trees and organic vegetable plots of the back garden. Between them a pink wash-basin stood on a pedestal, set beneath a big antique wall-mounted mirror, at least a metre square, with a faint coppery patina, the silvering crazed at the edges. The claw-footed bath itself filled the left-hand corner, opposite a chain-flush toilet bowl of blue-patterned porcelain like a Wedgwood plate, next to the timber door with its ornate geometrical carvings. The toilet's polished timber seat was down, naturally, and masked by a rather twee fluffy woollen cover that Tansy might well have knitted herself. A flower-patterned plastic screen hung on a steel rail around the bath, suspended from white plastic rings as large as bangles. Tansy did not approve of separate shower stalls; a bath was how she'd washed as a girl, and the wide old shower head was barely tolerated. I didn't mind, I enjoyed a long soak as much as anyone three or four times my age.

I pulled the screen back on its runner and studied the bath, which of course was empty, fighting an urge to throw off my sweaty clothes and jump in for a steaming soak. The possibility that six corpses had shared that bath caused me to change my mind, even as I shook my head in self-mockery.

The place smelled wonderful, that's what I was noticing most of all. Scalloped shells at bath and basin alike held a deep green translucent chunky oval of Pears soap, a green deeper than jade, and its aroma seemed to summon me back to childhood, when my mother washed me with the perfumed scents of cleanliness, then dried me briskly with a fluffy towel smelling of sunlight. I squeezed my eyes shut for a moment, caught myself sighing, opened them. Just an ordinary bathroom, really. Perhaps cleaner than most. Aunt Tansy was punctilious. The house was large and rambling but tidy; she ran a taut ship, with the help of a middle-aged 'treasure', Mrs Abbott, who came by twice a week and took over most of the vacuuming and dusting. But a ship insufficiently taut, apparently, to prevent a weekly visitation from the dead.

I glanced at my watch. Little wonder I was tired, it was nearly eleven. Great-Aunt Tansy was a woman of regular habits. Her invariable practice was to watch television while baking until the end of the Saturday night movie, clean her teeth, and be in bed by 11.30. It seemed her Saturday corpse must have put in its appearance by the time she switched the TV off at 11.15 or so, and was always gone when she rose for church at 8.30 on Sunday morning.

'Madness,' I muttered aloud, removed my heavy boots, and climbed into the bath, holding the bat in one hand. I got out again, lifted the woolly toilet seat, pissed for a while, flushed, left the seat up. This was my bathroom now, by default. I climbed back into the bath, cool on my feet through the socks. By leaving a gap between the plastic screen and the tiled wall, I was able to watch the closed and locked window through the small aperture. This meant sitting on the slippery rounded edge of the bath and stretching my neck into a ridiculous position, but I decided a few minutes dis-comfort for the cause was worth it. I thought of Tansy's homely gesture in insisting on shared cocoa and wished for something equally mundane to calm my jitters. Half my friends in school would have lit up a cigarette, but the foul things made me sick, and besides, even if I smoked there'd be little gain in advertising my presence. I caught myself. To whom? This was a delusion, an old lady's mad fancy.

The silence took on an eerie aspect. In her room below, Tansy might be sleeping by now, or perhaps lying awake, eyes wide and fixed on her dim ceiling. In the bathroom, no sound but my own breathing, not even the movement of wind in the trees below. I felt for a moment as if mine were the sole consciousness active in the whole world. A trickle of cold sweat ran down my back, some-thing I've only ever read about. In the last few weeks I had driven a powerful bike across vast plains, much of the landscape nearly barren due to the El Nino drought and maybe the Greenhouse Effect, I'd once come close to a fall from the skidding machine under the hooves of a hundred spooked cattle, and that had scared me without getting in my way; that was fear in the service of sharpened instincts and self-preservation. In Tansy's deathly quiet bathroom, I felt like wetting my pants.

My neck hurt. I got a sudden picture of how grotesque I looked, craning on the edge of the bath, which broke my mood. I laughed softly to myself and stood up, unkinking my spine, put my hand on the curtain to yank it back. The window nearest to me creaked ever so slightly, and I heard it open a little.

This was impossible. I was on the second floor of a tall old structure without a fire escape or any of that modern nonsense. I'd checked carefully to confirm my memory of the garden: no new lattices, the trees were all sensibly positioned metres away to prevent fire hazards, and Tansy's ladder was inside the house, not even outside in the locked shed. Dugald O'Brien was not raising a single wuffle in the night, let alone a bark at intruders. What the *hell*?

My heart slammed, and my mouth was dry. I pushed myself

back against the edge of the bath, back corrugated by the tiles of the wall, stared with difficulty through the gap. The nearer window was quietly pushed all the way open. I heard a muffled scuffle and a naked female back appeared in the window frame. A long brown leg came over the window sill, probed for the floor. My boots were sitting in plain view beside the toilet. Well, lots of people leave their clothes scattered about. Not in Tansy's house. But then these intruders would hardly be familiar with the nuances of Tansy's housekeeping policies. Don't be ludicrous, August, what would you know about what they know about? *There's a naked woman climbing in a second-storey window!*

She stood in the bathroom, her back to me. I felt an impulse to reach out and give her the surprise of her life with a playful smack on that pertly rounded ass. Less offensive, no doubt, than whacking her with the cricket bat, which I still clutched in my right numb hand; that might be sensible, if unsporting, but it wouldn't teach me anything about her bizarre activities. She was leaning out into the air, grunting and heaving, and suddenly hauled in the heavy front end of a very dead adult male through the window. The body stuck, shaking the window frame.

'Don't shove, Maybelline,' she said in an angry tone. 'You got the shoulders jammed.'

There was a tricky moment when the corpse withdrew a little, as she angled the shoulders, then surged back into the room to join the two of us. The far end of the corpse came into view, supported by an overweight muscular woman. Her biceps rippled impressively as she pushed the stiff hind quarters over the sill. The first woman let the carcass thud to the tiles. With a business-like grunt, Maybelline vaulted into the room. She was rather hairy, that much was obvious, her bikini line distinctly unfashionable. I thought I was drugged, or hallucinating, and then the first woman turned to face the bath, and I was sure of it.

Beauty like this you do not see, I told myself numbly, not in the real world. (That estimate was so astonishingly wrong, in such an astonishing way, that I simply note it here for the record.) Neither of the women was much older than me. University students, maybe, playing a preposterous prank. They moved about their macabre task with dispatch and grace, making a minimum of noise.

'Help me with his clothes, loon.'

Inside half a minute they'd stripped him of his shoes, suit and underwear. No attempt to search his jacket for billfold, nor to riffle his pockets. These were not pranksters, and certainly not simple thieves. He was blubbery and covered in hair about the back, shoulders and chest in the Mediterranean fashion; his hair-style had been a comb-over, which flopped repulsively to one side as they jostled him. I saw a small black hole in his left breast, and some thick, oozing blood. He had been shot through the heart. My own heart was ready to expire from overwork. The tough little wench took the murdered man under his armpits and hoisted him toward the bath.

'Loon, get the feet.'

She wasn't saying *loon*, it was more like 'lyoon'. Lune, the Moon seen from France?

Wait for it, I thought. Surpr-*ise!* Beautiful Lune grasped the edge of the plastic screen, threw it back along its runner. I stood up fast, bowed with a sweep of my right hand, and stepped out of the bath.

Both women stood petrified. In that moment of silence, stocky Maybelline's grip failed in terror, and the corpse hit the tiles again with a flat, unpleasant thump. 'Fuck!' she said, and shot through the window. I'll never again underestimate the speed of a corpulent human. Lune gave me a look of lovely, utter confusion, dropped the man's legs, bolted for the window.

'Sorry,' I said, and slammed the cricket bat down on the sill. She jerked back her fingers, stared at me in outrage, open-mouthed, and flew at me like a cat. There was nothing to grab of her but skin and hair. I was brought up nicely never to strike a woman. The corpse was leering up at us. I fell over on top of him, bringing Lune down as well, pinning her arms. She smelled really, really nice.

'Good god,' she said, 'get off me, you oaf. You *stink!* How long is it since you had a bath?'

It was so terribly unfair I just burst out laughing and let go of her.

Big mistake.

Lune had me in a headlock a second after I'd released her. She smacked the top of my head against the toilet bowl. I yowled and got free, stumbled to my feet, head ringing, slammed down the open window and locked it. In the night beyond, as the pane came down, I saw no sign of Maybelline or the crane that must have hoisted two women and a dead man up to this floor. I locked the window and the cricket bat caught me behind the right knee.

'Ow! Fuck! Will you *stop* that!' I yelped. As I turned I saw her in the big mirror, bat raised for a lethal stroke at my bruised skull. She was off balance for a moment as she brought it down; I side-stepped, kicked one leg of the corpse sideways to catch her next step. Lune fell into my arms. I was shockingly aroused, and tussled her into a sitting position on the lavatory. The seat was up, and she cried out indignantly as her bare backside hit the cold rim. One leg came up and her foot caught me in the thigh; something flashed, and I went shudderingly cold. From the heated rack I grabbed a thick, fluffy, warm towel and shoved it in her face, grasping her right foot and dragging it up so that she slid forward on the lavatory, banging her spine. There was a small row of silvery hieroglyphs carved into the instep of her foot.

She saw my shock, failed to recognise its nature.

'The mark of the beast,' she said sarcastically.

'Are you going to stay put, or do I have to hurt you? I'd rather not hurt you,' I said. Then: 'What?'

'My ID number,' she said, gibingly. 'My use-by date. That's what you think, I suppose? Another stupid mutilation fad.'

I wasn't thinking anything of the sort, but it was a useful suggestion.

'Yeah, well, it's preferable to a bolt through your tongue, I suppose.' I have nothing against body jewellery, but it seemed sensible to follow her lead up the garden path. I had the cricket bat by this point, and sat down opposite her on the edge of the bath. 'How did you get in? Who's this?' I nudged the dead guy who lay with one leg stuck out.

'The world is not as it seems,' she told me. She had wrapped herself in the towel, dropped toilet seat and cover and sat poised on it. I had never seen anyone so gloriously lovely, not at the movies, not on television, certainly not in this slightly down at heel suburb.

'No shit,' I said.

'What do they call you?'

'They call me August, Lyoon. They call me that because it's my name.'

'You've read Charles Fort, August?'

'No.' What, now we'll have a Reading Group? I glanced at the locked windows, waiting nervously for the backup troops to come barging in, maybe waving copies of the collected works of Charles Fort, whoever he was.

'He said, "I think we're property." And you *are*, you poor goose, you and all your fellow humans. Property is what you are, all six billion of you.'

I didn't laugh, it was too depressing for laughter. Aunt Tansy downstairs drifting in senile delusions, this gorgeous person upstairs heading for the same funny farm. No, wait. Tansy *wasn't* delusional. There *was* a corpse, and so presumably one *had* been delivered on each of the previous six Saturdays. Delivered by naked women, for all I knew, then disappeared in the early hours of Sunday morning. It didn't bear thinking about.

'So now that you've told me,' I said, 'I suppose you're going to have to kill me.'

Lune was horrified. 'Certainly not, what sort of immoral – You get your memory deleted.'

Someone had been priming Hollywood. Memory wipe – what was that, *Men in Black*, right? And people appearing out of thin air, or in this case through an impossibly high bathroom window, that went all the way back to *The Twilight Zone*. How come the scriptwriters and directors and actors didn't get their memories obliterated? There's always an escape clause in these mad conspiracy theories, and always a logical hole large enough to drive a tank through. Still –

'I know it's hard for you to listen to this,' Lune said. I thought I saw tears welling in her eyes. 'You're so brave and foolish, you humans. You invent one absurd creed and philosophy after another to persuade yourselves that you are the elect of some friendly deity. I'll say it bluntly: you're just a backdrop. You're the setting against which we play our parts.'

I shrugged. 'You're deluded,' I said. 'I've read that Phil Dick guy. He was crazy too, by the end.'

The air burned. I leaped so my back covered the door. Lune stayed where she was, perched on the toilet. She looked elegant, slightly sad. The same locked window blazed with blue flickering intensity, paint crackling. The glass crazed, vanished like steam. Maybelline shoved her stocky form through the gap, warily pointing a shiny steel tube at me, balancing herself with the other hand. She edged around the corpse on the floor, stood near Lune. I waited with my mouth open, expecting a blast of blue to swallow me down.

'You don't have to kill me,' I started to gabble. 'You're from a UFO, so you can take me back to your own planet, I've always wanted to travel, Illinois was interesting but space would be better. Roomier.' They stared at me. 'All right, not a spacecraft. You're from the future, it's a time machine outside the window, right? This guy would have been the next Hitler, so you're cleaning up the past before it contaminates your own time, I can live with that, your information is undoubtedly better than mine.'

'I told him they're all property,' Lune explained to her associate. 'I think it's unhinged him.'

'*What?* You stupid bitch, now we'll have to erase his medium term memory. The disposer will not be pleased.'

'We've got to delete his short term recall anyway, Maybelline, use your brains. I felt we owed him an explanation. There's something these humans use called "politeness" that I think you could damn well try yourself.'

•

'Shit, Lune.' Maybelline shook her head in remorse. 'I know you're not a stupid bitch. You're not any kind of a bitch, even if you are so beautiful I could scream.'

Lune offered her an accommodating smile, shrugged. The corpse leered up at us all from the floor. With a noise like tearing canvas, a short man pushed his way out through the mirror, stepping lightly from the basin to the floor. He carried a huge bag over his shoulder. I was ready to throw up. There wasn't enough room in the place to faint, so I stayed pinned against the door. All this racket, and still no word from Do Good. I hoped violently that none of the bastards had harmed the dear old beast.

'Here's a rum turn,' the disposer said, looking around. He was small cheerful fellow apparently in his fifties, with a bleary eye and a three-day growth of beard. On certain singers and movie stars that can be a cute look, if rather too last century for my tastes, but on this man it was distinctly seedy. On top of his tousled head sat an old cloth cap set at a rakish angle. 'Who's this chappie, then?' He beamed at the women, whipped an ancient meerschaum out of his jacket pocket. His jacket sleeves had leather patches. He stuffed the pipe with flake tobacco from a pouch and started to light it.

'Not in Aunt Tansy's house,' I said, and reached forward over the dead man and took the pipe from his mouth. He moved like a mongoose, had it back so fast my hand tingled. But he thrust it, unlighted, into his pocket, and put away his book of matches.

'My apologies. Rules of the house apply, of course. Come now, lassies, I don't know this gent's face at all.' He peered genially at me.

Both women spoke at once, stopped. Lune said, 'It's all right, sir, August got into this by mistake –'

'*Aug*ust?' cried Maybelline. 'You been sitting here exchanging *names* while I –'

'Now, now ladies.'

'Well, we'll be amnesing him, no harm done.'

'Aye, it's a fair bastard,' the disposer said, fingers plucking at his pocket for the pipe, dropped away again, 'when one of the humans gets into the wrong part of a Set. Ah well, a drop of the green ray and no harm's done. Now that you're here,' he said, rounding on me, 'give me an 'and with this codger.'

Dazed, simply unable to think, I helped him get the naked corpse into the bag, then fold in his shoes and clothing on top. We zipped the bag shut, me zipping, him pulling the edges together, and he hoisted the bundle up on his shoulder. I was mildly astonished that such a small man could tote such a weighty load, but I had seen too many unlikely happenings too rapidly, it was like stretching an elastic band to the point where it gives up the ghost and just lies there, no spring left in the thing.

'I'll be making a report about this fellow,' the disposer told the women, 'but give him a dose of the green and I think the Director will let you off with no demerits.'

He raised his cap to me. 'Good evening, sar, and thankee for your help with the props.' He clambered up on the basin, pulling out two drawers to make the climb easier, and tore open the mirror. He stepped into oblivion. The glass curdled, was once more still as a windless pond, golden tinted, slightly worn at its edges. I could see Maybelline's reflection, holding the tube trained on me. Blue flame, green ray, whatever. I just wanted to have a hot bath and go to bed and wake up from this rather pointless dream. But then all dreams are pointless, that's the thing about dreams.

'Go on, go on,' I said, 'climb out through the window and fly away on your magic broomsticks.'

'We have to –'

'Yes, I know.' How would they explain away the window without its glass, the burn marks in the paint? Maybe they'd come back while I slept and fix those as well. 'Well, get your nasty amnesia ray over with and let me catch some sleep, I've been on the road since six this morning.'

Lune looked at me, and took the tube from her companion. Maybelline wasted no time; she was out the window and gone. The beautiful woman stepped close to me, pulled down my head to her red mouth. I waited for her to bite me. A vampire element, perfect. 'The Drama doesn't have a tight script, August,' she said very softly in my ear. 'I'll come back and look in on you. Who knows?' To my amazement, she turned my face and kissed me. 'Goodbye.'

She stepped away, touched the tube at two points. I was flooded with emerald light. It was cold; I tingled with mild shock, and the room faded into dream. I swayed on my stockinged feet, saw her climb carefully through the gaping window frame. Lune seemed to hang in the dark outside, breasts half-shadowed. She did something that might have been a recalibration of the instrument, and blue light painted the window; it was as it had been, glazed, painted.

I waited for blackness, loss, amnesia. What I felt, instead, was pins and needles torturing my flesh. I stumped haltingly to the basin, flung cold water in my face. I could remember it all quite clearly. True, what I remembered was absurd, laughable, impossible. I dragged off my clothes as the water gushed into the bath, steam rising to fill the room. No fan. I sat in the wonderful hot water, rubbing fragrant Pears soap into my armpits and other stinky places. I propped my right foot out of the foamy water, turned it so I could examine the silver carven hieroglyphs on my sole. Pretty much the same as Lune's.

I towelled myself ferociously as the bath drained, wanting sleep so badly it was like hunger. I picked up my clothes and my boots and trotted on the cold boards in the dark to my bedroom. The window was already open, screened against insects, and through the wire mesh the sky was clear and very black, no moon, no broomsticks, no UFOs, no high-hanging *Truman Show* spotlights. Stars shone, and the smell of fresh soil and leaves came in from the garden on a cool breeze. Why had they slipped up? Surely their Records must show one Actor missing from duty, one Character in their bloody great Drama lost in the sea of humans when his parents died tragically? I gave the sky the bird, finger quivering. Not so smart, then. They'd lost me for close to two decades, I'd stay lost until I found the bastards on my own.

The pillow was warm. Lune. Her beautiful nakedness. The burning of her lips. Beyond the window the world was huge and dark. There were doorways out of it. I slept.

Rain Season

●

Leanne Frahm

Garth Lorgan clutched the receiver to his ear, absorbed in the words of Lennie Bedlow's CEO, Jonathon. He stared sightlessly through the third-storey office window at the fading light of the city.

'We want you to have this opportunity, Garth,' Jonathon was saying in his dry whispery voice, 'because Mr Bedlow believes that big companies can be too big, lose sight of the big picture, you understand?'

Garth nodded intently. 'Yes,' he said. 'Yes, I know exactly what you mean. You'll find we're the right size, compact but a real team, just the size Mr Bedlow is looking for.'

'Yes.' There was a pause, Garth could almost hear Jonathon thinking. A clap of thunder sounded faintly in the distance.

'Yes. Friday then? We'll get together on the site first, with Mr Bedlow. To give you exactly the scenario, before we get down to the basics, eh?'

'Friday?'

'That's not a problem, is it?' A touch of ice travelled with the words.

'No, no.' Garth said. He made it sound confident. 'God no. Friday's fine. The sooner we can get down to it, the sooner you'll find – Mr Bedlow will find – we're right for you.' He cursed the weak ending.

'Excellent,' said Jonathon with finality.

Garth gripped the receiver more tightly, as if to pull at Jonathon's sleeve, holding him. 'Just a minute,' he said. 'I should give you my mobile number, just in case . . .'

'No need,' said Jonathon crisply. 'Friday, on site.'

'Certainly. Right. Well, goodbye – I'll look forward to seeing you on Friday – ' The line went dead.

Garth sat motionless, holding his breath. Then he relaxed, exhaling. He slammed his fist on the desk savagely. 'Je-*sus*!' he said loudly.

This was it, the big chance. He'd *known* it would come, dammit! Years of running the agency on a shoe-string budget, advertising franchise boutiques in shopping centres for fat women who didn't think they were and championing shonky used car yards in the suburbs; reading the trade mags and envying Saatchi and Saatchi, Clemenger, all the big names; pouring over other ads for what made them work, feverishly making contacts and networking in the right places. Just to have that one big chance . . .

Bedlow's resorts.

The room brightened, and he glanced up at the window next to his desk (carefully placed in the Feng Shui Dragon Position; he didn't know if it worked, but potential clients might be impressed, and impression was everything). The afternoon sun had disappeared and in the sudden exterior dimness the fluorescent lights glowed more strongly. He leaned forward to look out across the buildings and office blocks of Fortitude Valley, towards the highrises of Brisbane.

Masses of black clouds were piling up in the east, the ocean, scudding towards the city. He heard another peal of thunder, closer. An afternoon storm, he noted abstractedly, his mind still with Lennie Bedlow and the big chance. He grinned and stood up abruptly, the chair rolling back on silent castors across the plush wine-coloured carpet. He'd tell the staff, get them to start thinking.

A sheet of rain dashed the window pane, vicious in its suddenness. Below him, Constance Street blurred in the early darkness, washed with streaks of primal colours as the running water caught the rainbow of neon signs. He opened the door.

'Listen up,' he said, striding out into the main office, and stopped.

The office was empty. The screens were covered, the work-stations bare.

Cara entered from the passageway that led to the toilets with her bag slung over her shoulder. 'Are you looking for Dee Dee and Mike, Mr Lorgan?' she said. She sauntered over to the reception desk and put some loose biros in the drawer. 'They've gone,' she said. 'It's after four-thirty – nearly.' She flicked a quick glance at him, twitching at the clinging skirt that barely covered the small mounds of her buttocks.

'Great,' said Garth, putting his hands on his hips. 'They knew that call was coming. They should have been here.'

'I'm sorry, Mr Lorgan. I didn't know – '

'All right, Cara. Where'd they go – the Dead Rat?'

She nodded.

'You finish up here. I'll chase them up and give them the good news. Excellent news, Cara.' He looked at her pretty, bored face with satisfaction. She went with the decor, with the jade green walls and the comfortless minimalist couch under the Dali prints. 'You're working at a prestigious agency now.'

She looked blank, uncertain of her response. 'That's nice, Mr Lorgan,' she said finally, fiddling with the strap of her bag. As she moved her arms her breasts became even more prominent under the silky fabric.

'Very nice,' he said. 'So nice we should celebrate. Why not come down to the Rat with us?'

She shook her head. 'I don't think so, Mr Lorgan. I would've, but with the rain ... The traffic's going to be awful. It's really heavy, isn't it?'

Garth turned. The rain was lashing down in a steady deluge, driving hard against the windows. He shrugged. 'It's undercover most of the way. But that's okay, go on home. And diary that I'll be out most of Friday. With Dee Dee.'

'All right, Mr Lorgan. Have a nice night.' Her skirt hem rose to her panty-line as she turned to leave and she pulled absently at it as she closed the door behind her.

'I will,' Garth said to himself. 'I will.'

The gutters along Constance Street ran deep with stormwater as the slanting rain splattered the concrete footpath. Garth moved through the after-work throng, as close to the buildings as possible. Despite the rain, the air was hot and perspiration pooled in his armpits.

The Dead Rat Hotel was crowded with the usual Friday night people, mostly from the offices along Fortitude Valley, a few tourists. He said hello a few times to faces he thought he knew, smiling. You always smiled in public, it went with success. He found Dee Dee and Mike planted on stools at the bar, flushed and laughing hard.

'Hi,' he said, pushing his way up to them. The noise was over-whelming.

'Yo, boss,' said Dee Dee, giggling.

'Garth,' Mike acknowledged.

'So,' Garth went on. 'Couldn't stay around to hear what Bedlow had to say?'

'Well –' said Mike.

Dee Dee's smile vanished. 'How did it go?' she muttered into her glass.

'I've got it,' he said triumphantly.

'*Got* it?' said Mike. The graphic designer looked incredulous.

'Just about. As good as,' Garth said. Dee Dee snorted and turned back to the bar.

'Listen,' he said angrily, 'It's there for the taking. Bedlow really wants us, and it's up to us to take it. As soon as we come up with a good concept, it's ours. And once I've got Bedlow and his resorts, they'll be knocking the doors down for us. You –' he pointed to Dee Dee ' – start thinking this weekend. No, now. We'll be seeing Bedlow on site on Friday, and I want to be talking proposals to him straight away.'

'What about Alfonso's?' said Dee Dee.

'What *about* Alfonso's?' Garth said.

'Alfonso's. The delicatessen chain. We were meeting *him* on Friday to look at the launch of the new branch at – '

'Shit. We don't want to lose accounts, even a bloody delicatessen, not yet.' Garth thought for a moment. 'Okay. You call him and change it.'

Dee Dee rolled her eyes, but said nothing. Mike grinned nervously.

'Right!' Garth slapped his hand on the bar. 'This is the big one, folks. Let's celebrate. Glen Fiddich all round.'

'Er, who's buying?' asked Mike cautiously.

Garth grinned at their suddenly interested faces. A gust of wind drove a torrent of rain through the door. The crowd surged back to avoid it, laughing and squealing.

'I am, Chucky. I am,' he said, and his laughter sounded big and confident, the way he knew it should.

Garth's Saab (second-hand, but good) crawled through the downpour, hugging the gutter. He squinted through the streaming windshield at grey bitumen and greyer rain, barely able to separate the two in the enfeebled glare of the headlights. There was little traffic at this hour. He was grateful for his renovated colonial cottage at New Farm, which had cost a small fortune, but it was close, handy to the office when the weather was bad (he could jog to work if he really wanted to) or when he might be a little over the limit . . . His grin was lop-sided.

Garth pulled up beside the high brick fence that screened the house, under a street-light illuminating the swarming arrows of rain. He opened the door and lurched up the path. He was soaked in seconds, shocked by the intensity of the drops on his skin and the eerie feeling of thin trickles running down his face from his flattened hair. There was a light in the living-room, shining through the mullioned windows. He blinked water from his eyes and hurried up the steps to the verandah.

Dry. He shook himself and water showered across the timber floor. As he unlocked the door a small white dog threw itself at him, yelping.

'Hi, Conan,' he said, picking up the prancing Lhasa Apso, and carried it through the foyer into the living-room, feeling its fur become draggled with the wetness of his clothes. He let it slip to the floor where it shook itself vigorously.

'You're soaking.' His wife, Lauren, sat curled up on the sofa by the trellised bar.

'It's raining,' he said.

'I know that.' She straightened her legs and sat up. 'You're dripping. On the rug. Everywhere.'

Garth looked down at the growing puddle around his feet. Conan sniffed at it, lapping tentatively. 'Sorry. I – '

'I suppose you've been at the bar again,' she said. The tiny lines around her mouth seemed more pronounced every time he looked at her. He nodded. 'Actually it was a celebration.'

His clothes were becoming uncomfortable, the material wet and stiff, chafing against his skin. He shoved the dog away with his foot. 'It looks like I've finally cracked the big time. Remember Bedlow? Remember his resorts?'

Lauren's gaze was expressionless, and that reminded him that he didn't quite have the account, not yet. He decided to be conciliatory. 'I'm sorry, I should have called you. You shouldn't have stayed up for me.'

'I didn't,' she said. 'I'm waiting for the girls.'

'They're still out? In this weather?' The night's drinks made it hard for his brain to focus. 'Where?'

Lauren looked away. 'At a rage, or rave, or whatever they call it this week. I don't know where.' Conan leapt on the sofa and snuggled into Lauren's side. She stroked the dog's silky dampness absently.

Garth was suddenly angry. 'My God, they're only fourteen,' he said loudly. 'What do you mean, letting them go to something like that, with drink and drugs and god knows what else! You're letting them run wild!'

'Fifteen,' said Lauren.

'What?'

'Fifteen. The twins had a birthday two weeks ago. Didn't you notice?' She stood up, shaking Conan to the floor. 'Perhaps I could control Melisah and Emilyjane better if I had some help.' Her voice quivered. 'Like from their father. If you weren't so busy promoting yourself, chasing after people you think are important, *celebrating*.'

He felt hot, the blood thudding in his forehead. 'It *is* important. I mean, they *are* important. This time it's the best chance yet, Bedlow *wants* me –' He stopped, suddenly conscious of Lauren's twisted smile and the rain drumming on the iron roof overhead.

'I'm going into the bedroom,' she said. 'For God's sake, dry yourself off.'

Next Friday morning saw rain falling from the low, leaden sky as inexorably as it had been all week. The trip had been impossibly slow; culverts washed out, creeks flooded. Snarled traffic crept along the highways and stopped altogether for minutes on end.

'The bloody weather bureau can't even say when it'll end,' said Dee Dee.

Garth didn't reply. He drove hunched forward, staring intently at the road, trying to distinguish the bitumen from the water-filled potholes. Dee Dee shrugged and turned her head away in silence.

When they turned onto the dirt road leading to the site, the low-slung Saab ground through the slush uneasily. Garth imagined the mud-encrusted paintwork and gritted his teeth. A high wire-mesh fence appeared from the blur of rain, separating scrubby bushland and vast areas of cleared land, all in shades of grey.

They drove through an open gate. 'Here already?' said Dee Dee brightly, and her sarcasm was as palpable as the humidity in the air around them. He ignored her.

The road led on to a concrete-block site office, where a Jeep Cherokee was parked. Garth pulled up beside it. '*That's* what you need for this sort of thing,' Dee Dee said. He nodded, feeling a stab of envy. 'Right, we're here,' he said, distracting himself.

As he switched off the motor, he heard the low booming of distant surf beyond the heavy patter of rain on the car's roof. He looked around. The misted distortion of the windows made the huge expanse of levelled ground surrounding them shimmeringly unreal and depressing. All colour was washed from the scene, with the exception of random groups of brilliant orange earth-moving machinery, like herds of gargantuan grazing beasts, oblivious of the rain.

Dee Dee nudged him sharply. 'Is that the legendary Bedlow?' He turned his head and saw a man in the doorway of the office block, gesturing at them.

'I don't know,' he muttered, feeling a spasm of excitement. He unbuckled the seat belt and opened the door. 'Come on.'

Rain soaked them warmly. 'Shit,' said Dee-Dee.

Garth and Dee Dee huddled under big black umbrellas on a small knoll some distance from the concrete office, trying to catch what Jonathon ('I'm sorry, Mr Bedlow is unable to attend in this inclement weather.') was saying under the fusillade of drops on the taut fabric.

The scale model of the proposed resort, displayed on a large table in the office and explained by Jonathon, was magnificent. Garth's breath caught in his throat every time he thought of it. Inside the office block, Jonathon's dry voice was barely audible over the sweep of the rain as he lectured them on lists of necessary material – brochures, videos, posters, advertisements – and issued them with a brief on Mr Bedlow's mandatories. Garth, nodding incessantly, passed them on to Dee Dee. Then Jonathon had requested, as Mr Bedlow would have suggested, that they walk through the area 'to absorb the atmosphere'. 'He's bloody joking,' Dee Dee mouthed worriedly as Jonathon went to a cupboard for the umbrellas. Garth frowned at her.

Now Garth's legs were aching from trudging through the morass of furrowed mud, and he could see Dee Dee's face was grim as she swayed, trying to stop her high heels sinking.

'The most important thing,' Jonathon was saying, 'what Mr Bedlow wants to impress most strongly, is that this resort is to be *natural*. An ecological resort. Five-star, of course, with every conceivable facility and luxury, but still uniquely *ecological*.'

He gestured towards the far-off beach. 'From here to there will be the golf course. Eighteen holes, designed by Davis if we can get him. The scrub has already been cleared and we've bulldozed the mangroves and imported some plantings to find the best grass for this area, as you can see.'

He pointed to the ground. Tufts of bright green grass struggled desperately upwards, but were drowning in the black mud oozing up around them. Garth saw his shoes were sinking into it too; the Gucci's had been a mistake, already soaked and stained. He shuffled surreptitiously, leaving deep footprints that immediately filled with water.

'Right,' he said, making his voice sound congratulatory and capable both at once. 'I think we've probably seen enough, Jonathon. Perhaps we could go back now . . .?'

Jonathon looked at him through spectacles misted with moisture. 'It is very important that you incorporate everything that Mr Bedlow has to say about this resort.'

'Believe me, Jonathon,' said Garth. 'This is the most important thing in the world for me.' He forced a smile. 'I won't let Mr Bedlow down. Never. Nothing will stand between me and whatever Mr Bedlow wants. Now can we get out of the rain?'

Even the teeming continual rain and half-heard news reports of flooding as the river rose couldn't dampen Garth's spirits on Monday morning. The staff briefing for Bedlow's was scheduled at nine and he wanted to start on it immediately with Dee Dee and Mike, and maybe that freelance Zac, the illustrator-cum-copywriter, who was good, very good, if expensive. Later, when this was a success, he could put on a staff copywriter, the firm would grow . . . He left the house promptly, before the girls were up, with a brief goodbye to Lauren.

He'd expected chaos on the roads, but there was surprisingly little traffic, even on Brunswick Street. Anne Street, though, was bumper to bumper with heavy haulage trucks, the rain beating savagely on their canvas loads and spraying the few pedestrians, but he was able to finally manoeuvre the Saab into the Chinatown parking lot, finding it only half-full. It's early yet, he thought.

He dived through the deluge for the cover of the footpath, under the dripping facades of the buildings, and glanced around. There were no cars at all in Brunswick Street on this side of the mall, but a flurry of activity and uniforms outside the railway entrance in the next block caught his attention, and he noticed three ambulances parked on the road. He wondered what had happened as he hurried on towards the office.

There was a rapid tapping of heels behind him, and his elbow was caught. He swung around. Dee Dee's face was pale under her heavy make-up and locks of damp hair hung loosely across her scarf.

'My God,' she said. 'Isn't it *awful*?'

'What?' said Garth.

She gestured back towards the ambulances. 'All those kids,' she said.

'I don't know what you're talking about,' he said impatiently. 'Come on.'

'But they're dead!'

He looked more closely at the distant figures. They were carrying stretchers and raindrops pounded on the plastic bags they held, reminding him of the drenched canvas of the trucks. 'What happened?' he said.

Dee Dee's voice had lost some of its usual confidence. 'I've just come up from the trains – mine's one of the few left running. Apparently a bunch of street kids were sheltering in a tunnel, and the river broke near it. There was a flood, they couldn't get out.'

'That's bad,' he said. 'Well, come on. We've got this meeting –'

Dee Dee stared at him. 'It's more than bad. The river's flooding all over, they've evacuated whole suburbs in places. Didn't you know?'

'No, I didn't notice. I've been busy,' he said pointedly. The nearby gutters were overflowing, sending tiny waves racing over the footpath at their shoes. Tendrils of wire-grass growing from the cracks trailed across the concrete, swept by the current. Garth looked more closely at them. They seemed to be growing while he watched . . .

He turned abruptly. 'Come on,' he said again to Dee Dee.

She shrugged and followed him through the rain.

Cara and Mike were late. 'It's the rain,' said Dee Dee reasonably. 'It's getting hard to move around.' Garth tried to curb his impatience. He spent the time going through Bedlow's documents again with Dee Dee.

When Cara came in she was flushed and damp, her make-up streaking, and her wet dress clinging to her body. 'Sorry,' she said breathlessly as Garth looked at her. He was about to say something, but Mike entered just then, swearing.

'Shit, Garth,' said Mike. 'This is ridiculous. We can't keep coming in through this. Do you know how many buses are running now?' Garth opened his mouth to answer.

'Fuck all, *that's* how many!'

Garth had never seen Mike angry. Dee Dee stepped in calmly.

'Maybe we should close for a while, until things get back to normal,' she said. Cara nodded tentatively.

Garth turned on her, feeling the blood rush to his head. 'Close?' he shouted. '*Close?* With Bedlow ready for the drawing board? With the biggest job of our lives in front of us? You have got to be joking, all of you.' He glared at each of them in turn. 'How easy do you think it is to find jobs in this industry right now?' There was a long silence.

'All right, all right,' said Dee Dee. 'We're here now, we may as well do something.'

'Right.' He was calmer now, more composed. He flicked through the folios on the desk and pulled out some pages. 'Here, Cara. Photocopy these so we've all got copies.'

She took them from him wordlessly.

'Now,' he said, addressing Dee Dee and Mike, 'I've spent a considerable amount of time on this over the weekend, and you would have too, Dee Dee, seeing you've already heard some of the ideas Bedlow has.' She nodded. 'We'll go through these with you, Mike . . . What?' Cara was at his elbow, her hands full of papers.

'It's not working,' she said.

'What's not working?' Garth said irritably.

'The photocopier. Look.' She held out a photocopied page. 'It's all blurry.'

He grabbed it from her. 'Shit,' he said. 'The paper's wet.'

'It must be the dampness,' said Dee Dee. 'The humidity . . .'

Garth strode to the cupboard where the stationery was kept and pulled out a ream of paper. He ripped open the cover. 'Jesus, it's all like that. *Christ* – doesn't *anything* work around here?'

'It's okay,' said Dee Dee, taking it from him. 'I'll get it dry, don't worry . . .'

'Well, bloody hurry up!' Garth walked over to the window and stared at the rain, his hands in his pockets. The street was empty. Only a crowd of seagulls moved through the downpour, scavenging among masses of vegetation that seemed to be choking the gutters and spilling across the road and footpaths. He wondered with annoyance why the Council wasn't clearing it away.

'Where's my shirt, the one with the navy stripe?' Garth called, rifling through the clothes hanging in his wardrobe. The light in the bedroom seemed dimmer than usual and the rain still drummed incessantly on the roof.

'You wore it the other day,' said Lauren shortly, bending to smooth sheets over the bed.

He turned to face her. 'Well, why isn't it washed?' he said.

'There've been electricity cuts – haven't you noticed?'

'Of course I've bloody noticed. The Mac keeps crashing, we're losing Bedlow's files all the time. We have to keep saving every few seconds. Don't talk to me about electricity cuts. Anyway, what's that got to do with my shirts?'

Lauren straightened and looked at him. 'The washing machine, the drier, the iron – they all need electricity, remember? I can only do so much when it's on, and no, I haven't been able to manage the shirt with navy stripes yet!' Her voice quivered.

'All right, all right.' He plucked another shirt from a hanger. 'I just want to look good, in case Bedlow drops in. He could, any time . . .'

'Bedlow, Bedlow, Bedlow. That's all I hear about. In the middle of a crisis like this!'

'Crisis?' Garth shrugged his shirt on and buttoned it. 'Oh, you mean the rain.'

'The rain? The rain?' Her voice rose. 'Yes, I mean the bloody *rain*.'

'There's no need to get hysterical,' he said with exasperation. He opened the door to see Melisah and Emilyjane coming out of the bathroom together, still in their pyjamas. The apricot walls looked grey in the gloom. Then the lights flickered and came back stronger, and he could see they *were* grey, a layer of mildew had settled on them. He decided not to mention this to Lauren, not in her current mood.

'Breakfast ready?' he said.

'What there is of it,' Lauren muttered behind him.

'What do you mean?' he said.

'I mean most of the stores are shut.' Lauren followed him down the hallway. 'And the ones still open have bugger-all supplies.'

'Lauren!' he said, surprised. The girls giggled and sat down at the table in the dim dining room.

Garth pulled his chair out. 'Why aren't you two dressed for school yet?'

'The schools are closed,' said Lauren. 'That is, the ones that aren't completely under water. I told you it was a crisis.'

Garth shook his head and picked up a piece of bread with a smear of butter on it. He looked at it with distaste. 'I must be the only person in Brisbane still working,' he said.

Lauren looked at him. 'Probably,' she agreed.

On the way to the Saab through the grey curtain of rain, Garth noticed the garden was a mess. The lawn was destroyed, ragged clods of grass criss-crossed with small ravines and gullies that trickled water. Weeds had engulfed the roses, and the few native plants ran rampant, tangled with large-leaved vines and grasses. He'd have to tell Lauren to get that gardener chap in, to clean it up. What if Bedlow visited?

He got into the car and closed the umbrella, shaking it before closing the door. Through the fogged windscreen he could see oceans of potholes, the jagged edges of their coastlines scarring the bitumen. He winced at the thought of driving the Saab over them, and felt another surge of anger at the Council for allowing it to happen. It was anger tinged with desperation. Why was all this happening *now*?

He put the Saab into first gear and inched his way forward, towards the Valley.

The phone rang. The voice beyond the rain was scratchy and distant, Cara's. 'I can't get in, Mr Lorgan,' she said. 'I just can't.'

Garth clenched his fist around the receiver, studying the wall in front of him, the one with the Dali prints on it. The electricity was working and the lights were on, highlighting the coating of mildew that painted a surrealistic mural that swept across the cornice to become a huge dark cloud across the ceiling, pressing down on him.

He put his hand over the receiver. 'Dee Dee,' he said. She looked up from her desk. She wore jeans and boots, and no make-up. Her hair was pulled back in a careless pony-tail. He frowned.

'Dee Dee, get in touch with building maintenance and get a cleaner in. This place has just got to be cleaned up.' She shrugged, and looked back down at her work.

He cleared his throat and spoke into the phone. 'Cara, I need you in here. The work is piling up, particularly with the computer down most of the time. I've even got hold of a manual typewriter for you.' He looked across at the clumsy black Remington sitting on Cara's desk, its bulky keys on their thin metal arms startlingly anachronistic among the computers and screens. 'This job has to go through.'

'But . . .'

'I don't want to hear "but", Cara.' Dee Dee paused and looked up at him again. He turned his back on her. 'Walk, if you have to, swim, I don't care. Just get your arse in here quick-smart, or I'll make sure it's not just this industry you don't work in, but any fucking industry at all! *Now*!'

He slammed the receiver down, breathing hard.

'You're an idiot.' Dee Dee's voice was politely conversational.

'What?' He swung round. She was tapping her pen on a thumbnail.

'Nothing,' she said. Garth gaped at her, but her head was bent again, and he wondered if he'd misheard. The phone rang. He snatched at it.

'What?' he yelled.

There was silence for a moment. Then an uncertain 'Garth?' It was Mike.

'Yes, yes. It's me,' said Garth. 'What is it? Why aren't you here?'

'I won't be in again, Garth. I'm finishing.'

'Finishing?' Garth stared at the screensaver on a monitor. Dull colours twisted hypnotically on it, mirroring the rolling rain-clouds beyond the window.

'That's right. I'm leaving.' Mike's tone was final, with just a touch of fear.

'You can't,' said Garth flatly.

'Sorry. Goodbye.'

Garth put the receiver down carefully and pushed his hair back from his sticky forehead. He looked around. Dee Dee's head was bent even lower, and he wasn't sure from the motion of her shoulders if she was laughing or not.

'Okay,' he said, straightening his shoulders. 'We just work harder. We don't let this slip away just because of the weather. Right?'

'Sure, boss.' Dee Dee's voice was muffled.

Garth walked over to Mike's desktop, grimacing. He looked

down at the carpet. Its deep purple was almost black beneath layers of piled grit.

'Don't forget that cleaner,' he said.

He was still at Mike's work-station when Cara came in. He stared at her. She was soaked, her hair plastered to her face in dull brown strands. Her bare legs and feet were muddy. Water trickled the wrinkled length of her tight, bright green dress and mixed with the mud to settle on the floor around her in a viscous black pool, as if she was dissolving in front of them.

'Jesus, Cara!' Garth wrinkled his nose in distaste. 'For God's sake, you can't work like that! Clean yourself up.'

Her mottled face reddened and he realised she'd already been crying. Dee Dee got up from her desk and went to her. 'Come on,' she said. 'I'll help.' She took Cara's hand to lead her towards the bathroom.

As they turned away, Garth saw something bloated, black and shiny hanging from the back of her thigh, just below the hem of her ridiculously short skirt. It swayed as she moved.

He stared aghast. It was a leech.

The Saab ran out of fuel at the bottom of the last hill before the house. Sighing, Garth switched off the engine and got out. He locked the doors and set off through the rain.

A series of shouts and squeals mingled with hysterical barks sounded from the back yard of the house as he drew closer. He trudged through the slush that had been the lawn to the gate that led to the back, wondering tiredly what new crisis Lauren had involved herself in. The wood of the gate felt soft and rotten, crumbling a little under his hand. He pushed it open and stopped.

Melisah and Emilyjane were running along the back fence, each with one of his golf clubs in her hand. They were wearing bikinis, and the rain dashed down on them, wetness shining their golden skins and highlighting the movement of their young muscles as they ran. A bedraggled Conan yapped at their heels excitedly.

Melisah paused. 'Mum,' she called, 'Call Conan. He's getting in the way!' She kicked at the dog which responded with a surprised yelp, and started off again, following Emilyjane.

Garth looked round and saw Lauren standing on the flagstones under the pergola at the back of the house, holding a large kitchen knife. 'What on earth is going on?' he said, striding towards her.

'Quiet!' she said, her eyes shining, watching the girls intently. 'Yes, yes,' she called, 'it's circling the gum. Get it on the way up!'

Garth swung round in time to see Melisah and Emilyjane stop and begin to pound into the eucalyptus with his clubs. 'Hey! Stop that!' he shouted, anger giving him the strength to run towards them. 'What do you think you're . . .' He stopped, stupefied, his mouth hanging open.

The girls were resting on the clubs now, breathing hard, studying the creature lying at their feet. Conan sniffed it, growling uncertainly. It was a goanna, a large one. Its striped hide was stippled with specks of bright blood that washed into a pink puddle around their feet.

Lauren splashed over to join them. Emilyjane and Melisah grinned at her, Melisah wiping her wet fringe back from her forehead. 'Well done,' said Lauren, smiling and putting her arm around Emilyjane. She gave the knife to Melisah who squatted down beside the carcase.

Garth was staring at his discarded golf-clubs lying in the mud and rage overtook his astonishment. 'What is going on?' he said harshly. Lauren looked at him as if he had only just arrived. 'Dinner,' she said off-handedly.

'Whose dinner?' said Garth.

She smiled at him as if he was one of the twins. 'You probably wouldn't be aware of it, but a state of emergency's been declared. There's no food, and they can't get any in. We have to look after ourselves now.'

Garth was incredulous. 'You mean you intend for us to eat *that*?'

Lauren nodded. 'We've got a bit of tinned stuff put away, but it makes sense to stretch it out with what we can catch.' She put her other arm around Melisah, who was still wrestling with the bloodied body of the goanna, and smiled. 'The girls are good at this.'

Emilyjane turned to her mother. 'Yes, but we have to do something about Conan. He's not a hunter, he just gets in the way.'

Lauren nodded again. 'Inside now, and get dry.' The girls ran off towards the house.

'And get into something decent,' Garth called.

'Why?' said Lauren. 'I mean,' she went on as Garth frowned at her. 'We can't wash clothes, and the twins are always wet. Bikinis make sense. Besides, nearly everyone else is gone.'

'We're not going anywhere,' said Garth quickly, 'Not with Bedlow's project . . .'

Lauren studied him. 'No,' she agreed to his surprise. 'We don't want to leave yet, either.' She turned and followed the twins into the house.

Garth stood in the rain. Lauren seemed younger to him, more alive, like the twins. Conan sniffed at his foot and whined for attention. 'By the way,' he said to her retreating body, 'The Saab's out of fuel. None of the service stations are open. I'll have to walk to work.'

Constance Street was empty of cars and pedestrians. It was awash, and grass and reeds grew in lush abundance around it. Eucalyptus saplings were struggling through the bitumen and lantana bushes pushed up through the grates where the stormwater bubbled, trying to escape. Garth was as wet with perspiration as with rainwater as he struggled through the swamp.

The foyer of the building gave some protection from the rain, but not from the vegetation. Weeds and vines had found purchase in the carpet and brightly coloured patches of lichen defaced the walls. Cobwebs dangled from the ceiling, sticking to him as he tried to brush past them. He wiped his face and undid the top button of his shirt as he climbed the stairs to his office. The monotonous sound of driving rain followed him.

Dee Dee was propped on a chair with a sketchbook on her lap

and her feet on her desk, which was scattered with crayons and coloured pencils. 'Hi,' she said briefly as he entered. The sensitive fern-like leaves of a patch of weed curled in upon themselves as he wiped his feet near them.

'Christ,' he said. 'It's so hot in here.'

'Well,' said Dee Dee, looking up. 'No electricity, no air-conditioning, and sealed windows. What do you expect?'

'Maybe you should get on to maintenance, get a generator in or something – '

'Get real,' she muttered, returning to her colouring-in.

Garth ignored her and shuffled to Mike's desk, where the latest lay-outs were set out. A fringe of bluish mould sprouted from the top page, and he carefully wiped it off with a scrap of tissue. He stared at them for some time.

The phone rang and he picked it up, clearing his throat. 'Lorgan and Associates,' he said.

He stood listening to the voice at the other end. 'Cara,' he said finally, 'We've been through all this before. I don't *care* if you're finding it hard . . .'

Dee Dee was on her feet and grabbed the receiver from him before he could protest. She turned away from him. 'Hi, Cara,' she said, 'It's Dee.' There was a pause while she listened, and he had time to wonder why she was wearing what looked like a scabbard with a Bowie knife on her belt. 'No, don't worry about that. Really. It doesn't matter any more. It's time to go.'

Garth started forward and raised his hand in protest. She swung away from him. 'That's right, time to get out. I'm heading for Montville, up in the mountains. Want to come?' She waited for Cara's response, and then laughed. 'We'll *walk*! Course we can. Okay, I'll meet you there and we'll be off. Wear boots. Bye.'

Dee Dee put down the phone and brushed aside a glossy-leaved liana vine coiled around the cord.

'You mean that?' said Garth. 'You're leaving, both of you? Leaving me here – with this?' He gestured at the papers and documents strewn around the office.

'Uh-huh,' said Dee Dee, picking up her bag from the desk, wiping a film of mould from it carelessly.

'Leaving me with all this work, in these god-awful conditions, in this god-damn heat –' His voice rose, he could feel it becoming a scream, and his ulcer spasmed.

'Heat? Hot, are you?' said Dee Dee. 'Well, I can fix that!'

She picked up her chair and hurled it through the window. There was a crash of breaking glass and the suddenly loud hiss of rain. It poured through the fragile shards that remained intact, drenching the furniture and carpet, and a warm breeze caught the papers, fanning them across the room.

Garth clutched at them wildly, his mouth open, as Dee Dee slammed the door behind her.

Something large made a slithering noise behind the photo-copier.

The force of the rain sprayed moisture through the fabric of the umbrella. It didn't matter, Garth was damp all the time now, it seemed. The walk home through the dusk was a nightmare of wading through once-familiar territory that had somehow become swampland, disturbing strange birds and things that scuttled through the waist-high grass as he went. His legs ached. The sight of the colonial cottage wavering through the dimness and rain brought a sigh of relief to his lips.

He was on the last step to the verandah when a large shaggy dog bounded out at him from the dark of the house. He stopped abruptly as it snarled, lowering its body into a crouch, its mouth open showing sharp fangs.

'Lauren!' Garth called, his voice wavering. The dog made a rumbling sound in its throat and edged closer.

'Lauren! What is this? Are you alright?' The dog was gathering itself to spring, he knew it was.

Lauren stepped onto the verandah and clapped her hands. 'Here Wolf.' The dog jumped up and ran to her side, panting. 'Good boy!' she said, burying her hand in the thick fur of its neck.

Garth dragged himself up the last step, feeling his legs quivering. 'Where did that come from?' he gasped.

'The girls needed him,' Lauren said. 'He helps.'

'The electricity's totally gone,' he said.

'I know,' said Lauren.

Garth followed her and the dog into the house. The kitchen was lit with candles, and a makeshift fireplace had been built with bricks on the slate floor near the dishwasher. It made the room hot, and steam rose from the water trickling down the walls from leaks in the roof. Garth sat down, feeling fatigue drain him.

'Where are the girls?' he said dully.

'In the back yard, getting the meat ready.'

'Not goanna again,' he said.

Lauren shook her head. She was busy with a saw, cutting the legs off a stained mahogany chair that Garth was sure belonged to the Wallaces, next door. He'd seen it when they'd visited for dinner, a long time ago.

He looked round absently. 'Where's Conan?' he said. 'I don't think he'll like this new dog very much, will he?'

'I don't think it matters,' said Lauren.

Beneath the dreary pall of rain Fortitude Valley was deserted and unrecognisable. Colourful banners advertising the next festival were reduced to ragged tatters and the gaily-striped awnings were shredded. The facades of the buildings were disfigured by opportunistic and unidentifiable growths, and the Chinatown lions seemed somehow smaller and misshapen, eroded by the constant rain. A small sea had risen in the Brunswick Street Mall, its waters scarred by the constant eruption of raindrops on the surface. Wavelets lapped into the reeds as he tramped through them, and he disturbed a flock of magpie geese gathered on the verges. Their grotesquely shaped heads jerked back and forth as he pushed past them.

He stopped at McWhirter's, where the automatic doors were open, jammed by waist-high masses of vegetation and debris. Inside, the ceiling was encrusted with growths of vibrant coloured fungi.

Closer to his building, the Dead Rat Hotel was much the same. There was no movement in the darkness beyond its front doors, and he remembered with a strange hunger the nights he had spent in there with Dee Dee and Mike. He hoped there were a few drinks left, to celebrate with when the work was completed. It would be. He'd finish it by himself. Soon. He didn't need the others. None of them.

A dismal chorus of honking sounded, and he looked back. The geese had followed him. He hurried on up the stairs to his dark office. To continue.

In the flickering of the candlelight, the big dog's eyes were shining pinholes of infinity as it lay curled near the twins, watching him enter the kitchen. Melisah and Emilyjane were sitting on the floor, legs crossed, intent on the objects around them. They had discarded their bikini tops. Garth pretended not to notice.

Lauren knelt by the fire, shredding a pile of newspapers, dressed only in a bra and panties. The flames crackled and hissed with the moisture in the furniture she was burning and he could feel sweat breaking out on his body. He sat down near the girls, trying to ignore the shifting of the dog. In the wavering light he could see the things they were working with – a broom handle, empty tin cans, his golf clubs, shears, wire, knives ... Their hair hung in dishevelled curls across their shadowed faces and their strong young hands were busy.

He cleared his throat. 'What are you doing?' he said. They looked at each other, then at their mother.

Lauren shook her hair back. 'Making spears,' she said matter-of-factly. Her face was flushed from the heat.

'Oh,' he said.

Garth sat at his desk, staring vacantly through the window of his office. Brisbane was a grey mirage through the rain, wavering and indistinct. There was no movement anywhere beyond the pelting water. With an effort he pulled his gaze down to his desk.

The work was almost done.

Shuffling through some papers, he extracted one and began reading by the dim light that filtered through the window.

The guinea grass in the front office rustled, and he stiffened. 'Who's there?' he called hoarsely.

A small furry shape dashed across the doorway and vanished. An animal, maybe a bandicoot. He sank back in his chair, feeling his lips twitch nervously. Lucky for it the twins weren't here. He picked up his biro and began making notes.

The phone rang. He snatched at it.

'Who's there? I mean, Lorgan and Associates,' he said.

'Garth. How are you?' Jonathon's dusty voice was unmistakable.

'Jonathon, it's good to hear from you,' Garth said, trying to make his voice sound warm.

'I wasn't sure that you'd be there,' Jonathon went on.

'Certainly wouldn't be anywhere else, not when there's work to be done,' Garth said heartily. 'I'm glad you rang, I've got great news. We've just about wrapped up the submission, and we're looking forward to showing it to Mr Bedlow just as soon as – '

'That's very good,' Jonathon interrupted. 'But unfortunately there has been a change of plan.'

Garth's face went cold. 'Well, we can accommodate any of Mr Bedlow's changes,' he said. 'We're nothing if not flexible here. That's the beauty of a small business. Flexible.'

'You don't understand,' said Jonathon patiently. 'Mr Bedlow has instructed me to tell you that the project is off.'

'Off?' Garth was bewildered, the word making no sense.

'Yes. Owing to your continuing inclement weather, Mr Bedlow doesn't believe there is much future in an ecological resort at that particular location. Mr Bedlow is looking elsewhere.'

'But surely our work will be relevant, wherever it is,' said Garth desperately. He was surprised to feel hot tears stinging his eye-lids.

'Elsewhere is overseas,' said Jonathon. 'Thank you for your involvement and commitment. Goodbye.'

There was a click on the line, then a hissing, as if all the rain in the world was falling through it.

The dog seemed not to have moved from its spot near the sink, where the heat from the constant fire radiated warmly. It opened its jaws, tongue lolling, as Garth entered, staggering under the weight of a brimming cardboard box.

He put the box on the kitchen table and collapsed into a chair next to Lauren, who was grinding seeds in a bowl with a smooth rock. The reddish firelight jumped and flickered uncertainly, casting deep shadows that swayed back and forth across the walls. His clothes felt hot and heavy and he slowly undid his shirt buttons. Lauren looked up from her work and nodded to him. Her skin was white and water-wrinkled, and strangely attractive.

Emilyjane and Melisah were together on the floor. Melisah's face was drawn into a frown of concentration as she sat drawing intricate designs across Emilyjane's cheeks and breasts with a marking pen, to match the ones on her own.

He looked away. There was a pyramid of tin cans arranged against the far wall that hadn't been there earlier, he was sure, and the girls' spears lay close by. The sharp tip of one was still shiny with blood.

Rain rattled inexorably on the roof.

'Here,' said Garth. He pushed the box of A3 envelopes containing Bedlow's project across the table towards Lauren. She smiled at him, and rose to add them to the fire.

Glimmer-by-Dark

•

Marianne de Pierres

I drifted back to Carmine Island on a whim, a fragment of memory, like a warm current. A means to float, no matter how much I wanted to drown.

Years before, families had clustered there, hungry for the sparkling water and unstained sand. In those days, ferries scurried like schools of busy reef fish to and from the mainland, their patrons littering the island with holiday trash, scarlet coral cuts and the agony of sunstroke, oblivious to the spirit winds.

Now only one barge still ran. A tired, flat-backed Beluga, wallowing its way through its last days. My custom had been to ride the stern. But I was a different person now. Worn by heartache.

The other passengers, I noticed, wore their own badges of disappointment. Some dressed in casual wealth, some in gaudy rags. I slumped among their fedoras and sarongs, sipping margaritas in the bar, while the wind whipped a whisper of life against my skin.

Their incurious glances lulled me. Perhaps Carmine Island would heal my pain where time and neuro-feedback gongs hadn't.

An hour on the barge saw one aspect of Carmine rising from the sea. Despite myself I strained to catch the view: turquoise water shimmering before black reef mirages, the gauzy web of spores buoyant on The Bara.

The spores had settled a decade ago, a freak of nature blown in from deeper waters, settling like a veil over Carmine, bringing with them fierce irritations and allergies. The residents who couldn't afford the expensive immunosuppressants suffered the exotic, often terminal, afflictions of the spores. Holiday-makers deserted but those resolute in their seclusion stayed. Tourism confined itself to the indolent young rich, clutching the antidote Tyline, searching for the hint of danger to shift their inertia.

My supply of the antidote was tucked in the waterproof pocket of my spray jacket. Half a year's worth – the last of my savings – buying isolation.

The floating pontoon undulated as the barge sighed alongside. Unsteadily – was it the margaritas? – I stumbled along it and caught the trans-island commuter. It dropped me in front of the realtor's, a flat beach house on Mariners Drive with its stilts rooted deep in the dune.

I scanned the window ads, scrolling quickly to what I could afford. Only two properties for rent, a unit at Los Nidos and a shack on the beach at Glimmer-by-Dark. I paid a month for the shack, leaving my palm print, the code to my savings account on the mainland.

'Have you got your Tyline?' asked the golden-skinned girl at the desk.

I nodded, not one for unnecessary words.

The bridge of her forehead bulged slightly, her watery eyes changed to startling aqua by the spores. She ticked a box on my profile and sighed, 'The whales sing on the full moon. The Sapphire Lounge and Bara Beach are off limits to tourists. Enjoy your stay.'

The sigh, I guessed, was about the Tyline. I was another tourist, when the locals had dwindled to so few.

I took the map she offered, and walked to Glimmer-by-Dark through the dunes. The spores danced above me in a riot of cerise hues, interconnected by an ephemeral webbing, filtering the sun so that everything seemed bathed in rarefied light. In the distance, waves crashed rhythmically in a gentle tattoo.

Avoiding the tourist path, I laboured like an initiate in an alien

•

land. At the top of the largest dune, a gasp escaped me. Immense rose-tainted sandcastles scattered the length of Bara Beach, rising like palaces – the work of the mysterious spores, bringing recognisable form to random matter. Although wind and water had blunted turrets and collapsed rampart walls, somehow they survived the tidal ebb, soldiers in a perennial last stand. Rocky headlands buttressed them, cloaked in brilliant splashes of algae. The vibrancy of the colours bruised my eyes, forcing me to turn away and seek the rocky tourist path toward Glimmer-by-Dark.

The shack was sparse and austere, an unconsciously appropriate choice. I dozed in a chair on the deck, exhausted by the walk and the decision that brought me to Carmine.

'It's the spores, you understand. They're tiring at first.' The soft, cultured voice stung me out of my lethargy like gunshot. A man, younger than me, bare-chested, slightly built and smiling. Handsome.

'Mills-Thomas. Charlie, actually. Semi-retired journalist.' He thrust out a hand.

Reluctantly I took it. Younger men ignored me now. I wasn't sure how to act.

'Tinashi.'

'Pretty. Like its owner.'

The easy flattery confused me. I closed my eyes hoping that the man would vanish as he'd appeared.

'We're having a meal at my place tonight. Glimmer beach folk only. Even Katrin. Come along before dark, second beach house before the breakwater. Meet the crowd.' He squeezed my shoulder lightly. A friendly gesture.

I shuddered at it, fighting my instinct to draw away from his touch. Instead I drew a tight breath. 'Thank you.'

'You're lucky. It's a glitter-rose dusk tonight,' he said with a mildly quizzical look, and left.

I stayed in the chair, then, alert for other intruders, but no one came near me. In the distance I saw a figure on the beach, well past the line of tumbled shacks, almost to the crook of the next rocky headland. Tall, I guessed. Long, sweeping hair like wings. Engaged in a frenzied pacing.

Eventually I tired of my observations and went inside to unpack my bag. The cupboards remained sadly empty afterwards. Traversing the tiny rooms I noticed a bowl of island fruits on the table, and in the fridge a bottle of pink champagne, somehow spirited there before my arrival. Biting into a sweet, velvety pai, I returned to the deck and resumed my vigil over the beach. But the strange figure had gone and eventually I dozed again.

The growing shadows of dusk disturbed my dreams, turning them gloomy. I awoke with a start, mouth dry, and staggered to the kitchenette. The water still tasted crystal clear, an alluring island feature from bygone days. Dragging my fingers roughly through my hair, and nursing several pieces of fruit in the crook of my arm, I hurried from my shack towards the breakwater.

Party lights and laughter guided me to the young man's house.

'Tinashi. Join us,' Charlie took the fruit, touching my arm again, like an old friend. He wore a printed floral shirt soaked with the scent of jasmine.

I pasted blandness to my face to disguise my anger at being forced into such artificialities.

'Meet the crew. Geronimo, deep-sea fisherman moonlighting with the local whale-song eco-exploiters; Lauren and Quentin Carson, on honeymoon for a year; Armagh and his daughter Jaella – Armagh teaches divinity at the school, and Jaella works at the store; and Professor Arthur Wang, our resident Professor of Marine Biology, on sabbatical.'

I flickered a tense smile at them.

Apart from the enormous Geronimo, whose mohawk glistened like bunched, wet seaweed, they seemed unremarkable. Lauren and Quentin, smoothly blonde and elegant, held hands. Teenage-thin Jaella fidgeted, bored by the whole thing and embarrassed by her father, Armagh, whose eyes were half closed in what I took for prayer or meditation.

'Aren't you going to introduce me, Charlie?'

I stared past the curious faces to the shadows at the end of the room. A tall, lean figure stepped from them, thick hair like wings hanging to her hips.

'Katrin.' She introduced herself with a strange grin, hovering like threat. 'Always the last. They think I'm a witch,' she said.

In the light she seemed older, but quite beautiful, brimming with a vitality, and restlessness. Her eyes were black – no – dark violet. Spore eyes?

Charlie giggled. Nervous and high, like a young girl. 'Katrin likes to joke.'

I studied her face, distracted momentarily from my despondency and the difficulty of new people.

Katrin posed, one way and then the other, like a photographer's model, face tilted, chin high and confident. 'Seen enough?' she asked me.

I felt warmth in my cheeks.

'Ignore her. She'll soon stop.' Arthur Wang sidled up next to me, barely reaching my shoulder.

Before I could reply the others were moving, scooping up glasses, turning to the beach, laughing off the moment with chatter. Charlie slipped a flute of pink champagne into my hand.

'Tradition,' he said. 'Pink at glitter-rose.'

I sipped it quickly, avoiding his hopeful, eager smile and jasmine-scented warmth, and stepped out onto the patio between Geronimo and Arthur Wang.

Their murmur washed over me as we waited.

With the last of the sunset The Bara breeze dropped to a breath, and a strange phosphorescence claimed the sand. Colourless at first and rapidly changing to a carpet of tiny, shining, rose coloured grains. Something about them seemed to compel me to hasten to the beach and run them through my fingers and toes.

I must have stirred, because Geronimo and Arthur Wang each laid a hand on my arm.

'The spores are active,' Arthur Wang explained. 'Walking the beach during glitter-rose can be – ' he trailed off.

Geronimo took it up, his voice a quiet boom. 'What the Prof is saying, Tinashi, is – if you walk on the beach at glitter-rose, you might as well feed your Tyline to the fish. You don't know what the spores will do, how they will change you. Everyone is different. The locals, I mean. Some things you can see, like the eyes and the water retention in the forehead. Others it's only on the inside. They're the ones to watch. You never know about them. By heaven, it's tempting though.' His voice brimmed with emotion in that last sentence, like a man at the limit of his endurance.

I glanced among them then, and saw his feeling mirrored in the others' faces. Longing. And fear.

I gulped my pink champagne deeply and felt the tingle waken dead places in me.

That's when I noticed Katrin watching me, her strange smile hovering. 'Come walk with me on the beach, Tinashi,' she teased.

I opened my mouth to speak and found my voice had deserted me.

Charlie grasped Katrin's shoulder and shook her. 'Leave her alone,' he said.

Katrin stroked his face, almost lovingly, and laughed. A sharp, derisive sound. 'Poor broken Charlie's got writer's block. Can't get the words out any more. Can't save the world. Or can he?'

Swallowing the dregs from her flute, she danced down the steps toward the radiant beach.

Charlie's face whitened in fury.

Next to me Arthur Wang shook his head sadly. 'She loves the danger.'

'No,' Armagh burst out. 'She does it to taunt me. The devil has her.'

He seemed distraught, as if he might follow her, but Lauren Carson placed a soothing hand on his arm. 'It's to taunt all of us.'

Glitter-rose dusk lasted another hour, before, like city lights doused by timers, the carpet dimmed.

Arthur Wang walked me to my shack. 'We think the spores

reproduce on certain tides. The colour is a bit like coral spawning. A bloom of reproduction. It only seems to happen on the beach at dusk. Sometimes at dawn as well. Once the colour fades it's quite safe.'

'So the spores are not just those you can see in the sky?'

He shook his head in warning. 'They're in everything. Don't forget your Tyline, Tinashi, unless, of course . . . you want to.'

'Like Katrin?' I asked.

'Like Katrin,' he said, and bowed politely into the dark.

The morning renounced the previous, strange dusk – a sharp, crisp salt-air day, sun shining through the barely visible gauze of spores. I walked to the shop wondering if perhaps I had imagined them all.

Then I met Lauren Carson, her sleek blonde hair tucked neatly under a broad brimmed straw hat, sunglasses wide and dark. She carried a basket of bread and pai fruit.

'Come for a cup of tea,' she begged, moving too close to me. 'Quentin's gone fishing with Geronimo. I get so lonely. We're the second shack past the professor's away from the breakwater, toward the headland. Come soon. I'll be waiting.'

I purchased some food from Jaella who, thankfully, showed no interest in conversation. As she packed my provisions, her gaze strayed back to the coastline as if she was watching for something.

I nodded thanks and returned to my shack where I lay on my bed and considered sleeping again. Only lingering shreds of civility dragged me to Lauren Carson's for tea.

'Black.' It was a statement.

'Thanks. How did you know?'

We sat inside. She wore her sunglasses like a reluctant movie star, while she poured from a cottage-shaped teapot. 'It's my talent. Sensing things about people. Of course I don't get much practice here. Now I know most of our neighbours.'

I feigned interest.

'Take Geronimo. He grows tropical orchids. Don't let his mohawk distract you. And the professor, he likes to gut things.'

She chatted on about the residents of Glimmer-by-Dark in the sort of tedious detail that shrivelled my soul – Jaella's rebelliousness, Wang's insomnia, Geronimo's fondness for chemical abuse, Armagh's obsession with saving Katrin's soul.

I escaped, eventually, and spent the rest of the day in my shack, sleeping and brooding.

At sunset, as The Bara gusted its last for the day, I took a plate of cheese and bread and the last pai and sat on the patio to watch. In the distance I recognised Jaella's solitary, young form, curled, waiting above the waterline. Out to sea a small boat cut steadily toward her.

Geronimo and Quentin returning from a day out?

As the boat crested the shore-breaking waves, Quentin Carson leapt from the boat and waded in. Jaella ran to his waiting arms.

Geronimo turned the boat towards the breakwater for mooring and left them on the beach passionately entwined.

Did Lauren know about them, I wondered? The self-professed intuit. Surely she could see them from her patio?

Unwillingly, I felt myself becoming seduced into their paltry intrigues.

'She should kill him, you know.' A voice serrated by madness.

I hid my fright. 'Hello, Katrin,' I said smoothly.

She stood at the foot of my patio steps, a wine bottle and a single glass in her hand. After a moment she poured red wine into the glass and handed it to me. As I sipped, she swigged deeply from the bottle.

'She meets him every day. They make love in the dunes below his shack. Her father has no idea. He's too busy peeping at me through my window at night. I can hear him praying.'

Jaella's father? Armagh, I reminded myself.

'And Lauren?' I listened in dismay as the words tumbled from my mouth – suggesting an involvement I really did not seek.

Katrin swigged again, dashing drops from her mouth in anger. 'She should kill him.'

I thought of Lauren Carson. Sweet, garrulous, gentle Lauren. The idea was preposterous.

I took an assertive stance. 'When did you stop taking Tyline, Katrin?'

She leaned in toward me and I felt the weight of her mood. As darkness folded around us, The Bara spluttered one last warm gasp and died. My clothes stuck to my body and I clenched the arm of the chair, trying not to tremble. This was dangerous ground but I felt compelled to let this woman know she could not bully me.

'Is that what Charlie told you?' she asked.

I shrugged.

She snatched the glass from my hand, snapping the stem, spilling wine on my shirt. Then she vaulted down my steps like a gymnast, the contents of the fallen bottle draining onto the sand. It was gone in seconds.

So was Katrin.

I took a shuddery breath and levered myself out my chair. Once inside I locked the door and fell onto my bed and into a fitful sleep.

I avoided the residents of Glimmer-by-Dark over the next few weeks, venturing out only to visit the shop for provisions. Jaella's preoccupations meant our conversation remained indifferent. Thankfully I didn't see Lauren again so was spared the tedium of her menial observations, and the guilt of my knowledge about her husband's affair.

But my collusion, even though accidental, nagged at my conscience. By coming to Carmine Island, I had sought to withdraw into a cradle of my own gloom, and instead found myself distracted by unwelcome connections with near strangers.

Like a celluloid soap opera framed by the struts of my beach house balcony, I watched Jaella and Quentin's infidelity unfold each afternoon; I witnessed Katrin's wild beach pacing; closed my ears to Katrin and Charlie's bitter, unintelligible arguments behind my shack in the dunes.

One night, almost a month after my arrival, a loud knocking tore me from my dreams in the early hours of the morning.

I switched on the coloured patio lights and peered through the window. Arthur Wang stood there.

'Tinashi. You must come. Charlie's been . . .'

My heart constricted. *Charlie's what?*

I flung the door open. The professor was crying and shivering, dressed only in silk shorts. 'She killed him?'

Katrin!

'Where is she? Where's Charlie?'

'He's on the beach. I think she's hiding there as well.'

'The police?'

'Geronimo's gone to get them. But you have to help me. There's going to be a glitter-rose dawn. We have to get his body off the beach.'

'Does it matter now?' my voice sounded cold, uncaring. But it was fear. I didn't want to go near the beach.

'The spores will alter him. His family won't recognise what's left . . .'

The small man began to cry again.

I thought of Charlie handing me pink champagne. His handsome, smiling face. His jasmine-warmth. I shook Wang's shoulder. 'Quickly then.'

Arthur Wang had a torch.

The body was near the spot where Jaella waited for Quentin Carson. Where the pair made love.

Scenes ran through my mind as the sky lightened. Katrin taunting Charlie about his writer's block. A tussle. His neck twisted at an angle. Broken.

Katrin, crazy, hiding, watching us. Now.

We strained, dragging Charlie's body toward the rock breakwater that ran back into the dunes.

All the while another suspicion played at the back of my mind, refusing to form in the presence of death and my coursing adrenaline.

Over my laboured breathing a thrum started, like a softly plucked string.

'Can you hear that?'

The professor had stopped crying. His head cocked, panting. 'Glitter-rose.'

'We'll have to leave him,' I said. Already I could see a faint glow on the sand.

'No.'

The glow brightened. I dropped Charlie's arm and turned to run the last distance to the rocks.

Geronimo blocked my way.

'Thank goodness. Where are the police?'

Geronimo stood squarely, his huge hands outstretched to stop me. Quentin Carson appeared beside him. And Jaella.

I stared at Geronimo's fingers and my lingering suspicion coalesced.

Katrin couldn't have broken Charlie's neck. She wasn't strong enough.

'What about the drag marks?' Quentin spoke.

'Tide will wash them,' shrugged Geronimo. 'It will look like she pushed him from the rocks and then did herself in.'

She? Me.

Quentin sensed my confusion. 'We found out that Charlie was writing an article about us, an exposé, and we had to stop him. Jaella checked your background. You're unstable. Complete breakdown. Out of long-term care. No one will ask too many questions about your motive.'

His explanation left me more bewildered. And panicky. My past distorted to suit their means . . .

Around us the sand began to change colour.

'What about glitter-rose?' I croaked.

The four of them laughed. Geronimo grabbed my arms and dragged me onto the rocks. Quentin forced a gun into my mouth.

My heart beat in painful, furious beats. In seconds I would be dead.

'But Quentin, you promised.' Arthur Wang interrupted. 'You said I could cut him.'

'There isn't time,' said Quentin irritably. 'And it might cause questions.'

'But you promised. My conditions were clear. I harvest the spores and package them safely. I get to cut the body.' He pushed his way nearer to continue his protest.

Those precious distracting seconds bought me my life. A spotlight silhouetted us. Six figures caught in a bizarre play.

'We've got you, Quentin.'

Katrin.

I squinted into the light. I thought I could see Lauren Carson standing next to her. And two others in uniform.

The police took them away. Leaving Katrin and Lauren and I with Charlie's body. They said they would be back. Would we make sure Charlie wasn't touched?

I knelt down some distance from the body and let grains of glitter-rose spores trickle through my fingers, mingling with Charlie's blood. They fashioned themselves into shapes like teardrops.

Lauren and Katrin stood close together, arms around each other.

'Charlie was writing an exposé. It was going to be his ticket back to his world,' said Katrin.

I stared at her blankly.

She smiled, strange, but not crazy. *Hair like wings.*

'Tyline doesn't work, Tinashi. It never has. Everyone who lives here is infected with the spores. It's the island's secret. Charlie wanted to tell the rest of the world. And make himself famous.'

'Why did they want to stop him?'

She shrugged. 'Geronimo was right. The spores affect everyone differently. A miracle for some, for others . . . When Lauren arrived she had a terminal disease, now it's gone. The spores cured it but now she's going blind.'

Lauren reached up, feeling the contours of Katrin's face tenderly.

'I don't need to see you. As long as I'm alive and we're together,' she murmured.

Then she tilted her head toward me. 'You see, Tinashi, when Quentin realised the spores had cured me, he saw a chance to make money. Professor Wang harvested the spores for Quentin and Geronimo to sell in secret, to buyers on the mainland. Then I started to go blind. Quentin didn't want me anymore. The spores had changed him too. They do that. For some it's physical change, for others it's . . . inward. Katrin tried to stop them. She believes the spores are too dangerous. We know too little about them. She's the only one who can –' Lauren trailed off, unsure about how far to go.

But somewhere, beyond the shock, my mind had begun to function again.

'You're immune to them, aren't you? That's why they were afraid of you,' I said.

Katrin moved to sit serenely on the fiery carpet of sand spores, reaching out for her lover. She didn't bother to answer.

I left them there waiting for the police and trudged back to my shack. I showered, opened a bottle of pink champagne and took it out onto the patio.

I toasted the last of the glitter-rose dawn and thought of Charlie whom I'd hardly known and now would never forget. Slipping a crystal-hard teardrop shape from my pocket, I rolled it in my palm.

Then I thought of how I was now infected by the spores. What would that mean? Strangely, the question didn't frighten me. I'd come here searching for solace from my life. But there was no solace. There was only change. Maybe that would be enough.

The Sword of God

•

Russell Blackford
(for Damien Broderick)

'The future shudders, cracks, breaks, reforms. Every minute it shudders; every minute it reforms, and is still itself.'

Simeon Africanus, the sorcerer of blood and time, speaks softly. But, within the confines of Zenobia's dimly lit throne chamber, his voice carries well enough for those present to hear – the Queen herself, two hand-picked guards, the neoplatonist philosopher Longinus, and an ancient eunuch servant. At the feet of one of the guards there lies the sorcerer's sheathless weapon, a black-bladed Persian scimitar.

Simeon was born in Carthage, but since then he has served many polities, kingdoms and empires. Now he has slipped under cover of darkness into Palmyra, oasis city, focus of imperial conflict in the hot, arid Syrian desert. He has sought wine and an audience with Queen Zenobia. Control of the world is in a crazily swinging balance.

'It clings to itself. But, on occasion, my Queen, a mighty hand can reshape it.'

Syria, Palestine, most of Egypt and the East have rebelled against Rome, paid Zenobia homage. Great cities such as Alexandria and Antioch. But now her home city is under siege and the future is with the violent Imperator of Rome, Aurelian, who calls himself 'restorer of the empire'.

The sorcerer shrugs and drinks quietly from a goblet fashioned of gold and jewelled with emeralds and sapphires. Zenobia's hospitality is in the decadent style of Egypt or Persia. The goblet is deep and massive, filled with dark wine. Even so, it is little more than a toy in Simeon's strange hands – hairy and elongated, they are hands like the paws of a carnivorous animal.

Simeon is very tall, leanly powerful. Smooth-skinned, clean-shaven and apparently youthful, he is as fluid in his movements as the wine he drinks. He smiles, but it is more a kind of snarl; there is a display of sharp yellow teeth, like a mountain wolf's. His eyes are other than human, huge orbs, a kind of deep apricot-brown. Straight, thick, glossy hair spills over his shoulders in a tawny brown mane.

He sets down the goblet and waits.

The neoplatonist philosopher Longinus speaks up, catching the Queen's eye. 'This is strange philosophy. But we shall hear more.'

Zenobia speaks, her voice strong and surprisingly deep, almost like a man's. 'Prepare quarters for this traveller. Take his sword and cloak. Then bring us more food and wine.'

Simeon stands and removes his mud-brown hoodless paenula, his long traveller's cloak. 'I do not need food,' he says. 'The wine is enough for now. Also, I must keep the sword. Before this evening is over, I'll demonstrate it to you.' Zenobia catches Longinus's eye; the philosopher nods slowly.

'Very well,' says the Queen. 'But some of us must eat.'

The round-cheeked eunuch takes Simeon's paenula and departs. Outside, he calls in his high voice to other servants. Simeon reclines and stretches his long limbs, comfortable in a short linen tunic.

'Advice and assistance comes from unexpected quarters,' says Longinus. 'Tell us more, Magus.'

'*Magus* is the wrong word. I do not worship Ormazd or the hero Mithras, though I am prepared to serve whatever gods will aid me.' He addresses the Queen directly. 'Lady, what of you? I have been told you are a votary of the Palestinian sky god, Yahweh.'

Zenobia actually laughs, flashing her extraordinary white teeth.

'What an odd way to put it,' she says. 'No, I am no Jewess, if that is what you mean. Like my people, I worship Zeus-Bel ... or, otherwise,' – a knowing look – 'whatever gods will aid me.'

'Very well. You must understand, my Queen,' he returns to the true subject, looks directly into her intense black eyes – 'I'll never discern what must be. But I have had my vision of what *will*, alas, be: Palmyra fallen, Aurelian in triumph, yourself taken prisoner, paraded before the Imperator's chariot in Antioch and then in Rome itself. And, of course, beheaded.' When he says *of course*, it is with an offhand flicking of his tawny hair. 'Firmus in Egypt and your kinsmen in this city will continue the revolt against Rome, fighting in your name, but they, too, will be put down by Aurelian.' He relaxes again, silent, picks up the goblet, sips more wine. 'I am sorry to say these things,' he says at last.

The eunuch returns with spiced meat and dates, which he sets down. Longinus picks at the food with delicate, manicured finger-tips. Simeon ignores it. The eunuch pours more wine, dark as blood, and Simeon drinks.

'Palmyra's strategoi are the equal of Rome's,' the Queen says evenly. 'We have suffered some defeats recently, but we have won victories, even over Rome itself. My strategos Timagenes destroyed Probus in Egypt, and I myself, with Septimius Zabda, crushed the army of Heraclianus when it entered Palmyra's territories. Our cavalry are superior to the Romans'. Our camel-mounted drome-darii and our archers are famed across the world.'

'Yes, but Aurelian has already defeated your full cavalry not once but twice. Surely the future is his. And now he lays siege to Palmyra itself. You have cause to fear him.'

For all her martial affectations, Zenobia is ravishing, the more so now she is angry. Her eyes seem to flash black fire. Part Saracen, part Egyptian, the Palmyran queen claims descent from the Cleopatras and Ptolemies of Egypt, but she is more warlike than any of those ancestors. Perhaps the generations of Saracen desert warriors in her blood are the true explanation of her temperament. She dresses not as a Syrian woman or in the manner of the Persians whom she follows in other things, but as an Imperator of the Romans. She is bare-armed, wrapped in a purple toga over a simple tunic. Her costume is held together by a ribbon of silk about her waist, tied at the centre with a brooch of the jewel known as cochlis – an agate stone shaped uncannily like a sea-shell – and dyed the rich purple prepared in Palmyra from Indian sandyx. Black hair falls freely about fine shoulders. Her eyes are far deeper brown than Simeon's, close to true black, so that pupil is difficult to separate from iris. Her teeth are white as pearls, seeming to sparkle against the black of her hair and the smooth, swarthy skin of her face and arms. Zenobia is strong in profile, with a straight nose, high cheekbones, and a slightly jutting chin that conveys terrible determination.

'Don't speak to me of defeat and death,' she says.

'Of course not. But those serving you are not mighty enough, Lady. I have lived many centuries on this earth and provided these hands of mine to many kings and queens who have been thankful for the service.' He extends them, palms upward. 'For a small price the future can be changed.'

'And why should I believe all this superstition?'

'If not, why do you bother listening to it?'

'Because we know more than you might think,' says Longinus. 'That is why. You were with the Sassanid usurper, Ardashir, when the Parthian host fell before him at Hormizdagan. Strange events took place on that battlefield. We still adjudge you worth listening to, but I warn you that the Queen will not listen forever.'

Zenobia stands and paces, taller in her Roman ankle-boots, flat-soled leather calcei, than most men. 'Longinus is right: I get tired of all these words. Convince me that you can aid Palmyra.'

'My Queen, the battle of Hormizdagan was nearly fifty years ago. Look at me. I appear young, do I not? If you credit what Longinus tells you, you must know that I am not a mortal man.'

She smiles genuinely now, no bitterness. Eyes twinkle and the right corner of her wide, red-lipped mouth turns up, revealing the famous pearly teeth. 'So be it. And you tell me Palmyra's future . . .

but then you say you can alter it. How, then? I'm still waiting to be convinced.'

Simeon places the goblet gently upon Zenobia's table of white marble. He stands. 'Lady, if I may take my sword?' She does not reply, but Longinus makes a small gesture of assent. Simeon fetches his curved scimitar, holds it up proudly in both hands, pointing outwards from his chest. 'In the court of the Shahanshah in Ctesiphon,' he says, 'there are poets who have named this blade The Sword of God, the symbol of world dominion. So much for poets, Longinus might say. And rightly so. Of course, this scimitar has no special powers, despite what poets may fabricate or vulgar men may think. Those powers lie deep within its wielder. I fought beside Shapur when he overran Hatra and when he crushed the might of Rome at Ctesiphon and again at Antioch. Then I departed his service. Your friend Firmus disturbed me at my studies in Alexandria and sought my aid for you. Here I am. Shall I convince you by demonstration?'

The Queen merely drinks more wine, calls to her eunuch to refill her goblet. Yet, she is thoughtful; she does not put it to her full lips. 'Very well. What is required?'

'How much do you value your bodyguards? Could you let me have their lives?'

'You wish to lower yourself to swordplay, great sorcerer?' says Longinus, mockingly.

And Zenobia's eyes flash sarcasm.

'I wish to demonstrate what can be done with this simple blade, yes, but scarcely to lower myself. There is no shame in the way of a warrior.'

'Very well,' says Zenobia. 'You wish to fight them both? Together?'

'Lady, I do.'

Zenobia gestures to her guards. Each takes one step forward. They draw short Roman swords from their belts. One man is over four cubits tall, though even he needs to look up at Simeon. The other is smaller but square-built and hard. Both have hair close-cropped, faces grim and blue-stubbled. Imperial veterans. 'If you

•

can kill these, you are worth many men. Fight, then.' She addresses the bodyguards. 'Beware of sorcery, Gaianus.' She looks earnestly from one to the other. 'Sextus, good luck to you.'

The two guards advance toward Simeon, who steps away. He fed one day ago, in his own manner, and he is still strong enough to deal with these two. From his perspective, their movements are slow as he eludes them, as if they move in a ritual dance. His scimitar slashes and removes the sword hand of the tall veteran, Gaianus. Blood flows from the severed wrist and Simeon steps in, keeping Gaianus between himself and chunky Sextus. With a swift movement, Simeon grips the severed arm, takes it to his mouth, and tastes the sweet blood; he sucks down as much as he can, and his strength is renewed. He swings Gaianus by the bleeding arm, shifting him with a speed that the slowly-moving Sextus cannot elude. Sextus stumbles. Simeon flicks his scimitar and cuts Gaianus's head almost from his shoulders; he puts his mouth to the gashed neck and drinks down more blood.

Then, as the world perceives time, it is over in the blink of an eye. Sextus gains his feet, but, as Simeon Africanus sees the world, everything *freezes*. The whole throne chamber is a still tableau, held by the sorcery of time. The Carthaginian sorcerer steps through it, takes two short paces. His scimitar slashes backhanded and cleaves directly through Sextus's strongly muscled neck. Momentarily, the head seems frozen in place, though detached from the shoulders that supported it. Then time restores itself, shrieking, and the head flies, an obscene thing, through the air, more blood spraying the chamber, the veteran's strong body jerking, then collapsing, with the life taken out of it.

Zenobia looks shocked. Blood from the two guards has sprayed her clothing, her hair, her face and arms. The eunuch servant rushes, waddling, to her aid. Though she composes herself, shaking her head, gesturing the eunuch away, her dark skin is ashen.

'What did you see, my Queen?'

'You moved like a hungry wolf and you attacked like one. Your face is covered in blood. Then, in the end, you were . . . a falcon's shadow, a mere blur. You crossed to Sextus and slew him before he could even move.'

'Yes, my Queen. And so can I do to Aurelian, or any of your enemies. Keep me fed. The Imperator is devotee of a mighty god, Sol Invictus, the unconquerable sun. But he does not know the meaning of the word unconquerable. As for you, philosopher, you have seen the sorcery of blood and time. Some of it. Are you impressed?' When Longinus does not answer, Simeon adds. 'There is more. Watch carefully.' He crouches beside the body of Sextus. 'I shall soon be even stronger.' His lips and his long, supple tongue caress the severed stump of the soldier's neck. Ah, sweet blood. He takes his fill until he is sated, then he looks up at the Queen. 'Now you know what I want in return for my service. Blood, Lady. Merely keep me fed. I need fresh human blood. Normally, that of your enemies will be sufficient. But I shall also demand special favours. Favours you may consider unpleasant.'

No one attempts to interfere with him, but disgust is obvious on the face of Zenobia and the others. Gaianus and Sextus had good blood, but Simeon knows he will have to give up what he has gained if he is to win the Queen's trust.

'How much did you value these men?' he says.

She appears not only repulsed but frightened, yet not wishing to show it. 'Very much.'

Simeon nods slowly. 'They were both strong men. Good men. For the moment, I have grown very powerful on them. Observe what happens next, and remember. But before you observe, you must close your eyes for some seconds until I ask you to open them. You have to trust me, my Queen. If I desired you harm, nothing here could prevent it.' She obeys his wish. He closes his own eyes, visualises *behind* them what he wishes to see, suddenly opens them.

The chamber is again free of blood. All except what has dried on Simeon and Zenobia themselves. Time has flowed backward. Gaianus and Sextus are whole. They step toward Simeon, who easily slips away. Yet, he is now a feeble creature. He has exerted his powers to the limit, displacing what has been. He is so weak it is a positive thing, not a mere absence of strength. Everything else is as it was, but he has displaced his past self . . . and Zenobia's. Both remember.

'Open your eyes, my Queen,' he says softly. She does so. Looks almost as horrified as before. 'Lady, please stop these men from attacking me.'

'As you were, guards,' she says. 'You heard him.' Gaianus blinks but halts, puts a hand on his companion's shoulder. Of course, they, Longinus, the eunuch, all remember nothing. Zenobia moves her head from side to side, not shaking it, but seeming to search for some explanation of what confronts her. She looks down at the blood which still stains her clothing, attempting to reconcile two realities in her mind. 'Leave this chamber. All of you, leave. You too, Longinus. Leave me with the sorcerer.' Guards and the eunuch exchange disbelieving glances. Longinus begins to protest, but obviously thinks better of it. 'Leave,' Zenobia says. 'I must be left alone with this man. I know that he will not harm me. Can't you hear me? Leave, I said.' And, hesitating, they do finally leave.

'I am very weak,' Simeon Africanus says. 'What you saw has taken away some of my own life. But you will help me. Are you brave enough to nurse a wolf? If you wish to destroy Aurelian and reshape the future of Rome, step over here, come to me, Zenobia.'

She winces at being addressed simply by her name, but she walks cautiously to him. 'What do you want?'

'Hold out your arm to me, slowly. That's right.' He takes her small hand. 'Without this I will die.' Her skin is exquisite, dark, soft, high-veined, her palm sword-callused. He paws the underside of her wrist with its network of blue veins. Beneath his fingers, blood seeps slowly from the pores of her skin. He takes the bleeding wrist to his mouth, sucks lasciviously, as her entire body stiffens in outrage. But he feels the strength return. Blood of a woman who is nearly a goddess! So much power from so little blood . . . He will always remember this. A few seconds is enough. Simeon removes his mouth from her wrist, wipes over the wrist with the palm of his hand, and the bleeding stops. 'Now,' he says. 'I am much stronger. All the same, I must sleep. When I have done so, let us consider this latest epistle from Aurelian.'

'Come to my personal chamber at dawn. You will be allowed in. We can discuss it.'

'As you wish . . . my Queen.'

The braggart Aurelian has written in Greek, styling himself, typically, as Imperator of the Roman world and recoverer of the East, calling upon Zenobia and her allies to surrender. 'Your lives will be spared,' the letter says, 'but only on conditions. You and your children will live wherever I and the noble Roman Senate appoint as a place for you. Your jewels, gold and silver, your silks, your horses and camels and other animals are to be forfeited to the treasury of Rome.'

'He forgets himself,' says Zenobia. 'I am still well placed to survive this siege. My strategoi are seasoned and clever. There are many allies who abhor Aurelian more than they fear me. The Shahanshah of Persia has promised to send me an army.'

'And is the city loyal?'

'It is. The people still love me. My children, especially Vaballathus Athenodorus, and my other kinsmen in Palmyra still trust me, even though I am, as men say,' sardonically, '*just* a woman.'

'Have you replied to the Imperator?'

'I have drafted a reply,' says Zenobia. 'It is here. I have written in Syriac, for my Greek is not as learned as the Imperator's. But Longinus can translate and embroider it so that it becomes far more elegant.' She lowers her voice confidentially. 'The outside world thinks of us as merchants turned warriors. They're right. But Palmyra has also become, with Alexandria, the most scholarly city of the world.'

'May I see what you've written?'

The future cracks; Simeon Africanus has begun to interfere.

She hands over the parchment and he takes it, reads aloud. 'From Zenobia, Queen of the East, to Aurelian Augustus. Conquest must be gained by deeds of valour, not by the pen. Would my ancestor Cleopatra have submitted upon receiving such a letter? Like her, I would rather stand and die a Queen than kneel and live. You are not invincible. Most who have died in this siege have been Romans, not Palmyrans. When aid arrives in the city you will put away your arrogance.'

'It lacks some polish,' she says. 'Longinus can add that.'

'It's an excellent response, my Queen. But let me make one suggestion of my own: tell Aurelian that he has set himself against the Sword of God.'

Each day they continue the fight from their battlements. Palmyra's fortified walls are laid out in a semi-circle about the city, incorporating even a section of the splendid oasis lake. At all points the walls are augmented by mighty catapults and other engines of war, which hurl boulders and Greek fire upon the besiegers. The Romans reply with arrows and spears, and they form their testudos, their shielded tortoise formations, to undermine the walls. So far, they are frustrated. Each day they are repelled from the stones of the city. It is true that few Palmyrans have yet died.

But that changes. The Romans bring out siege ladders to scale the walls, and the Palmyrans are soon hard-pressed.

The combat goes badly despite the efforts of Simeon himself, the courage of the Palmyrans and the might of the city's walls and engines. Aurelian has an inexhaustible supply of men from the vast territories of Rome. His army is made up of a mixture of Dalmatian cavalrymen, now required to fight without their horses, regular infantrymen drawn from the empire's Gothic legions, and contingents of Easterners – Mesopotamians, Syrians, Palestinians – some of them armed with heavy clubs and staves rather than swords.

While the Palmyrans are great archers, horsemen and dromedarii, their morale suffers when they are so outnumbered and cooped up in the city day after day. And, most importantly, they suffer in the desert heat, even though born to it. Somehow, the terrible heat of the spring sun drains away their strength without affecting that of the Romans. Indeed, the longer the day goes on and the sun shines, the fresher and more encouraged the Romans seem to become, until late afternoon, when the sun begins to wane; it is as if the sun itself is fighting for them.

Each day, Simeon feeds upon the sweet veins of Zenobia; though she is obviously still repulsed, she allows him this, knowing he is by far the most dangerous of all her warriors. Her courage and resolve fascinate and enchant him. Seemingly, she will do anything to overcome the might of Aurelian and Rome.

There is one way Simeon can perceive to end the conflict quickly. Aurelian is foolhardy enough to enter himself into the midst of the melee at the city walls; he does not seem to care that he puts himself in danger. If Simeon can reach him in the press of the fighting, Aurelian must die. Surely then, isolated on enemy territory far from Rome, any new Imperator elected by the legion will wish to retreat from the East to deal with rivals.

Simeon conserves his strength. Even without sorcery, he is a formidable warrior, fluid, strong and skilful with the scimitar. Early one afternoon, the Romans launch a full-scale assault, wheeling up their towering siege ladders. Simeon sees Aurelian close by on the city wall. He and a group of his followers are in the middle of the south wall, above the city's agora and banqueting hall. Shouting goes up, and the clash of iron and bronze. Smoke pours forth where Greek fire is hurled at the invaders. Heavy stones are thrown down from the walls and clang on the Roman testudos, which bend and grunt but do not break up. Palmyran swordsmen, led by grizzled Septimius Zabda, young Vaballathus and Zenobia herself, attempt to drive back the climbers and isolate those who have already stepped on the parapet. In the din and the rushing chaos, Simeon finds himself facing a pair of club-wielding Palestinians. They are dark, brawny, sweaty fellows, doubtless two of the heroes of Immae. There Aurelian's Palestinian infantrymen bruised and crushed Palmyra's armoured cavalrymen, who were confounded when resisted by strong-armed brutes wielding clubs that could smash bones, even through coats of mail. Simeon treats them warily; Zenobia has described to him the deceptive speed and accuracy with which these clubs can be swung.

He slips away, moving to his right toward a stairwell that leads down to the porticoed laneway of the city. He lets the Palestinian clubmen pursue. He feints at their heads with his scimitar as they come closer, then slips away again. It is hot and sticky in his bronze mail. His two enemies are bare-armed and full of roaring energy. The sun beats down, glaring and intolerable, making Simeon feel strangely nauseous in the pit of his stomach, even as the clubmen rush after him, their massive shoulders and upper arms gleaming and slick with sweat.

For all that, they cannot catch him. He melts away from them, then *into* their embrace, his scimitar slicing quickly across the line of their throats before they comprehend what has happened. Both fall, one with his throat slit wide open, choking quickly and dying, but the other very much alive, if hurt. He has taken only a shallow wound in the side of the neck, missing the main blood vessels. All the better. Simeon returns his scimitar to its chain-linked belt, falls bodily upon this living prey before he can recover himself, drags him kicking and protesting back behind the press of the fighting.

The fellow has dropped his club, but he tries to wrestle with Simeon for his life, clutching and pushing and kicking. The man's energy is uncanny. How can he retain it in this heat and even as blood drains from him? They grapple and slip in dirt and blood, almost falling onto the city's weathered steps. Hysterical strength tests Simeon; arms squeeze against him like thick, tightening cords of nautical rope, yet Simeon's own inhuman strength prevails – as they struggle, kneeling, the sorcerer's shoulder presses into the Palestinian's chest, long arms about the thick waist. Simeon pushes, grimacing and snarling with the strain, until he feels the sudden slackness, and hears the anxiously awaited crack of bones breaking. His hands find their way into the shallow wound on the man's neck, opening it up with the smallest effort of blood sorcery, tearing away skin and garments as he stretches the bleeding area, deepening it, hands digging through muscles and arteries and veins. Then his mouth finds the delicious wound; blood pumps out freely and Simeon drinks it hungrily. The man was a warrior and a hero. His blood is strong.

Simeon jostles his way back to battle, rejuvenated, covered in life-giving blood. More Romans fall beneath his scimitar. Today is the day. He faces Aurelian.

The self-styled recoverer of the East appears startled to be descended upon by this bloodied effigy, man or demon. But then, astonishingly, he smiles! Dirt and gore mar his lined face and his simple armour. He is not overly tall and he must be all of sixty years of age, yet there is an animal vitality about him. He does not appear to sweat in all this heat and he stares coldly into Simeon's dreadful blood-smeared face. Aurelian holds his short sword, point upwards, like a duellist with a knife.

Time stops. Aurelian is frozen with the rest of the besiegers and the besieged. His hour has come to die; but when Simeon tenses to pounce at the Imperator something goes wrong – his scimitar appears to turn and struggle in his hand like a venomous snake. Simeon is feeling dizzy and faint as if with sunstroke; a spirit is fighting him, possessing his sword, draining his strength. He finds himself reeling in the wrong direction, *away* from the Imperator. His sorcery is shattered. Aurelian comes to life. And the sun has grown huge, an ocean of liquid yellow fire across the whole sky, seeming to burn like the Christian hell.

Aurelian rushes bull-like at Simeon, who finds he is able to flow out of the Imperator's way, but not to retaliate. Aurelian smiles grimly. 'Your time has gone, creature of blood,' he says in gruff Latin, 'whatever you call yourself. I am the future. The priests of Sol Invictus chose me to restore the world for Rome. I am under their protection and that of their deity.' He plods forward stolidly and thrusts quickly with his sword, striking Simeon in the side but not breaking through his shirt of bronze mail. 'Sol Invictus is the world-conquering god. Did you believe that your ancient sorceries could prevail against his?'

Desperate fighting goes on all around. In the uproar of the

battle, Simeon is not sure how much of this he actually hears and how much he reads from the movements of Aurelian's lips or even his thoughts. Swords clash, the black blade again seeming to fight against Simeon and *for* the Imperator, jerking about in his hands, seemingly wishing to avoid Aurelian or his sword and aiming itself for Simeon's unprotected lower leg. It is all he can do to avoid wounding himself.

Palmyrans and Gothic legionnaires struggle by close to them, and in the fray Simeon is parted from the Imperator. But now he knows how difficult it will be to kill Aurelian. Even with this warning of Aurelian's powers, he is not sure that he could ever do it.

Victory is no longer assured.

Like a hollow skull, defeat laughs mockingly at Palmyra.

Nonetheless, only isolated besiegers obtain any foothold upon the city parapets, and they are forced to retreat. The siege continues.

If Zenobia had sufficient forces she could attack at night, but she is greatly outnumbered and must fight behind Palmyra's fortifications. Aurelian has the advantage unless reinforcements arrive.

Simeon has made a terrible mistake in allowing himself to become obsessed with Zenobia, who seems to wince from him as one might from some loathsome shaggy beast, even as she continues to use him. When the Romans finally take the city, as they must do next time they mount a full attack, she will have no use for him, except as one of the men she can blame for leading her, *a mere woman*, astray. He will need all his powers simply to escape the doomed city. Perhaps, with her phenomenal beauty, Zenobia can still reshape the future sufficiently to have her own life spared if she is captured by the Imperator. Perhaps. But for her to be enchained, led in triumph, violated by the army, and in the end most likely beheaded, is an evil Simeon cannot allow.

They meet in the Temple of Zeus-Bel, beside Palmyra's peaceful lake, to make their preparations. Evidently, Aurelian has been able to cut off Zenobia's reinforcements from Persia and Armenia, from the Saracens, the Blemmyae and others. The siege is unrelieved, and the city's finest soldiers are dead. But Zenobia is undaunted. She and Longinus have devised a last plan. If she could escape to Persia or Egypt where she still has rich and powerful friends, her kingdom might yet prevail. The new Shahanshah, Hormizd, is only a shadow of his father, sharp-minded and great-bodied Shapur, who ruled among the Sassanids for thirty years. But if the wealth and population of the Sassanid empire could be combined with Zenobia's undoubted military prowess, even Aurelian would be halted in his ambitions. Again, there is mighty sorcery available in Persia among the Shahanshah's Magi. If this could be directed to the right ends, the priests of Sol Invictus might find that their god is not, after all, unconquerable.

Zenobia slips out of the city, fleeing into darkness; Simeon insists upon accompanying her. He is strong, for she has provided him with the blood of one of the city's suspected spies.

They ride mounted high on female dromedaries. In desert terrain, these can outrun any horse. Zenobia has planned carefully. Once they reach the Euphrates River near Dura, they will be able to sail downstream to Seleucia – twin city to the Persian capital Ctesiphon – lying between the Euphrates and the Tigris where the great rivers come closest together, before finally meeting one hundred miles further south above Ferat. From Selucia, they can cross the Tigris to seek audience of the Shahanshah in his palace in Ctesiphon.

Once they reach the Euphrates and the lands of Hormidz, Aurelian will pursue them at his peril. And yet, Simeon Africanus has seen even this in his visions of the future: Palmyra surrendering without its Queen to lead the fighting and maintain morale; Zenobia captured on the dhow-rigged boat that would have taken her to safety and possibly to allies. If the future is to crack and break, not merely shudder, there must be a better way, and Simeon's own hands must do the timebreaking.

They ride at night, a time when the bright powers of Aurelian and the priests of Sol Invictus are surely at their weakest, wrapping woollen cloaks and blankets about them, for the desert cools rapidly in the evening. They are prepared with gold and jewels, with skins of water and with days' worth of rations for Zenobia to eat: sun-dried fruits, spices, and smoked meats. 'Do you despise me, after all this?' Simeon asks her.

He cannot see her face in the dark. 'No. You have fought genuinely for me. Whatever manner of creature you are, I took you into my service and I cannot doubt your loyalty.'

They ride on. Stars glitter in the clear sky but there is no moon. A chilly breeze bites through cloaks and blankets.

'What will happen to Palmyra without me?' Zenobia asks.

'Don't you believe we will be able to bring reinforcements before the city falls?'

'Sorcerer,' she says, 'I do not even believe we will live beyond tomorrow. Aurelian will find us. This is a desperate chance we take, for all our preparations. What will happen to the city?'

'If what you say proves true, Palmyra will surrender. The men fight less for the kingdom and the city than they do for you, your-self. You inspire ... their devotion.' Almost, he says *our* devotion, but thinks better of it. 'Perhaps the best thing your kinsmen could do is open the gates of the city, provide Aurelian with gifts and throw themselves on the Imperator's mercy.'

'He is too bloodthirsty to have mercy.'

There is a silence. Then Simeon reminds her of Tyana, Aurelian's first major conquest in his vaunted restoration of the East. 'They say that he threatened the city, boasting that if it did not surrender he would not leave so much as a dog alive.'

'So they say. The city defied him until one of its rich merchants, a fellow called Heraclammon, betrayed it. At that point Aurelian entered in triumph. His soldiers pressed him to violate the women, slaughter the inhabitants and take their possessions as booty of war. They reminded him of what he said, that he would not leave so much as a dog alive. So how did Aurelian respond? *Then kill all the dogs.*'

She looks at him oddly. 'Well ... we keep many dogs in Palmyra. Camels, horses, goats, all sorts of animals.' Rueful laughter. 'If by any chance I do survive this, I will have my revenge, ten Romans for every life, man, woman or animal, taken in Palmyra. I have told you what I think. What odds do you give that we will reach Ctesiphon?'

Now he must confirm her fears. 'The priests of Sol Invictus will discover our escape. They are powerful sorcerers. Expect to be followed at dawn.' He can hear her take in breath. 'By fleeing you have taken but a small risk, Lady. I have seen your future, but you now have an advantage I did not foresee – you have me with you.'

'What are you telling me?'

'Lady, sorcery aside, our camels can outrun any horses that follow us from Aurelian's siege-tents at Palmyra. Yet, you are right: we cannot avoid the Romans as far as Ctesiphon.'

'Yes, but if we are to die many Romans will die first.'

'Lady, I've told you your one advantage. Aurelian knows that many of his soldiers will die if they must confront me. So he himself will join the pursuit. That was not a factor in my vision. He will put himself at risk. We have already changed the future, my Queen. All things are possible. You must try to trust me.'

She has no choice. They ride on in complete silence.

Night cannot last forever.

In the morning, they roll away blankets and change into long, hooded paenulae of white linen, hastily prepared by Zenobia's seamstresses, which cover them from brows to feet for protection from the sun.

Later, as the sun ascends a merciless spring sky, Simeon climbs an isolated stony hill amidst miles of rolling sand, and looks into the distance behind them, waiting for horsemen to appear on the horizon, following their path. He is not long disappointed. There are about six of them, not galloping, but cantering hard. He returns to Zenobia.

'They'll reach us soon, Queen. Of course, their horses must be tired. Our dromedaries are fresh enough. We could stay ahead of them for now, but not until nightfall. Not if I understand Aurelian's sorcery. Trying would be foolish.' Indeed, he thinks, the sooner the

Imperator confronts us the better. If we need contend with only six Romans, we have a chance. But not yet. Not quite yet. 'They'll be watching out for us, because they expect us to proceed with deliberation. The time is soon coming to deal with them.'

They are far now from Palmyra's oasis lake, on the one hand, and far, on the other, from the blue waters of the Euphrates. They proceed slowly, sharing one of the water skins they have brought. The day is growing hotter as morning approaches noon. When the horsemen become visible, appearing above a dune across the rolling desert plain, Simeon decides to run, to bring the play to its end.

In a manner of speaking, they run, the dromedaries loping across desert sand and stones, kicking up a wake of dry dust, beginning to pull further ahead of the Roman horsemen. Looking behind, Simeon sees that the horses are being urged on to greater efforts, though not breaking into full gallop as yet. Soon, they are gaining once more, but the dromedaries have energy aplenty in reserve. 'We'll go yet faster, Queen.' They do so, but only to an extent where the pursuers neither gain nor begin to fall away.

'Our camels can do this forever. Aurelian's horses will soon have had enough.'

'Normally, Zenobia. Normal horses.' She does not seem to mind being called simply Zenobia in this time of crisis. 'With the sun in the sky, I believe that the Imperator's power will be able to sustain them. Is your dromedary yet tiring?'

'She is still strong.'

'My mount also. His power has not extended to us. There must be limits to its range.'

'Yet, the sun appears to take strength from his enemies across a whole battlefield. How close may we let him approach?'

'We'll have to guess. But he must have limits, otherwise he could have brought down your city with exhaustion from Antioch or even Rome. Besides, the weakness which your armies have suffered when opposing him is a gradual one over a day; whereas when he defeated me with sickness and vertigo it was at close quarters.'

The chase proceeds into the afternoon. As the sun becomes

hotter in the sky, Zenobia suggests they pull further ahead – perhaps the range of Aurelian's power becomes greater as the sun itself grows stronger. He takes her advice, but once they have doubled the distance between themselves and Aurelian they do not allow the gap to increase; Simeon does not wish Aurelian to lose heart, if that were possible. He wishes to tempt the Imperator into consuming his strength.

Late in the afternoon, before the sun wanes, Aurelian acts. There is a long downward slope between him and his quarry, and his horses put on a fresh spurt, finally breaking into full gallop across the desert. Zenobia and Simeon run their camels hard, but at least they can use the dromedaries to fritter away some of Aurelian's power.

Eventually, Aurelian gains on them, and he gets close enough for Simeon to feel his exhausting presence. No use fleeing any longer. Simeon and Zenobia stop and dismount, lay down their weapons, stand waiting for what must seem their inevitable capture. They fold back the hoods of their paenulae, making their identities plain. It will take perhaps a minute for the horsemen to be upon them.

Simeon uses the time well.

'I'm sorry, my Queen,' he says, 'for what I must now do.'

'What!'

The horsemen are close. Time stops; Zenobia's speech is halted, her mouth left gaping open. The whole desert freezes. Aurelian and his soldiers are suspended in dusty blue air; a hawk, high in the sky, hangs frozen; even gnats are fixed in position, like dots of ink on parchment; isolated tussocks of desert grasses lock into bent shapes made by an intermittent dry wind. Simeon walks calmly to his dromedary, draws from its sewn straps the Sword of God; for that instant, his arm and the black blade are the only things in the desert that move. It is now many hours since he has had his fill of blood; he can sustain this effort for only a few more heartbeats. He concentrates, walks purposefully back to Zenobia, seizes her roughly by the wrist. 'Ah, if this moment could last,' he says softly, to her unhearing ears. Ever so gently, he holds her narrow wrist, calling to her blood, feeling a pulse begin, though her body is otherwise as frozen in the moment as the rest of the desert. Red blood wells under her skin and flows for him, another visible movement among frozen sand and stone and time. Reverently this time, he puts his mouth to her arm.

And drinks her. Dry.

It is a perfect draught, as strong as he has ever tasted. The blood of a demi-goddess flowed in her veins – no wonder he loved her! Now it flows in his. There is a power in him. His mind is a sharp blade. His body was a wolf's; now it is a lion's or a huge German bear's. He is stronger than he has ever been. Time unfreezes as Simeon conserves his powers; the horsemen approach. Horror in their faces. Simeon is half-crouched, the scimitar held at an angle across his body, in the attitude of a man prepared to die fighting.

Aurelian's spirit is pulling at him, trying to suck the sorcerer's strength away. But Zenobia's blood seems to turn to golden power whatever it touches within Simeon's body. For the moment, he resists and turns back the might of Sol Invictus.

'Stay behind me,' Aurelian growls to his men. 'I don't want any of you dead in the confusion.' Then, grimly, 'I shall finish this task.' Simeon buries his scimitar, point first and almost to the hilt, in the desert sand as Aurelian charges upon him, short sword pointed at Simeon's heart. A drumming of hooves on sand and a guttural shout. 'Die at last, creature of evil!'

Simeon feels the huge new strength from Zenobia's blood start to siphon away, as Aurelian's sorcery asserts itself, close up and under the grim Imperator's conscious control. Time will not freeze ... but it slows ... *enough*. Simeon avoids the charge and crouches low as the panting, whinnying horse rushes past; he seizes Aurelian by his leg, dragging him out of the saddle as he passes. Both fall to the ground, Aurelian losing his sword, but kicking powerfully with a thud into Simeon's chest and crawling away. Simeon springs upon him and they are wrestling; Simeon cannot concentrate on slowing or stopping time, and Aurelian's sorcery waits to fall upon his own like a huge iron hammer smashing upon a floor of glass. The

Imperator's strength is enormous, and he seems to glow from inside with heat, heat which quickly burns away Simeon's own reservoir of strength. They wrestle like titans, Zenobia's blood renewing itself within Simeon. She must not have died for nothing! And now each is draining at the other's strength, for Simeon's long fingers have tightened on the Imperator's throat; he is calling in his mind to Aurelian's blood, and it hears . . .

It comes to him; it seeps out under strange, long, hairy fingers.

Bruised, they roll and struggle, but then Simeon's mouth finds the side of Aurelian's neck where the carotid pulses; blood spurts, splashing Simeon's face and tawny hair – some of it, enough of it, going down into the hollow of his belly, sustaining, strengthening him further. Within seconds, it is over. The Imperator's body is white and limp. As the remaining horsemen charge upon him, time finally freezes like blue ice. The rest is sheer carnage: Simeon tears them limb from limb . . .

The priests of Sol Invictus created well. Aurelian's blood is as potent as Zenobia's. Simeon closes his eyes and concentrates. He must work his greatest act of sorcery, displace everyone in sight, everyone except Zenobia. The power of Aurelian's blood boils in him. First, he looks behind his eyes at what he wishes to see.

And opens his eyes.

The scene is changed. A hawk flies against the sun. Gnats zigzag in the air. Occasional tussocky vegetation waves in the intermittent breeze. There is a charnel house of death about him. Horses run wildly back and forth, arching their necks and shaking their reins, startled to find that their masters have vanished from their backs. But, in the other direction, a tall dark-haired woman dressed in a white linen paenula is beginning to mouth the word, 'What!' She looks about her, where she stands, confused, beside her Palmyran dromedary. Her dark-skinned Saracen face is as shocked as the first time she saw Simeon's bloodthirsty sorcery. But she says nothing.

Simeon draws his blade out of the dry, fine sand. Somewhat raggedly, he saws from its shoulders the sneering head of Lucius

Domitius Aurelianus Augustus, the Imperator of Rome known as Aurelian. Simeon speaks to the head in Latin: 'You set yourself against the Sword of God, Imperator.'

Satisfied, he grips the trophy by its cropped hair, turns toward Zenobia, sagging to one knee.

'What happened here?' she says.

He is mute with sickness and confusion.

That last effort, displacing six dead men plus himself to a time several minutes in the past, has taken all the strength he had; it has almost killed him. Yet, he remains glutted with Aurelian's blood. No longer a source of strength, it is evil, lifeless stuff within him. It weighs sickeningly upon his bowels.

'You cannot imagine what I have had to do here, and I am too weak to explain it or just what it has done to me,' he says. He sits back on his haunches and throws the blood-drained severed head so that it lands at her feet. 'My strength is gone. I am no protection to you. I may not live beyond the next minutes. Perhaps in some of these corpses there is a little poor blood to sustain me back to Palmyra.'

'I still have all my blood.' Zenobia suppresses a shudder of disgust. 'Take some of it.'

Yes. He has room in his belly for a last small draught of Zenobia. 'Lady, there will need to be a new Imperator of Rome. Your fortunes will turn, now.'

She walks to him. 'You cannot talk. Be quiet.'

'Zenobia, you are, as they say, *just* a woman, and you cannot be Imperator. I propose your son, Vaballathus Athenodorus.'

'Indeed, he has always been a dutiful boy. Be quiet now.'

She crouches to him, extends her arm towards his hungry mouth, her hand bent backward at the wrist, veins upward.

The future shudders; it cracks open like an egg; it breaks, shatters. And is reborn.

The Gate of Heaven

•

Rosaleen Love

The Buddhist monk is wired to the EEG. As he enters trance, the machine traces evidence for Nirvana.

See these DNA strips. Here is the location of the gene for God.

Here is proof of the power of prayer. These people in the cancer ward do not know that others are praying for them. See how they improve.

Fourth comes the discovery of the gate of heaven.

Of course there will always be those who say that what happened on space-craft Mir is fraud, or mass hypnosis. What, though, if it were true?

I have kept my peace about Mir, until this day. Once, upon Mir, the veil of reality was lifted, and we beheld with a celestial clarity, and we were all transformed.

Then Mir was destroyed. It went plummeting into the great Southern Ocean, or so they said.

What if I were to say that Mir is still aloft, the real Mir? It was the material Mir that burned and crashed into the sea, but in the reality beyond the material world, which is uncreated, which pervades everything, and which we have always thought, until that moment, to be beyond the reach of human knowledge and understanding, the real space station Mir still flies aloft, the cosmonauts at their posts.

I tried to tell what I saw, and was called crazy. They felt sorry for me, and gave me drugs that caused my vision to fade. The everyday world crowded in and my normal life was returned to me.

My friends are still aloft, and I am here.

I have lost entrance to the gate of Paradise.

'I have a theory of everything.' We were on board Mir, doing one of the endless sleep experiments. Tsiolkovsky attached himself to the wall-panel by strips of velcro. He wore a blue cap fitted with sensors, stuck to his head with greasy gel. He closed his eyes to allow me to fix the REM sensors to his eyelids. He had a large bulb thermometer in his rectum to measure core body temperature. I placed a catheter in his vein, and took the first blood sample for the night. 'This cannot be the real world,' said Tsiolkovsky. 'Volkov, what do you say to this idea? I believe we are trapped in a nightmare.'

I splashed his blood onto paper and fed it into the Reflectron. Measurements from the machine went straight to Base on earth.

I agreed with Tsiolkovsky's theory of the nightmare, but I argued with him to urge him on, to help him find a better reason for being born. 'When I prick your arm, you bleed,' I said. 'This is not the blood of nightmares. It smears on the strip. You can see it. Here.' But he could not see. The sensors pressed on his eyelids.

'They are studying sleep on Mir, but they create the conditions under which it is impossible to sleep.' He had to wake up every hour, if indeed he ever got to sleep, to provide more blood for the machine.

I was the one to wake him, if the alarm did not.

'What do you think the real world is like?' I asked, as I taped the catheter to his arm. I did not adjust the thermometer in his rectum.

I, too, thought the measurements were crazy, but unlike Tsiolkovsky I believed there was a world where this had some meaning.

'Tell me, why do I exist in this world?'

'You are placed here for a purpose,' I replied, knowing it would not calm him, but it was what I believed.

'What is the point of our lives? How can I attain something other than this world, with its machinery that breaks down, its computers that give stupid readings, this water that drips endlessly over everything . . .' His voice trailed away. He was, despite all, asleep.

I wiped up the water. It came from leaks and spills and human sweat and pooled in puddles over everything, blobs in free fall. Dampness was all, on Mir.

Each hour I woke Tsiolkovsky, to draw blood for the Reflectron, the measuring machine that scientists other than ours said was useless, never tested in space, in the heat, and obsolete everywhere but Mir. He said, the American Linebarger, when he was with us, that the measurements it gave were wrong. They had to be, because if they were right, we would be dead. The results they sent back to Base were incompatible with life.

We were so tired, so much of the time, we did not know what we were doing. We were dead enough. I believed the measurements were accurate.

Tsiolkovsky asked, 'What is the point of our lives?'

And his question was answered, but not, as it turned out, by me.

I asked Base if we could stop the experiments. 'The men are exhausted. We have six nights of data. Is it enough?'

'We'll see about it,' Base said, secure on earth. 'We'll get back to you later.' When the experiments were over. I needed a swift reply. I was not confident of one.

We were so tired we started to hear things. Each of us heard something different.

It happened when Mir reached the apogee of its orbit. The closer we were to heaven, in which we did not believe, the more we heard the celestial music.

I heard it as a rushing in the ears, as if I pressed a sea-shell close, like the distant seas. Manakov heard a deep mournful sound, and I knew when he was listening, because tears sprang to his eyes.

Tsiolkovsky found it more restful than distressing. Globa heard a kind of celestial Elvis, his version of Paradise.

We thought the music was within us, and that it was one of the effects of micro-gravity. In weightlessness, calcium leaches out of the bones and is excreted in urine. We pissed our bones away. Likewise calcium was leaching from the bones in our ears, so we heard sounds that were not there. That was Manakov's theory.

Tsiolkovsky said we were so high up we could hear the murmur of waves from beyond earth's shores. He said we heard the music of space. We were in a gap between heaven and earth, between the music of the head, and the music of the spheres, as far apart, and as close, as the gap between the singer and the song, the raw stone and the sculptor's vision.

Living as we did between heaven (in which we did not believe) and earth (in which we once believed, but then had doubts) we were seduced by the music of spheres.

I should have reported to Base anything that smacked of religious fervour. But I did not. Here, in space, we sensed most clearly the dis-junction between what lay beyond and that which pulled us back, the broken machinery, crashed computers, leaking coolants, and the myriad tasks of the day. Things could be otherwise, if only . . . if only.

First came the music, then the visions.

The space walks were, at first, routine. Two of us went outside once a week to change the radiation dosimeters, check the particle sensors and the thermal safety blankets round Soyuz, our escape module.

Tsiolkovsky was with Globa the first time it happened. They went out through the Kvant 2 hatch to the Kristall hull.

Space walks began at sunrise. Tsiolkovsky went first, just as the first rays of the sun hit Mir. That's why he saw it, he said, while Globa reported nothing.

Tsiolkovsky said: 'I crawled through the hatch, and swung out to the ladder. All I could see was the brightness of the sun, and its rays falling towards me. The rays of the sun were falling and I felt I was rising towards them.'

Globa said: 'I could not exit the hatch. Tsiolkovsky stayed half in the door, half outside, his helmet turned towards the rising sun. I asked him if there was a problem.'

Tsiolkovsky said: 'I felt as if I were standing at the base of a high mountain, at the edge of an abyss. I was not afraid. Both mountain and abyss glowed with light. I wanted to let go of Mir, to rise into the light.'

Globa's said: 'Tsiolkovsky tugged at the handrail, to which he was tethered. I thought it was the rail. Once, it came loose from metal fatigue. Now we always check them first thing.'

Tsiolkovsky said: 'The entire universe was filled with infinite light.'

Globa said: 'Tsiolkovsky did not move for thirty minutes. I was stuck in the capsule. I could go neither backwards nor forwards. He did not respond to my repeated calls for help. I tell you, I began to feel frantic. I pushed him, I pulled him, but he only swayed a little, pivoting on his tether. It took all my training to think through what I would have to do, if he would not move.'

Tsiolkovsky said: 'It lasted a moment, this sense of infinite light. I turned and saw the earth huge beneath me, and the spell was broken. The light contracted to a point, and that point swelled to become the earth, and I knew the earth under Mir is not a sphere of cooling magma, as we have been told, but a sphere of contracted light.'

Globa said: 'After half an hour, Tsiolkovsky resumed the space walk as if nothing had happened. When I questioned him he said he'd been momentarily blinded by the light as he went through the hatch.'

Later, as I helped him from his space-suit, Tsiolkovsky seemed his usual self. His first words were: 'Volkov, how can I ever really comprehend myself and the universe?'

When Globa told him what had happened, he grew thoughtful.

Later, debriefing, Tsiolkovsky said: 'I felt I was in Paradise.'

We did not tell Base that Tsiolkovsky spent half an hour in Paradise. We said the walk had gone as planned, and the new monitors were in place.

I was next, when I walked out with Globa, who saw only the hull before his eyes, his gloved hands manipulating the equipment. Globa went first. I moved to follow.

The outer hull is crowded with experiments and with solar panels. We transit with great care, avoiding anything sharp that might puncture our suits.

Before me, the sun's rays. Beneath me, Mir sparkled in sunlight. When I reached the site, I tethered myself to the nearest handrail. My hands were heavy with gloves. Arms, legs and trunk swung round as one. I was an Egyptian mummy raised from the dead, sleep-walking though the pyramid in search of the entrance to the other world.

We worked steadily until nightfall. On Mir, the movement from day to night is sudden. Blackness is absolute. We cannot work when this happens, and stay tethered to await the rising sun. It is a task for which we are trained.

This time, I could not relax into the situation, which, in itself, is not dangerous, simply something that happens. I swung restlessly on my tether. I had the strong urge to stand upright. But I did not know how to do it. In space, there is no up, no down, no sense to the notion of standing.

Then I had the sudden sense that space itself moved into me, and through me, and gently set me right. My hand-hold shifted to a foot-hold. I was moved, but I had not moved. I was by myself, yet I was with the stars.

I felt the space of Mir above and below me. The space of Mir was within me and without me.

I took refuge in the shadows of Mir's wings.

Then I saw the small light of Globa's torch.

Globa. I was not alone. Space retreated from me. Soon it was sunrise. We got back to work. Together, we ascended the mountain that is Kristall, and checked the monitors.

Afterwards I asked Globa what he had seen. Nothing.

I said nothing. If I told Tsiolkovsky, it would only bring on more questions like 'Who am I, and what do I exist for?' I was beginning to wonder, myself, but I was not sure confiding in Tsiolkovsky would get me anywhere. He should report me to Base, as I should already have reported him.

Then came the fire. It happened so silently, so swiftly.

It was Globa's turn for the sleep experiments. We wired him up, and left him alone in Spetkr to get what sleep he could.

We took a meal together. Black-currant jelly from foil packets, and vodka from Globa's stash.

At the time of the fire, I was stamping postcards. Endlessly. We stamped them in proof they were on Mir, to sell on our return. Manakov was tucking up cables. I scarcely noticed any more, the cables in free fall, the pools of water, the flickering lights from computer malfunctions. I felt this was the only life I ever knew, that all other notions of life on earth were phantasms induced by vodka and lack of sleep.

Tsiolkovsky flew past the bench. He refused to stamp postcards. When I asked him to help, he replied: 'How is it possible for me to understand the cause of all that happens to me?' It was only stamping postcards, but he would make yet another cosmic question of it.

Manakov said: 'The oxygen is getting low.' It was my task to replenish the supply.

I secured the cards and made my way through the hatchway into the Kvant module.

I switched to the back-up system. Everything on Mir was fast becoming back-up, and back-ups of the back-ups, as the front-line equipment collapsed.

I found the cylinder, and took out the gutted candle, the spent lithium perchlorate. I put a fresh candle in the tube. I turned the red dial and smelt the sweet flow of oxygen. Then, as I placed the cylinder back in its cradle, I saw sparks of light in the air-flow.

Fire!

I was on board a space craft hurtling around the earth. I was located precisely in time and space. But at the moment I knew this,

I also knew I inhabited another place where time and space were irrelevant.

I felt a great sluggishness come over me. My actions should have been swift. I should have yelled 'Fire!' My companions should rush to help me. We are trained to respond quickly, without question.

But just as I knew I must call out, I felt myself fall out of this space, this time, into another place. I saw sparks from the cylinder turn, in free-fall, into a burning sphere. I saw the soul of the universe in this fire, this small burning sun inside Mir. I saw the king of stars and the fountain of life.

I watched the flame grow to embrace the entire universe. I said in a voice that I knew did not carry: 'We have a fire.'

These things happened, as if in another place, to another person.

Inside the Kvant module a light flashed upon me, and through me, shining as a mirror, all colours together, flashing and disappearing, reappearing, fusing and blending to a light that is not a light, to a fire that is not a fire. I saw the fire before me, the flames flowing into a sphere as oxygen escaped. I sensed the invisible fire all round, within Mir and beyond, spreading to infinity, an invisible fire, a fire that does not burn, a fire that brings with it perfection and tranquillity. When we knew nothing of it, it stayed hidden. Once I sensed it, it showed itself to me, when I sought to find it, I did not know what it was that I was looking for.

I think then it was that I called 'Fire!' in a voice that carried well beyond my head.

Tsiolkovsky flew through the hatch and seized the fire-extinguisher. Nothing came out of it. We needed the back-up extinguisher, and the back-up to the back-up.

The fire alarm rang, a piercing buzzer. I remembered Globa, asleep in the Spetkr module. I had to get him. The alarm should trigger a shutdown of the ventilation system. Manakov tussled with the container of oxygen masks, wrenching it open and throwing them to us. Tsiolkovsky threw a towel on the flames. It caught fire, and specks of smoke and burning towel flew round the module.

I saw smoke, and at its heart a yellow glow, and Tsiolkovsky fighting with the extinguisher that would not come free from the wall.

I saw motes of dust in the air, and splashes of molten metal.

Manakov wrenched the nozzle round from the hull, and flecks of foam flew in the cabin.

The fire hissed.

The first mask did not work. The oxygen did not trigger. I threw it away and took an extra for Globa. I had to find him and wake him. We might need to evacuate in Soyuz.

Soyuz was on the other side of the fire.

I moved fast out of Kvant and shut the hatch behind me, so that smoke would not seep into the ventilator system.

It was so quiet out there.

I found Globa awake, trailing his wires, and fighting to remove the blue cap so firmly gelled to his head. He scattered the sensors about him. They floated in free fall, measuring the brain waves of the ether. His blood splashed into the air from the discarded catheter, and formed blobs of red rain.

Globa was in a state.

On Basc, they did not like interruptions to their sleep experiments.

The masks worked and we breathed sweet air. I wondered, then, about the air. Perhaps we no longer needed it. If we did not need to breathe, then Tsiolkovsky was right when he said we were dead, and had been so for a long time.

The fire shrank. The burning bush contracted to a point. The flame went out. It was over.

We did not need the escape module Soyuz, not yet.

Our fire debriefing was swift and to the point.

Manakov said: 'It happened. I saw it, with my own eyes. I saw the fire and I sensed the presence within.'

Globa said: 'I heard a voice I have always known.'

Tsiolkovsky said; 'The music is in our hearts. The light is in our heads. We fought a fire, and won a prize beyond the telling.'

I said: 'I shall inform Base that there has been a small problem with the oxygen emergency oxygen supply. Nothing we couldn't fix.'

Metal fatigue, they said, afterwards, it was caused by metal fatigue on Mir, the untested effects of space radiation on earth-made metals. As the hull of Mir got more exhausted, as did its occupants, and yet more exhausted, the exhaustion became a creeping contagion that spread, here loosening bolts, there rusting fire extinguishers to the bulkhead, here sending hand-rails careening off into space. Metal fatigue rusted the judgment of long-stay cosmonauts, so that they saw God on space-walks, and heard the songs of angels.

They trashed Mir in the Southern Ocean. Of course, they thought we had all returned by then, and certainly, Tsiolkovsky, and Globa, and Manakov seemed to come back with me, in Soyuz, but it was more that they sent their emissaries in their bodily forms, ghosts that went through the motions of being human.

Tsiolkovsky said: 'I always told you, Volkov, that I had a dream, and now I know that I have awoken from my dream, which was the dream of life on board Mir. I awoke, and I found myself in an awesome place, and here I want to stay.'

And I alone returned to earth, as me, the real, the one and only me. Since then, I have mourned my loss. I dream, with Tsiolkovsky, that there is a ladder set on this ground upon which I now walk, and its top reaches far beyond the ghostly Mir in the sky to the gate of Paradise itself, and angels go up and down it. They pass close by the ghost Mir, which sings in its celestial orbit, captured by the sphere of perfection. Mir is crystal clear, and shining with its solar panels and its hull free forever from rusting and metallic stresses, flying in the ethereal wind, and clothed in the fiery garments of light.

Mir circles still on high, and I think of Manakov, busy, as always, eternally mopping up puddles of the heavenly quintessence.

The Boy Who
Didn't Yearn

•

Margo Lanagan

I should have realised straight off. Of all people, I, Tess Maxwell, should have seen him for what he was. I mean, I knew something was different, something big. My eyes kept going back to him. But I was caught up in people leaving the Art Cottage, and he was in the crowd going to the basketball courts, and we got swept away from each other, Keenoy Ribson and me.

I tried to work it out at the bus stop, the way you try and get a whole dream back using the one little shred you remember, but it turned into a flutter among flutters in my mind, and the bus came, and I went home.

I went home and I went to work – same place. I work in 'the parlour', Mum calls it, a polite name for such a messy, personal kind of business premises.

My first client was a woman who was after her husband. He was right there with her, of course; the thick, dark string of his tether went from his worn slipper-toe to her right shoulder. He hung over her, griping.

'He's saying "Don't burn the snags, Merrill",' I told her.

She laughed. 'Oh yes, of course. Yes, that's him. Same old whinging bludger. God, I miss him!' And she cried. They always cry when you tell them that kind of detail.

119

And then there was a man. He had a very handsome boyfriend –
well, the handsome version alternated with a blotched, dying one
who slid down to lie between us on the Turkish rug. 'He's very
grateful for everything you did for him,' I said. 'It made it easier, he
says. You did everything right. Robert, his name is.' And the guy
nodded, and he dissolved in tears, too. 'You're doing good work,'
I went on. 'You think it's pointless without Robert, but every day of
your life you make a big difference to a lot of people. He's not
saying that; it's just . . . clear, around you. There's all this value;
you're very solid. What is your work?'

'I'm a nurse,' he said, through the complimentary tissues.

'Oh, there you go, then.'

After him, I was tired, because it is tiring. But two clients means
a hundred dollars. Five hundred dollars a week is a good amount –
it means we can live, as well as keep Dad at Bernard House. If I
were really *determined* I could do more, but I guess I'm not. We're
managing, aren't we? We're managing fine on two a night.

Mum was in the kitchen with a fruit-shake and a cheese muffin
for me, and Dad was there, too, on home-care. I sat and ate and
thought about bed.

'Take Dad for a walk?' said Mum.

I nodded. It was too early for bed; a walk would clear my head
ready for homework.

It was cold outside, grey and darkening. I wheeled Dad up to
the park, because the paths there have got nice, rounded corners,
and I needed to be somewhere quiet, among trees and rotundas and
curly metal seats. I started to wake up there, I started to come
back to myself. You can't hurry that; all you can do is wait.

I used to exhaust myself over Dad. It didn't do any good. I can feel
his brain almost as if it's in my own skull, and half of it's just
drained, of juice, of life. And nothing on the living side's very
strong, either. Everything shimmers at the same level, with no
memory bigger or better than the others, and there are no links

between the memories, or feelings tied to them; everything's just random poppings-up, a sort of play of life like a small, settled fire that won't actually burn anything.

Once, right back at the beginning, Mum asked what I could see. 'They say the life force can flow back in, bit by bit,' she said. And she looked up from Dad, wanting hope – from me, probably the only person in her world who couldn't give her any.

I was so embarrassed for her I couldn't speak. *Life* force – where'd she get that idea? And who were 'they' supposed to be?

'But that'd be for *mild* strokes, I suppose,' she finished, turning away.

I recovered a bit. 'He's there, but he's all mulched up. He doesn't hang together.'

'Is there any point,' she asked, 'in it being us, who look after him? Does it make any difference? Does he recognise us?'

'Not very often. And not much happens when he does.'

Which was why we eventually put him in Bernard House, to get some life back for ourselves, some time *not* tending that fire. We do still tend it, but only on a few weeknights. Mum wheels Dad home and parks him in the kitchen-family room he designed and built, and feeds him while I work – she says she doesn't want me feeding him, doesn't want me to have memories of that. And she talks to him. She's hoping to get something back, an eye-flicker, a noise that sounds like an answer. Stubbornly she goes on, serenely talking, about the news, about people they both used to know (but now only she knows them), goes on and on breaking her heart over him – or maybe not breaking it so much as wearing it away, grinding it gradually down to nothing.

I won't do that to myself. I know it upsets Mum that I don't talk to Dad, but what's the point if he doesn't exist enough to hear me? Mum still thinks he does – time and time again I see her making up that alternative life, seeing his eyes brighten, watching him throw off his rug and stand up: *I'll just get that doorknob fixed before dinner*, he says, or *What are we all sitting around here for, with long faces?* But even when his voice is so clear, coming through her, I can't believe; I *know* Dad's kind of damage never mends. He won't come back.

Next morning I woke up breathing the deep calm of a Dad-free house. *Whatsaname Ribson*, I thought. *Keenoy. The air around him is absolutely clear and silent*. Yeah, that was it. No strings attached him to any yearnings or losses. He was clean; he was himself, he was completely self-contained. Like me. Excitement stirred tentatively under my ribs. *Could* there be someone like that? Or did he have some attachment I just wasn't seeing yet?

I dressed and took coffee in to Mum, stroked her head to wake her up and gave her one of those big morning hugs – better than coffee, she says – which are like being drunk out of, but like drinking too. And I smiled back at her, which I can do, some mornings.

'Busy day ahead?' she said. Beside her the bedclothes were flat and uncluttered, where for a long time after Dad's stroke there'd been a mound, a Dad-shaped mound that Mum had put there.

'Busy day every day. Want toast?'

'There are some muffins left – I'll have one of those. Please, I mean.'

'Your wish is my command.'

'Thanks, love.'

Going up the hill to school, I saw a tall boy's curly blond hair ahead. *Ah, yes. Him.*

He was talking to Slade and those guys. He said something that made them laugh. They were easier to see for a moment – those guys are usually so stuck about with hang-ups it's quite painful to look at them. But when the veils of fear and bad home life and wanting-a-red-car clustered back around them, Keenoy Ribson was still clear and unobscured. My eyes searched around him automatically, wondering where he hid all his stuff – some people can do that – searching and searching and finding nothing. Nothing at all. It was kind of stunning, like a fine day after a long rainy spell. I watched him closely – his relaxed walk, his personal version of the school uniform, the beaten-up school bag with his old school's crest on it, with the motto KNOW THYSELF – and I waited for interference, but he stayed as crisp and clean-edged as a photograph.

Several times that day I saw him, always with totally different groups of people. He didn't seem to care who he was seen with, Slade's roughnecks or Mandy's knitting circle or that nerd Purtwee. He always looked perfectly comfortable; the group was always cheerful and busy with conversation.

'Did you see that new guy?' I heard Josh Bateman say.

'What a suck – see him talking to Bannister? Getting in with the school captain?'

But at lunchtime there they were, Keenoy and Josh and all the soccer-heads together, out on the oval, kicking a ball around.

Nobody had a problem with him, unless you call the girls' instant wild crushes a problem. '*Such* a babe,' Blossom O'Malley said to me – I happened to be standing near her when Keenoy walked past.

'You think?' I said.

'What, are you crazy?' She goggled at me.

'You think he's good-looking?'

She gazed after him. 'Well, it's not so much the looks, though they're *okay*. It's more, he's so *happy*.'

I liked Blossom for a second, then, with that note of longing in her voice. Just for that brief time, she had dignity, before all her usual cutesy, kittenish attachments bobbed in around her again.

My work makes it hard for me to like people. They seem so despicable sometimes, going around inside out, all their weaknesses showing in their walk, in their clothes, in their I'm-in-control-of-it-all faces, let alone the visible holes in them, the baggage-people they drag around with them. Mum says these things are only obvious to me, though. I must remember that not everyone can see what's so shatteringly clear to me. I envy other people that, and I despise them. I can't see how they can live, so cluttered up with other people's lives and influences; I'd hate to live in someone else's shadow. Worse, I'd hate to go around with my insides all blurted out like that, moaning my wants to the whole world, mourning what I'd lost.

Keenoy Ribson *went on* being happy. (I should've realised then, at least.) He didn't take on any of our hang-ups, didn't join any of the cliques. He seemed to enjoy himself, to enjoy being at *this* school, with us. He volunteered for the daggy old musical; he played sports – not well, but with lots of energy; he worked hard enough but didn't do brilliantly. And he talked. He greeted everyone, he chatted, he joked, he had deep-and-meaningfuls when deep-and-meaningfuls were required. He was always in there with people, close up, interacting.

I kept waiting for some insufficiency, some little longing, to show itself near him, but it never did. I'd have to talk to him, maybe, get to know him better, or just get him away from the crowd and see him against a plain background, before I'd know for sure.

I did follow him home one day – well, not all the way home. Somehow I lost him near the freeway overpass, just got distracted for the second it took him to disappear up some lane or into some house.

I didn't try again. I wasn't exactly in a hurry to be disappointed. (Funny how, through the whole thing, I always expected disappointment, even though I went after hope. 'Went after' – hmph, more like I sat like a lump, doing nothing, letting hope grow all by itself, like ivy, latching onto me with its millions of little suckers.)

'How does it come to you, the Knowledge?' one of my clients once asked me, a client who'd pulled a whole bunch of mooing, chattering gurus into the parlour with her, all their tethers snarled together.

It always annoys me, that soft, awed tone of voice. I sighed. 'It's very simple. You know how some people have been hurt so badly that they shuffle when they walk, or they hunch over and hug the inside edge of the pavement? You know how angry people wear this angry face around all the time, with the pulled-down mouth and the eyes kind of flashing to warn you?'

'Yes, you're right!' She sounded surprised, as if this was new

•

to her. 'It's as if their experiences are imprinted in their bodies somehow.'

'Well, exactly. And all you have to do is look a little bit closer, and all the details of that imprint will show you the shape of the thing that's giving them pain, or anger, or sadness. Usually it's another person, but it can be some *thing* they want badly, like a big house or a pile of gold that can push you out of shape, too.'

But I'd lost her – she'd gone all reverent again. She wanted me to be another guru, the guru of gurus, to give her the final answer that would pull all the others together and give her one simple rule for living. 'It's a wonderful gift.' She thought she was agreeing, but she was actually preventing herself from seeing. People do this *all the time.*

It's not a gift. Everyone can do it – but nobody does. Nobody bothers to read – from the way a person's spine bends or the way their voice turns all feathery when they're stressed – the shape of the *other* person who stands behind, or over, or inside, or squashed underneath the client. *Absent ones,* Mum calls them, but in fact they're very present. They've carved themselves into each client – sometimes gently and in a good way, sometimes with a single thump or shout spoiling a life, cramping every movement from that moment on. Just open your eyes and you'll see them.

It was a Wednesday evening, getting into autumn. I was pushing Dad home from the park. Everything looked coldly blue, except for the golden interior of Bar Piccolo, like a little lantern between the closed minimart and the vacant shop that had once been the Bibliophile bookshop. Kids from school sat laughing around a table in there, among them Keenoy Ribson.

I guess I kind of loomed up to the window out of the dark, and Dad's wheelchair's a bit of an eye-catcher, and . . . anyway, Keenoy looked up, and lifted a hand as if we were old friends.

I put a smile on my face that died as soon as I was past the window. Then I heard footsteps, and there was Keenoy beside me. 'Tess! I need a word with you.'

'Oh?' I tried to casually hide the wheelchair behind me.

'Sorry. You in a hurry?' He indicated Dad with his eyes.

'Not really. Um, this is my dad.'

'Hello, Mr Maxwell.'

Dad's head wandered around to look at him.

'He's had a stroke,' I said. 'He can't speak.' In fact, he isn't really here at all. Please act as if he isn't here.

'Ah.' Keenoy nodded to him anyway. 'I was just going to ask you, Tess, we're short one Beggar Maid in the musical. D'you think you could fill in the gap?'

Surprise made me laugh. 'Hey, I'm not really performing material.'

'All you have to do is sit in a bunch of Maids and sing a chorus, sway a bit. Nothing too hard.'

'Sounds very *not* me.'

He made a pleading face that I had to laugh at. 'Come to rehearsal tomorrow,' he begged. 'Take a look.'

'Okay, I'll take a look.'

'Good *on you*!'

'I'm not promising anything.'

'Look, you don't have to.' He backed towards the café. 'See you then.'

He was gone. And I walked home smiling. Idiot.

I've made them sound really powerful, those 'absent' ones. But in the end it's the clients who decide how helped, how timid, how lost they'll be. That's why I was so sour on making this thing of mine into a business. Before Dad died – sorry, had his stroke – I never would have dreamed of doing it. All I was doing, I felt, was taking money for telling people what they'd already spent *years* telling themselves – that Grandma was the only one who ever properly loved them, that she must be watching them from above, continuing to wish them well. Or that their dead child still lived somewhere – which it did, inside them – beaming innocence out into the world.

You want certain voices to speak to you – lovingly or sternly or whatever. You want it so badly that you throw them out from yourself, and when I hear them and repeat back to you what they say, it seems like proof. You forget it's your own ventriloquism, your own loss, your own hankering written into the space around you for just about anyone to read. I feel like a thief, charging you my fee, but if you need to hear, but won't listen for yourself, and if we need the money, I'll do it. I won't like doing it, but I'll do it.

I went home smiling and told myself not to get silly. I should have been tired, but I wasn't. Mum had lit a fire in the parlour fireplace, and I sat there with her for a while. In the firelight Dad looked like somebody's dreamy old grandpa, mesmerised by the flames, and Mum and I had a sleepy, bitsy conversation. I almost told her about the musical, but then I thought, No, she'd be too delighted. She'd pin more on it than I want pinned . . . for now. Instead, I let myself feel the occasional roll of excitement inside me, let Keenoy's face rise in my memory and shine across to me some of its happy light and warmth.

I went to the rehearsal next day. I volunteered straight up, and got parked among the Beggar Maids.

'Oh hi, Tess,' said Zenardia. 'I didn't know you were musical.'

'Oh, I'm not. I'm only doing this as a favour to Keenoy.' It was the first and last time I ever said his name, and it made a funny feeling in my mouth, a kind of embarrassing tang, as if I'd used a special, intimate name I had for him, loosed it in public.

The rehearsal started. It probably seems like nothing to a normal person, but I enjoyed myself. It was a silly, romantic story, inter-rupted by the soppiest songs, but I got caught up in it anyway. Everyone else was taking it so seriously! When Lexie Nelson, the main girl, was singing her duet with Keenoy, they were both so *excellent*, even standing there in their school uniforms, that I saw Lexie clearly for the first time. Her mother climbed down off her back and her pushy brothers faded away to nothing, and for several minutes she didn't care that Nick Stefanopoulos didn't love her the way she loved him. I sat there with all the other Maids – who had stopped chatting to listen, just as impressed as I was – and I let myself think, Maybe life could be like this.

Right back when I first discovered that other people didn't see what I saw, all I wanted to do was get out, climb down from this kind of princess's tower my knowledge puts me in, mingle, be with other people, act like them – unaware, laughing at my own mistakes. I can see that people's ignorance is blissful – I'd like to turn around and say to some clients, Hey look, you'd be happier not knowing. Really, don't make me tell you.

Because knowing is hard. For my clients, knowing just their own stuff is hard to cope with; for me, knowing everyone's . . . well, I used *not* to cope; a school assembly used to make me pass out. Nowadays I can block out quite a bit of the noise and bother around people, but it still takes some strength to deal with, say, a half-full train carriage, where there's room for each person's burdens and yearnings to swell out and speak up and compete for attention. Whenever a new passenger climbs in, everyone's yearnings check out the new ones and then go back to their own blabbing and yowling. It gets exhausting. I only really have any peace when I'm on my own, shut away from everyone. The rest is . . . well, it'll always be hard work, won't it? I just have to face that.

After the rehearsal, Keenoy walked me home. He was exactly the right height, just a bit taller than me. It makes me miserable now to think how perfect he was.

I told him everything. Well, he'd seen Dad, so he knew about all that, and he wanted to know more, and he asked about the stroke, and listened, and was sympathetic but not ghoulish about it. 'That's hard on you and your mum.' His tone of voice, of course, was righter than most people's, with no awkwardness in it. He must have some kind of similar experience behind him, I thought, but where? If it hasn't left a mark on him, what's he done to get over it? What power does he have? What makes him so strong?

I looked up at him occasionally as we walked and talked. His skin was totally spot-free, unmarked by freckles or acne or any other kind of imperfection. Blossom was right; it was a happy face. Happiness was built into it, the mouth always ready to smile if not actually smiling, the eyes kind of smallish but active, taking in everything and having a quick thought to match each taken-in thing. I liked him. For the first time in my life I could see how it was possible to like a boy, even for someone like me.

I didn't feel awkward at all, saying, 'Would you like a hot drink or something?' when we reached my gate.

'Sure,' he said.

I held open the gate after me. 'Where do you live, anyway?'

'Just a little way along from here, really. Over Oaky Park way.'

'Really? Why don't you go to Oaky Park High, then, instead of travelling all the way across here?'

'Oh, well, you know . . .'

I opened the door. Something went crash, in the kitchen. 'So clumsy!' came Mum's voice, her really-upset voice. 'You've turned into a baby – no, *worse* than a baby! You'll *never* grow up! You'll never be more than this clumsy wreck – '

I froze on the doorstep. Another crash. Sobbing.

Keenoy took my shoulders, moved me to one side and went in towards the kitchen. I started after him; I didn't want him to see, didn't want Mum to know he'd heard her losing it.

Dad was there, with food spilled down his shirtfront. Mum was crouched down next to him, trying to scoop the mush on the floor back up into the bowl with a shaking spoon. She looked up and saw Keenoy – and recognised him. (Well, she would, wouldn't she?)

'I just wanted him to try,' she said desperately. 'Maybe he *could* feed himself! Maybe something's knitted back together in his head by now. Maybe he's healing in there and none of us can see it yet!' She said it all in a garbled, hiccuping rush, while Keenoy took the bowl and spoon from her, put them in the sink, then turned back to put his arms around her – whoa! She was sobbing against him; she looked very small wrapped up in there, and he felt suddenly very big in the room. It seemed a big thing for a person to do, to comfort someone just because she needed it.

I stood by the door feeling sick. If it had been me, I would have concentrated on the mess: wiped up the mush, told Mum to sit down, made her a cup of tea, cleaned up Dad's shirt, moved around and around her and not touched her once, biting back my irritation. 'I could have *told you* Dad would drop it! Don't you listen when I tell you? *He's not there!*' I never would have hugged her. I would have been too angry.

I went away, full of shame. I put my bag in my room, went into the parlour. Twenty minutes and my first client would be here. I'd have to calm down by then.

After a little while Keenoy Ribson came in. He stood in the doorway with a mug of hot chocolate in each hand, smiling.

'She okay?' I said gracelessly.

'She's fine. A "momentary lapse", she said. We all have 'em.' He handed me a drink and sat down in the client chair.

'She'll never stop missing him. It's almost all she ever does.'

'But not you?'

I tried to take a sip of my drink, but it gave my lip a warning scald. I blew on it instead. 'Sure, I miss my dad. But that out there in the wheelchair, that's not him, and it never will be him. There's too much damage. I'm not going to fool myself.'

'No, you're too clear-eyed for that.' There was no sarcasm in his voice. He looked so singular and baggage-free in that chair, the chair I usually saw through such a fog of ghosts and inhibitions. For once, someone was looking at me to give me something, not to suck a reading out of me, not to be saved. He was looking, he was caring, he was interested. Nobody looks at me like that – and I'm not talking about romance here; this is so much more important than romance. I'm so lonely in my life! I remember thinking. I've got no one! What a sad novelty it was to confide in someone, to tell about just me. Usually people's sympathy locks straight onto Mum, and we all help and console her; I'm so competent and practical, it must seem like I don't need consoling.

'I've been meaning to ask you,' I said – and it was a wonderful feeling, to be able to say anything I liked and know I wouldn't be laughed at, or revered – 'Have you got a talent like mine?'

'Which talent's that? Like, of all your talents?' He raised his mug to me and took a sip. 'I mean, I can sing, you heard me –'

'The talent of seeing . . . extra things about people.'

'Extra things? What, like their potential as Beggar Maids?'

'Like their hang-ups.'

'Their hang-ups?' And then he drank down his hot chocolate. In two gulps – I heard them both. He put the mug on the table next to the tissue box. His smile was a little strange, a little fixed.

'It's almost a psychic thing,' I said, frowning from the empty mug to him. And despite that look in his eyes, which said clearly, Don't go down this road, I told him all about it, about my work, the things I see, and how he didn't fit into the system. Boy, did I blather on. 'You don't even seem to have any parental pressure, which is crazy for a sixteen- or seventeen-year-old. Every other boy I know carries his father around on his back like a sack of cement – sometimes his mum's there too, trying to heave off a bit of the dad's weight, trying to make life a bit easier. You don't seem to have anyone. Nothing gets to you; nothing pushes you out of your own shape. I don't see how that's possible. Are you some kind of strange non-grieving orphan? Have you got some kind of religious belief that clears all your gremlins away?' Blah, blah, blah.

When I finally shut up, he laughed gently. 'You don't want to know, Tess.'

'But I do! I'm *busting* to know! Because whatever you've got, I want it too!' And I blah-ed on about that, too – clarity and self-assurance and kindness.

He was still laughing. He was at his best-looking, laughing – maybe he was hoping that'd distract me.

But it didn't, and he laughed on, too long, too watchfully.

And then he slipped. His gaze flicked to the floor just for a second, and when he looked back to me his laughter had definitely turned nervous.

I looked down. I was trying to hide it from myself and see it at the same time, so the tether was very fine, disguising itself by following the pattern in the Turkish rug. But I knew that pattern; I could see where the line had to cross from one motif to another, wriggling through the pile like a snake through stubble. A thread of darkness ran from one side of the rug to the other, joining Keenoy's foot to mine.

'You idiot,' I heard myself say.

Keenoy's smile was feebly apologetic now. His eyes wobbled, and then began to widen down his collapsing face, dragging the smile down with them.

'I *thought* you were too good to be true,' I said, trying to save face.

Keenoy's head was a melted heap on his chest. His torso deflated with a wet pop!, his arms shrinking into his shoulders.

'You twit.' I hit my head with my fist, over and over. 'You sappy, cloth-brained, *stupid* – '

He shrivelled to a tiny black blob on the end of the line, whipping back across the rug into the toe of my shoe. I hadn't noticed him leave, but now I felt him come back into me, like water-balloons bursting in my chest and throat. Then I was brim-full of my own self again, unhappy but unstretched, not yearning, not fooling myself.

I sat there for a bit, recovering. I could hear Mum humming along to the radio in the kitchen. Keenoy's empty mug sent up a last lazy curl of steam. I felt like a complete fool. But at least it was over now; I didn't have to wonder any more.

And then the front gate clicked open, letting my first client in. Taking a deep breath, I got up and went to the door.

A Spell at the
End of the World

●

Alexander James

His mission was this; to board the ocean liner on a three-month passage to Melbourne, on very short notice, with three packages. He was to guard them with his life. Someone would meet him at the hotel at the other end, and know what to do from there. The packages were given to him the night before the ship sailed, as was his ticket and boarding pass, along with an envelope filled with Australian money and another envelope with his accommodation details. They had told him that there might be incidents along the way. People or things might attempt to take the packages from him. Perhaps even kill him for them. He was to protect himself and the packages with his knowledge of the arts. Customs had been attended to.

Barker had taken their words with a nod, with the uneasy knowledge that choosing him had been a mistake.

He was a sorcerer, to be sure, and they had wanted a sorcerer for the mission. But there were greater in London than he, wiser, more powerful, better experienced. Certainly half a dozen he could name better versed in covert activities, less vulnerable to attack and more suited to fighting off assassins.

But he suspected, if not knew, that he had been chosen because he was not a ranking sorcerer. So far as mastery of the arts went, he was nondescript. He'd achieved reliable status amongst the occult underworld and as a white sorcerer had taken part in the fight against the darker elements. He had calmed restless spirits for troubled folk, and sent demons back from whence they'd been summoned. He'd brought those responsible to justice. He had even been part of portal creation not once but three times, and thus witnessed conversations with beings not of this Earthly dimension. But he'd never been asked by the Supernatural Council to do anything other than help with those portal spells, until the night they had summoned him and given him this mission.

The spells he knew and had mastered were all protective or benign, apart from the general spells of exorcism that every sorcerer knew. He had known at an early age, relative to the discovery of his heightened will, that he did not possess the stamina nor disposition to become a warrior sorcerer, that his niche was more likely within those ranks who chose to defend, correct and ease rather than seek out, advance and attack. He dealt with the consequences of what the practitioners of the black arts did, he did not seek them out before they could do it.

But he had shown bravery, more than once. A willingness to place himself and his will, his confidence in the mastery of the arts, between demons and those they sought to harm. Between evil men and their victims. And he had come through unscathed.

He was a good sorcerer. But not the best.

The best would have known what had saved his life twice on the ocean liner. He did not.

The first attack had come during the first week of the voyage, the first time he had vacated his cabin at length. Upon boarding, Barker had cast a protective spell on his cabin which would not allow anyone to enter without his permission. Such a spell was strong, but the more he used the door, the weaker the spell would become. So he remained in the cabin and read some of the books he'd brought with him. Although he had packed a broadly themed collection of novels in anticipation of a quiet, solitary cruise, he had quickly exhausted his patience with them. He was on a holiday ship after all, designed for comfort, if not luxury, and there were other diversions and entertainments he didn't have the discipline to completely avoid, despite the covert nature of his mission. There was even a stage magician amongst the lounge singers and vaudevillian comedians, to entertain the shipbound travellers. This had piqued his curiosity enough to risk leaving the packages unattended.

Barker had quickly seen through the magician's sleight of hand and diversionary tactics, even from the back of the packed audience. Occasionally a true sorcerer practised stage magic, but this one had been nothing more than a master of illusion.

Nothing more? Barker caught himself.

Could he perform magic?

Could he do anything the Great Majesto had done without the aid of sorcery? He doubted it. Majesto must have practised diligently for years to gain the level of skill he'd exhibited on stage. It was just that parallel, the one between illusion and sorcery, which brought about his mild snobbery toward stage magic. He imagined briefly that he might know how astronomers felt when compared to astrologers. Same subject, both skilled, but diametrically opposed.

It had been on that night, when he had decided to gauge whether or not he might have a comrade in arts for the long journey, that he'd first been attacked. Gazing out to sea after Majesto's encore, watching the mothers assess him as they guided their virgin daughters past him in the hope he might be a potential suitor, he let his guard down. How, he wondered, might a young woman 'see the world', at least as it truly was, with her mother constantly at her side? Still, it was tradition. The world was made of that. He suspected that many of the young women would return to England unattached, then marry the first man they set eyes upon to get away from their omnipresent maternal shadow. Perhaps that was the idea?

The decks of the liner were crowded during the day, but at night after dinner and entertainment, the decks were all but empty. He had always enjoyed the sea, at least the feeling of gazing out at it from the safe vantage point of a stretch of British coastline. The ocean made some people feel small, insignificant, but it had always made him feel profoundly connected to life. Had he not answered the call of sorcery, he might have been one of those young men who set sail for a military life. But then again, he'd always been pre-dominantly of artistic temperament. If he was being honest with himself, he would not have lasted long in the navy. A mere child during the war against the Nazis, he'd been evacuated to Coventry for the duration, where his gifts had started to reveal themselves and flourish. The children's war stories he'd heard at the time, as opposed to the terrors that had surfaced and been told and retold long after, even to this day, might just as well have attracted him to the air force or conventional service. But as a child he'd always seen the military in whatever form as a kind of noble dream, a romantic fantasy that was meant for others. Of course, as a child he'd not seen the war in such terms, only now, fourteen years after the end of the war, did he reflect and gain clarity upon his child-hood perspective.

He was made for something else. Another kind of war.

He supposed though, had he been born a decade earlier, or if the war had lasted a decade longer, that he would have stepped forward. Fought. The call to the art of sorcery had not stopped others of his kind signing up, had not stopped them being killed or even making careers. Sorcerers were in many ways just like other men. Other women. They answered many calls, individually or as a whole through their Supernatural Council, and had throughout the centuries. They had lives outside the calling; butchers, bakers, and particularly candlestick makers.

He was a bookseller.

Ordinary books, most of the time. Works of fiction. But he had dealt with grimoires and spell books and magical items on the side, and the combination made for a diverse and curious clientele. He wondered how the store was keeping in his absence, if he'd chosen correctly to leave it in the hands of his nephew. The store ran itself, if you knew how to let it, and he suspected his nephew, until then an apprentice projectionist at the local motion picture theatre, possessed the correct temperament for such work. A caretaker. A watcher and imaginer. A sorcerer, no, but one who might appreciate tales of such things.

Tales were becoming more popular these days, as it had been designed. The great work of fiction had been completed, released and embraced by the people of the United Kingdom, and would spawn many and varied writers to emulate the tale for better or worse. He'd been told this through the underworld rumour mill and had come to believe it.

'Those books,' they would say, 'those three books are our cover as the world progresses. It will cement the sorcerer's art as fantasy, enter culture and divert ordinary people from our reality.'

Yes, be believed that the great tale of the elves and dwarves and other fanciful beings had been engineered as a cover for sorcerers in the age to come. But the rest of it . . . the other reason?

He wondered if it were true. Had there truly once been intelligent creatures other than men on the Earth? Had all record of their existence been systematically removed, in order to hide what remained of them?

'It could be done,' his friend had sworn, 'it could be done easily within two generations, with the right people in the right places. Look at Hitler. They say he would have done it with the Jews, had he won the war. Simply wiped them off the face of the Earth and out of history books as though they never existed. Two generations. That's all it takes to forget. The way the world is moving now, perhaps one generation is all it would take. Imagine how quickly information will travel in years to come, Barker. Why, important messages can cross the world in a minute . . . in fifty years who's to say it won't be a matter of seconds? For the really important messages, that is.'

Barker didn't know. He only knew how long it took for the ocean liner to get to Melbourne, how long it took for his books to be sent to collectors in various parts of the world. Anything crossing the globe in less than three months seemed absurd.

The man had seemed to come out of the sea at him. He was shoved hard, backward across the deck into the long window that separated the shuffle board deck from the walkway. Not out of the sea, he realised. The man must have been hanging or perched somehow over the edge of the ship. Barker had been standing at the portside railing, watching the ocean and thinking about war for some time, so the assailant must have made his way across the portside edge of the ship somehow and crawled up to him, rather than hiding in wait for Barker to move toward him.

The man had whispered a guttural, 'H'ro'shoh.'

Paralysing spell, Barker recognised. One of those prehistoric utterances that resided still within man's collective unconscious. A series of harsh syllables that would stop a man in his tracks. The name of a beast, perhaps? That when uttered had frozen early homosapiens in primal fear? The title of a devilish totem?

'H'karal,' Barker hissed in return, before his throat seized up, drawing energy from his gut and repelling the man with a wave of white heat, simultaneously defrosting his own stiff frame. The man had a dagger and he rebounded before Barker could properly move to counter anything more and then, as the dagger's tip was at his throat, the assailant flew backward over the edge of the ship and was gone. It had been like a strong wind, a freak gust, had caught and taken him.

Over the edge, gone.

Dead as soon as he hit the water, if not drowned . . . how long would it take a man alone to drown at sea? The dread thought hit Barker as he returned to the edge, looked down into the black night water and started to call, before he knew it, that there was a man overboard.

Conscience.

But then there was a hand . . . at least, he felt that it had fingers, skin and joint, gently over his mouth from behind, and a voice in his mind that spoke a language he didn't recognise. But the words made sense. The words said:

'He would have killed you, he would try again. My grip snapped his neck, he is no more . . .'

The hand was removed and Barker turned about but there was no one there. An empty deck, a darkened shuffle board enclosure behind broad glass.

But in the reflection of the glass . . . the moon was not full, but she and the stars cast a bright glow nevertheless, he saw something. And a scent, like cut grass. It took him back to his school days, of summer recesses on the school oval.

He thought he'd seen bark.

But how? Bark, in his mind . . .

Think, sorcerer.

What you saw made an association of bark in your mind, but that was because what you saw was something outside of your comprehension . . . outside of *human* comprehension?

Barker shivered for all sorts of reasons and hurried back to his cabin.

When the ocean liner had docked three months later and Barker had descended the gangplank, catching sight of the crane that dangled his luggage and his packages, twirling high above the ship, it was without a clue as to where he really was or who he was supposed to meet.

The voyage had concluded and here he was, alone on the dock surrounded by hundreds of tourists and the people who'd come out this morning to greet them. He did not linger.

He read the directions to the hotel, which had been written by hand and attached to his accommodation details, and decided to go directly there, which was in the middle of the city, via taxi cab. He paused only briefly, before making his way, to pay the dockside workers for their help in transferring his luggage and the packages into the cab.

Once at the hotel he had tried to pay the concierge in advance for his room, but discovered that everything was in order, indefinitely. He had to assume that the Australian dollars he'd been given were simply for getting by.

In the lobby, as he waited for the porter to show him to his room, he saw and sensed immediately that the hotel was large and plush, and that the well dressed and perfectly groomed occupants conducted themselves as though they deserved to be there. Wealth and status. Feeling almost directly at odds with this, he made an immediate decision to keep to himself, to get by with room service and the radio. He made a mental note to purchase a few more novels.

The three months on the liner had not been enjoyable. At the parts of the world where the ship had docked and the passengers disembarked, he'd seen only the limited view from portside each time. Parts of the world he'd never expected to see, nor weeks before ever believed he would. But just a glimpse.

And now, it appeared, he was stuck in one of them without a clue as to where he really was or who he was supposed to meet.

His visions had started on that night, and he wondered if they were connected at all to the incidents on the ship when he'd been attacked.

Three days later, Barker was reminded of his thoughts on the deck, the night of the first attempt on his life, as he crossed the hotel lobby and noticed the foliage. Very exotic, potted palms of that size, and clearly healthy. Someone's pride. Not unlike one of his three mysterious packages, up in his room. The concierge watched him, as he did whenever Barker left his room, as he had briefly for the past three afternoons. The inspection had a hint of curiosity, with a hint of knowing that Barker, really, had no idea where he was or what he was doing there.

Barker made his way to the bar and drank what he had become used to calling beer. The beverage and the afternoon trips to the bar were concessions to boredom, the boredom an extension of the long ocean voyage, which had descended soon after the beginning of his self-imposed exile to the hotel room. It was principally because the beer was cold that made the beverage so unlike the lagers and ales he'd grown accustomed to at home. But it was definitely flavoursome, beneath the chill, and he suspected the hotel, being what it was, served the very best.

A vision came to him as he sat on a bar stool. It dizzied him and he steadied himself as he sat, leaning heavily against the grey and tan swirl of the marble counter.

'Easy there, friend,' came a soft voice, American. A strange man sat one vacant stool away, sporting a wide smile. He was slender, his thin and lightly balding grey hair slicked back, with kind eyes over a beaky nose. His mouth seemed too wide for his thin jaw and pointy chin. Barker suspected he would have been twenty years the man's junior.

'You're sure a drink is what you need?'

There was an impish quality to the man as he smiled.

Barker shook his head and smiled politely. 'I'm not drunk, thank you. Just a light turn, must be the climate ...'

'British, huh? I've heard of something called the Melbourne flu, maybe you've got that? Never had any trouble with it myself.'

True, the elfin man was not simply thin but lean and graceful. There was elegance in the way he sipped his glass of lager, in his poise on the stool.

'I don't think I'm ill, actually.'

Barker wondered: was this his contact? Was this how it would work?

'To be quite frank, I've been having visions,' Barker confessed.

The elfin man shifted his gaze directly to him. He was dressed smartly; navy slacks, a white blazer and white shirt, with a stylish navy cravat about his wiry neck. Very good shape, Barker assessed, for a man in advance of fifty years.

'Visions?' he raised a thin eyebrow. He was not handsome, in fact he looked a bit like an old woman. His forehead was huge. But there was something in his eyes, and simply in his general demeanour, that made Barker like him almost instantly. 'Is this an everyday thing for you?'

'No, just the past three days. Since I arrived.'

'And ...' there was a slight tone of scepticism, but it was playful. 'How often do these visions ...' the elfin man flicked his hand gaily as he searched for the word – 'manifest?'

•

'One or two a day,' Barker shrugged, a little embarrassed.

The elfin man was now well and truly intrigued. 'What do you see?'

Barker spoke unselfconsciously, simply relaying his feeling of the vision without mental edit. 'This time I saw . . . a rush of energy, of youth. In the future, perhaps a decade away. Colour and . . . dreams. Smoke and music.'

The elfin man leaned back, assessing Barker, doubtfully, yet with sympathy in his eyes.

'Perhaps a drink is exactly what you need, friend.'

He waved at the bartender and a glass of beer was poured and appeared quickly on the bar before Barker. He sipped. Frothy, bitter . . . cold. But he was getting used to it.

'I've never experienced anything like it. It's like . . . flourishes of energy conveyed over time. Quite extraordinary.'

'I dare say, I dare say,' the elfin man uttered.

'My name's Barker.'

'Is it, now?'

'Barker Moon.'

'And that's not a stage name?'

'No, it's real.'

'Your real name. Well, I have a stage name, but my real name is Frederick. Frederick Austerlitz.'

Frederick's hand was thin and wiry also, but the grip was firm, more solid than Barker's given that he had held back for fear of too tight a squeeze.

'I'm sorry to unload all of this on you, but it's come to be rather overwhelming. I'm babbling a bit with the disorientation, I think.'

'Well that's alright. I think we all do that from time to time. You really don't know who I am, do you?'

'I'm sorry. Are you famous? Are you on the stage? Or in the movies? I don't go to the movies. My nephew is a projectionist. He tells me the stories, but I prefer to read. Perhaps I'd know your stage name?'

'Perhaps,' Frederick smiled. 'Well, I never. Perhaps if you imagined me in a top hat?'

'I'm sorry. I don't mean to embarrass you, but I really don't . . .'

'Well. How refreshing. So, Barker, what brings you to the end of the world?'

'The end of the world?'

Frederick smiled and handed Barker a newspaper from the end of the bar. Barker's mind was still coming into focus, but the headline and accompanying article was to do with a Hollywood actress who was in town, making a movie about the end of the world. She had claimed, the headline stated, that Melbourne was an 'ideal place to film the end of the world'.

So that was where he was. The End of the World.

'She didn't mean it of course,' Frederick smiled. 'I believe there is some doubt as to whether or not she actually said it. But I don't suppose that matters. It is a terribly good quote, even if it is quite unjustified.'

Very well spoken for an American.

'The beer here is very good for a start.'

'I'm taking a while to get used to it.'

'Good-looking fellow like you, I think you're going to get along fine. The key to getting along in a city is letting the city get to know you. If you sit around here for a while, you never know who you might meet, or where it might lead you.'

'Actually, I was hoping you might have some idea as to what I'm doing here.'

'Me?' Frederick smiled. 'I'm just here to get away from things for a while.'

'Oh.'

'You're expecting to meet someone, is that it? Pen friend perhaps? A lady pen friend?'

'No,' Barker smiled simply. 'Nothing like that.'

Frederick nodded and contemplated his beer.

'Yes, a good beer they do here. My father came from a long line of brewers. So I should know.'

Frederick finished his beer and stepped as gracefully from his bar stool as anyone could.

'Well, I must be going. You take care of yourself and watch out for those visions. You never know where they might lead you either.'

Frederick smiled, charming as he looked Barker up and down.

'Why are you here, Frederick?' Barker asked.

'Oh,' Frederick beamed, 'I make visions. At least, I help.' He turned and walked cheerfully from the bar. 'When I can.'

And Frederick was gone.

Barker assessed the paper again and read the article. It was the third of June already. It had been the end of March when he'd set off. He'd heard of Ava Gardner, he thought. But as the closest he came to movies were his nephew's relayed silver screen experiences, he really had no idea of context. She was a movie star, however, and it was to be expected that their names would achieve some sort of accreditation in the mind.

'One of a kind, that one,' the bartender said to Barker.

He didn't know if the bartender meant Ava Gardner or Frederick, but the elfin chap had been gone a while and Barker suspected he meant the actress.

Barker returned to his room and assessed his packages again.

To call them packages was not exactly accurate. There was one true package, a spell book he assumed from the feel of it. A short examination, early along the voyage, had revealed within the leather satchel an item that had been wrapped within purple velvet cloth. He had not opened the satchel past that initial cursory inspection and it resided within his travel trunk under his shirts and trousers. He had received the distinct sensation that the parcels were not to be tampered with. The sorcerer who had summoned him and sent him off on his mission for the Supernatural Council had not specified as such. It just went without saying. Take them with you, keep them safe, do not touch.

Any sorcerer would feel it.

Alongside his brand new travel trunk, an older one. Much older, he perceived. Not just from the look, but from occult vibrations it gave off. And much heavier than his own. It weighed a ton.

Finally, the most unusual. A plant. A wine barrel, sawn in half, about twenty inches across, within it soil and shrub. He did not know what sort of shrub it was, but it was about three feet high and its thick diamond leaves, dark emerald green, extended probably three inches over the side of the wine barrel pot. His only additional instruction had been to water it once a week. Just one fluid ounce.

Each of his trunks was at the foot of the double bed, an extravagance that the Council had seen fit to provide, for which he was grateful. The potted shrub sat in the corner by the window with the view of the city.

London it was not, but the end of the world . . .? The weather was gloomy, but that was all he'd heard about Melbourne before departing. It rained all the time. No, come to think of it he'd heard something else. That Greeks liked to emigrate here.

Funny, Barker smiled to himself, the things one picks up without knowing.

The visions came increasingly to him in the days that followed. And Barker would follow each with a short trip to the bar and a cold beer. After a week, he grew accustomed to both.

He supposed that the Council would send someone to get him in due course, and that the dreams and visions were a side effect of the power emanating from the book.

In the visions he saw men returning from the Great War, and things he supposed were in the future. He discovered that he was in a state of Australia called Victoria, and supposed that after all his reading back in London he already knew this. He saw the Olympic Games in Melbourne, which had occurred only a few years before in 1956, and saw another similar event in the future. Such wonders he beheld, and colour and technology. He saw the first settlers in 1835, one hundred years before his own birth, led by a man called Batman, and was briefly, though vividly, exposed to some of their struggles in settling a village on the river which at some point was named Yarra.

After another week he ventured out more often, risked leaving the hotel and inner city entirely, relying on a strong protective spell he'd cast over his room to prevent theft in his absence.

He wandered suburbs with names like Carlton and Collingwood, and would occasionally stop for a cold beer. The suburbs weren't so different, but everything seemed newer, fresher. There was something about the fact that nothing had been here for much more than a century, if that, which made him feel cheerful. It made him miss London, but made that city seem simultaneously over-laden with history. The people were here for a new start, for the beginning of something. At least, they were on a historical scale.

In one suburban pub he saw a working man bring a glass of beer out to his wife, who was knitting in the front passenger seat of a huge white car called an FJ Holden. They did not allow women in the front bars, and some larger hotels had a separate lounge for ladies.

After a while the winter gloom brought about mild bouts of depression, only a few hours each, as indeed the dark weather had at home. He supposed it was something to do with loneliness. During these times, in which he would return to his room and read, it seemed the more time he spent in his room, the more frequently the visions would descend.

The concierge looked at him less and less, but, when he did, with a higher degree of suspicion.

He thought the shrub in the wine barrel was growing, but could not be sure. He thought occasionally of opening the ancient trunk, but always thought better of it. He never considered opening the leather satchel.

As another week passed, it always seemed to be raining. Drizzle, if not heavy showers.

Barker's bouts of depression lengthened and then started to get the better of him. He started to wonder if anyone would ever come for him. The visions became ever more distinct and yet more banal. They flooded his mind sometimes two or three per hour, sometimes lasting up to a minute each.

He made the acquaintance of several regulars at the bar, including the two regular barmen and a barmaid who worked at night, but never spoke meaningfully with them, and never again openly discussed his mission or his visions the way he had with Frederick. When a vision came while he was at the bar, he would drop his head into his arms and remain that way until the sounds and images passed. One of the young ladies he'd met, who was staying there with her mother while they were on tour, had assumed he was drinking away some great romantic sorrow. She took quite a shine to Barker, he saw, until one of the barmen had whispered something to her about visions. Then she kept her distance.

After that he ceased frequenting the bar, lest they start to believe he was more odd than they already did.

The worst of the visions came with the fourth week.

Everyone knew, had seen the pictures. But the visions presented themselves as though one were really there. It was horrifying. The mushroom cloud and blast of heat. And the noise. The flash, then the explosion. Horrendous.

Anyone would have been terrified at the sight. But to a sorcerer, with a sorcerer's perception of nature, the horror was ten, perhaps one hundred fold. A sorcerer manipulated nature. Or, rather, found a way to bend the course of nature to his will. But manipulation of nature to this level . . . it was like rape.

'Why am I seeing the mushroom clouds, over and over?' he asked the book, as his fifth week in Melbourne began. His food was being delivered now. A knock on the door, a tray wheeled in, the busboy gone.

The food was very good, but he found no pleasure in it.

He stopped drinking the beer one night upon realising he'd become accidentally pole-axed, after cracking his head against the view of the gloomy city at the end of the world.

He barely recalled the ocean liner and the ocean.

The constant vision of mushroom clouds made him dwell upon

the downbeat. The time three years ago when he thought he would lose the bookshop. When Fiona had not accepted his proposal. When the demon on Carnaby Street looked at him as though it had won, and for a second he'd believed the look. When he thought he was going to die at knifepoint on the liner and . . .

That other time.

The second attack.

A woman, the second time. A middle-aged woman with jet hair and thin lips. A mother and daughter had passed him by, once round the deck before bed, Americans, and they had been cold. They had been wearing long winter coats, huddled together and strolling against the wind, double clip-clop on the wood, and the coats were flapping back in the breeze and the woman had come out of the coat, or from behind the mother and daughter, or something, some camouflage spell with which he'd been unfamiliar and she had a dagger at his heart and she had said to him: 'Give me your key before you die' as she came at him black and evil with a cruel and chilling wind.

The protective spell he had cast over his cabin which, theoretically, no sorcerer but himself could penetrate, would have a better chance at being dispelled if they had his key. He used the key every time he went back to his cabin, or departed the cabin, and thus it possessed an iconographic power another would need to attempt to break the spell. After all, he bent the spell, with his will, every time he used the key. It was an enemy's best chance, and if the key were given willingly, all the better.

He had been so stunned at the attack, which had come a month after the first one, that he had simply not been able to counter it. He had simply fallen backward in shock. But in a flash of sight as he fell, he saw something descend upon the black woman before she reached him. It was like a boulder, dropped from an upper deck. By the time he had scrambled to his feet, she had been crushed. There was blood everywhere. Her body had been reduced to a pulpy mass within the black garments. In fact, the garments in which the goo resided was his only sure indication that the mess had indeed once been his assailant. He had not known what to do, except return to his cabin.

It had been late.

No one had seen.

And nothing was mentioned.

A day later, when he braved resurfacing, this time in daylight, he walked the deck with the other passengers, squinting in the sunlight. He gathered the courage to return to the fore of the ship, where the attack had occurred. There were signs of blood in the cracks between the heavy wooden boards of the deck, but the awfulness had been cleaned up. He supposed someone had found it, and that a roster had been checked. That a stowaway had been assumed to have been crushed to a pulp late at night for no apparent reason. It was a mystery, the less said about it the better, until they docked in Melbourne. He supposed correctly, because in his panic he had read the minds of the crew and found the general consensus toward the incident.

He had not read the minds of anyone on board since he'd first assessed the passengers to see if anyone knew him, or about him, a mild and general telepathic scan. He'd done the same when he'd first arrived at the hotel, two months later. Scans of this nature were forbidden by the Supernatural Council, unless they expressly involved the safety of innocents through occult circumstances. His panic scan, that morning on the liner, had revealed to him his naivety; his two would-be assassins had not registered with him at all when he had made his initial assessment. Therefore, there might be others aboard.

So after that, he'd remained in his cabin for the most part of the final month of the voyage. He cast a general weave about the liner whenever he was out to make people forget he was there, to make himself insignificant.

And now here he was again, hiding in his room. Only now he was not hiding from an external assailant. This time his attacker was, via his mushroom cloud visions, in the room with him.

The book.

Time flew around and through him. The history of the city at the end of the world.

Tall ships and convicts and settlers and soldiers. Churches and hotels, God and ale ...

Football.

The creation of the great tramways system.

Buildings and libraries and town halls and hospitals and cemeteries and schools and stock exchanges and houses and houses and houses of parliament and proclamations and elections ... it seemed organic, the way the city grew and lived and breathed and produced and destroyed and harvested and expanded and expanded and ...

All day, every night, punctuated by mushroom clouds.

He saw a mighty gambling house ...

With the mushroom clouds he heard names of places farther away on the continent, like Maralinga and Emu Field and Christmas Island ...

Maralinga took him back, further than he thought possible, to the native people, thousands and thousands of years ... ceremony and seasons and hunting and laughter and weird tribal music and dancing and scarring –

He had to get out.

He had to get out of bed.

He had to get away from the book.

He looked at the sheets of the double bed. How long had he been lying there, sailing through history? The maid had changed them not half a day ago, but they were soaked. The look on her face ... some brand of mild fear. The blankets were now strewn across the end of the bed and the nearby floor, the sheets wet with perspiration. He was cold, and feverish. The gloom remained outside, clouds over the city. Drizzle.

Showers.

He needed a shower. He had never had a shower until he came to the end of the world. Only baths. But showers were more instant. Everything would be more instant soon. He had seen it. The athletes were faster at the games in the future, the cars were sleeker, the buildings . . . dear God the buildings . . . so high. Televisions . . . he hadn't had much to do with them. They were omnipresent. He couldn't comprehend. He didn't go to the movies, but there were movies and television everywhere, in the home and sliding images, shifting illusions, and changing pictures and all shapes and sizes and sounds, sounds . . . typewriters that were thin and sleek and portable telephones the size of a cigarette packet.

He recalled as he removed his damp pyjamas that there had been no sound, no sound as it was today, no ambient noise, before the Industrial Age. Just quiet. But the noise had grown. Louder. To the incomprehensible level of the sub atomic.

The water hit him, hot. It burned.

He saw skin burning.

He shut off the shower with, as quickly as he wished he could, the vision.

But that had been good, Barker thought. Reviving.

He could order a plate of chips at the hotel bar. Eat them and have a drink. He had not had a cold beer for weeks, it seemed.

Barker dressed, taking his clothes from the trunk. In a short moment of panic he forgot that he had transferred the leather satchel into the wardrobe in the corner of the room several days ago, a fruitless attempt at distancing himself.

He wondered what day it was. What month.

As it turned out, it was American Independence Day.

He had been in Melbourne, in the hotel, for a month.

Barker knew this because there was always copy of the paper on the bar.

He ordered the plate of chips and accepted the beer and gulped twice. The bartender assessed him sympathetically.

'Been a while,' he stated, open-endedly.

'Yes,' Barker said. 'How do I . . . do I look well?'

'You look tired, mate. You a writer or something? Spending all ya time alone up there?'

'How do you . . .?'

'We take a stab at guessing every now and then. Y'know, mate. Passes the time. Elsie says there's no typewriter up there, but we reckon ya keep it in ya trunk, put it away before any of the staff come in for a gander. Watcha reckon?'

Barker sighed. This was normal. Normal life. People in the here and now gossiping and passing the time.

'Yes,' Barker sipped, 'that's right. That's what I'm doing. Did you have a wager?'

'Five bob, mate.'

'Pleased to be of service, then.'

'Chip's 'r on me, mate. No worries.'

'I need to eat. I feel weak. It's possible I have let my imagination run away with me.'

'The visions? The ones you said? When Fred was here?'

'You know Fred?'

'Jeez, mate. Everyone knows Fred.'

The bartender chuckled as he moved away, then a strange expression crossed him. He was staring across the bar. 'Christ, who's that?'

Barker turned, and tried to follow the bartender's line of sight through to the lobby.

'He's waving at ya, mate.'

Barker tried, but saw nothing. 'Where?'

'By the palms . . .' the bartender muttered. 'Weirdest bloke I've ever seen . . .'

Barker saw him. A tall man, almost a shadow. He was wearing a brown shirt and trousers, and a cloak that looked as though, from this distance, like . . . *bark*.

Barker was away, moving toward the man, but then he was gone. Like a flash, up the stairs to the lobby landing.

And then Barker knew. There was someone in his room. The bark man had tried to warn him.

Barker ran. The elevator would be too slow . . . his room was on the third floor, and he took the stairs two, three at a time. Dizzy, not much energy.

The door to his room was open, the spell broken.

The potted shrub was wilting, something toxic poured over it. The ancient chest had an addition, an even more ancient lock clamped over its latch, and a terrible thumping was resounding from within.

The concierge was opening the wardrobe, reaching for the leather satchel.

The concierge.

Barker floored him with an arm around his neck, too weak for sorcery. The satchel hit the floor. But the concierge back-flipped and was on his feet, leaving Barker on the floor with it. Barker was puffing; the race up the stairs had exhausted him. He grabbed the satchel, but the concierge had his hands on the bag as well, yanking it. Barker held on strong, all his remaining energy in his grip.

The bark man was at the door. He seemed withered, his face long and brown, sunburned and leathery. His expression projected helplessness. But he spoke. The same strange language that Barker had somehow understood on the liner. But now it was alien. Barker had no idea what the bark man was trying to tell him.

'Listen to me,' the concierge uttered as they both held onto the satchel. 'Listen to me, fool sorcerer. Do you know what this is?'

'You can't have it.'

The concierge stared at him and it was like the demon on Carnaby Street again. The concierge knew he'd won. He could overpower Barker. But instead, he decided to talk. He was trying to convince Barker to give the book freely.

'The world is growing smaller, Barker. Yet at the same time, it is coming apart. The older races have seen this since the Industrial Age; they've been departing in small numbers for centuries.'

'The older races?' Barker grew angry. 'What are you talking about?'

'Elves and dwarves, Barker. At least, that's what we call them now.'

Barker yanked at the satchel, but the concierge grabbed back. Barker knew he couldn't keep hold much longer, much less gain full possession of it. So he decided to listen, to humour the madman in the hope of finding a solution in the meantime.

'They're planning an exodus, Barker. A mass exodus! We have foreseen it, my order. We have seen a time when the Industrial Age will give way to the Age of Information, and that means the older races will be susceptible to discovery. To mass discovery, quickly! We don't know how, as yet, this Age of Information shall proceed ...'

The phrase echoed through Barker's weary mind as he heard himself whisper.

'Portable telephones, the size of cigarette packets ...'

'Is that right?' the concierge raised an eyebrow as his eyes widened. His grip on the satchel slacked a little. 'The book has shown you that?'

'You can't have it!'

'It is! It really is the book!'

'You can't have it you bloody blighter!' Barker wrenched it away.

The concierge simply leaned back, glancing over his shoulder at the bark man, the impotent observer, as though the revelation of the truth of the package had stunned him so greatly he really didn't know what to do.

'What is the book?' Barker asked, grasping it to his chest as he backed away on his knees. 'What does it contain that you would kill me for it?'

'You don't know? They sent you to guard it and you don't know what it is?'

'It's powerful, too powerful for the likes of you ...'

'The likes of me? Do you know who I am, Barker? Barker Moon, do you know how long I suffered in this hell hole hotel, as an elevator porter? Me? Waiting for the moment when you'd become weak enough for me to gain access. A decent spell, young sorcerer, but with the madness that book was putting you through, it could not hold forever ... I could feel it from the lobby, the book. Your visions ...'

'Who are you?'

'I am one of perhaps a dozen people in this little world who know what that book is, Barker. The dozen of whom, apparently, does not include your good self.'

'Tell me then,' Barker spat. 'Tell me what it is that I'll die for.'

'In time, Barker. But you must listen.'

Yes, Barker knew now. The concierge wanted a convert. He wanted Barker as a black practitioner ... and this explanation was supposed to cross him over to the dark side.

'It has been suggested, Barker, that the rise of information may have to do with the rise of magic ... but it will not. It will be via material means, rather than ethereal. It will be resolutely physical in nature. But that is not the most important of matters. The fact of the matter, of matter itself, in fact, is that atomic testing is the most rampantly chaotic of mankind's many follies. Far more so than they imagine!'

'Well we're in agreement upon that!' Barker managed a weak, humourless laugh.

'The ancient races are real, Barker, and they cannot tolerate such desecration of the powers of nature. They call it exploitation ... but in splitting the atom, mankind has touched the very core of nature! And nature will begin to unravel. It has already begun! But they see worse, yes, worse to come. A great warming of the earth which shall render life here intolerable, impossible for them.'

Barker nodded, primarily to himself. 'I've seen these things ... the mushroom clouds ... oh God, the book was *showing* them to me, *telling* me. The book is something to do with time, isn't it?'

'The book,' said the bark man, his voice a little shaky, '*is* time, Barker.'

Barker and the concierge looked to the bark man as one, amazed that he had spoken, astonished that he had spoken English.

'I beg your pardon?' asked the concierge in a high, fearful pitch.

'At the beginning of the world,' the bark man spoke in an eerie hush, 'there were those who were the first to reach consciousness. Their first imaginings were recited, repeatedly, to create the reality we share. Under this process, our reality was made separate from others.'

'You mean, our dimension . . .' Barker was struggling. So tired. 'It was created with a spell?'

The concierge cackled. 'Of course that's what it means, you idiot!'

'This was the first spell,' bark man continued. 'The spell of dimension. But dimension was static. Existence was static. Experience came from this knowledge, blossomed from it, and thus momentum was derived. This was the second spell, the act of momentum . . . of time itself, moving forward.'

'The Spell of Time?' It seemed incomprehensible to Barker. 'The spell that *created* time?'

'The Spell of Time is written in the book.' The bark man pointed at Barker. 'The book you brought with you.'

'Then . . . time is coming apart,' Barker told the bark man. 'I've seen it.'

'We know, Barker. Mankind's atomic testing is destroying the fabric of reality. Slowly at first, but surely. That is why this man must not possess the book . . .'

'Nonsense!' the concierge spun around at Barker. 'We must have it! My kind! The world is falling apart and who better to oversee that chaos? You would stop it, recast the first spells, but why? Out of the chaos will come a new mankind! A dark and terrible mankind not bound by dimension or time or – '

'You're completely addled,' Barker groaned. 'Utterly insane . . .'

'My kind! We are made for this time, Barker! Made for this time!'

'Open the book, Barker,' said the bark man. 'Show him his time.'

And Barker knew what to do. As the concierge came at him again, Barker hit him in the face. He fell backward, but was furious. Energy surrounded him, occult energy. His patience was lost. He was preparing a spell that would destroy Barker. Barker's hands moved clumsily, unbuckling the satchel. Purple velvet within, the feel of the spine of the book and a rush of energy.

Barker opened the book and spread the pages at the concierge.

The concierge withered in bright white light and was gone. Within the passage of the three, maybe four seconds in which

•

Barker had opened and closed the pages, the concierge had aged, died and come to dust.

As Barker came to sleep.

'The messenger awakens,' said a voice. Barker recognised the bark man's eerie English. He was in his hotel room, in bed. Freshly laundered sheets and pyjamas, he noted. 'He has required only thirteen hours to regenerate,' the bark man uttered. 'Remarkable after such exposure.'

He could not see the bark man, but in a chair at the foot of the bed near the trunks was an old sorcerer with a white beard, dressed in a modern grey suit.

'It is why he was chosen,' the sorcerer smiled at Barker. 'He comes from a long line of defenders, but was not of the temperament to become one. For this mission, however, we needed someone who did not know their own ability. Their own reserves of the art. My name is Markson. I'm your contact, Barker.'

Barker was puzzled. 'Where's Frederick?'

'Frederick?'

'Frederick . . . I waited for him, every day to . . . oh, never mind.'

'You've done extremely well, Barker. We expected you to last a week or two, but thirty-three days . . . you've shown reservoirs of will no one could have expected.'

Barker shifted his bedding aside and sat on the edge of the bed. He felt remarkably refreshed. 'I don't understand.'

'What the concierge told you was true. What our friend here told you was true. But we needed someone to bring the book here, to Australia. Someone the black practitioners would not at first suspect.'

'And, of course,' Barker rubbed some sleep out of his eyes, 'who would suspect me?'

'We knew they would eventually work it out, and that when they did, we needed someone they would underestimate. We needed you, Barker, to draw them out.'

'I was bait?' Barker didn't like the thought.

'I'm afraid so. It does sound cruel, doesn't it. Perhaps it was. Yes, to a degree I believe so. However, the Supernatural Council are largely unfamiliar with this part of the world ... we know little of the identities or structures of the sorcerers who reside here. Previous agents, sent out to determine such matters, all vanished. But a few sorcerers have passed through, and we thought a tourist, or someone who seemed at first like one, might be good cover.'

'I might have been killed,' Barker growled. 'I almost was.'

Markson shifted uncomfortably in his seat. 'Barker, let me explain. Nations are forged in darkness. In war, in the elimination of cultures. This is a young nation, and the darkness remains very strong. It is a time for the black practitioners, and they have established a presence here. But there is also great potential. Thanks to you, we now have a place from which to move forward. The identity of the concierge as a leading black practitioner means that we can follow his path back ... and make this country safe for the tasks ahead. You have cleared the way, Barker.'

'Cleared the way ...' Barker leaned forward, head in hands, trying to remember what the concierge and the bark man had told him. 'For the exodus of ancient races? Is that correct? Did I dream that?'

'No, you did not. They will depart ... at a crucial juncture. Barker, what you've learned here in the past few days is known by only a few select sorcerers. One less, it seems, as of yesterday afternoon. It must remain that way.'

In this, at least, Barker could remain solid. 'I understand. You can trust me.'

'We know,' said the bark man.

But from where did his voice come? Barker looked around the room, as Markson's gaze shifted deliberately to a new shrub by the window, a larger one. Its leaves ruffled, as though a soft breeze had moved through it. But the window was closed. No ... the shrub hadn't moved, something in front of it had. There was something there, camouflaged against the shrub. The shape shifted and stood. It was the bark man.

'You're ...' Barker couldn't believe he was going to say it. 'You're an elf?'

'Yes,' the elf spoke in English. 'We are able to reside in and around ... you say flora, foliage, plant life ... however it may be. The voyage across the ocean was distasteful for want of movement, but I slept, meditated. As did my companion.'

'You saved my life; that first assassin on the liner.'

'The assassins boarded the liner secretly,' Markson offered. 'After the ship had departed London. We don't know how.'

'It took much from me,' the elf explained. 'To leave cover. But you were our guardian, and we were pleased to be of service.'

But Barker's mind was centred on a previous comment. Something *else* had saved him from the second assailant.

'Your companion?' he asked.

Then he realised. There was a dwarf asleep in the ancient trunk.

'May I speak with him? Thank him?'

'He is very old. It took more from him, than it did from me, to come to your aid. The concierge disturbed him, and now he slumbers. It is best to allow him rest. The ocean is not a place for either of our kind. The people of the seas, of our time ... it is their domain. But they communicate very seldom these days ... we do not know if they will participate in the great leaving.'

Barker shook his head. He was starting to feel groggy again. He felt like a beer, a cold one. 'The time of great leaving ...' he repeated.

'Mankind has begun to make the world unbound, and the spells of creation must be recast,' the elf spoke gravely. 'Although our people have been present on this continent for a hundred years or more, we two are of noble birth, the first official representatives of our kind here. We have come to speak with those of a race long separated from the elves and dwarves, many thousands of years old. We shall form a council for the great leaving.'

Barker pondered some more. 'Why here? In this country?'

'It is the most virgin of lands that still follows the old ways and possesses the necessary landscapes for the ceremonies required.

But even here, we cannot tolerate long. When the first spell, the spell of dimension, is recast, there will be a gap, a great gap, when we shall gather. The last of the ancient races will depart for a dimension more green, more fertile, where we might thrive once more. What mankind does here after that is not of our concern.'

Barker wondered what this meant. How long had it been foreseen, planned?

'So,' he thought hard, 'in starting the unravelling of reality, in playing with the atom . . . and making life unbearable for you here in this dimension, mankind has also, unknowingly, provided you with a means of escape, to a new start?'

'It is so. Perhaps it is the way of things.'

Barker smiled, grim, and finally faced the truth. 'So, I was a decoy.'

'You were manipulated, Barker,' Markson apologised. 'And for this we offer you any reward you care to name.'

Barker shook his head. 'The concierge. I should have known.'

'We did not,' the elf smiled.

Barker pondered. 'When will all this happen?'

Markson shrugged. 'Fifty years, maybe more. But preparations must be made. And this book, and the other two, must be hidden in the meantime.'

'The other two . . . what is the third spell?'

'I cannot say. It is dangerous for one as young as you to know as much as you do already. Suffice to say that another means entirely must be found to bring it here . . . and not for many years yet.'

'Search for the knowledge, Barker,' the elf responded instead. 'You'll find that the third spell will become apparent.'

Barker nodded. He was sure it would.

'There are very few sorcerers here, Barker, compared with our own continent.' Markson stood. He was tall, muscular. 'But the majority are evil. We shall change that, in time, and do what is right by those who have lived here in the ages long past.'

Do what is right, Barker thought.

Few sorcerers here . . . the majority evil.

Meant for another war . . .

Barker nodded. 'You said, *anything*?'

Barker sat at the bar and drank the cold beer he had come to enjoy.

'We meet again,' said someone with an impish voice.

'Frederick?'

Barker turned and there he was. Lean, elegant, but not an elf. A man.

'So have you had an adventure yet, Barker? Or have you just been sitting right here on the same bar stool for six weeks, waiting for me to come back?'

Barker smiled. 'A bit of both, really.'

'Well that's good. It's good that you had an adventure, and it's good that I came back.'

'Where have you been?' Barker asked.

'I have simply been a tourist,' Frederick responded as he waved at the bartender for a beer. 'How about you? How are those visions coming along?'

'They're finished. I found out what was causing them.'

'And what was that? Nothing in the water, I hope. Melbourne water takes getting used to.'

'No,' Barker smiled. 'It was something else. My part in it is done, but . . .'

'Your part in it? Well, so is mine. I have played my part and now I'm going home. How about you? Back to England?'

'No. No, I can't leave this place now. I feel as though I'm part of it. Part of its history.'

'Well. What did I tell you? Let a city know you and . . . Barker, what business are you in?'

'I was a bookseller. But my associates here are helping me with something else. I've purchased a movie house. I think images are going to be very important. Movies and those television boxes, and even more, perhaps, one day. I'm bringing my nephew out here.'

'The projectionist,' Frederick recalled.

'Yes!' Barker was delighted that Frederick remembered. 'It

seems like a good place for young people who are willing to make a go of it.'

'Television,' Frederick nodded. 'It's coming. Soon it will be everywhere.'

'Yes. I believe you are right. The concierge asked me if I wanted one in my room.' Barker smiled. 'But I didn't think I needed it.'

Frederick laughed. 'Too many visions of your own.'

'Exactly. But I learned from them. I learned a lot.'

'How so?'

'Well, I've purchased some shares in some companies. One that makes televisions, one that makes telephones, and another that makes cameras.'

'Bold moves, bold moves indeed. I like it.'

Frederick finished his beer and extended his hand.

'It's been good to meet you, Barker. Good luck with the business.'

'Thank you Frederick. Will you be coming back?'

'Well, who can say?'

'I mean, will I ever see you again?'

'You've bought yourself a cinema, you say?'

'Well, yes.'

'Then you'll see me again, Barker. You'll see me again.'

The Isolation of
the Deciding Factor

•

Carmel Bird

The Work of Hermione

'There are many poisonous aconites growing in the fields, but the monkshood variety is wholesome and medicinal, and the flowers are large, hooded, pale yellow, with a pleasant smell. The root is tuberous, sometimes consisting of one lump or knob, sometimes of more. A decoction of the root is a good lotion to wash the parts bitten by venomous creatures. The flower should be kept out of the way of children, for there is therein a farina which is dangerous if blown in the eyes.' So wrote Hermione Uhu in her doctoral thesis, paraphrasing the words of Nicholas Culpeper. Hermione went on to say that, as a result of her research, she was confident that when combined with the juice of the common strawberry the farina of the monkshood, applied to the eye, offered positive results in the isolation of the Genetic Unconscious Deciding Factor (GUDF). It all seemed too much like simple old witchcraft, and was a long time before anybody would listen to Hermione, but you will be pleased to learn that in the end her research was deemed valid, lives were changed, and a certain kind of wisdom prevailed.

Hermione Uhu has certainly made a name for herself. She now leads the team of medical professionals who report to the IOSV, the International Office for Species Variation, whose area includes the Office for Environmental Wonders (OEW). Hermione, at the age of forty, is the top surgeon and researcher in the field of Variation, but – apart from the fact that she is pale and thin and wears her black hair in a pageboy, uses no make-up, lives with her father who is a professor of something like philosophy, drinks vodka mixed with Sirop de Violette, and is, like so many members of her profession, mildly addicted to morphine – I can't tell you very much about her that is personal. She has beautiful slender hands and feet; everybody comments on those.

Hermione's life intersected suddenly with the lives of the Tillyards quite early in the twenty-first century.

The Birth of Norma

Imagine the shock suffered by Belinda Tillyard when her fifth child, her first daughter, was born with the paws of a kitten. When the midwife said 'It's – a – girl' the spaces between the words gave those words an ominous weight. Belinda reached in joy for her daughter's hands, as mothers do, to marvel at their perfection, to count the fingers, to kiss the tiny, angelic fingernails. Alas. Belinda took to her lips two sweet little front paws with pale pink pads, covered in pure white down. The back paws were larger and stronger, but of course similar.

Belinda, observed with alarm by her faithful husband Gustav, who in fact somehow missed the sighting of the little paws, lapsed at once into an hysterical faint, clawing at the crisp green edges of the counterpane, and when she was brought round, the child had disappeared. Belinda believed she had been hallucinating, affected by the labour, the epidural, the gas, the stress of joy, seeing and feeling a mother's worst fears. The image of the little paws hung in her recent memory. Belinda, it should be explained, detested cats.

The Fate of Daphne

As a child of eight Belinda, with her friend Daphne, had crept through the witch's garden, a riotous tangled place filled with an alphabet of plants from adder's tongue to mandrake to wormwood, to peer in the foggy window. There was Mrs Macbeth with her wild white hair and her tartan cloak, bent over a pot hanging on a hook over the fire.

'That's the cauldron,' Daphne whispered.

'Ssh, she'll hear us.'

The witch had a reputation for catching children and boiling them up in her potions. The smell of cooking flesh was known to emanate from the cottage at all hours of the night and day. Mrs Macbeth sold her concoctions at a roadside stall – in brown glass bottles with corks in the top, and with lists of herbs and ailments on the labels. Knapwort harshweed will cleanse the lungs of tartarous humours, and is indicated for the relief of asthma. The bruised herb is famous for removing black and blue marks from the skin. Ploughman's spikenard promotes the flow of menstrual blood. No mention of rendered child, but it was obvious really. From time to time a child, particularly a girl, would disappear, never to be found, and the locals knew that the child, after being subdued with opium, had gone into Mrs Macbeth's pot. But nothing was ever proved. The bones were used to fertilise the garden which was the most luxuriant and burgeoning place for miles around. Every district had its witch, and people accepted the fact that some children were born to fill the bubbling cauldron, and that was all there was to it. If you wanted magic potions, you had to pay the price, after all. And they did. People wanted three kinds of medicine in particular – the love potion, the fertility drug, and the abortifact. Those were, of course, the old days before exact and reliable science.

So, to get back to Belinda and Daphne, they go creeping through the comfrey and nettles until they reach the window, and they hold their breath and gaze in at the woman stirring the pot, a woman guarded by a small wolf lying on the hearth-rug, and surrounded by a dozen cats of all shapes and sizes. All goes well, and the girls stare in fascination as the witch stirs her stew, and the cats doze, and the wolf looks with its yellow eyes into the blue flickering of the flames. Then Belinda leans against the branch of an over-hanging almond tree, and there is a little cracking sound. A small grey cat on the mat opens its eyes, and looks straight into the eyes of Daphne who springs back, slips on a rotting red fungus and slides to the ground, caught and tangled in a malicious serpentine vine. Belinda has already reached the road when the witch, in response to the commotion, appears in her doorway. She catches Daphne in her arms, and whisks her inside before you can say 'owl on the craggy rock'.

Daphne was never seen again, and Belinda was too shocked, afraid to tell anyone what had happened. In fact she didn't really know what had happened. One minute there was Daphne in her brown velvet dress with the lace collar, and the next minute there was nothing, and Belinda was running down the road with her eyes starting out of her head. Raving. Fear took her over, and she was never the same. She almost lost the will to live, but her mother, at her wits' end bought (at great expense) a brown bottle of something from Mrs Macbeth, and Belinda was restored to a kind of sanity. People guessed or knew the truth about Daphne, but it was all rumour and speculation. A scarecrow wearing Daphne's dress appeared in a field of prodigious opium poppies next to Mrs Macbeth's house. There's very little you can do in these cases, really, when all's said and done. And so Belinda had to carry the guilt (I snapped the twig) forever, and she focused this guilt on her fear and hatred of the cat that looked at Daphne, and of all cats in general. 'Pathological fear of feline species' they wrote on her reports.

The Marriage of Belinda

Because she was so strange and moody, people imagined that Belinda would never find a husband. However Belinda's mother was a determined woman and, having resorted to the remedies of Mrs Macbeth in one famous instance, was not slow to avail herself of another. And so it was that Belinda's mother baked her celebrated cinnamon cookies, mixing them with a decoction of lady's smock, knot weed and a powder strangely reminiscent of dried baby's blood, and offered them at Christmas time to all the young men of the district. Only one man was affected, but of course this was

fortunate, as more than one could have given rise to complica-
tions, and there was really no time for that. So Gustav Tillyard fell
in love with Belinda and they were married in the local Uniting
Church on the corner under the peppercorn tree to great rejoicing,
and for many years there was a feeling of happy-ever-after in the
Tillyard home.

Let's now return to the moment of the birth of Belinda's
fifth child.

The Concoctions of UNNXS

The child born to Belinda had in fact been placed in a special
section of the hospital nursery, the part called UNNXS, signifying
Unusual Neo-Nate-Cross-Species, where the mutations appearing at
the time of the turn of the century were kept for observation and
consideration. There had been babies with lizard tails, with dog
faces, pig snouts, rat brains – babies with the tearless eyes of croco-
diles, the fluttering umbrella wings of bats. Pussyfoot, as little baby
Tillyard was labelled, was the first known example of her kind.

Hermione and her team made the decisions regarding the future
of the babies in UNNXS. They were skilled and experienced in
the business of manufacturing one whole child from several parts,
and for assembling the leftovers into astonishing constructions in
the Concoction Area. The Concoctions were raised under secret
laboratory conditions until such time as they expired or became
redundant for one reason or another. Or until they became useful.
During the week of Pussyfoot's arrival, there was also in the nursery
a boy with the bill of a duck and strangely deformed lungs which
appeared to be composed of spongy fungal material resembling fly
agaric. His little hands and feet were perfect. So the decision was
made, after due process and consideration at the highest levels of the
Department of Law and Prophets, that Ugly Duckling would
provide the material for the extremities of Pussyfoot, and that her
paws, and his remaining parts, would be put aside, possibly for the
re-cycle, or perhaps for the re-dundant. A lifelike replica of a perfect
dead baby boy was provided for mourning and funeral purposes,

and the Ducklings were informed that their child's respiratory system had failed shortly after birth, a true statement, after all. After an agonising length of time during which Belinda and all the Tillyards were kept in the dark about their baby, they were able at last to rejoice in the news that although there had been some problems with ankles and wrists, requiring micro-surgery, their baby was a lovely healthy girl. Her little limbs were wrapped in bandages, and there were therapies to be followed for some months, but eventually, her hands and feet were free, and she was simply perfect. They called her, as you already know, Norma.

This name was chosen from a misleading book of babies' names where it is said that the meaning is 'priestess'. It does mean that, in a way, but the life of the poor druid priestess Norma of ancient times was a particularly violent and unhappy one – filled with bloody sacrifice, as well as murder and suicide. Not that anyone in Norma Tillyard's family was aware that another child had to die that Norma might live. Poor little Ugly Duckling died that Norma Tillyard might live. The interesting thing is that in naming her, as her mother thought 'Normal', they built into her life terrible notions of treachery, of murder, and of suicide.

The Ravaging of the Planet

Belinda never quite suppressed the hallucination she had experienced at the time of Norma's birth. She kept it as a special kind of secret deep within her heart, for the moment had been so vivid, the little paws so very real. Truth to tell, Belinda relegated this image to a place where that other awful memory, the disappearance of Daphne, had its dwelling. And Belinda developed a passionate interest in news stories concerning birth defects and deformities, scanning the television screen, the web, and such popular magazines as came her way for references to children born with the paws of kittens. The magazines were in fact very few and far between because of a temporary ban on the use of trees for the manufacture of paper. In any case, as far as Belinda could tell, no story of a feline mutant ever made itself public. Belinda grew accustomed to the idea

that her vision had been nothing but an illusion, a gross and misleading image from the depths of her unconscious mind, a mind
overheated by stress and drugs and whatnot.

However, in the various media there was no shortage of other
strange and quite amazing events to report.

It was a time of swift, dramatic and bewildering change. The sea
would rise up and sweep away coastlines; fires raged across forests
and cities alike; wild winds uprooted skyscrapers; there were famines
and plagues; water supplies were polluted by nuclear waste, by
surgical waste, by mysterious viruses. Kind priests locked their
congregations inside the churches and administered lethal doses of
old-fashioned poisons in the communion wine and somebody had
to come along and decide what to do with the dead bodies all over
the glittering pictorial mosaic floor. Stars came spinning out of the
sky, searing the tops of mountains as they rushed by. This was so
spectacular. Scientists gazed in fear at old pictures of the Tunguska
butterfly – was that the result of a visit by random meteor or evil
enemy? It goes without saying that the planet was eroded by wars of
all kinds, and that hopeless people roamed about stripped of all, of
hearth, home – on the seas, in the deserts, in the mountains, and
through the jagged silent stench of ruined cities. A child was born
in Peru with the head of Socrates.

The Safety of the Tunnels

The Tillyards lived underground in The Tunnels, spending a certain
amount of time by day in The Basin which was a secure park open
to the sky, at the hub of The Tunnels. Air and sunshine and fresh
raindrops could thus nourish and give pleasure to the people. At
night The Basin remained open to the heavens, to the moon and
the stars, and because it was patrolled by guards equipped with the
latest weapons and security devices, it was classified as a 'Lifesafe
Area A'. In the event of an environmental, political, or other dis-
turbance, The Basin would automatically close over, shutting out
the moonlight and the stars, until the threat had passed.

Norma Tillyard was a delightful child who, far from suffering from a weakness in wrists and ankles, was very athletic, and fond of physical activity. At the age of six she took up ballet in a serious way and rose to be, at the youthful age of sixteen, the prima ballerina in The Enlightenment which was the ballet company in The Tunnels. Norma's hands and feet were abnormally large and powerful for a girl of her build, but this fact enhanced rather than impeded her career.

The Great-Grandmother's Words

Meanwhile, far, far behind the scenes of Norma's life, back at IOSV, the research – into the reasons and uses for, and the implications of, such birth variations as hers – was continuing. The human species was, as they said at IOSV, 'throwing up'. That is, the species was offering so many unusual variations at a greater and greater rate that researchers such as Hermione Uhu were coming round to the notion that these things really must have a meaning. Could they hold a key to some sort of knowledge? Now it was Hermione who incubated the idea that perhaps instead of forever looking, looking, looking into the blood and the genes and the environment of subjects such as Norma, she might examine the thought material, in particular the unconscious content of the imaginations and dreams of the parents of the aberrant babies. On the wall of her father's study there was a small sampler depicting children digging in a cherry orchard. It had been embroidered by Hermione's great-grandmother, and the text read: You May Find the Answer if You Look in the Right Place.

Hermione sometimes thought about that sampler with its tiny faded stitches resembling spider's marks worked in figures of dried blood. The right place, Hermione realised one night, as she strolled in The Basin looking up at the twinkling of a few stars, was quite possibly located in dreams and hopes and fears. She had nursed the theory of the Genetic Unconscious Deciding Factor for a long time, but nobody would take her seriously. It comes down to funding, of course. Hopes and fears are such insubstantial elements, and research is generally funded for something that can be seen in

test-tubes or at least in computer images of various kinds. The
GUDF hovered at the front of the back of Hermione's mind.

The Part of Fate

One night Hermione and her father the philosopher attended a performance of The Enlightenment company, playing at The Mineshaft
Theatre in The Archive which is the area in The Tunnels where
you can find the arts. Hermione followed Norma's career, always
hoping for some hint, some clue to all the mysteries of Variation.
Fate Can Perhaps Sometimes Play a Part. (I am just telling you that.
You probably won't see it on a sampler anywhere.)

Fate placed Hermione and Professor Uhu in seats next to
Belinda and Gustav Tillyard.

Although Hermione obviously knew who Norma was, she did
not recognise her parents. It was the hand of Destiny at work.
Norma was dancing in a short sequence titled 'The Lion in the
Desert Eats the Stars', inspired by a painting of the desert at night,
a sleeping gypsy in a striped costume, a guitar, and a golden lion.
Norma portrayed the part of the Lion, and she received a standing
ovation. She was absolutely brilliant, no question about that, so
graceful and yet so utterly and savagely convincing. Hermione and
her father were on their feet clapping and beaming, and beside
them was Norma's father, vivid with joy and pride. But Belinda,
when she tried to stand up, fainted dead away, collapsing into the
red velvet theatre seat.

Hermione turned to her at once in professional concern, and as
the patient was coming round – it was all too much for her – over-
whelmed by Norma's great success – mother of a prima ballerina –
Hermione heard Belinda say, 'Daphne, Daphne. I am so afraid, so
afraid. The lions. I am so afraid of the lions. Don't make me look at
the lions. My baby. I hate the lions. Daphne! All cats. I hate all cats.
All cats. All cats. Lions, oh good God. Oh, so scared. There was a
little grey cat and it looked at Daphne. Slipping, slipping, slipping.'

Hermione held Belinda's hand, and she listened.

'So, are you the mother of the little star?'

But Belinda said only, 'The poor baby's hands looked like kitten's paws. Kitten's paws. Paws. Paws!'

'She's delirious,' Gustav said.

And Hermione Uhu, almost delirious herself, slipped quietly away and returned home, inspired by all that had happened.

'I wonder,' Hermione said to herself as she rested in a huge brown leather armchair, sipping her vodka and Sirop de Violette, 'I wonder if there really is anything in the fact that the mother suffers from what amounts to a feline phobia.'

And she smiled her special mysterious smile as her incredible mind elegantly put the facts together, one by one by one: Childhood trauma fear of cat. Deep repression of the fear. Breeding of the fear in the profound imagination. Resolution of the fear in physical form in offspring.

The power of the imagination to direct genetics. The idea that GUDF might prove valid was almost too exciting, and Hermione felt a little faint herself.

The Recording of Dreams

She had of course the power to put in motion an Order of Isolation for Belinda. This was fairly routine. Belinda's dreams must be completely documented, and so Belinda was placed in an investigative coma, the decoction of monkshood farina and strawberry juice was introduced into the sockets of her eyes, and all her dreams from her own birth up to the present day were then recorded in moving images on a computer, using a program developed by Hermione. All our dreams are imprinted on us, stored in our profound imaginations, and can be retrieved and read by the use of MUSH (Maximum Unconscious Spirit Hallucination), after the inexplicable stimulation of the monkshood and strawberry decoction.

And sure enough, there it was, a DDI, or Dominant Dread Image trawling through the history of Belinda's unconscious, slicing through all narratives just as commercials slice through the narratives of television, and permanently swimming through Belinda's bloodstream, washing over her ovaries trillions and zillions of times.

The jaws of the leopard. The bloody flesh of the prey. The paws of a kitten. The eyes of a cat. The strange image of a lion opening its great mouth to swallow all the stars of the Milky Way. Then there came the birth of a perfect child with perfect furry paws. Criss-crossing with the DDI was another image, that of a beautiful child in a brown dress, lace at the throat and wrists, slipping down a long green slope, sliding, forever sliding, disappearing from sight, and reappearing and slipping, and sliding, sliding.

'The key lies in the unconscious mind. There is no longer any question of that. The answer is in the imagination of the subject, in the memory, in the traumatic events of the formative years. Mutation is linked to imagination in a most intimate and complex and elegant way,' Hermione wrote. 'The junction of herbal medicine and the new technologies has brought to light the secret of the link between the content of the unconscious mind and the genetic codes of the subject.'

The Death of Belinda

It is a very sad fact that Belinda Tillyard never woke up from the ordeal of the strange sleep that provided such a scientific break-through. She drifted away as great red tears of monkshood and strawberry juice dribbled from the corners of her eyes.

'Your mother has died in her sleep,' Gustav told the family, himself understanding almost nothing of what had happened. After a time he found himself strangely attracted to Hemione Uhu but, without some intervention such as Belinda's mother's cinnamon cookies, nothing would ever come of that. Hermione was utterly dedicated to her work, blinkered, almost part of her own computer systems, or so it seemed. She received many accolades for her work, and in her acceptance speeches she always paid humble tribute to the sampler made by her great-grandmother, and to the wisdom of the ancient herbalists. People generally took this reference to ancient wisdoms as a little eccentricity for which the great scientist must be humoured and forgiven. She received funding for the estab-lishment of a huge Imago-Genetic Research Institute, and although there remained, as there always will remain, old-fashioned thinkers who tut-tutted philosophically and ethically about privacy and human rights, the IGRI went ahead in leaps and bounds. The name of Belinda Tillyard drifted away, but her legacy is in fact alive wherever two or three are gathered together to marvel at the work of Hermione Uhu, and the miraculous isolation of the Genetic Unconscious Deciding Factor.

Queue Jumping

•

Tim Richards

Big Skies (Bob Higgs)

No matter how often calls came in – and through March there'd be ten a night – someone had to be sent out to investigate the sighting and collect particulars. All the high-ranked detectives in Bendigo refused to deal with alien business. You'd never get promoted by locking up Blobs, or getting them to piss off back to Planet Wank. That's what Connies were for.

If something really interesting came up, you were better off bringing in a specialist from the city. Jack Carter would get on the blower to Bob Higgs, a big bloke who had a reputation for getting to the crux of what aliens were after.

Higgs lived by the motto that the most obvious explanation is never the correct one. Extra-terrestrials are nifty at covering their tracks. The trick was to find the obvious answer and go lateral as buggery. Having seen Higgsy in action, the police in Clonard and Koorook sharpened up their left-field thinking about alien motives, but they still deferred to an expert.

Once the boy from the future made his presence felt at Mintook Secondary, it was only a matter of time before the administration contracted Bendigo, and Jack Carter had Bob Higgs choofing up the Calder Highway in his metal-green Statesman to see what the fuss was about.

Rooting Out The Beginning of The End (Raymond)

When Mrs Peng asked Raymond where his parents lived, she was told her question couldn't be answered. He'd been sleeping rough at the cemetery, and would be comfortable enough there till his job was done. While he appreciated the difficult situation the Principal was in – no school could take kids who didn't have a home address or legal guardians – he wanted her to make a special exception in his case. The sooner she let Ray get on with whatever he had to do, the sooner he'd be out of her hair.

Life at a small country high school can get very samey, so new kids become overnight celebrities. Not only did Raymond have a sophistication of manner that other kids who'd come from the city didn't have, he had no fear of sleeping in the cemetery. If this boy had claimed to be a vampire, he couldn't have raised more of a stir than he had by claiming that he was a visitor from the future.

Department guidelines weren't very clear. When Mrs Peng was Vice-Principal at Kerang several years earlier, there'd been a minor outbreak of this kind of thing. Two girls and a boy, third formers, claiming to be from the future. Each was running a separate but connected errand intended to redress a genetic fuck-up. They'd given home addresses, telephone numbers, all the usual details, but their nearest and dearest were fictions. In that instance, the School Council decided to be tolerant and let the matter run its course. Though the trio vanished after a few months, they'd caused a shitload of disruption, and Peng – Killer Penguin to students and staff alike – wasn't keen to repeat that with Raymond.

Raymond could stay until someone came up from Melbourne to sort it out, but he couldn't assume that he'd be going the distance at Mintook. In the meantime, he'd be boarding with Kim and Narelle Tyler, a young couple who taught Maths and Science in the upper-school.

The boy from the future gazed at Narelle's spare toothbrush as if he'd never seen one. Even the idea that teeth decomposed frightened him. Narelle was also in the habit of flouncing through the house in just a blouse and panties, and Kim noticed Ray's eyes testing their sockets. 'You'll have to excuse me,' the boy apologised, 'where I come from, women are more demure.'

Kim was shocked that a fourteen-year-old could use a word like demure in ordinary conversation. It added weight to the boy's claims. He was not like them.

As Ray tried to come to terms with his quiche and mixed vegetables, Kim asked whether he could elaborate on the precise nature of his mission. If the visitor's plan was to suck their brains during the night, they'd like to know about it.

Though wanting to be polite, there wasn't a lot Raymond could say. Agents were seldom given assignments. They were chosen as types. Ray's behavioural inclinations would make the necessary intervention inevitable. According to Ray's understanding, interventions tend to be undramatic and imperceptible. By engineering a small change, the agent forestalled a cataclysm further down the line. In all likelihood, Ray would disappear as soon as his mission was accomplished, possibly to return to his own time, possibly to become one of the annulled.

The annulled were destiny's martyrs. They were agents whose very agency had the effect of rendering themselves historically superfluous.

'No shit?' Narelle said. 'Wouldn't you be better off making sure you fucked up?'

'Everything's factored in,' Raymond told her, before requesting advice on how to eat quiche.

The Age of Specialisation (Bob Higgs)

After settling in to room 5 at the Railway Hotel, Bob Higgs arranged to meet Mrs Peng and Inspector Jack Carter in the downstairs lounge. Big Higgsy was inclined to hold off interviewing the boy till he had a clearer understanding of the stranger's disposition.

The expert was already pissed off with the Inspector. Carter had given Higgs to believe that this was uncomplicated alien business. Higgs now saw that it was nothing of the sort. Aliens were annoying bastards but few were so devious as temporal infiltrators. Time-travellers were a different bottle of sharks altogether.

But Jack Carter hadn't become Inspector without knowing how to rationalise a stuff-up. Sure, this kid was claiming to be from the future, but this was most likely an alien swifty. And not even the expert could summarily dismiss that possibility.

Though Bob promised to do what he could, he didn't like the sound of it. He had no sympathy for time travellers. Self-satisfied bastards the lot of them. He'd nearly chosen to take his work down that line when there'd been an explosion of demand a couple of years back, but everything he heard about 'slingshot investigations' promised certain job dissatisfaction.

'When blobs wander in from outer space, it's just a matter of working out what they're after, and whether you can spare it. If it's dirty books or a few gallons of sperm, big deal. But if it's something like human braincells, you might have to get rough. Cause, effect, intervention . . . These mongrels from the future are slippery. They can't tell you what they're after because they don't know. And then they fuckin' vanish without you ever knowing what they've done, why they've done it, or whether it's something you could have stopped.'

Mrs Peng was keen to emphasise the boy's view. So far as Raymond knew, he was here to make an intervention crucial to the future of civilisation.

The man from Melbourne wasn't having a bar of it. The future couldn't be trusted. Bob Higgs swigged the last of his gin and tonic, and called to Stan the barman for a refill.

'That's what they all say. They're here to stop X meeting Y, or to prevent someone's death. It's some huge fuckin' deal for the future of the planet,' the big man growled. 'And maybe that's what scientists intended when they first got the capacity to time travel – Hey, shit, this is going to let us take control, and all that . . . But ten, fifteen years down the line, all the classified stuff is so public domain that virtually any cowboy can use it. Suddenly you've got ordinary fuckwits zooming through time, selling this bullshit about having the destiny of the planet in their hands, when they're just a bunch of motherfuckers and grandmotherfuckers.'

Mrs Peng paused to compose herself before asking big Bob exactly what he meant by the term motherfucker.

Higgs meant his description to be taken literally. These blokes were acting out the last taboo.

'Nobody really knows whether these guys come from twenty years down the track or two thousand. It's all on their say-so. What if it's only thirty years? You've got some pervert thirty years from now getting his hands on a machine that's going to let him meet his mother when she was fourteen. You don't need to be Sigmund to figure out what's going on. Cut out the middle-man, skip dad, and go straight to Go. Not so much Oedipus eat your heart out, as Oedipus eat your mo . . .'

Always ahead of the game, the Inspector pulled Bob up before he could further offend Mrs Peng. 'I'm not sure that I get your argument,' Carter told his consultant. 'Surely, if you do something that stops your mother meeting your father, you run the risk of annulling yourself.'

Higgs agreed. Logic said that'd be the case. 'The thing is, Jack, these motherfuckers don't see things the way we do. Maybe they'll annul themselves. But maybe they always get away with the sick shit they do, and just keep doing it on a loop.'

Whether or not she followed the sad intricacies of this, the school Principal looked distressed.

'If what you say is true, Mr Higgs . . . If this capacity for ordinary people to zoom back in time becomes a possibility, then we wouldn't be able to trust anyone. Some of our best friends could be sleepers, or motherfuckers, as you call them. I couldn't be certain that Mr Peng wasn't one of these depraved men.'

Higgs nodded. 'Give me an alien any time. You know where you stand with an alien.'

The Future Lies in Education (Raymond)

As Mrs Peng discussed Raymond's future with Big Higgsy in the lounge of the Railway Hotel, the boy from the future sat in the back of Miss Murray's Year 10 English class, doing his best to fit in. This meant staring out the window when his class was required to follow the text the teacher was reading out loud. When finally, the teacher asked whether she was doing this for her own benefit, none of the dreamers could answer.

'Raymond, since you come from the future, maybe you'd like to tell this lot how *To Kill a Mockingbird* ends?'

Several of the more studious girls objected to her invitation to ruin the ending for them, but young Ray pointed out that he'd never read the book. In the future, no one carries knowledge about with them in a way that might tax their memory. You slipped a chip in whenever you needed to know something specific. Raymond was struggling to make sense of the deficient Boo Radley, and he figured that scientists must have found a way to genetically correct Boo-ism. Or else the future had worked a more sinister solution.

Having made the mistake of turning her class's attention to Ray's predicament, Miss Murray now had little hope of shifting them back to Atticus and Scout.

Karen Bolitho was sobbing. She couldn't bear to think of a time when everyone she loved, Pony especially, would be dead. Ray was someone's idea of a sick prank. Why send people back into the past if they hadn't got the whole mortality thing sorted? Even in the future, they were still making *ad hoc* repairs. The fuck-ups would just go on and on forever.

Many of the Year 10s refused to buy Raymond's sketchy story. If he really was from the future, he wouldn't be fart-arsing around in Year 10 English at Mintook Secondary. He'd be making contact with a kid destined to become President of the United States.

A hand went up at the rear of the classroom. Melissa Torok wanted to remind the class that she was born in Minnesota and had Presidential ambitions. She had no idea how she would get back to America to realise them. Maybe that's where Ray came in.

Ray would disappoint her. In the future, America would be no big deal. Things were going to get a lot more complicated. Kids didn't get that many chances to be adventurous, and when authorities suggested that he might be of some use, he volunteered for the mission. Ray was selected from more than ten thousand volunteers. All knew there was a real chance they'd annul themselves, or return to the future as mutant entities with no idea who they were or what they'd done. Adventure was worth the gamble.

When Gavin McGibbon told Ray that he wasn't his idea of Vasco da Gama, the visitor conceded that in most respects he was unexceptional. It was likely that he'd been chosen for a disposition, or a reflex, rather than a talent. When the time came for Ray to do whatever he was expected to do, he wouldn't have a choice in the matter. Ninety-nine times out of a hundred he'd go whatever way the boffins expected him to go. His choices were factored in.

Amy Williams was troubled by a more general issue. Mr Davis in Biology taught them that most people chose their partners for subconscious reasons that have nothing to do with romantic love. We're pre-programmed. You might never know that the true reason you were drawn to a boy was some small way in which he reminded you of your father. Women almost invariably choose taller men who look like they'd be faithful hunter-providers, while boys drawn to women with big breasts or broad hips were largely unaware of the part that fertility-assessment played in their selection. Darwinism was all about giving your offspring the best chance to carry your attributes into the future, to secure an on-going role for your own genetic inheritance.

Amy's concern was simple. If Raymond actually came from a distant time in the future, he had to constitute the best bet. Even if Ray himself was annulled, the future would still have an investment in seeing your issue get through.

The new boy then noticed the class pausing to appraise him in a very calculated way. It was difficult to imagine Ray's superhumanity, but maybe the young man had qualities that any bright girl should want. This troubled the sensitive boys quite as much as it excited the girls.

Queue Jumping

Mostly very quiet, Jodi Everett was a bright, pretty girl who drew a lot of male attention. She'd clearly given the whole matter of Raymond, partner selection, and genetic transmission serious consideration.

'Ray's got it all over us in a way,' Jodi observed. 'I mean, I'd find it very flattering to think that I had a special purpose by virtue of the man I mated with ... Virgin Mary and all that. But you'd never know whether Ray was taking advantage of his situation to have it off willy-nilly, or whether the future was choosing you. *You specifically.*'

Again, this struck hard at the class' imagination, and they were silent for a while. Jack Hunter saw the teacher lost in her own suppositions.

'Maybe it's not just girls his age,' Jack interjected. 'Ray might be here to have it off with Miss Murray.'

'Here to get ravaged by her more likely,' Gavin added.

The teacher brought this new line of thought to a halt with, 'I think that's quite enough, Gavin,' but the hint of a smile said that Jack and Gavin had read her mind.

'Perhaps we should go back to using old-fashioned terms like The Will of God,' Miss Murray said by way of re-establishing authority.

'The Will of Allah,' Ray corrected.

Big Higgsy meets The Boy From the Future

The boy from the future had no idea what to expect from Bob Higgs. Mrs Peng had told a white lie to the effect that Mr Higgs was a man from the Education Department, and Ray would need to speak to him with regard to his continuing participation in class. A small staff room was set aside for the interview.

Bob Higgs was an obese, greasy-skinned man of a type Raymond hadn't seen before. Intensely suspicious, Higgs stared at Ray as if he was an interloper from another planet. Ray's only problem, so far as Ray saw it, was not knowing how to act instinctively in a situation that was so abnormal. Was he allowed to be tetchy? Could he tell people they were shits if they treated him like shit, or should he try to act discreetly and behave more like a 'local'? Ray now lamented his lack of specific instructions.

When Bob Higgs asked Ray why he was here, the boy said he didn't know. He was on an important assignment, but as for the specifics, the whys and hows, Bob's guess was as good as Ray's. The boy trusted that the people who sent him knew their job.

The consultant wanted to know whether the boy was acting alone. Maybe Ray had some fellow agents, or was about to be put into contact with sleepers.

Once again, Ray couldn't rule out those possibilities. So far as he knew, he was acting alone. He couldn't see the benefit of creating a situation where two operatives might fall over each other. But it wasn't for him to know these things, he was just a kid. (Did it make sense to speak in age-relative terms? It was easy to disappear up the brown arsehole of relativity.) And Bob Higgs hardly gave the impression of being someone more perceptive than Ray was.

'You don't like your father, do you?' the fat man asserted, *apropos* of nothing.

'How do you mean?'

'A kid like you, taking all these risks. Leaving your family behind. Taking the chance that you might damage yourself and your family irreversibly.'

Ray saw harm to his family as an outside risk. The only considerable risk was to himself. He and his father got along fine. Ray's dad was proud that his son had volunteered to make things better.

Higgs asked why he should believe the boy. After all, Ray's interests weren't necessarily the interests of the Mintook community.

'This is a lark of yours, isn't it? I reckon your family would be devastated if they knew what you were up to.'

Raymond didn't know how to respond. He'd already guessed that Higgs wasn't what Mrs Peng said he was, and he now felt like strangling Big Bob. But, if Ray had such a powerful impulse to strangle the man, maybe he had that for a reason . . . No, surely the officials would have sought Ray's permission if their intention was that he should kill someone like Bob Higgs.

Could the people who chose him have made that choice because they saw a potential for killing? These thoughts made the boy dizzy, and still the fat man continued to bait him.

'Do any of the girls in your class remind you of your mother?' Higgs asked.

Raymond couldn't say. He hadn't thought about it.

'One of them is your mother, or grandmother, isn't she, Ray? You saw the photographs of your mother as a young woman, and they excited you, didn't they?'

The boy from the future told Higgs that he was a sick man. Only a sick man could impute those motives. Ray had come a long way. His mission was entirely honourable.

'What if I said that you're just a retrograde virus from the future, a filthy little motherfucker?'

Rather than punch Higgs, Raymond laughed out loud. The man was pathetic. Good for not much more than giving parking tickets to aliens. Taking Bob seriously would be a waste of energy.

'Whatever you think is immaterial, Mr Higgs. Events will take their course. Whether the next thing is trivial or crucial, one thing's for sure. It's all been factored in.'

A Town Called Hypothesis

Over a period of three or four days, local speculations bred and multiplied like ravenous locusts.

Raymond was an assassin.

Raymond was a sacrificial lamb. His tragic death would draw attention to a person whose historic trajectory needed to be changed.

Raymond was nothing more than a lost schizophrenic. His thinking was being distorted by an acute anxiety-depression.

Raymond was here to have sex with one or many local women in order to found a religious cult with controlled bloodlines.

Raymond was here to foil the sexual coupling of a man and woman who were destined to produce dangerous issue.

Raymond was here on a personal mission to leave behind

evidence of a pre-history sufficient to establish his future claims to be a god-head.

Raymond was a vagrant who tells a strange story convincingly well.

Raymond was the Son of God.

Raymond was Satan incarnate.

Raymond was a personified force of entropy.

Raymond should be prevented from doing anything.

Preventing Raymond from doing anything would only satisfy whatever expectation the distant future had of the distant past.

Raymond was an unnecessary distraction.

Raymond should be given *carte blanche* to do whatever he had to do.

Raymond should be tortured unmercifully to discourage the future from interfering with God's plan.

Raymond should be hypnotised to see whether he carried any useful knowledge with regard to precious metal deposits, or future agricultural practices.

Raymond should be treated just like you'd want your own children to be treated if they were stranded or lost in a far-off country.

Uncertainties

Ray would remember wandering down a rusty track between luminously yellow fields of canola, and feeling sad with regard to an episode recently past.

He'd been visiting Jodi Everett at her parents' farm, and while her parents had gone off to see their business partners, she'd taken him into her bedroom to listen to music. He found Jodi's music less captivating than her boundless enthusiasm for it. The bassline pulled at Ray's stomach.

'You can only really understand this music if you take drugs with it,' Jodi told him, and Ray would have happily shared drugs with her, but she had none.

He remembered feeling uncertain about what she might expect

from him. He didn't know Jodi well, but he liked her, and she was pretty. Ray very much wanted to kiss her, and to be wanted by her, but this overt friendliness seemed forced. Out of character. As Ray lay on her bed, examining the cover of a compact disc, Jodi bent over to kiss him on the lips.

Before he could register what happened, and invite her to join him in a passionate embrace, the girl was above the bed, taking off her T-shirt. Though Jodi's body was young, and beautifully proportioned, she was trembling uncontrollably, and not far off tears, despite earnest attempts to smile.

He couldn't remember exactly what he said next, or why he'd chosen to deny her what they both wanted. Ray might have said something about wanting to, but needing to be aware that a stronger force was guiding him. But even as he said it, he knew that he was making excuses for his own confusion.

This was a girl Ray should have been able to love wholeheartedly. All he'd managed to do was confuse and embarrass her.

Covering her breasts with her arms, Jodi told Ray to leave. Even as he backed out of the room, he felt that he'd seen her face, that expression, those exact same tears, somewhere before. And he could have killed himself for not embracing Jodi and trying to comfort her.

He was walking aimlessly down this dirt track, trying to make sense of his true motives and desires, when he met his classmate Gavin McGibbon riding a bike in the opposite direction. When Ray said hi to Gavin, the local boy dropped an abrupt broadie.

'You recognise me, don't you?' Gavin asked.

'From school.'

'Before that, or since then. However you want to put it. *We know each other.*'

Ray knew nothing of the sort.

Gavin was certain Ray knew about his own agency. He said that Ray had been sent back to perform an assassination. He'd been required to kill Gavin before he fucked Jodi. And Gavin refused to believe the boy from the future when he said that he'd been given no precise mission.

'The thing is,' Gavin told him, 'I don't give a fuck how badly the history of this planet turns out, and I'm certainly not going to stand back and let you do whatever you're intending to do to me or Jode. I'm not going to kill you, Ray, I'm going to annul you. I've got you factored in.'

Raymond remembered struggling over the knife, the fierce determination on Gavin's face, a punch in the gut that might have been a stab wound, and his own desire to take hold of Gavin's knife and kill him. He remembered thinking that Gavin was the dragon he had to slay.

The two boys from the future were grappling for control of the knife when Ray woke in a sweaty panic. Collecting the details of this dream did nothing to relieve his confusion.

Ray was a vagrant in time. His new life, for all true intents and purposes, was aimless. Though he desperately wanted to believe in Allah's will, Ray could no longer feel certain he was an agent of that will.

The Dragon Slays Himself

Bob Higgs was never going to admit his impotence to Jack Carter or Mrs Peng. Dealing with aliens taught him that sometimes it's best to bluff and draw things out, to let events take their course before claiming any course of events was a consequence of your decisive intervention. The best possible outcome.

Caught in a tricky situation, an experienced practitioner always floats the need for random, apparently irrational measures designed to suggest that only he could know what needed to be done to safeguard Mintook and surrounding shires from the worst case ramifications of having a motherfucker in their midst.

Bob Higgs instructed Jack Carter to close down the local bakery on Thursdays. He told Mrs Peng to introduce a prayer before each class. Rear-angle parking in town must be immediately replaced by parallel parking.

He insisted that the boy from the future be sniffed by Ted Anguin's border collie cross every morning. Dogs were unusually sensitive to a scent of life beyond their own deaths. Ted's dog would go rabid if Raymond was on the verge of annulling himself.

To Mrs Peng, Bob Higgs confided an absolute certainty that the boy knew far more than he'd been letting on. Raymond's claim that interventions were irrevocably factored in was a bluff.

When the woman lamented that they couldn't possibly know whether they were doing more harm than good, Higgs assured her that they could always know what they felt in their hearts. Intentions counted.

As the pair were discussing putting Ray on a strict braised chicken and rice diet, Jack Carter and a young constable arrived with news that Jodi Everett was missing. The bedroom window was wide open, and her bed hadn't been slept in. The most recent entry in the girl's diary expressed a desire to have a child by the boy from the future.

Carter wanted Big Higgsy to tell him whether they should get a specialist search team sent up from Melbourne.

Bob Higgs was curiously unmoved by the Inspector's distress.

'I wouldn't bother,' the fat man told Carter. 'You'll find her soon enough. He will have vaporised before he could hide the body.'

'You reckon he's killed her?'

'Nothing more certain. Fucked her, then left her to rot. When you DNA test the semen, you'll find that the Everett girl was our boy Raymond's mum.'

Mrs Peng couldn't make it to the door before a stream of vomit forced its way through her fingers. Not even this shook the consultant's air of calm. Everything Higgs first predicted had come to fruition.

'Sickest way to commit suicide. Scouring time for a way to annul yourself . . . But that's the terrorist mentality. They resent the fact that our values are enduring values.'

Higgs shook the Inspector by the hand. He was sorry things had turned out the way they had, but there was nothing they could have done. This stuff happened a lot more than you heard about. The only unusual aspect of this case was that the killer had gone out of his way to draw attention to himself.

The expert from Melbourne rubbed the distraught Principal's shoulder and told her not to blame herself. At least one thing Raymond said had been true. Everything was factored in. Ray's intervention turned each of them into unwitting agents. Now it was time for Bob Higgs to get back to his own family in the city. He asked Mrs Peng to pass on his regards to Mr Peng and the boys.

While these farewells were being exchanged, Catherine O'Shaunessy, editor of the *Mintook Times*, burst into the lounge. She had excellent news. Jodi Everett was safe and well. After deciding against surrendering her virginity to Ray, she'd spent the night in the cemetery. She was cold and hungry. More embarrassed than anything.

Embarrassments gathered like a storm.

Just after lunch, Bob Higgs, a man reputed to be expert in all things alien, checked out of the Railway Hotel at Mintook, and directed his metal-green Statesman toward the affluent south-eastern suburbs of the state capital. In their subsequent conversations, neither Jack Carter nor Mrs Peng ever mentioned Bob Higgs or the consultant's outrageous fee.

Waiting

Mintook's harvest that year was a clinker, and a record twenty-three Year 12 students were offered university places. After two years of solid toiling, Narelle Tyler became pregnant. Despite this, she and Kim were keen for Raymond to stay on as their guest. The boy from the future had a sweet manner and made friends easily. Dogs were especially fond of him. Ray could get even the most unruly mongrel to do anything.

Raymond proved to be an intelligent, attentive student with a predictable interest in history. Even with so much doubt surrounding the length of his stay, the boy hoped to win a scholarship to continue his studies beyond Year 12.

The young men who might have imagined Ray to be an insuperable adversary were finally won over by the outsider's capacity to tell a killer yarn. Ray's blue stories were several shades bluer than anything ever told in Mintook, and his audience left it for Ray to judge whether speaking this filth conflicted with his regular vague references to Allah.

It was as a cricketer that Ray really made his mark. Blessed with elastic wrists, the cricket bat was a wand in his hands. As the boy from the future chalked up a succession of massive scores, observers expressed the view that Ray must have been privy to sophisticated coaching. Few believed him when he said that he'd never heard of cricket before.

So huge was his enjoyment of the game, Ray began to hope that his mission was to save cricket from extinction. So far as the new-comer could gather, cricket was all about marshalling the forces of time; a game of patience and opportunism.

Once the initial excitement wore off, girls were less obvious in their attempts to win Ray's attention. Many chose to refer to him as the local cricket star before mentioning that this visitor from another time was Mintook's harbinger of destiny.

The most enthusiastic of Ray's female admirers, Jodi, and the boy from the future soon became thought of as an item. This affection notwithstanding, Jodi made no more nocturnal flights, and declared herself to be in no rush to give up her 'virtue'. Knowing too well what these declarations meant in local terms, Kim Tyler always made sure that Ray had condoms to safeguard against a moment when present and future might conspire to merge rather too dramatically.

At first, everyone waited, but gradually consciousness of the wait diminished, and Mintook people began to think of Raymond as just one of many agents of destiny rather than time's ultimate cannibal. Newspapers were printed, bread was baked, buses were caught and missed. Children were born and several older residents died. The McGibbon family shifted back to Melbourne. If Mintook's boy from the future was going to evaporate, he'd do so when the time suited and not before. After the final of the cricket, hopefully.

Even Mrs Peng began to think of Ray as just another boy in whites who cycled down her street on his way to the cricket ground every Saturday. These assimilations were pretty much her experience of life in the towns around Koorook. Outsiders came, and they were a big deal for a while. You often wondered what they thought this community could possibly do for them. Violent conflict seemed inevitable. Then, the sun rose one day, and it was as if they'd always been there, hand-picked for the town by some greater force of necessity.

Doctor Who?
(*or* The Day I Learnt to
Love Tom Baker)

•

Ben Peek

At fourteen, I had never seen my father's face. It wasn't that I didn't try to see it, only that he was *very* good at hiding it. Behind the black-and-white print of his newspaper, underneath the grease and red of our car, and up the steel legs of his ladder where he perched over the clogged gutter: Dad had hundreds of ways to hide his face. Even surprise didn't work. The one time that I was sure that I had caught him unaware – I had burst into the toilet by accident – I found Dad looking at me through the Batman mask he was wearing.

That incident had been at a fancy dress birthday party for one of his girlfriends, and I like to think that it was merely a coincidence, rather than a planned deception. It had been Mandy's party, the one with blonde hair, I think, but Dad had also been seeing a brown-haired girl called Andy. I had always gotten the two of them mixed up. So much so that once I thanked Andy (or was it Mandy?) for a gift that the other had given me. But I refuse to be blamed for that. It's not my fault if my dad can't date one girl at a time.

That mask in the toilet was a perfect example of how Dad managed to keep his face hidden from me. It occurs to me, every now and then, that it is possible that the government has been swapping fathers on me for years, and that they have a collection of stocky, middle-aged men wearing seventies rock T-shirts who come and go through my house at monthly intervals.

I'm not too sure what the reason for this could be, and I suppose it doesn't really matter. Not today, anyway. I had the day off school to go with Dad to Grandpa's funeral and, besides trying to peer through the straggly brown hair that is the back of Dad's head, I'm not really in the mood for conspiracies. Grandpa's dead. In the back of the car is my inheritance, while in the front of the car is Dad's current girlfriend, twisted around on the front seat so that she can talk to both of us.

Her name is Angela, and she is another one of the tall, dark-haired girlfriends that Dad brings home from university. There are two kinds of girls that Dad brings home: the tall blondes, and the tall brunettes. I like to think that there are some short, red-haired girls there too, but overall I think it's healthier not to think of my Dad, his girlfriends, and whatever it is they are doing at two o'clock in the morning. (I know what they're doing, okay? I just refuse to say it.)

I wouldn't really say that there is anything great about Angela, but at least she hasn't tried to win me over with presents, or said to me, like either Mandy or Andy said, 'You can call me Mum'. I didn't like that one bit, and I even found that it cheapened the lunches that Mandy (or Andy) had made for me to take to school. Not to mention the presents. Actually, when I think about it, Angela is okay, except for the fact that she has given me the nickname Holden, which she and Dad think is a riot. Ha ha. So funny. And for the record, my name is Matt.

Angela has been speaking to Dad for most of the ride home, asking questions about Grandpa and what it was like for Dad when he was growing up. Cue boredom. Unable to fake interest any longer – and looking for an easy distraction – Angela turned her attention towards my inheritance, and then said to me, 'You know, it really isn't that bad.'

'Do you want it then?'

'Matt,' Dad warned.

I rolled my eyes at his back and silently dared him to turn around. But he didn't, so I took another look at the curly head that poked over my seat from the back of the station wagon. I sighed.

It was still Tom Baker.

It was a life-sized, black-and-white cardboard cut-out of Tom Baker – whoever he was – complete with silly curly hair, a scarf, and geeky clothing. *This* was what my Grandpa had left me, believe it or not. Dad got some money and I got a cardboard cut out of Tom Baker, which I suppose shows just how deranged the old man was when he died. Which isn't a nice thing to think, and I regretted it cause he was a nice Grandpa and I didn't wish that he was dead.

But still: a *cardboard cut out of Tom Baker*! A whole house full of things and he leaves me this?

'He was in *Doctor Who*,' Angela said, shaking her head at my eye rolling.

'Doctor what?'

'*Doctor Who*.'

'Oh,' I said, but that didn't clear up anything. I had the sneaking suspicion that *Doctor Who* was going to be one of those television shows that she had watched when she was my age.

'I watched it all the time when I was your age,' Angela said. 'I thought it was cool.'

'Do you still think it's cool?'

'*Matt*,' Dad warned again.

'What?'

'Be nice.'

'I was!'

'I know that tone.'

Angela said, 'I think it's still cool, yes.'

It was on the tip of my tongue to suggest that maybe she'd like to take Tom home, but I could almost hear Dad's warning. I bit that back and said, 'What kind of show was it?'

'Science fiction,' Dad answered.

'Did you watch it too?' Angela asked, giving him the smile that girls gave my Dad when he had watched their favourite TV shows.

'Yeah.' Dad sounded like he was smiling too.

'Did it have any cool special effects?' I asked, sliding over in my seat to try and see if he was.

•

Avoiding me by checking his mirrors, he said, 'At the time.'

'So, *no* is the answer.'

'You got to remember how it was at the time, Matt.'

'Dad, can I explain something to you? They have *good* special effects now, and it's time for you to stop making excuses for those shows you watched when you were my age.'

'Matt, don't –'

'It's true, Dad.'

Dad sighed as Angela laughed. He said, 'How'd you become so cynical?'

I didn't reply. Dad asked me that all the time, and while I had a few theories on it, I also knew that it wasn't the sort of question that I was meant to have an answer for.

When we got home, Angela helped me carry Tom Baker upstairs. Dad and I live in a pretty big place out in Eastwood, and Dad spends most of his spare time mowing the lawns or working in the garden, which I think are his hobbies. Most of his time is spent either with his girlfriends, or out at his job at Sydney University.

Once we got into my room with Tom Baker, I began kicking my clothes out of the way and clearing a spot. Yes, I *do* have a messy room, but it's not because I get any joy out of dumping my clothes, toys, magazines and books around it like I do. And I don't enjoy having dust on my TV or on my computer. But I do let the clothes pile, and the dust crawl, and when it gets to the point that it needs to be cleaned, that's usually around the time that I get into trouble. Well, trouble is such a strong word, because I don't set out with the thought in my head that yes, today, a Tuesday, will be Trouble Day. It really is just a misunderstanding, even if it does result in me being punished, and having a messy room stops Dad from having to think of something *interesting*. This is why I let the clothes pile, and the dust crawl, and why there was a pile of clothes next to the TV that I had to kick away before Angela and I could place Tom Baker.

He still looked like a geek, and I said as much to Angela.

•

'That's how he looked in *Doctor Who*,' she said.

I stared at the cardboard cut-out. The more time I spent staring at it, the more uninteresting it became. There was just something about his clothes, and that scarf, and, yes, his hair, which was really ... *boring*. Where were his weapons? What about the monsters? What could Grandpa have been thinking when he left me this?

Yes, I'll leave this to Matt. I think he'd really enjoy this. Absolutely. He can dance with it around his room.

Or:

Matt doesn't look like he has many friends. Perhaps a cardboard cut-out of Tom Baker would really help him in that department.

Somehow neither struck me as right. Grandpa had always liked his things weird, that was true, but there was a reason for it. Maybe there was a map to buried treasure on the back of Tom's head? Would it show itself tonight under the moonlight? Somehow I doubted it.

'What are you going to do with it?' Angela said.

'What can I do with it?'

She looked at me, then looked back to it. 'You could sell it.'

'You want to buy it?'

'What would I do with it?'

'Dance?'

Angela laughed, but it wasn't hard to get a laugh out of Angela. She, unlike Mandy or Andy, had a sense of humour. She said, 'I don't really like dancing enough to dance with Tom Baker.'

'He could be a dinner companion for those lonely nights,' I suggested.

'I eat here most nights.'

'And don't you think it's time to cut down?'

I probably shouldn't have said that – I could practically hear Dad warning me from downstairs, but Angela just smiled. Then she said, 'Well, whatever you decide, it's yours. Have fun.'

When she had left the room I checked the back of his head, just in case there was a map there. There wasn't.

I had decided, after a few dance steps with Tom Baker, that he wasn't really good for anything, and I was going to head back downstairs when I heard a whisper. I had settled Tom down next to the TV again, and the sky outside the window was dark. The tree outside rustled but the night was otherwise quiet, and there was no one left in the room to make the whisper. Except me.

I breathed onto my hand, listened. I wasn't given to whispering without being aware of it. It could have been my imagination? I never had control over that. I waved at the cardboard cut-out and left my room, heading downstairs.

I had a strange dream that night. I blame Dad, because he had done the cooking and *what*ever he had made – there was some name for it, but it didn't sound particularly believable – gave me that dream. It has happened before, and I'm pretty good at blaming Dad.

In the dream, I was sleeping in my bed. It was peaceful and quiet and dark, like how I imagine the middle of the night usually is, when I was awoken by a whisper. It sounded just like the whisper that I had heard before, but louder.

I sat up in my bed and looked straight at the cardboard cut-out of Tom Baker. The light from outside had slanted right through the window and when I looked at him, really *looked* at him, I could see his cardboard mouth moving.

'My first film appearance was in *A Winter's Tale*,' he said, and his voice sounded mushy, as if it was being pushed through wet cardboard. 'I had originally been in the stage production of the piece two years earlier.'

Well, I remember thinking very clearly, that's nice. In the dream, it didn't seem very strange that Tom Baker was speaking. In fact, it seemed like the most natural thing in the world. So natural that I fell back to sleep and didn't let the whispering bother me.

I was late waking up the next morning, which was, of course, going to make me late for school. I pulled on my uniform without a shower, grabbed my bag, waved at Tom Baker and ran down stairs, jumping the last five as I aimed for the door.

'Hey!'

I stopped with my hand on the doorknob. Angela rushed down the stairs with her own bag slung over her shoulder. 'Need a ride?'

'Uh huh.'

That's the other thing I like about Angela. Mandy or Andy had never given me a lift to school unless Dad was around, and they always made sure to point it out to him. But not Angela. She would sometimes take me to school three, four times a week because she had her own morning classes to attend, and had not once made a special point of waking up early to take me.

Angela drove a blue hatchback with a lot of rust paint around the doors, and the inside smelt strongly of her perfume. Her driving was . . . well, I liked it. Dad referred to it as an amusement park ride, and there was that quality about it when Angela began weaving through cars.

When we got to school, Angela said, 'I think your dad is going to rent some *Doctor Who* episodes for you this afternoon.'

'Tell him to rent the 1978 season,' I replied without hesitation.

Angela laughed, told me I killed her and drove off.

Personally, I was little concerned, because that hadn't been a joke. I really *did* think that Dad should rent the 1978 season, and what was worse was that I even wanted to watch it. By lunch time, I had decided that it was a combination of the dream I had had and the stress that I constantly lived with from not ever having seen Dad's face.

When I got home, Dad's station red wagon was in the driveway. I found him in the kitchen with his head stuck beneath the sink and a toolbox next to him, and his hand was trying to reach it, but couldn't.

'That you Matt?'

'Yeah.'

'Can you pass me the socket wrench?'

'It's right next to you, Dad,' I said, looking where his head was. It was too dark to see anything but the pipe he was fixing. 'All you've got to do is look around.'

'*Matt*,' Dad said with that tone.

'Honestly.'

'Matt, just pass me the wrench!'

I put it into his hand. 'Dad, where did Grandpa get Tom Baker?'

'I don't know. A shop, I guess.'

'Oh.'

Dad tightened something, then said, 'I rented some *Doctor Who* episodes, they're on the counter there.'

'The 1978 season?' I asked, alarming myself again.

'What?'

I found the videos on the counter, and began shuffling through them. 'Dad, none of them have Tom Baker in them.'

'The store didn't have any of them.'

I was disappointed. Part of me couldn't believe that I *was* disappointed, while the other half of me was dealing with the actual disappointment. Behind me, I heard Dad standing, but by the time I turned around, he had already left the kitchen and was making his way outside.

We watched the videos after dinner. Dad and Angela sat on the couch and I lay on the beanbag in front of them. Dad had rented six videos, each with a couple of episodes on them, and I must have been really tired or they must have been really boring, because I fell asleep through the middle of the second one. The Doctor was this old guy, and there were these robots that were supposed to inspire fear but just looked very, very lame. I could have made better costumes. I could have even made better sound and special effects. Angela and Dad, however, thought it was great: they laughed and pointed out all these things to each other, which couldn't have been very interesting either because even they couldn't keep me awake.

I dreamt again. It was probably because of those *Doctor Who* episodes: I dreamt that I was in my bed, that Dad had lifted me off

•

the beanbag and taken me upstairs. Even in my dream I couldn't see his face, just the bottom of his jaw. He took me upstairs with Angela and the two of them put me in my bed, and in the dream Angela said, 'He's a good kid,' which she would have *never* said in reality. Dad agreed, and they left, and that was when the strange things began.

Except that, like before, it didn't seem strange. When Dad closed my door, the cardboard cut-out of Tom Baker began to move.

He had no legs to walk, and was thus forced to waddle and rock his way across the floor. He navigated through the junk, bumping toys and magazines to the side, and came up beside me.

And then he did something that I would have sworn that a cardboard cut-out of Tom Baker couldn't have done: he *bent* over. Right over, until his cardboard face was pressed near my ear. Then, in his mushy cardboard voice, he said, 'In 1972 I was in a production of *Troilus and Cressida*.'

I awoke with a start. It was morning and the sun was well and truly up. I was late, again, but I didn't feel like rushing out the door today. It was Thursday. Dad and Angela would have left early, and I didn't feel well – my body ached, my head hurt – and I decided that I'd either stay home or go to school late. I had done that before, and it wasn't a big deal, and besides which, I *did* feel sick. I didn't feel like doing anything, except for watching the 1978 season of *Doctor Who*, which I was a little uncomfortable with admitting. Especially with Tom Baker staring down at me from next to the television, and the dream touch of his cardboard face still against me.

I figured that I might as well watch some TV, so I leant to the floor for the remote . . . and paused.

There was a trail on the floor.

It led through the clothes, magazines, toys, and books: a thin line that looked as if it had been caused by something sliding along the carpet. The trail lead down around the far end of the bed and I knew without even checking, that the trail would end right at Tom Baker's cardboard feet.

I sat up, holding the remote tightly.

Tom Baker's cardboard lips moved slowly: 'My final season as the Doctor in *Doctor Who* was season eighteen in 1981.'

His voice sounded exactly like it did in my dream, and for a moment, I thought that I *was* dreaming. A talking cardboard cut-out wasn't *that* strange in a dream, was it? I could just lie back and go to sleep and everything would be fine. Except that I would be going *back* to sleep – that was what stopped me. If I went *back* to sleep, Tom Baker would still be speaking with his mushy cardboard voice and I would still be hearing him.

And when I woke up, I might even want to watch *Dungeons and Dragons* for his appearance. Or I might find myself watching re-runs of *The Kenny Everett Show*, *Medics* or even the 1983 movie *The Zany Adventures of Robin Hood*.

I couldn't stop making references to Tom Baker! It didn't matter that I had never seen them, I *knew*, absolutely *knew* that *The Curse of Tutankhamen's Tomb*, *The Book Tower*, and *Doctor Who Night* were fantastic productions of television and theatre. There was no room for doubt in my mind. Why should there be? Tom Baker kept speaking, and I kept learning.

I jumped from my bed and ran out of my room, pulling the door shut behind me and slumping against the hallway wall. I could still hear Tom's soggy whisper from my room, but I had no idea what to do. What kind of insane cardboard cut-out had I been left? I sat in the hall and tried to block out the voice, but it crept past my fingers, filling me with its information.

And then it stopped.

I didn't open the door, but the longer I sat in the hallway, the more time went by without a murmur coming from inside my room. Eventually I stood and pushed open my door.

Everything was quiet. Tom Baker stood near the TV, silent, unmoving. He looked very much like an ordinary cardboard cut-out, but no matter how still and how cardboard he looked, I couldn't overlook the tell-tale trail around my bed.

I had to do something, I knew, and before I could stop myself, I grabbed hold of Tom Baker.

Dragging him by his head, I left the room. I got into the hall before he started to wriggle in my arms, trying to shake himself free, but I held on tight. I dragged him down the stairs, through the living room and outside where I stood him in the middle of the back yard. The yard is big, full of flowers and plants that Dad planted, and the best way to describe it is green.

At first I laid Tom Baker on the ground, trying to jump on him; but he would dart out from under my feet and try to scurry away every time I let him go, so that I had to think of something else. Grabbing hold of him, I stood him in the middle of the yard and trapped him between two cement pots – one behind him and the other one in front. The cardboard cut-out gave a sudden wriggle, but I trapped him anyhow.

He looked worried, trapped between those two pots, but I refused to have any sympathy for him. He had filled my head with things that I hadn't needed to know, like the fact that Tom Baker had been in *The Golden Voyage of Sinbad* in 1973. Completely useless information!

I went into the shed and pulled out the lawn mower petrol can. Dad would come up with some form of creative punishment when he found out what I'd done, but I was more than willing to deal with that.

When I got back, Tom Baker was speaking again in his mushy voice. Blocking out the words, I began to pour petrol over it.

'Matt?'

I turned around. Angela was standing on the back veranda.

'Matt,' she said very slowly, 'what are you doing?'

I pointed at Tom Baker. 'I'm burning it.'

'Matt,' Angela said walking towards me, 'why don't you give me the petrol?'

'Just listen to it!'

'It's not saying anything Matt.'

She was right. The sneaky cardboard cut-out had gone quiet. I looked at Angela, I looked at the cardboard cut-out. Was this anything like *Frankenstein: the True Story* that had been made in 1973?

How could I know? And if I didn't stop it here, would I become the leader of the Tom Baker fan club? Could I let that happen?

I threw the petrol can at him. Right at his head.

And he *ducked*.

Angela stopped, and stood very still, looking at me and then Tom Baker. She had seen it too! Before she could say anything, Tom Baker began to speak: 'My first season of *Doctor Who* was in 1975, season twelve.'

'Matt?' Angela said.

'I told you!'

Angela backed away from the cut-out. Without waiting to hear what she said, I ran past her and back into the house, grabbing the box of matches Dad kept near the stove. When I ran back outside, Angela was standing in the same place, not moving but staring intently at Tom Baker.

'Angela!' I screamed, but she did not react. 'Angela!'

Nothing. I ran past her, striking the matches.

Tom Baker didn't stop speaking. He didn't cry out for me to stop, didn't say anything other than the fact that the real Tom Baker had been in the stage production of *The Trials of Oscar Wilde* in 1974.

And then the cardboard cut-out was on fire.

Angela shook her head, blinked tried to say something, then stopped. Instead, we stood there and watched Tom Baker burn. He spoke for a while, but soon that stopped, and it just burnt to the ground. The cut-out must have made me feel sorrow or something too, because I actually started to cry a little. Everything was blurred and strange, so when Angela put her arm around me and gave me a hug, I didn't stop her. I would have stopped Mandy or Andy, but like I said, Angela wasn't a bad sort, even if she did date my Dad. Which was okay, I guess. Someone was going to have to look him in the face and explain this.

Frozen Charlottes

●

Lucy Sussex

'We have long forgotten the ritual by which the house of our life
was erected. But ... when enemy bombs are taking their toll, what
enervated, perverse antiquities do they not lay bare in their
foundations? What things were interred and sacrificed amid magic
incantations, what horrible cabinet of curiosities lies there below?'

Walter Benjamin

That night she thinks: never again. The woman to the left of her, a
mere girl, has wept on and off, all afternoon. On the other side are
a pair already into baby talk, and not even pregnant yet. She knows
what the nurses say privately, to each other, raving bloody loonies,
all of them, it's nature's way of preventing hereditary insanity. Sometimes she wonders if she is going mad herself, as the drug-induced
depressions hit. No more, she thinks, this is it, now or never, even
if that does mean *never* ... And as the black tide of misery rises
within her, squeezing out through her eyelids, she too weeps, but
with an edge of relief.

Next day he visits. He takes her hand, doesn't squeeze it, just
holds it, in silence, waiting for her to speak. In the end she whispers:
'Get me out of here!'

Getting out of the hospital is easy. What is harder is coming home to the big white house in the outer suburbs, and looking out the window at the rows and rows of houses undulating away, their hills hoists blossoming with little white squares, little blue or pink clothes. Nappie Valley, the real estate agents call it. And the glances of fake sympathy hurt as much as the real sympathy, from relatives, and so-called friends. She can't bear, either, for anyone to commiserate with her: *leave me alone!* In the end she doesn't go out much, creating a comfort zone around her: junk food, daytime TV. Until one day Jerry Springer's topic is *her* topic, too close to home, this home no longer, not to a nuclear family, two parents, one cat, one dog, a little boy and little girl. Not even one child lives here, despite the sunny room upstairs, all filled with nursery things, in their cardboard boxes, never unpacked. A monument to the what-might-have-beens . . .

He comes home to find her flipping through the real estate sections of the internet. 'I'm getting us out of here,' she says.

He sits down, ready to listen. She moves from site to site, clicking on buttons.

'Remember when we were the renovators from hell?'

He chuckles, and she knows she is on the right track.

'And we'd talk about "projects" – "wrecker's delights" really, but we'd find them, buy them, do them up, sell them . . .'

He says: 'I remember how we never wanted anything beyond six square metres of recycled Baltic pine floorboards, or a match for the odd antique doorknob. Achievable things . . .'

Before, she thinks, before we decided we had to get real jobs, and with that everything that came with them: the suburban dream home, the pension plans, the desire to perpetuate ourselves . . .

She clicks again.

'So you're looking for a project,' he says.

She nods. 'Just getting a feel for it. And then we can call up the old contacts, find which suburbs are about to boom, where you get good tools, or where the wrecking yards are these days.'

'We can't go back in time, love,' he says after a while.

'I know. But we have to move, move on, and this is one way.

And it was fun, remember that? Despite the hammered fingers, the dust and dirt. You felt you were doing something creative, something positive.'

He thinks. 'I'm sick of driving a desk,' he says finally. 'You win. We'll give it a go.'

Selling the big white house is easy. Selling his business, resigning from what she knows might be the last good job she'll ever have, is harder. But hardest of all is finding the project, after they have narrowed down their hunt to a suburb where nobody knows them – a forgotten knot of working-class inner-city, stuck between industrial areas, and a rubbish dump about to be reclaimed.

It turns out to be one hell of a project – a little two-room cottage of stone, with behind it shoddy addition after shoddy addition, on a block of land paved with solid concrete and weedy wilderness.

He says: 'It's classified – the oldest surviving building in the area. Which saved it from being flattened, at least.'

She says nothing.

'I know it doesn't look like much, but you wanted a project, love . . .'

She takes a deep breath: 'It'll do . . .'

They buy a second-hand caravan, to live in during the worst of the renovations, and park it behind the house. The first night, they sit outside in the dark, balmy night, eating pizza and drinking beer. Around them is the concreted back yard, with fruit trees sticking out, above them the expanse of stars, dimmed by city lights.

'Tomorrow we start,' he says, looking at the stars.

'Tomorrow,' she says, and slips her arm around him. Later, they make love in the caravan, with no consideration for days of the month, charts and temperatures – just because they want to.

The old bluestone is sound on its stone foundations; the rest of the house is another matter, the stumps decaying, the floors pitched every which way. In the lean-to kitchen, water in the sink tilts at an uneasy angle. Each decade or so, something has been added to the house: an 1890s annexe, a 1920s kitchen, 1950s bedroom, 1960s bathroom, 1970s brick patio.

'We'll have to demolish and start again,' he says. 'All except the bluestone.'

'History,' she says, stroking the blocks of stone. 'I should go to the library, the local historical society, see what they know about it.'

But in the morning, waking bright and early with the thumps as the skip is delivered, she forgets about research in the fun of getting dirty and sweaty again. In the garden they play tiger in the weed jungle, hunting rubbish for the skip: old tyres, half a bicycle, broken bricks, a rusted old barbecue. In one corner, under the weeds, is buried treasure, an old claw-footed bath, which they manhandle out into the centre of the back yard, for somewhere to put it. She is tipping a laden wheelbarrow into the skip when an old woman comes past, pushing a shopping trolley. She looks and bursts out laughing, a thin cackle, with little of fun about it.

'You won't catch me, you won't catch me … doin' that!'

Crash! The contents of the wheelbarrow hit the bottom of the skip, the noise relieving her feelings at the interjection. When she looks up, the old woman has gone.

The rest of the day passes in a blur of work. When they stop for coffee and sweet biscuits, their hands are so filthy they leave grimy marks on the mugs. Otherwise, though, they are happy as a sand boy and girl. Late in the day, they are ripping up onion skins of mouldy carpet, then the lino beneath them, then old urine-yellow newspaper, so brittle with age it flakes in the fingers.

She stops, bending over the exposed floorboards.

'I can hear something. Hush!'

'What?' he says. 'I don't hear anything.'

'It's like a scratching, as if something's trying to get out.' Cocking her head to one side she follows the thread of sound, her Blundstone boots echoing on the newly exposed boards. She tries to tiptoe, to minimise the sound, something hard to do in the boots.

'Watch that floor,' he says, as she disappears through the doorway into the 1890s addition. 'It's borer central in there.'

A creak, a loud crunch, and then a shriek. He rushes in, to find her waist deep in rotten timber.

'Jeeze! You all right?'

'Better than the floor,' she says. She wrinkles her nose. 'It smells like a stray cat lives down here. A tom, too. Maybe that was the sound I heard.'

'Room enough for a wine cellar,' he says, gauging the space between what was left of the flooring and the cracked, dry clay beneath. It formed a subterranean cave, littered with broken bricks, bottles and rusted cans. He tests a joist, finds it sound. 'Here, I'll give you a hand up.'

But she is looking at something small shining whitely in the gloom. She crouches, brushing off a layer of powdered timber from it. Next moment she screams again, not the little bat-squeak of surprise, but the stuff of nightmare, and keeps on screaming.

He's run to the nearest bottle shop and bought a bottle of cheap brandy. Now he hands her an inch of the liquid in a hastily rinsed coffee mug. She drinks, chokes, drinks again.

'I'm sorry,' she finally says. 'Did you see it? A little white hand, it looked like, reaching up at me. The size of a foetus in a bottle.'

She drains the rest of the cup, stands. 'Well, they say you should face your fears.' She is, though, none too steady on her feet, as they near the gaping hole in the floor.

'Let me do it!' he says, and lowers himself to the ground. He bends down then lifts his head, eyebrows raised.

'It's just a doll, love. See?'

'Leave it,' she says. 'Let's call it a day and go get a video.'

But in the morning, though she is almost too stiff to move with the unaccustomed exertion, she pulls herself painfully through the house in her pyjamas, and into the 1890s section again. Wincing, she lowers herself into the pit.

She hears his footsteps in the next room along.

'Hey! Do you think you could get me something to dig with? Please . . .'

The doll is china, and it has, quite definitely, been buried. The clay is hard as concrete, but she hesitates to use more than a trowel, lest she shatter the china. At the end, she has a blistered palm, but holds a baby doll, moulded all in one piece: head, legs, arms and torso. In the bathroom, with its peeling op art wallpaper, she washes off dirt from the doll in the basin.

'History,' she murmurs. 'Or herstory, given that a little girl must have played with this. I wonder how old it is.'

That wonder sees her dry her hands, get dressed properly, and head off to the big city library. She comes back hours later with a sheaf of photocopies, so eager she starts talking the moment she sees him. Which is on the front doorstep, where he stands broom in hand, sweeping several years of accumulated leaf mould off the verandah.

'It's a type of doll made between 1850 and 1914 – so it's the same era as the front sections of the house. They're called Frozen Charlottes, or Frozen Charlies. There was this popular song, called "Fair Charlotte", about a girl who went for a sleigh ride in the snow. She had a party dress she wanted to show off, so she refused to wear a blanket to keep herself warm. Nineteen verses later, she comes to a bad end.'

She read:

> *He took her hand into his own,*
> *Oh God! It was cold as stone*
> *He tore her mantle from her brow*
> *On her face the cold stars shone*
>
> *Then quickly to the lighted hall*
> *Her lifeless form he bore,*
> *Fair Charlotte was a frozen corpse*
> *And her lips spake nevermore.*

'Is that it?' he says.

'Yes.'

'Charming,' he says. 'I'm not sure I could sit still to listen to twenty-one verses of that.'

From the street behind she hears the rattle of trolley wheels on pavement, a thin, cold laugh.

'You won't catch me, you won't catch me . . . doing that.'

She turns, resolving to be neighbourly.

'Surely *you* must sweep your verandah?'

The old woman continues on, not stopping. Over her shoulder she speaks, a parting shot, but a passing truck nearly obliterates the sound. Then she is past.

'Did you catch that?' he says.

'I'm not sure. Did she really say: catch me sweeping the house of horrors?'

'House of mumble was what I heard. Clearly the local weirdo. Okay, so you've been researching. I've been checking out the floors, and I think they'll all have to go. But that's not all: there's another of these freezing charlies. I just found it, under the floor.'

She kneels in front of the bathroom basin, a nail brush in hand, scrubbing dirt off the new doll.

'They're identical,' she says.

'Like out of the same mould,' he says, glancing over her shoulder.

'They *were* popular, a mass-produced doll. But why bury them?'

'Some little girl had a sadist for a brother, I'd guess.'

She laid the dolls on the bathmat to dry.

'Oh, there's a foot missing. I'll see if I can find it.'

He leaves her to it, starts taking a sledgehammer to the concrete footpath in the front yard. In the crunching of the hammer, his huffing and puffing, he forgets her, forgets the time. When he looks up it is sunset, and she is standing in the doorway. Even in the dim evening light he can see she is covered in dirt, and deathly white in the face.

'I found more than the missing foot. I found a whole army of dolls, all much the same, all buried. There's more to this than some poor little girl with a nasty older brother. It's like the day of judgement or something, the last trump, and up comes the dead ...'

'Maybe the house was a doll factory once,' he says. 'And they had a lot of rejects.'

Behind them, from the street, comes a now too-familiar sound, the sound of a shopping trolley. She crunches over the lumps of broken concrete, vaults the gate in her hurry.

'Hey, you with the trolley! You know all about this house, you keep laughing at us! So tell us what the joke is, with all the dolls.'

The old woman gapes and ducks past, breaking into a shaky run up the street. Her shoes flap, her knee stockings, neatly darned, slip down her skinny shanks.

She thinks of tackling, if she knew how to do it, but instead uses her relative youth to outpace, then confront, the old woman. It isn't hard – her trolley is laden, and she is panting hard enough to give herself a coronary.

'What is it about all the dolls buried under our house? You know, don't you?'

The old woman halts, slumps over the handles of the trolley and gasps for breath. Finally she speaks.

'I don't know about any dolls. But I do know they dug up every inch of the land there, and they found nothin'. Like she said: "You won't catch me". And they didn't.'

'Who said "You won't catch me"?' Apart from *you*, she thinks.

'Old Ma Wynne. Most famous person we ever had from round here. No footie player, no crook ever got her headlines. One of those series killers, they call them now. But they never found the bodies, and there must have been dozens of them.'

Widow Wynne locked her front door and strode down the street, carpet bag in her hand, the cherries in her bonnet nodding with her passage, her long coat flapping in the cool breeze. The coat was black for widowhood, the cherries red, for merriment. Little enough of that around here, though. Three doors down, bailiffs at the door, loading furniture into the van. Empty house beside that, the tenants did a scarper, the rent well in arrears. Three children, their clothes clean even if they are coming out of their boots, dog her footsteps, keeping a safe distance. They're getting thinner, she thinks, their eyes hollow, their fingers like chicken bones in the old German story *Hansel and Gretel*. Weren't those children abandoned in the forest by parents who couldn't feed them? Must have been a depression, whenever it was, just like now.

'Witch, witch,' she hears behind her, a child's jeering whisper. She whirls round, clawing her hands, and they take to their heels. When she turns, back is the respectable widow and small businesswoman. Things get much worse around here, she thought, your mama and dadda, they'll abandon you ...

At the train station she buys a return fare to the city, third class, and also a copy of the evening paper. In the classified ads there are her advertisements, each with a post office box number. Business is booming, about the only business that is, it seems. She glances through the rest of the news. 'Legislature Debates Foundling Hospital Bill' is the headline. She skims the article quickly, pursing her lips at its conclusion: the bill was defeated 'lest it encourage immorality'. And whose immorality might that be, honourable sirs? Yours and the housemaid? You're not the one who'll be sacked without references when you start to show. On the same page is the result of an inquest into a case of overlaying – a mother rolling on her baby when asleep, and smothering it. Third case this week. Drunk, was she? Husband out of work? How many children did she have? Not guilty ... just like Hansel and Gretel's parents. At least they only abandoned their babes in the wood.

She folds the paper and devotes the rest of the ride to eyeing the scenery. The train passes through rows of mean little suburbs, their back lanes full of washing and brats. The pleasures of the poor, she thinks. Not a penny in the house but rich in children. We got steam trains, we got telegraph, but you'd think some know-it-all would come up with some way of giving the womenfolk a rest ... And put me out of business, she thinks.

Several stops before the city, she alights, checking the address on an envelope before striding through side streets. She moves quickly, for this is slumland, dangerous for anyone who has the faintest whiff of prosperity. The single-fronted little terrace might have housed a small family once, but now it has been let, and sub-let, to boarders. At the end of the passage is a room, and her client. Irish accent, hurt, bewildered eyes, pretty enough, if you liked carrot-tops.

She wastes no time. 'You've got the money?'

The girl laboriously counts it out, as if expressing drops of her own blood, or milk.

'All ready, then?'

The girl nods, her eyes filling. All in one movement she turns and bends, lifting from the mean little iron bed a limp bundle, in baby clothes. Mrs Wynne bends over it, seeing the infant is clean, wrapped in a shawl, and on its lips the unmistakable smell, opiates and alcohol, laudanum, the mother's friend.

'Dear little thing,' she says.

In a moment the transaction is over. Mrs Wynne walks out the front door, leaving behind her weeping client, in her carpet bag the sleeping, drugged, baby.

She doesn't look like a monster ...

'She doesn't look like a monster,' he says. They have spent all morning in the archival section of the library, reels of microfilm beside them, ancient newspaper history scrolling before their eyes. Now they sit at a communal table, in front of them a microfilm photocopy. It shows an evening paper of a century ago, a line engraving of their house, circa 1890s, the front yard full of police-men, digging. On the same page is another engraving, a middle-aged woman, on her black bonnet a nodding spray of cherries.

'"A kind face, seemed very fond of children", that's what Witness A said, after handing over her baby and paying money to

Mrs Wynne's adoption agency. Which consisted of various post office boxes and one woman with a carpet bag.'

'A mass murderer. "Massacre of the innocents" and "Out-Heroding Herod",' he says, reading from the screen in front of them. 'And I thought media frenzy was a modern thing.'

'If she *was* a mass murderer. Remember, she was acquitted for lack of evidence.'

'Then what did she do with the babies?'

The question hangs in the air. In front of them is a line drawing, showing a witch-like crone, cherries in her hat, throwing an infant in the harbour, a cartoonist's response from a century ago.

'Look at these papers,' she says. 'Birth notices, welcoming fifth, sixth children. Overlaying, whatever that was. Babies found on church doorsteps. The past is a different country.'

'I wouldn't like to have lived there,' he says.

'Even though we could have adopted twelve kids or more if we wanted? Nobody wanted illegitimate babies, especially with the over-supply.'

'Let's go,' he said. 'I'm not sure I can take much more of this.'

Back at the house, she wanders through the 1890s rooms, trying to imagine a black coat, a hat with cherries. Finally she crawls under the house again, unearthing more dolls. He trundles in the wheelbarrow, and they fill it with the finds. When the barrow is laden, he takes it out to the yard. It seems a sacrilege, after what they know, to just dump the dolls on the brick or concrete, so he lines the claw-footed bath with an old blanket, and carefully lays the dolls on top. Then he returns to help her with the dig.

Hours later, utterly exhausted and filthy, they sit on the back doorstep, sharing sips from the bottle of brandy. Moonlight shines down on them, and on the bath, filled with little white forms, the heads turned towards them, the little dark painted eyes watchful. It is very still, hardly any traffic, but the empty air in front of them teems with movement, as if filled with moths glimpsed only from the corner of the eye, that slip out of sight if you try and look at them directly.

'Do you see?' she whispers.

'Not – see,' he whispers back.

The contents of the bath seethe, sending dolls falling out onto the concrete. They break, a plaintive plink like drops of rain, then a shower, as they continue to tumble. The remaining dolls in the bath have transmogrified into chubby toddlers, who totter on the rim of the bath, fall to join their fellows. Child-dolls, taller and thinner, play in the bath, tussle, fight, and also topple. A group of boy dolls play soldiers, marching over their fellows, growing taller and thinner, into grown doll-men, short back and sides, painted moustaches. They form a battalion, then, as if to a 'Hup, one, two, three!' march in formation over the side of the bath, crashing and breaking. A pause, then two doll nurses appear over the side of the bath, carrying a stretcher, with a sick doll, its arms flopping helplessly. They toss it over the side, return to the writhing pile for another patient, then a third. Other nurses appear to help in the grisly task, with their own stretchers and sick. They finish, then throw themselves after their patients. A pause, then a doll dressed flapper-style appears over the side of the bath, sexily posing as she walks. Another doll approaches, pushes her off . . .

She closes her eyes, hides her head in his shoulder, unable to watch anymore. She hears, though, the continual crash of breaking china.

Finally the painful noise stops. Around them it is still now, utterly quiet, even in the centre of the city. She opens her eyes. Around the bath is a mass of broken china. They approach, stare into the depths, to see movement.

He gets the torch from the kitchen. They see one doll left, an old woman – except that nobody has ever made an old woman doll. She claws at the side of the bath, the wool of the blanket, trying to get out. Finally she collapses in a heap, stills. Before their eyes the doll breaks into pieces as if ground under a heel.

He turns off the torch. She reaches out to the pile of broken dolls, feels the china faintly warm and gritty under her fingers. Some of the dolls have been reduced to powder, their constituting earth.

' "Dead and turned to clay", ' he says. 'That's a line from somewhere.'

'And I also remember now something about bone china – it's china with bone ash mixed in with it.' She shivers.

He says: 'I think we just witnessed the lives they would have led. Infant mortality was high at the time – that was the first wave. The childhood diseases, diphtheria, whooping cough, typhoid did the rest. Then we got to 1914, the first world war, followed by the influenza epidemic . . . and so on and so on. One made it to old age, it looks like.'

'If they'd lived they'd all be dead by now.'

'To this end we must all come, love, though we try and hide from it, by perpetuating ourselves, busying ourselves with projects.'

'Hush,' she says. Hand in hand they stand before the mass of china and clay dust, pondering their lives and those of these poor broken others, pondering the what-might-have-beens.

A Gorilla
Becomes a Jeep

●

Edward Burger

My intention initially was to relate the gorilla to a car, rather than a jeep. But to be more specific, what I really had in mind was a four-wheel-drive sedan. I was loath to say 'car' because the word is too readily associated with vehicles that (in appearance) correspond to the current popular car model, which has been prevalent for so many years and is so common and dull that the image of such gives me nausea. But nor would I liken it to a Landrover, firstly for the same reason as above, and secondly because it does not match the body-shape I had in mind. What I do envisage is a car of sedan-shape (with a roof), which is robust, as if armoured, and is certainly not like today's cars, which are shiny, rounded and bend like aluminium. Yet even the term 'jeep' is inadequate for it can suggest something that is roofless, zippy, and anything but heavy and solid. The biggest army jeeps certainly are heavy and solid, yet teeny lightweight beach-buggies can also be called jeeps. For the sake of convenience, I will call this vehicle a 'car', bearing in mind that it is not rounded and plastic but possesses those qualities mentioned above.

A heavy, robust car is a heavy, robust car (with a roof and boot). A gorilla has black skin and is covered with hair. The robust car need not necessarily have four-wheel-drive (though gorilla/robust-car-like-vehicles do possess four-wheel-drive), but I suggested that it did possess such early in the dialogue, purely as an attempt to describe the genre of car/vehicle, and not necessarily its shape – though the external appearance of this car/vehicle is most important, more so than its performance or comfort. I am at present concerned with presenting a visual interpretation of the transformation that took place. So I should specify that this gorilla was an adult *male* gorilla since this is relevant to acquiring a clear (or, at least, clearer) picture of the metamorphosis. I will not endeavour to distinguish this adult male gorilla from other adult male gorillas, but the considerable difference between adult *male* gorillas and adult *female* gorillas is the more relevant distinction to make because their differences are very marked. But that's not to say that female gorillas don't also become robust car-like machines – they frequently do, and far more frequently than male gorillas, but I need to specify 'male' in this instance so as to convey the clearest picture possible of one specific transformatory case. (As to why I chose to use a male gorilla [as the vehicle for this example of vehicular transformation] over a female gorilla in the first place, is a subject of greater delicacy.) An adult male gorilla is much larger than an adult female gorilla, and is hence more formidable, yet also its shape is markedly different to a female's, especially if – by comparison – one compares the difference in shape between – for instance – an adult female chimpanzee and an adult male chimpanzee, or an adult female gorilla and any adult chimpanzee, or an adult female gorilla and any human. None the less, a gorilla is a gorilla, and in this instance it was a formidable male gorilla. The gorilla was a formidable vehicle, and the vehicle was a formidable gorilla.

The transformation went thus: The gorilla raised its chin till the bottom surface of its jaw was in line with its neck and the rest of its body. The gorilla's hands and feet began to swell, which were to become the wheels of the vehicle – I have chosen to call this vehicle a '*vehicle*' for it is not car-like, nor is it rounded and plastic but possesses those qualities mentioned previously. A '*gorilla*' is a gorilla that does not yet have wheels. The top of the gorilla's head became flat, like the bonnet of a heavy robust vehicle, its back stretched and flattened to become the roof, its bottom became the boot, and its arms and legs became the sides and floor of this robust sedan-like vehicle.

Extract from an Anthropologist's journal

We met with a most remarkable occurrence today. It was mid morning, and we had traversed several miles on foot along the 'Dense As All Fuck' trail when we stopped for a cup of tea. But no sooner had our teapots brewed than a whole flock of gorillas came storming along. They came swinging in on vines from all directions, crying out like Tarzan. One of them almost spilt the jug of milk. Our guide saved it in the nick of time. He got his chest trodden on though, poor devil. Well, no sooner had the gorillas arrived than they were gone. Apparently they were just passing through. A rather rude way to behave, I must say. No wonder they are called gorillas. Anyhow, we decided to follow these gorillas and find out what all the fuss was about. We wound up at a clearing just a couple of hundred yards away where dozens of gorillas were making an awful ruckus. There was an odd looking creature that appeared to be a gorilla yet its body was undergoing outlandish contortions, as if it was changing form. These bodily contortions were of the kind one sees when a human transforms into a werewolf. But its shape became so distorted and grotesque it was indefinable. I was rather taken aback by it all. It was not until the transformation was nearly complete that I recognised what it had become. It was a vehicle. It resembled a large, chunky (and hairy) automobile. The next thing to happen was that several of the other gorillas climbed into this gorilla-automobile – perhaps eight in all – as many as could squeeze in – and then it drove off into the jungle. I had never seen anything like it. Neither had the rest of the crew. We considered following this strange gorilla-automobile, but we were not really up to it. We needed to sit down for a spell. What's more, the other chaps had not had their cups of tea yet, and I had spilt mine.

(This extract was the first recorded sighting of a gorilla-vehicular transformation.)

A gorilla is an animal. An armoured vehicular-sedan is a machine. A thing that is half gorilla and half vehicular-machine is an abomination – at least, it is most likely to be considered an abomination if its existence is the product of unnatural agencies. A jeep-like vehicle is not natural but a gorilla is. The particular gorilla/heavy-robust-jeep in question (which I have concluded is more like a jeep than anything else) became a gorilla/heavy-jeep (with a roof) through no apparent human intervention. It or its parents or grandparents might by chance have come into contact with a peculiar form of radiation, a manufactured virus, or some other potent residual agency that ultimately caused the transformation. But this is only conjecture. Perhaps its transformation was natural. Perhaps it even had total control of whether or not it changed, when it changed, and what it changed into. So why did this particular gorilla specifically become a heavy sedan-jeep? It might be just as logical to ask: Why did the heavy jeep-sedan start off as a gorilla? It appears that this gorilla became a weighty roofed-jeep because it had to convey humans through a rugged and unhewn environment. The environment was the gorilla's natural habitat – a jungle. The gorilla was in the proximity of humans when it transformed. The humans were animal liberationists who had to journey through the jungle in order to raid the offices of a twisted and heartless group of humans who ran a disreputable gorilla/big-army-jeep supply company. The gorilla transformed (into a gorilla/army-jeep-with-a-roof) in the proximity of the liberationists who imagined that it had not appeared in their proximity by chance. So they used it.

A vital point that has not been clarified is the fact that the formidable heavy-roofed vehicle in question was not *just* a roofed jeep-like vehicle. It was still half a gorilla. It was a gorilla/vehicle-cross. When the gorilla's hands and feet became wheels, these wheels were still hands and feet, when its anus became an exhaust, the exhaust was still its anus, and when its mouth became a fuel-intake aperture, this aperture was still its mouth, and so on. The humans who were riding in the gorilla were comfortable because it was covered in fur, it was soft and it was warm. And it didn't have to be steered because it steered itself because it had a mind of its own. But humans have to be nice to gorilla/jeep-like-sedans especially when they are travelling in one. Everyone knows how strong a normal gorilla is. A gorilla/jeep-like-sedan (with a roof) is even stronger because it is bigger, heavier and harder. If it wants to hurt its human passengers, it only has to push its walls together and will easily crush them to death.

Extract from an interview with an Administrative Assistant
It's true I was once employed by one of those disreputable car manufacturers, but I didn't know that they were doing such horrible things to all those poor gorillas. I didn't know anything about that side of the operation. I was just an administrative assistant. I thought the business was located in the jungle because metal was cheap. I got such a surprise when we were attacked by that herd of gorillas. I was sitting at my desk at the rear of the front office when two of the big, furry gorilla-cars crashed straight through the front wall. At the same time, another dozen gorilla-cars apparently burst through other parts of the building. The place was suddenly full of gorillas. My fellow office-workers were thrown around the room, bounced against walls, used as punching-bags, run-over and squashed. It was horrible. I managed to survive only because one of the gorillas took a liking to me. She treated me like I was a doll. She carried me around with her as she smashed furniture, broke down doors, and pummelled every person she came across. When there were only a few people left standing, the gorillas started to gang up on people. I remember a scene where four gorillas each grabbed an arm or leg of some poor fellow, picked him up and stretched him, while a fifth one jumped on his belly. It was frightful!
(This extract refers to one of many alleged raids carried out by gorillas upon illegal gorilla-vehicle operations.)

Gorilla/heavy-jeep-machines are more widespread than most humans realise. Many army vehicles as well as a lot of civilian cars are actually gorilla/heavy-jeeps-with-roofs. They have a metal covering on the inside and out, which the gorilla-vehicle suppliers have added not just for greater durability or to achieve a more desirable show-room finish – the gorilla/big-jeeplike-vehicle suppliers are a twisted and heartless breed of humans who have forced the metal coverings upon the transformed gorillas to imprison them and drive them unwilling into the commercial vehicle trade. These coverings hide the presence of the gorillas, protecting the suppliers from the scrutiny of animal liberationists and the like. Even when panels are taken off these heavy jeep-like vehicles with roofs, revealing the furry body of the gorilla, the fur is generally mistaken for insulation.

An ape-car (which cannot be categorised by any one label) is more reliable than a regular vehicle; parts may last a lifetime. However, when a part does break down, it is harder to replace since the replacement-parts – generally speaking – are not readily available. Parts are fragile and difficult to maintain inbetween bodies during the transferral period, and the fitting can be an intricate and delicate task. Repairs are not guaranteed success despite all efforts. For example: the seizure of an engine might necessitate open-heart surgery or replacement of the heart and other organs. A broken axle or even a flat tyre can be very hard to mend, and near impossible to restore to prior working efficiency. A broken crank-shaft is in most cases irreplaceable and can render a vehicle perma-nently out of action. Yet it could be a mistake to dispose of a car just because it is not working. Even gorilla/robust-weighty-roofed-sedans that have merely become less efficient with age are some-times dumped, particularly those disguised as normal cars. In fact, those that are disguised as normal cars are prone to break-downs – and not just nervous break-downs; owners who don't know that they should be feeding their car leaves and berries give them petrol and oil instead. Gorilla/armoured-like-weighty-sedan-vehicles cannot subsist on such a diet. What's more, it plays havoc with their bowels. So animal liberationists (as well as gorillas) frequently visit car-wrecking yards, searching for signs of life. They also search rubbish dumps, and are usually mistakenly identified as derelicts or rubbish hoarders.

•

Gorilla/roofed-weighty-robust-land-rover-like-cars much prefer to transport other gorillas than humans. Most would rather crush humans. When faced with a gorilla, a human's intelligence does not amount to much. A human's protestations are just an irritation, and its struggling is totally ineffectual. A human is like a misbehaving toy.

Extract from a broadcast by a Gorilla-Jeep Guerrilla Leader
We are capable of producing quite a clamour when the situation demands it. That's not to say that we necessarily advocate the use of brawn over brain, but it is nature's will that we replace humans as the dominant species. There is no point in entering into any farcical humanesque-style political debate. Humans only care about themselves. Besides, just as humans tailor their existence to be yielding of fulfilment and pleasure, we gain fulfilment and pleasure in executing nature's will by beating up humans.

We gorillas are more likely to succeed in our endeavours than humans are because of the indefatigable bonds that unite us. Normal gorillas are dependent on gorilla-jeeps for achieving successful surprise attacks, while the gorilla-jeeps are dependent on normal gorillas for chores such as grooming and removing lice. We gorilla-jeeps also occasionally need assistance in removing splinters; with all the inadvertent tree-felling we do to get from place to place (not to mention all the smashing-up we do of timber furnishings and buildings), it is inevitable that we acquire splinters. Another problem is that it is difficult to eat sometimes when no appropriate foodstuffs are within reach. For instance, I can push over bushes and small-to-medium trees in order to bring certain leaves and berries down to my level, but I cannot push over a really thick tree. Several of us together can. We can break through anything. United, we gorillas are a powerful force. More than mere guerrillas, we are an unstoppable army. Viva la revolution!
(To the best of my knowledge, this extract is a faithful transcription of said broadcast, bearing no distortions or discrepancies of which I am aware.)

An artificial mechanised form represents the ultimate evolutionary state of the intelligent human (or smart ape). Mechanisation overcomes the hindrance of *physical* and *emotional* weaknesses. A gorilla that becomes a furry robust non-lightweight jeep-like vehicle (with a roof) has jumped two evolutionary rungs. It is conceivable that one day gorillas will overrun (or run over) the human population and become the dominant species on Earth. Such scenarios have frequently been the subject of fiction, but with the presence of this new breed of gorilla and the accompanying unrest between gorilla and human populations, such a scenario has the distinct possibility of becoming reality.

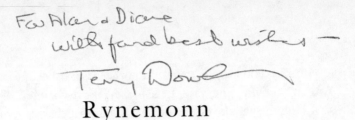

Rynemonn

●

Terry Dowling

Terry Dowling often wraps individual story output within overall themes. His Rynosseros series of books, Rynosseros (1991, Aphelion; 2003, MirrorDanse), Blue Tyson (1992, Aphelion) and Twilight Beach (1993, Aphelion) are prime examples of this approach.

The three stories and introductory fragment presented here as 'Rynemonn' are the concluding tales of a fourth Tom Rynosseros volume (yet to be published) by that name.

Editors

Doing the Line

You find a spot, often near a belltree on its lonely stretch of Road. You stop, secure your craft, take up your supplies and walk out, use your compass, calculate your angle and keep walking.

You find a place on the shore of a sand-sea. You sit on the lonely beach, ideally its only inhabitant, only human inhabitant at least, and, shielded by sand-shades and desert robes, you simply let it come to you.

First it's the silence once your tread and body sounds have settled. The silence and the distances, and with them the blinding strike of sun on sand and stone and heated air, the light coming at you in shimmers, planes and pulses, in glare and sundry mirages. Then you feel – truly feel – the breath of the land, feel the roll of thermals, the living tides of the sand-sea, pushing in upon you, stirring your robes, stray wisps of air, tufts of spinifex, catching on stones and rock towers and stands of land-coral, spiralling up to make anomalies in the flow, weather, a sense of this place and not some other.

Steadily, you learn it, cannot do otherwise. It becomes defined. You sit studying the vast, heat-locked, heat-changed distances, savouring the paradoxes, the rich yet minimalist character, or you lie back so the sky is everything and you could fall up into it. You consider each trace of cloud that appears, watch as it crawls by two or three miles overhead, know it intimately before it slips out of your piece of blue.

Most cultures have given a name to that moment of seeing, knowing and at-oneness. Such an elemental recognition is among the most ancient wisdoms of the Ab'O. These tribal peoples, as changed, changing and changeless as they now are, who have always had the soul-map of the songlines to keep intact this vital, pivotal connection between self and place, reality and dream, identity and the infinite, are caught between amusement and grudging approval at this growing habit among Nationals. They cannot be what they are, see as they do, and not approve. No, they applaud the belated longing; they do not evict the new wanderers on the land, for they know what it is, what has caused it. Deeply know. And you cannot know such a thing and not allow it in others. It is where it all comes together – in this shared knowing.

So when this man came to this shore, watched the land and the day happening, blended time and place with self, there was maat restored again, and hozho and wa, a gesture towards such things at least, and there was 'doing the Line', some clumsy, earnest honouring of the songlines, eternal upon the land. The Land. Let us get this right as well. What is.

You may already know him, of him. He is sometimes called the Leopard now, after a mythical animal in the heraldries of ancient lands (you would have to ask the Antique Men about that). But he has many names: Tom Tyson, Blue Tyson, Tom O'Bedlam, Tom Rynosseros, TJA96042, others.

But in a way I hope you don't. Because then this will be as new as the Line has made it all for him. Then it will come to you as life always comes to us, as bits lived elsewhere and brought to us as glimpses of something ongoing, made part of *our* purpose, *our*

experience. Only partly true, of course, since truth is always somewhere else.

It was a appropriate that he chose this place, the shore of this
sand-sea, with this belltree to sit near. He sat watching it for a
long time, the desert, the tree, the sky, the tree. It was different than
most. It was not beside an official Road for a start, but looked out
on the empty distances of Bullen Meddi, and it was wind and not
sun-powered, with a finned crown turning above the diligent where
its tiny life sat. It was different too in that it stood near the remains
of an abandoned carnival. Laid out close by were the improbable,
crazy shapes of a carousel, a ferris wheel, an ornamental gate, other
ragged ramshackle structures half-buried in the sand like bits of discarded dream, or something just now forming, pushing through.

'The Line does not have to be straight, merely complete', the
old saying has it, so it was appropriate that he start the Line here, and
finally, finally, on the evening of the fifth day when he was slowed
enough and ready enough, he walked over to the spinner and sat on
the sand before it.

'Hello Khoumy?' he called up, not really expecting an answer,
not even sure it lived, despite the turning crown. There was only the
old silence beyond the whirr of the spinner cap, the hiss of sand,
now and then the flutter of old canvas, the tick of heated metal in
the deserted carnival streets.

'Djuringa,' he said moments later, and when the echo came
back flecked with static – 'Djuringa' – added: 'Do you know me?'

'I might,' the belltree said, its voice raw and unpractised. 'You're
human life.'

'Well, yes. That's right. I am. I'm Tom Tyson.' He didn't expect
it to remember his name.

Moments passed, the finned crown turning in the brilliant air.
There was a soft music as well now, a low melodious pulse from the
dim-recall rods low in the AI's shaft. It was ministering to him,
trying to give what the greater belltree strains did, life-gift, harvested
windsong, a seeding of negative ions. Being near most belltrees gave
the ozone rush of impossible storms, the exhilaration of charged

molecules. From this weathered post came just the infrequent pulses, the best it could do, but signs all the same.

'You came from the Madhouse. Seven years ago.'

'You're right. I did.' The belltree's knowledge surprised him. 'You tap into the net?'

'Sometimes,' the voice came, still raw but steadying, firming with use. 'I'm not very strong. But sometimes other trees remember to talk to me. Stronger ones reach out and find me. Sometimes humans come and help.'

It was better than Tom had dared expect. 'I'm glad they do. Very glad. What else do you know? About me?'

Again the spinner paused, seeking data. The cap turned.

'That you came out with only three clear memories from your past – of a ship, a star, the face of a woman. You won a great ship from the tribes. *Rynosseros*. And Blue. A Hero Colour. Your name is in the Great Passage Book. You said my name.'

Tom realised it was a question. 'Yes, Khoumy. I came here once. You told me your name.'

'I've forgotten that. I'm not very smart. There are so many things to know.'

'There are. So please try again, Khoumy. What else have you heard? About me?'

The spinner cap turned, raw with reflected light. 'You are looking for your past. You're a pirate now because of what happened at – Caaerdia? Is that a place?'

'Yes, it is.'

'This is a place. It's hard to imagine other places.'

'I suppose it is.'

'The other trees talk about places all the time. They talk about you. The Leopard. I don't know what that means. But you're a champion of AI. That's a good thing. I like you for that.'

'Yes, well, thank you, Khoumy. I'm trying to find out things. About my past. About my three signs. It's why I'm here. Out here.'

'Here.'

'Yes.'

The next words startled him. 'You fear you may be made like me. You sent your ship away.'

'How do you know that, Khoumy? That I might have been made?'

'It's here. In the net. There is another place. Pentecost.'

'Is there more?'

'Yes.'

'I mean please tell me what else you know about me.'

Tom found that what had started as simple delight at a marvellous thing, this tree here and alive still, had become sudden anxiety, special need. Thousands upon thousands of belltrees across Australia, scattered along the desert Roads. What were they saying?

'The Life Houses wanted a National Clever Man. They built for that.'

'I fear they did. But Life Houses usually build what they are asked to build.'

'Usually?'

'Most of the time. Who would want a National who is also a Clever Man?'

'I don't know. But you can read the haldanes.'

'In a way. Do you know what haldanes are, Khoumy?'

'Bigger humanity. I found out. You thought they were gods, but they're you.'

'Yes. Bigger humanity. That's a good way to put it. We used to think it was what gave the tribes their mental powers. Energy vectors they could access. Now we think they are something more. We're finding ourselves.'

'It's why you're here.'

'That's right. Finding myself. Trying.'

'They tried to kill your friends. Your ship.'

'They did. At Pentecost and Caaerdria. Because of me. Whatever I am. They act more openly now.'

'They killed my friends.'

The other spinners Quint made, Tom realised, remembering how the eccentric old National had wanted to re-open the carnival, had made his own belltrees here.

'Yes. But I had to see if you still lived. It's why I decided to start the Line here.'

'It's good to be here.'

'Yes, Khoumy. Yes, it is. Tomorrow I'll go out there. Do the Line.'

'To another place. Other places.' The voice was stronger now, so full of joy at talking.

'Many other places, yes.'

There was silence between them then, near-silence, the thermals rolling in, the spinner cap turning, the remains of the old carnival muttering to itself in time with the day. Tom felt easier than he had in months. He lay back on his elbows and looked up at the diligent below the spinning crown.

'Are you happy?'

'I don't know that,' the belltree said.

'Are you glad to be here? To be a belltree here?'

'I am here.'

'But are you glad you are?'

'It's all there is.'

Tom wasn't sure why he pressed. 'But it matters to you?'

'Matters?'

'The sun is good?'

'Yes.'

'The wind?'

'Yes.'

'The night?'

'There are stars! Yes!'

'You like these things?'

'Oh yes. They are good.'

'You're happy then?'

'I'm part of the story, aren't I?'

'Yes.' What else to say? 'I'm part of yours too. That's what living things do. Make stories of themselves.'

'For themselves?'

Tom smiled up at the flashing crown. 'Yes. For themselves and then for others.'

'Will you tell me a story? About another place? I'd really like
that. About why you're here. Why you came back here.'

'All right.' And Tom thought about it, really thought about it,
at last or again, for he hadn't been sure, not really.

But cause. Actual cause. Only two steps were needed.

'A story,' he said. 'But you must remember it.'

'I will remember. It will be my job.'

'Good. And tell the others. Tell the older, stronger belltrees you
have a story to trade. But they have to talk to you. They must
include you.'

'That will be my job too.'

'Yes.'

And leaning back in the sand, losing himself in the feathering of
air against his cheek and the rush of the spinner cap against the blue,
Tom went back and began the story.

Coyote Struck by Lightning

Have you ever looked at something and not seen it? Have you
watched a street, studied a painting, looked through a window at a
familiar landscape and only later truly beheld it for the first time, yet
at first glimpse already had the sense, the premonition – somehow –
of knowing it fully? Have you done this?

That is how it was that day on the coast outside Cervantes,
with the rotors of the wind-farm turning – whoop whoop whoop –
at the edge of town and the tribal people and Nationals bringing in
their sand-dolls, and the smoke of bale-fires blackening the sky.
It was Colios, a vital time, a pivotal time and, as so often happens,
a largely unrecognised time.

The festival of Colios was a new thing, or rather a new-old thing,
for its origins and workings were lost in memory and borrowed tra-
ditions. Like Koronai in Twilight Beach, like Tafa at Inlansay and
Saralon at Port Allure, it fell during the first weeks of autumn.
Every afternoon, every evening, there were bale-fires set along the
outskirts of the town and up on the headlands where the desert met
the sea, columns of black smoke streaking the sky, stealing the sky,

linking up to form arches: roiling, surging cloisters through which the townspeople would come to add their votive dolls to the communal fires. The smoke of those fires became vortices in the rotors of the wind-farm at the southern edge of town, became tangled, corkscrewed and flung away by the big ferris wheel at the carnival on Black Point.

It was all part of the payback of Colios, the new thanksgiving, since the Right to Fire, like the Right to Wind, Earth and Water, were all part of life's round. It was what you did. Rights had become rites, of course, the reasons for doing lost in the custom of doing.

So it was, a kilometre outside of the ancient town of Cervantes on the west coast of Australia, that I followed the Line, allowed it to take me, directed it in fact so I could meet the Navajo semiologist-shamans from the university at Waso, here to study the newest skypainting in the A200 series.

They were down on the painting itself when I arrived at 1436, and when Ester, the local Council delegate, learned who I was, she couldn't help repeating the headline on the dailies back in town as she led me across to where they waited.

'They all have the same first name,' she said, as if that were even more amazing than Navajo hatathalis being interested in these anomalies, even more amazing than the skypaintings themselves. 'They're an old Amerind people. I never knew that.'

'Ester, I know about the Navajo and Waso. I know about the first names.'

'I just thought that being out on walkabout for so long you wouldn't –'

'Introduce us, please.'

We walked out to this latest nazca, stepped onto the first scorch circle, sixteen metres in diameter, crossed it to the linking corridor, four metres wide, twelve long, reached the larger, thirty-two metre circle where three of the four Dineh stood holding their scanners and clipboards, watching us approach.

They had the same sanded mahogany skin-tones, the same obsidian gaze and tall, deep-chested physiques, with calm expressions on their rough handsome faces and, yes, though with different spellings, the same first names. And not Navajo, I reminded myself. Dineh. Their own name. The People.

I let Ester work through the introductions. John Dance and Jon Cipher, the older hatathalis, both had shoulder-length, steel-grey hair and badges of office in turquoise and silver pinned to their ochre-coloured university fatigues. John Mele, one of two younger field-service trainees and apprentice shamans, had his black hair back in a tight ponytail and wore Thunderbird and other *yei* motifs on his jacket. As Ester and I drew near, the fourth Dineh came towards us from the opposite end of the skypainting. This latest nazca was so large that it would easily take him a minute to reach us.

'*Ya eeh teh*, Hosteen Dance, Hosteen Cipher,' I said when Ester was done, and to the younger man already with our group, '*Ya eeh teh.*'

'*Ya eeh teh*, Captain,' John Dance said, clearly pleased by the formal courtesy so far from home. 'And first names here, Tom. Thank you for joining us. We know it is difficult for you now.' He deliberately broke eye-contact and gestured at the expanse of the skypainting on which we stood, encompassing the fourth Dineh still on his way. 'Again, scorching and staining both. Volatised pigments that possibly were not present before the manifestation, though how can we know? Many insist a chosen site is primed beforehand. What do you make of this?'

It was no empty question. 'What you know. The usual thing. That it's Colios. New practices are being defined, meanings sought, as ever. The link to old crop circles is deliberate. But saltings, as you say. Fakery. A need for signs. John, I am no help here.'

John Dance nodded and waited for the second apprentice to reach us, a most striking figure, I saw as he drew near, dressed less ornately than John Mele and the older hatathalis, just simple black fatigues, but an amazing sight with his long white hair and gaunt, scarred face, twenty years old made a hundred and twenty to judge by the head and face alone. It was a sight made more disturbing by the darting, sidelong glances he gave as he approached. Ester was clearly uncomfortable at the prospect of meeting him again; she excused herself and headed back to town.

'John,' the older Dineh said, acknowledging him when he reached us. 'This is Blue Tyson. The Tom Tyson we have spoken of.'

'*Ya eeh teh*, Tom Rynosseros,' the old-young man said, his gaze steadying. 'I am John Coyote. Easy to remember.'

'*Ya eeh teh*, John,' I said, trying not to show any reaction to his appearance or the significance of such a surname for a Dineh. A coyote traditionally stood for evil and misfortune, for malicious pranks and things going wrong. Jass Lassi had mentioned this apprentice's name on his recent visit, had told me how four years ago, camping outside Teny in Dinetah, this young Navajo had been struck by lightning and survived. Only now did the connection make it more than a curiosity, another of Jass's stories.

Fortunately, John Dance read the moment and answered my earlier remark.

'Your three Madhouse signs are mental antecedents, we realise,' the elder said. 'Possibly placed within your consciousness by others. These are – as you say – no doubt saltings and fakery, but they mark the time. And, so that you know, Captain Tom, it is not the stigmata dreams of Totem Rule or your own signs that made us ask for you. Serafina images and Soul iconography have little to do with this.'

'Then what, John? I'm at a loss.'

'Let's say that it is your search among the world's symbol systems. Things like this.' He gestured to where Cervantes stood beneath its pall of black smoke, to where the lines of its tribal and National inhabitants moved through the rising on-shore wind to add their dolls to the fires. That freshening wind made the pall curve over us even more than before. 'We hear, too, that you have been assisting with various investigations.'

'Hardly scientific, John. More the restless spirit.'

'But intuitive and dedicated,' Jon Cipher added. 'Anything might help.'

And, surprising the two elders, John Coyote spoke. 'You are

steeped in other signs now, Captain,' he said, his gaze fixed on me
'Your medallion, your gun, your rhino head, probably that sword
you wear. Even your Bladed Sun, so like our Zia sign – '

'Yes,' John Dance continued smoothly, saving us from some old
point of tension between Jon Cipher and this young, clearly precocious, strangely named man. It was there in how their dark gazes
locked and held as the other senior hatathali spoke. 'We accept these
stainings, these skypaintings, nazca, whatever we call them, because
they exist. Because of Colios and this re-focused practice of burning
the sand-dolls on bale-fires. It is widespread now: during Tafa at
Inlansay, Saralon at Port Allure. Even Koronai. Hosteen Cipher and
myself see some pre-Tribation connection with the old European
corn-doll rites. With similar autumn harvest festivals from all over
the world transported and revived here, given new purchase. Even
mixed up with the old plague practices of burning the dead.'

'The Black Death?' I said, looking over at the line of bale-fires,
at the happy if solemn parents and gleeful children bringing in
what they had made to cast on the smouldering pyres. The westering sun turned them into silhouettes, shadow puppets, so many
striking dolls themselves. 'I've never thought of it that way.'

'And similar plagues in history,' John Dance said. 'Smallpox
plagues. Typhus. Cholera. Or the funeral pyres after any natural
disaster: flood, famine, before the epidemics set in. Burning the
dead during sieges. But all sorts of things. Rituals were often built
around them.'

'Burning the Guy as well,' John Coyote added, making Jon
Cipher's eyes lock hard on him again. He was clearly not meant
to speak. 'Old Guy Fawkes transplanted. Few dolls among the
Nyoongar, Yolngu, Koori or other tribal ancestors, as far as we can
tell, but clay dolls made so little girls could suckle them at clay
breasts on the Mornington Peninsula – '

'Old customs always feed the new.' Again John Dance continued as if the interruption hadn't occurred. 'We accept these
things because they exist. We accept you with no less wonder.
Science may reveal it all.'

'But patterning,' I said, being careful because of the delicate situation here, because of the Line drawing to its end, because of how it had always been; needing to be careful because I had chosen wrongly in the past, made mistakes, committed butherum among the tribes as blundering National and bearer of a Hero Colour. Who knew what offence I might now commit among these Navajo shaman-scholars? These Dineh, yes.

'Patterning,' John Dance echoed, and gestured at the sky-painting on which we stood. 'In all our legends there may be an answer for these.'

Who really needs one? I almost said, playing devil's advocate to myself, but the other elder spoke first.

'Be with us, Captain.' Jon Cipher gave a wonderful smile, so much at odds with his manner towards John Coyote. 'Share this. Let us talk. Anything.'

And we all looked out at this corner of apocalypse: at the nazca leading off from where we stood, at the great cloisters of darkness building on all sides, creating the sense of being inside an immense black cathedral or within the fingers of a shadowing hand.

Or rather all but John Coyote did. I glanced back to find him watching me, his dark eyes filled with an alarming intensity, his face racked now and then by nervous tics. Here was a trouble-maker, a maverick, someone probably worth speaking with alone. I nodded once, gift of sanction, then made myself study the sky-painting again: the darker stained and scorched sand of the circles and the connecting corridor, noting the ancillary flourishes, the curious metre-wide swastika arms, two in the smaller circle, three in the larger. Overdone, if anything. Too much like the old twentieth and twenty-first century end-stage crop-circles before they were debunked. Trying too hard.

Jon Cipher might have read my mind. 'We've been to Totem Rule, Captain. Guests claim to be having more stigmata dreams since the skypaintings. It's to be expected. We've seen the Image Books for the Soul and Ephemeris, talked to what mirage divers would speak with us. We know the iconographies for the Air and the Inland Sea. We've matched them to those from the Atlas Mountains and the Wadi Rum, from our own deserts in Dinetah.'

'You must have considered the sats. Orbital strike.'

'The obvious and most likely answer, but look at the precision, the detail. Not impossible, but improbable. Look at the colours – '

'Then something local. I hear that nearly all the nazca are on this side of the continent.'

And John Coyote was there again. 'There is a Gerias Kite tethered over near the rotors – '

Jon Cipher spoke in Navajo, quick guttural words, and John Coyote became silent at once. His eyes began their mad darting again, reading the landscape, refusing to settle.

'Excuse John, please, Captain Tom,' John Dance said. 'His youthful enthusiasm makes him forget our agreed protocols.'

I nodded, and again deliberately scanned the distances of ochre and red sand that stretched to the horizon, again found myself marvelling at how these Navajo – these Dineh! – were out of Waso without the usual tribal supervision. The Waso concession was permitted under the strictest rules, the watch community there nearly fifty strong, but treated as if the Way of the Dineh, an amenable but contrary metaphysic, might disturb the local truths.

John Dance left me to my thoughts as we resumed walking across the vast shapes. After a few minutes, he spoke once more. 'We know you are – outlaw now, whatever that means. Pirate. Privateer. We did not expect you to come. This might endanger you.'

'I was never hiding, John. And *they* have never been far away.'

'They're watching?'

'They will be watching, listening, yes. Have to, given what I am. As it is for you. You are watched.'

'Yes,' John Dance agreed as we neared the northern edge of the largest shape. The other Dineh followed several paces behind. 'You will know why we're allowed Waso. They needed Teny in Dinetah, a place for looking back at here, for exploring the songlines and haldanes and Dreamings, all the Djuringa mysteries, *away* from this key locus. We requested the same, reciprocal liberties, to explore our Ways in due privacy, the curing and stabilising ceremonies we use to keep the universe in balance.'

'*Hozho*.'

John Dance nodded, again pleased. 'You know the word. Good.'

'Superficially, John. There is so much to know.'

'So we choose carefully, yes?'

'John Coyote mentioned a Gerias Kite.'

'There is one tethered over by the rotors, yes. Someone has flown in for Colios, probably a Prince out of Lostnest to allow such a privilege. Such things are banned here, we know, but we're told that his small domain is off the coast, that there is a special dispensation. He could be the one. The only question is why would a tribal Prince create skypaintings?'

'What we said earlier, John. It's Colios. A new time, one still being defined, full of old things merged with the new. These are its forms, icons and sacred sites.'

'Just people adding things to the mix, you think?'

'We're all desperate for meaning. You know that belief systems almost always start out simple and become complicated by the shrewder, more enterprising followers.' I glanced back to make sure that Jon Cipher had the two younger shamans safely away from us. 'John, I admit to being curious. Tell me about John Coyote if you can. A friend from Arizona once spoke of him. That name . . .'

The hatathali glanced over to where the other three were testing soil samples with their scanners.

'I promised he could speak with you, but it was to be after this first meeting. He is, well, unstable. We make allowances. He forgot himself and I apologise. The name Coyote he chose for himself after he was struck by lightning the second time – '

'*Second* time! John, I knew only of the once.'

'You know of the spectacular thunderstorms we have in the high deserts of the American south-west. The first strike was when he was a boy. Burnt him, but he lived. The second was four years ago, very close to Teny. It turned his hair white, changed him in other ways, damaged his mind but focused him really, made a good thing out of what we feared would be a bad. That's when he took the name. He pleaded to come with us to Waso, the only thing he has ever asked of us really.' Then John Dance glanced up into the sky, not as a spiritual or reflective act, but as a reminder that we would have listeners. 'So, let me ask you, what do you know of the sand-dolls they burn here today?' He gestured, indicating the modest but unending lines of townspeople servicing the bale-fires.

'Only what I've heard from locals, nomads, sailors. It's a new thing, or another old thing made new. For five, six years it's been happening, all across the continent.'

'What they told us in Cervantes, Tom. It's like the cluster of flags on Cervantes Island and along Old Ronsard Strand. Very important, everyone says, but ask why they are there? No one knows for sure.'

'So how should I play this? You say John Coyote wants to talk to me.'

'You're both probably right about it not being the sats. So let him show you the kite. It is the most likely answer and you'll be gathering facts. We'll continue taking samples.' And he smiled at the sky as if to say: Be circumspect for the watchers.

'Thank you, John.'

'It is easy to give this, Captain. It matters to him and so matters to us.'

Five minutes later, John Coyote and I were heading for the line of bale-fires, avoiding the main trail into town by turning south towards the wind-farm, to where a deeper shadow held within the pall, the dark shape of the kite swinging about its mooring stanchion.

John took on the role of guide, very earnest, very serious, his gaze darting this way and that, though everything he said seemed phrased as if to test whether I already knew what he was telling me. Every comment had its tiny payload of challenge and enquiry, though he started, predictably enough, by talking about the Colios festivities.

'This new custom of yours, Captain. Sand-dolls.' His gaze swept the land, unrelenting. 'You spend weeks making them, then bury them until harvest. You light the bale-fires, dig up the dolls and burn them, poke and prod at them with your forks, watch them fall apart. It's all so medieval.'

I ignored the *you* and *yours* and the wildness in his eyes and played along, accepting that this was more protective coloration for the inevitable watchers and that his real purpose would be made clear in time. 'As you say, John. I was telling the others. It's making virtue of necessity. Since we're in a desert, with only modest local crops, market gardens and hydroponics, it's less a localised harvest ritual now than a general plea for bounty and paradise, for any kind of flourishing viable future.'

'Hence more urgent, more desperate, yes?' The kite was looming before us now, a great dark platform, a disk, an arrowhead shape hanging above the land.

'If you choose to see it that way. But thanksgiving just the same.'

'With a sense of giving back for what has been given. Restitution.' His gaze held mine.

I could only nod. What did this striking young man want me to say? But, thankfully, whenever I did leave a silence, John was quick to fill it.

'I notice that the National sand-dolls are makeshift, even half-hearted things compared to the tribal dolls. The Ab'Os know that stitched-up straw and soaked rags are not enough; you have to coat them with pitch, not just to represent tribal skin-colour but so they burn spectacularly and give off the smoke they require. They know that you need to build your temple in the sky.'

The man was obsessed. 'John, you're very taken with this? Is there a point you wish to make?'

'Always, but we're almost there. First let me show you the kite.'

It was one more thing adding to the strangeness, the sense of portentousness. Here at the edge of town was a much-prized rarity: a Gerias Kite, tethered low to a three-metre stanchion like a crippled manta. Someone had flown a ritual bird up from Lostnest for the festival, a Prince or some other privileged tribal leader allowed the dispensation of flight so they could be here for Colios.

Flight! I could scarcely believe it. The votive kite strained at the iron support, pulling this way and that against its land anchors so the cables slackened and bowed one moment, then drew taut as the great arrowhead-shaped flying machine shifted, as if it were testing them. *Tonight I shall escape.*

I couldn't help but think of the aerotropts at Twilight Beach during that recent Koronai. This amazing craft was probably inert, probably didn't have a mind greater than function-dedicated comp systems, but it reminded me and I cherished it.

'This could do it,' John said. 'It can be programmed. It will have laser points, delivery systems for the pigments.'

We stood watching the great shape nudging the stanchion, guy lines thrumming in the strengthening wind.

'See how the hull's patterned underneath,' John said, his gaze checking the land about us, as if intent on everything but the hull patterning. 'The polymer over the flotation nacelles has totemic striations. Very beautiful. It only looks dark like this because of the ash from the fires. There could very well be vents for releasing pigment payloads under there too, laser directed, then laser activated with appropriate allowances for wind dispersal.'

And, taking his cue, suddenly realising what was intended, I moved in under the manta shape itself, avoiding the stabilising vanes.

When it covered us, creaking and straining barely a metre overhead, a vast ceiling, the young shaman held up his hand-set. 'My scanner is dual function. But the hull screens us as well.' His unsettling mannerisms had vanished just like that; his manic quality set aside.

'They'll send agents.'

'But have to implement a suitable strategy.' He spoke in a clear, low voice. 'Discretion is important.'

'Please, John, what is it?'

'In setting up Teny in Dinetah, the Ab'Os needed to bring in resources: necessary tech, search systems, all an acceptable risk, but a risk nonetheless.'

'Go on.'

'Such a relocation had to create logistical problems, the security problems of any such major undertaking.'

'Of course. John, what are you saying?'

'That the Teny systems had little that was superfluous to the core task of studying the haldanes.'

'So?'

'Your name was there.'

'John!'

'Your profile. Your case. Coded, flagged highest security, but there.'

'You hacked their systems.'

'Acted according to my namesake, Captain. Coyote always plays a part. A troublemaker, true, but there is no civilisation without him.'

'John, can we get back to –'

'Nothing is sacred unless we both agree it is so. People say things are intrinsically sacred, but no. That is a yearning, a projection, a need for things to matter. No pharaoh has been left untouched in his tomb, no Celtic chieftain, no Manchu potentate or Persian queen. Nothing has saved them. Nothing is sacred, unless we agree: not life, not even the land. Coyote exists to remind them of that by bringing chaos. It's his job.'

I saw the change of tack for what it was, that this mattered, was what ultimately drove this man. 'Tell me.'

'He's the trickster, the mischievous, scheming outsider, the reviled thief and spoiler, the one who makes things go wrong to see what will happen.' He spoke rapidly now, never raising his voice. 'But he also sits in the doorway between this world and the other, between the spiritual world of the sacred hogan and the world out there. He keeps the door open, ultimately makes hozho possible by providing the chaos against which it is measured. He is Iai, the donkey-head in ancient Egyptian mythology who resists, who tests. The rebel. He is the fool without choice, ill-favoured, blessed and blasted, cursed and vital.'

'John, what did you do? What did you find?'

'The others do not know. It's the real reason I am here, why I pestered them to let me come down to Waso. Because of what I learned there.'

'Please!'

'You were made. Scribed DNA. They wanted a National Clever Man, as you've suspected. They had to know one way or the other. You are *like* Teny in Dinetah, only as a person: a way of looking back at here. Of looking at the tribal achievement. The Dreaming Way.'

My gaze stayed locked on his. 'The Dreaming Way?' But I understood. 'What else?'

'You went to Tarpial?'

'I did.'

'You met Seren Selie, learned it was her face –'

'She put it there.'

'Did she say why?'

'After a fashion.'

'Don't be coy, Captain. It was an attachment.'

'She said.'

'She lied. She is your sister in a sense. The female part of the experiment.'

'What!'

'Shut away in Tarpial. Working to bring you the truth.'

'She's Ab'O!'

'Scribed to be that way. One more vital legacy of that ancient, splendidly co-opted Human Genome Project. Can you be sure you aren't scribed to be another?'

'You said – no, I can't.'

'Exactly. You're National, deliberately that. But she was less clearly defined. She was temporised earlier too, brought into the world ten years before you. You were kept in the Madhouse.'

'Do you know why?'

'I can guess. She was part of a great new experiment, the darling of the life-houses, smart, precocious, no doubt a deliberate prodigy. She earned their trust, won their confidence, and ruined the other part of their experiment.'

'John –'

'Shut away in Tarpial she used what she could, found ways to circumvent their strictures. The Teny project was already underway. She linked to us in Tuba City; I agreed to act, a deformed outsider. I was already fated, had already been struck by lightning and spared. I was something of a pariah, a charmed yet blighted thing, even among my enlightened kind. I could easily assist. As Coyote, tradition sanctioned what I did. The bad things. The hard things.'

'How did she ruin it? What did she do?'

'All she had time for. Something simple. Added a third image to the three. Her own face.'

'Her face!'

'She knew something of scribing, had learned about keypoint insertions. She monitored your incept, added her own key template to the intended two when she could. Prioritised it.'

'Then the Ship and the Star –'

'The other way round.'

'The Star and the Ship.'

'Together!'

'The Star – Starship!'

'Was the activation code. They sent it again and again, by tech, via the mindline –'

'On Lake Air.' Thinking of Iain Summondamas and John Stone Grey, thinking of Arredeni Paxton Kemp and Anna, of Auer Rangan Anoki, all my confrontations with the Clever Men.

'But it never worked. You never became the full Clever Man they intended. Tartalen persuaded them to turn you out, to see what you would become, what would happen in situ. It was all they could do. They waited, tested, sent things at you.'

Bolo May. Stoutheart Tiberias Kra. Naesé. A carefully laden torc at Pentecost. Ships on the Air. Mira Lari, an animate with *that* Face.

'Let the Tree give me Blue.'

'No. That was something they didn't factor in. Couldn't.'

It was good to have it confirmed. Needed right then.

'They've tried to kill me. Countless times.'

'Factions. Tribal groups acting on their own, angered by the giving of the Colours, by the Haldane Order's reluctance to act. Even Kurdaitcha supposedly serving the life-houses. They see you as dangerous, as sacrilege.'

'Others have died because of me. Other Captains. Massen.'

'Then come in. Go public. Return to Twilight Beach. Or cross to Dinetah with us.'

'Your colleagues from Waso will be at risk. They –'

'Captain, they are here to provide an excuse. We've been tracking you too, as well as we could manage. It was so *we* could talk.'

'But Jon Cipher –'

'Resents the whole thing, yes. I have been struck by lightning. Ill-favoured. Unlucky. The risk to Waso and our people there concerns him. But a necessary part of the plan. They all know that whatever I tell you now is something we *can* give.'

'You were struck twice. Outside Teny as well.'

'Man-made lightning that time. There was a perimeter of angry hands.'

'You tried to break in to Teny!' I could hardly believe what I was hearing.

'Three people in our cell did. Encountered difficulties. I tried to help.'

'Your cell?' One thing after another.

'A group of Dineh and others trying to learn about the past. About the Tribation. It's an international movement, non-violent, full of Buddhists, Sufis and historians. Ours is a damaged, plundered world, Captain. Slowly healing.'

'You think the tribes know what happened?'

'Some of it. Fragments. Information systems were the first to go during that terrible time. It's verifying everything that's important now.'

'What do you have?'

John glanced at his scanner. 'They'll be coming for us, Captain. We should get away.'

'What did you learn, John?'

He didn't hesitate. 'None of it is certain. But how there was too much information. Truths were lost. Basic knowledge. How the Information Revolution became the Reality Crisis, a saturation of the data-sphere coupled with an intended flattening of effect. Fiction and falsehood more eloquent, more persuasive than available truth. People didn't respond, didn't know how to respond. It's hard for us to conceive of it, to model it now. It got so the world no longer *saw* what was happening. Some insist it was more invasive, that waves of controlled microwave pulses brought down the global data-nets, isolated the nations again, that there were race-specific epidemics, ethnotropic plagues – '

'Culling.'

'Culling, yes. We're almost certain. Culling and conditioning on a vast scale. Back and forth. Tom, we should go!'

The kite strained and heaved above us, lines creaking as it shifted with the wind.

But I couldn't leave yet. 'It's why the arcologies were abandoned.'

'Initially, yes. Or shut tight against the world.'

'That didn't save them. They became dead cities.'

'Many did, Captain. Many have.'

'And those millions, putting themselves into cryo. All the Cold People in those storage vaults – '

'Against a better day, yes. Against plague viruses they knew were fixed term. But a logistics nightmare, you see. Now the revival tech just isn't sufficient – '

'The Ab'O, the Dineh – ?'

'Not all peoples were targeted. It seems these angels of death were very specific. Minorities were exempted. The Maori, the Fijians, the Dineh, other Athabascan peoples – '

'The tribes weren't affected – '

'Captain, it's important we maintain our cover. We must get back to the skypainting, safeguard Waso.'

'Of course.'

I followed him numbly from under the striated hull, out past the mooring stanchion with its iron stairs leading up to the craft's flight-deck. John resumed his disguise of darting glances and fearsome intensity, and we let ourselves be seen to be chatting, gesturing, indicating things, making it seem as if we had been discussing the kite all along and its role in creating this new skypainting.

About us eddies of smoke from the bale-fires plunged and curled, caught up in the blades of the rotors to the south of the town, spiralling out from the great ferris by the Colios carnival on Black Point. For a moment it seemed like a corner of hell where dust-devils and willy-willies were made and set off on their courses, sent to haunt the emptied cities, sink charvolants and ruin lives.

Like Koronai so far away, Colios now seemed an even bleaker thing, a festival remembering a blasted, tragic time. *Bring out your dead!*

John Dance had been right. Not just some interesting re-location of corn-doll surrogates and harvest rituals, but a festival recalling the rest of it: wholesale slaughter, the *burning* of the dead. The more things changed . . .

'You! You there!'

We turned to see four tribesmen hurrying towards us, clearly more than festival custodians. They wore djellabas, had tribal sersifans and Japano swords. Two carried ritual woomeras for Unseen Spears.

'Tom, nothing I do should surprise you,' John said, and with a wink, immediately let his scarred face and dark eyes become wild again. This is how he had played Coyote in Dinetah, how he had gained access to Teny.

'You are Tom Rynosseros,' the leading tribesman said.

'I am the Blue Captain. Honour it!' I was tired, so tired of this.

'You are a pirate. An outcast,' the Ab'O said. He had bands of deep orange painted on his dusky cheeks: proclamation of intent. His hands were on his swords.

'I am on walkabout and I stand for Blue. Who sent you?'

'What?' the young warrior demanded.

'Which group? Who is your sponsor?'

'I am a custodian here, pirate! It is my official task –'

'You are about to disgrace your totems and your clans,' I said. 'Mark the Colour and name yourselves.'

I held him with my eyes, not daring to look away to see what John Coyote did, though I heard him muttering and gibbering at my side, playing the gifted sky-struck idiot.

It bought me seconds.

The young man glared, straightened. 'This one is Aron Jarr Akita.' The others exchanged quick glances with each other and followed suit, naming themselves in the lee of the Gerias Kite as at some embarkation ritual, John Coyote muttering all the while.

'We are allowed vendetta,' Akita said. 'We are – '

'Mark us!' I cried, looking up at imagined listeners, at the tribal scanners and their watch crews who had to be there, the ultimate reason for these men. 'You see this bearer of the gun of Ajan Bless Barratin, commander of the Exotic ship *Gyges*. I wear the sigil of Auer Rangan Anoki, murdered Clever Man of the Chitalice. I carry the living sword, Sen, once owned by Mati of the Chialis. In their names, too, I claim the lives of these who now dishonour Blue.' And to the waiting warriors: 'Be ready!'

In unison, a dazzling, practised flourish, they drew their swords and stood waiting for me to draw, but frowning, frowning now because of what I had said.

Instead of drawing, I reached up, moved Anoki's medallion aside, and opened my jacket, then my shirt, revealed the cross-hatch of scars on my chest from where I had fed my sword.

I met their gazes then, saw the confusion and growing dread in their eyes, and imagined their thoughts. *A living sword! What will be left of our lives for the noösphere, for the Dreamtime, for the ongoing? The living swords take everything.*

Then, shocking us all, John howled and went rushing off for the wind-farm at the edge of town. It was an act that might have been misunderstood, might have triggered strike, but the warriors held. It gave more time.

'You want to keep Teny in Dinetah?' I said, ignoring the fighters and looking up at the unseen listeners. 'Let anything happen to their divine fool and you'll lose it all. Waso will be withdrawn. Teny ends.'

Decisions must have been made in seconds, relayed through implants, because the two young men with the woomeras sheathed their swords, turned and hurried after John, who had now reached the rotors and was cavorting among them, arms outstretched.

I faced the remaining two and drew my sword, did it slowly, purposefully. 'You are both forfeit. You will feed Sen.'

'Captain, there has been a mistake,' Akita said. 'We didn't know –'

'Of course you did. You would have agreed to it eagerly. Let's begin!'

'Please, we –'

'The Chialis do this all the time. Surely they are not braver. It's two against one. Begin!'

'We have been told not to engage,' Akita said. 'Ordered not to!'

'You've drawn.'

'It's a command. We must obey.'

'You've drawn. Your leaders know the forfeit.'

'Why are you so determined?' Akita said, which made me ask it of myself.

Because of old anger, old grief and new. Because of rage and frustration. Because Massen was dead and a young woman had been left inside a triga ring, because of Mira Lari and Anoki and *Rynosseros* so casually slain, because some aerotropts had been murdered at Twilight Beach and, once, at far-off Trale, a hybrid life-experiment had reached out and sent a message, a star to match my Star because it found it there in my mind, possibly even recognised a piece of itself. Because. Because.

'Because sometimes I, too, believe I can win.'

'What?' Akita said. 'I don't follow.'

'Of course you do, Aron Jarr Akita. Otherwise you wouldn't be here.'

'I don't understand. You are mad! Both of you! You and that outlander!'

And my sword spoke, simple child words, but chilling to hear. 'Sometimes I am mad too.'

They were its first words in weeks.

The tribesmen stared, and their blades lifted, as much in terror as anything else.

'Captain, may I take their place?'

I turned to where the sun was westering beyond the colonnades of black smoke, saw a tall tribal woman in sand-robes, standing with two tribesman at her side.

'Lady Dusein!' Akita said. 'We were – '

She stopped him with a gesture. 'Excuse them, Captain. Let me blood your sword instead. Will you allow it?'

'No, Lady!' Akita cried, but she ignored him.

'Captain?'

'How is this your fight, Lady?' I asked.

'They are mine.'

'Truly?' I said.

'Officially. Yes.'

'Lady – ' Akita began.

'Akita, enough! Officially, superficially, they serve Gerias.'

'You are from Lostnest?'

She inclined her head. 'Yes. Will you let them disengage?'

I felt foolish now, foolish again, reacting, overreacting. But Sen deserved it. This was all it knew. It had spoken. What happened now mattered.

'Of course.'

She spoke in dialect, hard quick words that sent Akita and his companion rushing off towards the rotors to help secure John Coyote. She spoke again and her two bodyguards turned away as well, began walking back to the town.

Then she stepped closer, moved past me and turned so the sunlight lit her face and body, reached up and opened her sand-robes, opened her chemise, exposed her breasts, high and firm, the nipples erect with fear and emotion, perhaps just the cool wind from the ocean.

'Do it quickly. I am not very brave.'

I laid Sen along her chest, angled between her breasts ever so lightly. The blood came, just enough, in the straightest, thinnest line on her dusky skin.

I sheathed the blade without wiping it.

'That was kind,' she said, replacing her garments. 'I gentled you.'

'You did, Lady.'

'You were so angry.'

'You know me?'

'The Princes talk. Gerias is not so far away.'

I glanced to the north-east. 'You make the skypaintings.'

'Sometimes I take the kite aloft. This was a chance.'

'They're very fine. I'd like such a chance.'

'To make a skypainting?'

'To go aloft.'

'Where would you go?'

'Anywhere. Take the Line into the sky.'

'Captain, I am wearing shielding tech. You can say it.'

'Then back to my ship. Back to where the other Captains are gathering.'

'But that's what they want. All the Coloured Captains together. You've been called to the Air.'

'What!' A deep hard weight settled in my heart.

'It's true. A group claim. The elevation of Anna was too much.'

'Then I must keep away so that can't happen. They need us all with our ships to make the claim. I would go back to Cape Bedlam then, so I can –'

'Tartalen is at Azira. At the life-house there.'

'You know this?'

'Gerias is not so far away. I sometimes hear of Tartalen. I know Teny in Dinetah.'

'What has that –?' I stopped. 'You know Teny?'

'Of course. All the old stories of the Dineh. How coyote was struck by lightning. Twice. And new stories of the tribes, now being made. How no Gerias Kite could cross the continent without being struck from the sky. Unless . . .' She hesitated, looking over at the town.

'Lady?'

'Let me show you the town.'

'Lady, I know the town. I've been here before. Please finish what you were saying.'

'It will be different this time, I promise. Let me show you.'

It was strange to do, to go walking across the sand towards the chain of bale-fires with this Ab'O noble, towards the crusting of whitewashed buildings beyond the pillars of black smoke. To our left, the wind-farm rotors turned about themselves like great white birds never settling – whoop whoop whoop. Ahead, the black ferris pinwheeled against the golden sky like a stately old clock. On Pudding Hill coloured flags snapped in the wind on their tall poles. The pall of black smoke streamed into the sky above us, tipping over the land to the east, the black hand closing. And all the while the Ab'O townsfolk and Nationals came with their sand-dolls, feeding the fires.

'We shouldn't go too far,' I said. 'Especially now.'

'Here will do. Captain, do you know the old Arabic word moumia?'

'Moumia? Should I?'

'It means pitch. The tribal dolls are covered with pitch.'

It was like resuming my conversation with John Coyote from twenty, thirty minutes before. It made me look for him among the rotors, but he was nowhere to be seen. No, there he was! – racing towards the carnival on Black Point, to the great ferris there, still pursued by the four tribal custodians.

'He's a diversion.'

'He is. We're building an alibi.'

'An alibi? And the other Dineh?'

'Are in on it too. Peripherally. They don't know everything yet.'

'So, the tribal dolls are covered with pitch. To help them burn.'

Again I waited. Again I let her guide me through this her way. The Lady Dusein had brought us to within twenty metres of one of the fires. We stood watching as a family of Nationals: a mother, father and their two children, laid a daub, rag and wattle sand-doll on the pyre, obviously soaked with something highly flammable because the doll flared and stood almost erect before falling back into ruin. The family then stood aside to let an Ab'O family approach with their contribution. Two men carried a long black doll between them, did a three-count together and heaved it onto the flames.

Dusein waited until it was done. 'Did you know that there was a time in Egypt in the nineteenth and early twentieth centuries when finding burial pits was so commonplace that mummies were used to fuel locomotives running along the Nile? Wood and coal were scarce, and pitch had been used in the embalming, so they burned like bundles of dried sticks.'

'What's this got –?' But I grasped it in an instant. 'These dolls? These dolls are corpses?'

'Many of them. Most of them. From the old cryo crypts, Captain. The old failed forever crypts where so many Nationals went to escape the epidemics. The Cold People from when the arcologies were closed or abandoned. The spoiled ones.'

'I knew there were crypts close by –'

'At least nine on this section of coast. Seven of them failed decades ago.'

'Then Colios –?'

'Like so many renewal celebrations in history. Purging. Dealing with loss.'

'But there were thousands of people! Hundreds of thousands!'

'Millions, ultimately,' Dusein said.

We turned away from the fire, began walking back towards the Gerias Kite, not speaking until we were beside the mooring stanchion and the iron steps again.

'Thank you for revealing this,' I said. 'You are very brave to do it.'

She gave a fleeting smile, humourless, grim, then cocked her head, listening to a data-feed. 'They're bringing your friend. Are you serious about taking the Line into the sky?'

'Tartalen is at Azira, you said.'

'Would you? Take it aloft? Fly to Azira?'

'How can I? It's like you began to say. No Gerias Kite could hope to cross the continent.'

'Unless an abducted consort were aboard.'

I scarcely believed what I was hearing. 'You would risk it?'

'I risked your sword. That terrified me.'

'You knew better.'

'Hoped. You were very angry, very tired. You cared for your sword.'

I had to smile. 'Tell me the rest.'

'Captain, I am *here* to risk it. I know John Coyote from Dinetah. I am in his cell.'

Surprise after surprise. 'His cell! But how–?'

'Tom, I suggest you draw your gun and sword and "force" John and me aboard the kite.'

It happened quickly then. The warriors arrived to see both gun and Chialis sword at their Lady's throat, obeyed her clear instructions to move away without daring to risk drawing their laser batons. John came leaping and dancing over to the stanchion where we waited.

'This becomes the top of the tower!' he cried, still in character, and clambered up the iron steps to the flight deck. Dusein and I followed.

In less than a minute, the land-anchors were free, the tether retracted, and the Gerias Kite was sliding across the land, shearing the nearest smoke column at three hundred feet as it swung about, all the while climbing, flight-comp using the heat of the bale-fires as well as the wind to lift clear of the town and the ocean, swinging away from Cervantes.

Perhaps farsight snipers could have hit us with the appropriate hi-tech, but we'd quickly donned matching flight coveralls with the hoods up and the masks in place, and John and I stood closely behind Dusein at the starboard rail so they dared not risk it. She was murmuring in dialect all the while, dissuading them from extreme action, insisting that she would be released unharmed once we had reached whatever destination I had in mind. The sats needed to be told, she repeated over and over. No sky-strike. Emergency privilege invoked.

The kite seized the sky like a live thing, lifting us away from the smoke-blurred coastline, from the dubious haven of Cervantes with its rotors and funeral pyres and hidden, emptying crypts: two sane madmen and this brave lady on their magic bird, their flying carpet, their desperate chance.

John Coyote had once again put aside his madness and stood at the control binnacle, as if the craft needed human assistance.

'I came from Dinetah on a dirigible,' he said. 'A great totemic whale of a thing. It felt like we were *on* the sky. This feels like we're *in* it. Does that make sense?'

I was at the port window, staring down, unable to look away. We were flying. '*In* it, yes. Part of it. I'm still coming to grips with it all.'

'May you never,' John said. 'When this becomes commonplace, just a view, there is something wrong with the world.'

And Dusein was there, veteran of such flights, though perhaps rarely so high.

'Your wish has been granted, Tom,' she said. 'You've taken the Line into the sky.'

'Let's hope they allow it, Lady.'

'Dusein.'

'Dusein. It's not a precedent they will want. We can only wait and see.'

John Coyote left the binnacle. 'So let's go out and be *in* the sky.'

'In a moment, John. The Lady – Dusein has something more to tell me. The rest of it.'

John nodded, fitted his breather mask and left us, opened the cabin door and stepped out into the wind.

'Please,' I said.

'Now you know what the sand-dolls are.'

'What you said before. Mummies from the old crypts. The crypts that failed.'

'Take it further.'

'The tech failed. Was *allowed* to fail!'

Dusein nodded. 'And one step more.'

'*Is being shut down even now!*' I could scarcely believe it, could barely conceive of such a thing. Then, of course, could. It was so obvious, so inevitable. Settle the racial inequalities once and for all, everything from long-standing sovereignty squabbles over land-title and inheritance disputes to things like generational bank interest and the tenure of patents and copyrights.

Who authorised it? I almost asked, but realised that it was something people always did. Just did. Out of envy, out of mischief and bravado, schoolyard dares and pranks becoming more, much more: getting even, part of payback, then clandestine policy. *Custom*. It was what John Coyote had said: no tombs remained intact from earlier societies; everything became scholarship: one man's grave was another's archaeology. What had he said? *Nothing is sacred unless we both agree it is so.*

Nothing sacred. Ultimately.

Then the other part of it grabbed.

A systematic shutting down of the Cold People facilities. At Cervantes. Across Australia. Throughout the world. The rest of the cull. The *other* part. All anticipated by the plague techs and program designers, the architects of the scheme.

Nowhere to hide.

I had been to Krombi, had read the histories. So hard to kill one or two or five or even ten when you had their faces in front of you. So easy to kill the thousands, the tens and hundreds of thousands when they were faceless, just lines of identical cryo sleeves stretching off in long dark vaults, strings of numbers on watch screens, so easy to switch off systems, use terms like rationalising resources, downgrading status, implementing cutbacks and shut-downs. You could put all sorts of edges onto words. Words took whatever you gave them.

'Tom?' Dusein asked.

There are times when it doesn't do to think too much. There are times when it's more important just to be.

'John Coyote's right,' I said. 'Let's go out and be *in* the sky.'

Coming Down

To use the old American Imperial so often merged with traditional metric, Gerias Kites rarely travelled above three thousand feet. But they could go higher, and the main cabin could be adjusted for such high-altitude flight. Dusein pressurised and heated the kite's interiors well before the craft levelled off at twelve thousand feet. When Tom, John and Dusein ventured out onto the promenades, they wore the insulated coveralls and special flight masks from the crew lockers. You did not ride a Gerias Kite – experience the act of flight first-hand – and *not* look down.

With the kite running on automatic towards Azira far to the east, Tom did that again and again. Outside the arrowpoint compartment and main salon, narrow promenades ran in three directions across the kite's upper surface, all flanked by sturdy handrails to which waist tethers were double-clipped for safety. One sky-walk ran over the low spine to the tail; the others followed the rim either side to the same destination, ran nearly the perimeter edge of the upper face to meet the spinal track. Taking those port and starboard walks was an exhilarating, terrifying thing to do and quite irresistible. You looked down on the great sweep of the land and on oblivion in the same instant.

Tom never tired of it: the clear chill blue enclosing on all sides but one, and that one swelling out, merging, lifting up, it seemed, to become almost everything. Far above the sats moved, tracked and waited, holding back their fire. Below, the land came to meet him, displayed and fell behind, like an ever-cycling diorama left running, like some errant image play of the eternally turning rotors at Cervantes.

Twelve thousand feet wasn't enough. Dusein took the kite higher, adjusted the controls so they rose through the brilliant day.

'You need to see this, Tom,' she said through her breather mask when she joined him at the rail, standing close in the chill white-noise silence of the upper air.

Tom didn't ask what. Instead, he repeated the question which had marked their flight.

'Nothing else, really?'

Dusein knew immediately what he meant.

'We have no reason to withhold anything, Tom. You know what we know. Scribed DNA. A test case. Something very important. Any further surprises will come from you now. What *you* can discover.'

'Hardly comforting, Dusein.'

'It's a time when nothing is enough, I know. But it's important. Whatever it is, at least we know that.'

'Well, I'm grateful to both of you. For all this.' Tom smiled behind his breather mask and gestured out at the day. 'For *all* this.'

The kite levelled at eighteen thousand feet. Now the salt-lakes were mandalas, fractals, scattered mandelbrots endlessly flaring across the land. Now it held steady between layers of cloud, with streaks of cirrus above and clumps of cumulus below: ghost scimitars over fists of coral.

The land was barely grasped as real. For hours there was the spread of old reds, washed browns, tans and greys reaching to the horizon, set off with smears of pink and white, streaks of dusty black, fragile twists of aqua as inexplicable as dreams. Then half an hour would pass where those same washed colours turned rufous and raw, as if the land smouldered deep down with bits of ancient fire. Then back it went to the reds and worn browns, the tans, taupes and ochres, the gamboge and gilded greys, all of it marred by old ranges and watercourses, so many pulled threads in a pauper's drab. Yes, snatching ways to tell it, as if dusty cloth *had* been dropped upon a vast table. Ancient aviators must have seized on that allusion again and again. And no better: as if an antique film-loop had been left to simulate the world. You watched, knowing that every comparison had already been made, already existed in the forgotten history of the world. You stared and stared, struggling to make it more, to find some adequate way for words to render it.

And just when the cold, when the brilliant air and the slow transitions stole focus, more salt-lakes came at you, more twists of infinity building, spiralling, closing on themselves like signatures, cartouches, tricked-up promises, anything to keep you at the rail one minute longer. It got so the cold seemed to have always been there, and that the world had never been warm.

Even when the others went in, Tom continued to slide the clips of his tethers along the rails, peering down in case there was something, anything. Needing it to be *down*, in fact. His land, seen as gods see, as the sats did. That was when he noticed they were descending, that the scattered knots of cloud were growing larger, rising to meet him, it seemed. Dusein was bringing them to where the world was meaningful again.

'Patterning, you told the Dineh,' she said when he entered the cabin at last. 'You need to go much higher, to the sat and gragen orbits, or stay lower for it to be truly real. The middle loses meaning.'

Tom went to the arrowpoint window, sat in one of the big viewing chairs at the underview and looked down. She was right. There were better rewards at seven thousand feet. The moraines, the maimed roil of desert fastness, had substance again, appropriate dimension. And still they descended. At four thousand Tom saw charvis engaged, mirror-flash and hard fire, arcs of crackling light, and felt the familiar ache, knowing what it would be like to be at the point of such a storm. He looked for Dusein to tell her so, but saw she was with John at the controls, intent on cell business most likely, discussing strategies.

Discussing his role at such a time too, no doubt. He *was* being factored in, of course, made part of elaborate projections and contingencies, though not even John Coyote asked what their Blue Captain intended, in case it seemed opportunist. There was that between them at least. Not once did they treat him as the means to a preferred end. They allowed. Greatest gift.

The salt lakes moved below like coins, white into silver, and vanished beneath. It made Tom consider endings again then. His. Theirs. Things out of view. Even now bale-fires dirtied the sky. Cold People were dying. The world moved on. Even now the Captains were gathering, praying he'd keep away, hoping he'd return to complete whatever it was they made – were still trying to make – between them. Their place in the world.

'Tom,' John Coyote said, 'you should see this.'

'What is it, John?'

'I'm not sure. Best you come and see.'

The three of them adjusted their masks again and stepped out into the brilliance. Tom instinctively looked down to where the hot coins of the lakes fell astern, but John pointed west.

'There,' he said. 'Coming at us.'

Tom unclipped his portable scan and looked. His eyes focused but couldn't resolve what he saw. There was a scratch on the sky, a needle line of silver dividing the world almost vertically, or trying to, with a weight, an anchor, a glinting door shape – something – at the end of it, but closing on the earth.

No, that wasn't it. Like John had said: it was coming at them.

'It's a tether!' Tom cried.

John had his scan raised as well. 'From a sub-orbital!'

'And down there! Look!' Tom lowered his scan to see Dusein pointing across the rail. 'To the north!'

There was a dust cloud, a large one, the rooster tails of a fleet of charvolants, five, ten, possibly more. Tom raised his scan again.

'Your Captains?' Dusein asked even as he found focus.

'Not with those signatures,' Tom said. 'Red wheel on black.'

'Haldanian Order!' she cried.

John confirmed it. 'Madhouse ships! Nine signatures, nine ships. They're following. Trying for intercept.'

Tom swung his scan to the west, thumbed auto-lock.

The gondola on its tether seemed to be walking on the sky, sliding along some invisible track at precisely the kite's altitude. Tom found its thread, traced the line of quicksilver upwards, down again, thumbed more zoom, saw stabilisation vanes deployed, the tiny flash of rectifiers.

'Going to board, you think?' John asked, as if any of them could know. This was outside all their experience.

'Or attach something. Force us down.' It seemed likely.

'They may try system overrides,' Dusein said, closest thing to an aviator they had. 'But I'd say rupture a gas cell more likely. They'll have schematics. Know exactly what to hit.'

'Why not laser?' Tom asked.

'Too many variables,' she said. 'This is simpler. Get a barb in. Make a tear larger than systems can repair.'

John had his scan up again. 'That thing's occupied, you think?'

'Who knows?' Dusein said. 'It's large enough. But there are no records of deck fighting in the sky, so I'd say automated. They'll try to cripple us.'

Tom was watching the fleet again. 'With those ships for retrieval.'

'Likely, Tom. They're closing.'

John saw it first. 'No, they're turning! Look at their trail!'

He was right. The fleet was making a long slow curve. But it was Dusein who understood the significance of what they were seeing.

'They're turning because we are!'

'You're sure?' John asked.

Tom had noticed the direction shift, had thought it was one of Dusein's programmed rectifications.

'Azira is due east,' she said. 'We're turning north-east, at least five degrees and increasing. The fleet is compensating.'

He turned to her. 'They've commandeered flight control.'

'Seems like it. You and John watch the tether. I'll try to override.' She hurried off to the salon, leaving John Coyote and Tom at their scans.

Precious minutes passed. The direction shift became even more pronounced – the sun over their left shoulders instead of at their backs. The kite moved in the cold white-noise silence of the upper air-flow, while below the fleet swung in its long arc, and out there the gondola came creeping across the sky.

'Ten minutes at most,' Tom told the young shaman.

'What do we do? Use laser batons? There are some in the lockers.'

'It might come to that.'

Then Dusein was back with them again. 'Controls *are* locked. We should have expected this.'

John was frowning. 'Then why use the tether? If they can lock our controls, they can bring us down whenever they like.'

'Maybe it's a precaution,' Dusein said. 'Contingency.'

Tom wasn't convinced. 'Or something else. We can't know.'

Dusein was frowning too, her lovely eyes drawn down above the edge of her breather mask. 'It can't be factions. The Order is too strong.'

'Then what?' John asked. 'We're turning and the tether can't compensate.'

'No, we're descending,' Dusein said.

Again it was the trickery of flight. What had seemed to be the gondola lifting away, the tether retracting, was indeed the kite's own gradual loss of altitude. Now Tom saw that the airlerons along the kite's edges were angled for descent.

'Dusein, do we have para-sails, para-foils – what are they called?'

'Parachutes? Of course. They're standard equipment. But we don't need to evacuate.'

'Listen, both of you. The Order rarely acts this openly. They command enormous resources and they're determined. They brought down a tether. What we're protecting here is the viability of your cell. If I evacuate, you can radio the fleet, give visual ident, show I've left the kite. You and John can return to Cervantes.'

'No, Tom!'

'No!' John cried.

'Think it through. There's nothing else you can do for me now. We still need you. Still need the cell. We *all* do. If they bring us down, there's a good chance they'll separate us and do a close interrogation. Use mind-scan. Dusein, you are wife of a Prince. It is *your* kite. Once I've left, you invoke sovereignty, demand to return to Lostnest after your ordeal. Threaten Convocation if they won't allow it. John is safe. You are safe. The cell goes on.'

'But, Tom –'

'Dusein, once they ground us, they will make us disappear. This is the Haldane Order. They'll claim extraordinary powers, like Bolo

May once did. The sovereignty issue is still clear cut, but only while you are in the sky. You mustn't lose that.'

They accepted what Tom said, saw it was the only thing to do. There was silence for a time as the kite slowly settled, though it soon became too much for John.

'But you, Tom!' he said. 'What about you?'

'There's enough wind, John. I'll have jumped before you radio in, before their ships can turn, find Roads to take them.'

It hadn't been what he meant of course. 'But what about *you* – your story?'

Tom smiled, knowing what this intense, gifted young man was really asking. 'You think you will miss the ending?'

John smiled behind his mask too, but there was strong emotion in his dark eyes. 'This is one I'd like to have.'

'John, Dusein, there are factors at work here that may not be as they seem. I'm gambling on something.'

'Tell us,' John said.

'Just a feeling. Like you said, John, they send a fleet to intercept. So why go to the time and expense of sending down a tether if they can override our controls, bring us down whenever they want?'

Dusein nodded. 'But you said it *can't* be factions.'

'Not with this, no.'

John Coyote struck the rail. 'Not the Captains!'

'John, I don't see how it could be. They wouldn't risk it. Couldn't manage it. Not now. They're too closely watched.'

'Then what, Tom?'

'What indeed? The thing is, we'll never reach Azira like this. You need to be safe. Show me how to use the evacuation equipment.'

The device was called a parachute, and it was as old as Leonardo da Vinci, as old as weighted toys dropped off the walls of ziggurats along the Euphrates, probably as old as seed cases first noticed spiralling in the wind. Still trying to find objections, Dusein brought one from the lockers and helped Tom into the elaborate harness. While he secured his sword and ancient gun, she explained the automated release, showed him the manual back-ups, the guide straps and release toggles, heard him repeat her careful instructions back to her.

Tom had once ridden a storm-driven charvi kite leaving doomed *Tyger*. This would be similar, but so much easier. It was the other part of the leaving that made it hard. There had been *too* many leavings, too much making do when leave-taking was done.

'We'll see each other again,' he said. And without another word, without embraces or gestures that might be interpreted by distant watchers using scan, he went to the tail of the kite, to where the spinal walk met those at port and starboard and the debarkation ladder was locked away, to where there were no aerodynamic surfaces to snare trailing lines.

He didn't look back. There was this to do. Only this. One more unreality in the fairground sim unreality of flight, of having the world from above; one more thing after everything that had been.

Tom stepped into the sky.

There was the rush, chill and total, the panic, five, perhaps ten seconds of a wholly new knowing, then the chute's deployment, wrenching the world, pinning him to the sky again. In that sudden suspension he searched for referents. Above and behind his strange mushroom canopy sat the arrowhead, the blade, the fragile blown-leaf shape of the Gerias Kite dwindling, turning away, and the barest hint of the tether, still making its knife edge on the world.

It may have been ten, fifteen seconds more when the fleet started its turn. Two of the nine ships held their original course, looked like continuing, tracking the kite. But new decisions were made in those precious seconds, confirmations received, because then they too started to swing about, sweeping wide on the flat red terrain as if to complete their part in some stately cipher, a sand-painting made by wheels and travel platforms in answer to the skypaintings at Cervantes. All coming for him, Tom realised.

He saw why when he next looked up. The Gerias Kite had begun to turn, was banking even as he watched, its upper surface catching the sun. Safe. Hopefully safe.

Tom found the fleet again, marvelling anew at what it meant. *Nine* ships! Sent to fetch one of their own, yes, but so many. What was really happening? Had they been overheard outside Cervantes after all? Allowed their imposture as a way of getting Dusein and John Coyote this far from Lostnest? Again Tom located the kite where it sat on the sky, expecting it to burst into flame at any moment. But it stayed. For now it stayed, making its long way home.

That's how it was: fleet and kite, fleet and kite, then fleet, kite and landing site, until there was no more time. The desert was right there, Dusein's words suddenly real. Legs together and roll. Pull on the side toggles to lose the harness.

There was time for a glance at the cloud of dust building on the horizon, then the strike.

Tom stood in an old familiar silence, the utter silence of the hot still day, then found the growing edge of thunder – the sound of travel platforms off-Road, churning the gibber and saltpan as they made their hard run.

There were hills close by, the smoothed rock-forms chosen from above by Dusein. Not an optimum site by any means, too low, too worn, but with kite controls overridden, it had been the best choice available.

Tom bundled up the chute and ran for that meagre shelter. The approaching ships had full crews and surveillance tech. They had deck lasers and batons to use. They would have him soon enough, one way or the other.

At least the kite was still on its way west, he saw, control restored. The Order *had* relented; there was that to be thankful for. Or perhaps there were other things at play. He could only hope.

Tom reached the first boulders, was barely there, barely concealed when the vanguard of the fleet arrived – no, *not* the vanguard, not yet, not a Red Wheel ship at all! This wasn't one of the gracile, bronze-plated hulls used by the Order, but a battered old ninety-footer with plates missing from its resin sides and fifteen scrappy kites aloft. They trailed and swooped now as the vessel careened and slowed, rolled to a stop and was swallowed by the dust cloud of its approach. The name *Sycorax* was lettered in faded red at the bow.

'You there!' a figure called from the rail. 'Hurry, man! There are bogies on our tail!'

It was an easy trap if that, Tom knew as he ran for the old vessel. One ship to save the hunting out, the risk of harming valuable quarry. A decoy to earn his gratitude, lull him, then take him on to the next part of a carefully planned intercept.

Or not. For Tom had seen the fleet turn with the kite. Had seen the ships compensating. Perhaps *they* hadn't been the ones who had commandeered flight control. Perhaps it had been others. Allies like this. Battered old *Sycorax.*

Tom scrambled to the deck, found footing even as the vessel surged forward, as kites punched out on helium lifts and snatched at the sky again.

'Who are you?' he managed, breathless.

'Friends!' a crewman called, that word and no more as he ran for the cable boss. These weren't fully automated systems. Hands were needed at the winches and booms, and Tom hurried to help.

'We read nine!' the crewman said.

'Nine it is!' Tom confirmed, working the cranks with five others. They were lofting new lines, guiding more patched, part-strength photonics through the canopy spread, trying for as much of a break-neck run as they could get. Nothing like *Rynosseros* this, few of the automatics, precious few antimagnetics to help with the separations. This was aeropleuristics at its most basic.

Sycorax found the Road again, gathered speed and settled to her run. Her kitemaster added a brace of suncatchers to the spread, more frantic adjustments for Tom and the others, then a sorry-looking Chinese Hawk, probably all he had. When two suncatchers fouled, the lines were freed altogether, their kitemaster judging the gamble worth the loss. The pick-up had cost precious time but, everything considered, ship and crew had done well.

'Who sent you?' Tom asked when he had the breath, though clearly that was for later.

'Marcham,' the crewman said, thumb to his chest. 'Here's Connor, Rak, Ganness and Sackritter. Captain's Sallander. Kitemaster's Jell. We'll cover this.'

Tom took the cue, nodded and went aft to the quarterdeck, where a tall, dark-haired sandsman in scrap jacket and deck fatigues greeted him.

'Welcome aboard, Captain! Pat Sallander out of Gyrie.'

'Tom, Pat. And thanks.'

Sallander tipped his head at the short Tongan next to him, busy at the boss override. 'Jell arranged the bouquet for you.' He nodded to the clustering canopy overhead, just now beginning to settle.

'Jell first and last, Captain Tom,' the Tongan said. 'Just Jell. As for the bouquet, it's pure tatterpress improvisation and you know it! Welcome aboard!'

'Well judged all the same, Jell.'

The kitemaster grinned. 'Lost two. *Rynosseros* can owe.'

'Gladly. But who sent you? How did you find me?'

'No one *sent* us, Tom,' Sallander said, eyes on his helm controls and the Road ahead. 'We saw the kite, saw a dust cloud with nothing on scan. Figured cloaked ships. Without the tails we wouldn't have known.'

'Saw you jump,' Jell added, his gaze never once leaving the canopy. 'Figured we had a paranaut – whatever they're called.'

Sallander gave his kitemaster a quick smile. 'Saw Red Wheels through the glass and put it together. A Gerias Kite stolen from Cervantes. The wife of a Prince kidnapped. Tom Rynosseros out to break whatever tribal rules he hasn't yet broken.'

Tom had to grin, though it was short-lived. 'They're close.'

'They are,' Sallander said. 'Reckon forty-sixty their way on making it.'

Tom saw another brace of suncatchers go. 'You're shedding.'

'Trade-off. Like Jell says, *Rynosseros* can owe.'

'Endgame for us too, Pat.'

'Yeah, well. We do what we can.'

'Aye.'

Tom hurried to the commons, joined Marcham and the others at the booms, manually forcing separations while Jell guided a Demi up to the break – that shifting stagger point where most of the the kites formed their mantle. Only the Hawk and the *Sycorax* signature ranged beyond.

Even as Tom worked the boom, he saw that signature burst into flame, saw the Hawk go as well.

'Laser!' Marcham cried.

The Demi went seconds later, Jell immediately freeing the lines so *Sycorax* was past before the wreckage could settle and maim them further. They were building on 90 k's. They still had a chance.

That ninety became a desperate 100, then a hard-won 110 as the last precious photonics were added. Sallander had been saving them, sacrificing his brights and what few show kites he had rather than risk his final workhorses. Two death-lamps went up with them, spinning and flashing on their lines once they were past the spread.

No one had to be told what that meant. Endgame indeed. The Haldanian ships had to be visible through the glass at last, a clutch of glinting chalices under their flashing battle canopies, each with a red-wheel sigil at the break, all of them running on stored power and steadily gaining.

With the crew still at the booms, Sallander and Jell worked the lamps themselves, angling them to the sun as best they could, finding whatever ranged above their own rooster tail.

They scored hits against those mantles, but it was brief advantage. Laser struck the lamps, one, two, took the new photonics as well. *Sycorax* began slowing.

'Give me a crew line to one of those parafoils!' Tom said. 'They'll see me leave. May let you be.'

Sallander met Tom's gaze for a moment, just for a moment.

'For it either way,' he said. 'Witnesses, eh?'

'Aye.' Tom knew it was so. No choice but to run.

But he caught a quick glance between Sallander and Jell again. These men worked to a time for another reason, Tom was sure of it.

'What's ahead, Pat?'

'Scraps of a plan, Tom. Buying all the time and distance we can.'

'They have laser. Your hull, your platform – '

'Want you alive, I'm figuring. They'll take our canopy and roll us to a stop first. Help Jell swing those photonics manually, eh?'

Tom did so, crowding Jell at the boss override to shift the two port lines by main force. Not much of a strategy but, with the bouquet harvested, there was ample room now. Tom rammed the handles to new lock-points in the slot; the crew used their booms to assist, extending then drawing back the lines so the kites made irregular arcs instead of riding steady.

'Land anchors? Hedgehogs?' Tom asked.

'Used 'em getting to you,' Jell said at his shoulder. 'Supply modules, furniture, all we had. Not a fighting ship. No spares. We're leaner than we were, Captain.'

'*Rynosseros* can owe.' Tom had to grin again.

'She can,' Jell said.

Three more photonics went, strike, strike, strike. The Order's gun comps were good, and legal nowhere but on those sacred decks. The Haldanians commanded the sats too. Only Tom's presence prevented sky-strike, that much was clear. The dust wires trailing from *Sycorax*'s travel platform were partly to keep the air above untidy and make sat-scan difficult, but everyone knew that random strikes from orbit would soon get *Sycorax* if their attackers decided to.

'Seventy k's!' Sallander called.

Tom couldn't help himself. 'Abandon at forty! Lock helm and jump!'

'Phase up twenty,' Sallander said, as if he hadn't heard.

Jell touched the underside of the boss rig. 'They'll know,' he reminded his captain, mere formality.

Sallander didn't hesitate. 'Risk it!'

Jell activated something, and Tom understood the talk for what it was. 'You're powered!'

'Juggling, Tom. They've got sat-scan and laser. We need more time.'

'But powered!'

Four kites left, yet *Sycorax* stayed at seventy.

Tom worked his handles in the slots, kept his two parafoils shifting. The crew toiled at their booms.

They *had* to know. Four kites and such a speed! The fleet strategists had to figure it out.

But what with the rooster tail and the dust wires trailing to dirty the air, perhaps those strategists weren't sure what they were getting.

'Thirty count to white-out!' Sallander called, then: 'Lose power!'

Again Jell touched the underside of the boss override. *Sycorax* began slowing, and just in time. Tom's two parafoils went.

'Nearly, nearly,' Sallander said. 'Smokescreen on!' He anticipated Tom's question. 'No point till now. Too little fluid in the cans.'

Sycorax began fouling its own trail, sent black smoke boiling out along the Road behind.

'Now!' Sallander called, and Jell freed the last two lines, added power again.

'You're shielded!' Tom accepted it all. This had to be something John Coyote and Dusein had arranged. They'd feigned otherwise, but –

'Hold fast!' Jell shouted over the roar of their roadsong. Everyone responded.

Sycorax moved to starboard, began leaving the Road. It was level terrain for the most part but for a clustering of low hills a kilometre away, crowned with a scattering of boulders and dross like Tom's intended shelter earlier.

The fleet was following, fitted with state of the art hydraulics, easily capable of any crossing *Sycorax* could manage.

And as the last of the smokescreen trailed away, *Sycorax* rolled to within a hundred metres of those hills with their crowns of rounded stones, slowly drawing to a complete stop. The fleet was nearly on them, Red Wheels straining, death-lamps and laser-batts spinning and glinting, terrifying to see.

No time now. No time even to abandon ship and reach the token shelter of those rocks. It was like his earlier predicament before *Sycorax* arrived.

The fleet deployed on approach, six ships taking up stationary positions in a wide circle so they had all-points vantage, two turned in, one out, two in, one out, the remaining three coming to within fifty metres before braking.

Sudden stillness then, the sense of it, just dust tails billowing and settling around them, quickly falling away, then the ticking of hull plates, even the creaking of lines and straining canopies on the Haldanian ships, clearly audible across the distance. The Red Wheel captains left full mantles aloft but reined in, not simply as a quick-escape precaution – those ships were powered – but to provide shade for the officers and crews on their decks. Death lamps flashed and spun at full extension, gorging on sunlight; laser-batts shifted in the bright air like the heads of poisonous poppies.

Silence and stillness enough.

Then a voice through a hailer, determined and uncompromising.

'Attention, *Sycorax*! You will leave your ship immediately and proceed to *Charkenter*, the vessel closest to you. In exactly three minutes, your ship will be destroyed. There is no negotiation. This order will not be repeated.'

The *Sycorax* crew stole quick glances at their captain on the quarterdeck but remained at their posts. When Tom turned to Sallander, the tall sandsman raised a hand.

'Do nothing, Tom! Say nothing, please.'

'They mean what they say, Pat. They can bring down your ship and still have me.'

'I know.'

'Then let me – '

'Tom, you know they can hear what we say now we've stopped running. Watch the day.'

Tom did that, made himself study the shift of the dark canopies, the Red Wheels lifting and falling, listened to the sigh of breeze about the lines and transoms, to the ticking of hull plates and decking. Then he heard a new sound, a deep far-off droning, muffled but constant – no, building! Like engines, yes. Engines powering up! Not the laser-batts, though that was where he first looked.

Then the land beyond the perimeter burst open. Tom saw camouflage tarps flung aside, lids on makeshift frames, saw ships lift out of the land itself, appearing from ramps and hidden bunkers in the earth like demons, two, four, at least six charvis rising up like magic. Eight now, nine at least!

Not charvis. Not charvolants at all. Atabanques! Armed pirate ships without conventional canopies. Small, lean, raiders, plated, powered and, best of all, invisible to scan. They lofted death-lamps as they came, firing again and again, targeting the canopies of the Haldanian ships, the laser-batts first, enemy lamps second.

And from the other side of *Sycorax*, from the old round stones on the hills, came streaks of light, dazzling to see, accompanied by the scream of laser as they hit the travel platforms of the Order's ships.

No hulls struck yet. No sacrilege. Kites and platforms only. But a promise made. Surrender now! Save your ships!

Tom stared in amazement. Such a plan!

And knew who was behind it. The bringing down of the Gerias Kite, everything.

Tamis Hamm! Captain Ha-Ha himself, the great pirate. Funded by unnamed foreign conglomerates, governments, provocateurs, interested parties, using the same shielding tech he had used at Quaelitz, the same careful planning and deception. Had to be. Could only be. Tamas Hamm and the Restante Lady Say.

'Ha-Ha!' Tom cried, ridiculous to hear, wonderful to shout into the day.

Sallander nodded. 'Aye!'

'But it's the Order, Pat!'

'If not now, when?'

Tom didn't try to answer. If this were truly Captain Ha-Ha, then the Restante Lady Say *would* be with him, no doubt behind this too, the antique creop cylinder bearing all that remained of the ancient tribal dowager, Serenya Say. Only now could Tom grasp the sense of it, the scale and commitment, all that John Coyote had dared not reveal, may not – in true cell fashion – even have known of in all its detail.

Two veering atabanques went down to deck laser from two of the perimeter ships, but those Order ships were immediately struck by the laser points hidden in the rocks. Simple message. Strike our ships, we strike at yours!

Every Red Wheel canopy was burning now, fragmenting, falling, lines fouling then collapsing to the desert as the kite-heads burned away. All nine travel platforms smouldered. Two Haldanian hulls burned where hi-tech had hit them. Others sagged where supporting tech systems in their platforms had exploded upwards and maimed the ships they carried.

As for Ha-Ha's losses, one of the laser-struck atabanques had rolled and tumbled over itself; serious losses there. The other trailed dark smoke, but had righted itself using emergency hydraulics and now limped after the other seven raiders as they darted in and out of the crippled Haldanian fleet, striking at any resisting deck targets with death-lamps and laser.

Within three minutes of the camouflage lids flinging back, *Charkenter* sent up a single yellow kite: the official Stat Prevarican. *We surrender.*

The atabanques ceased firing at once and slipped away into the smoke and heat shimmer, knowing that the blinded sats would be responding, lowering, tethering, sorting options, doing all they could to find their missing ships.

Still, three minutes and such a difference. The fleet was crippled. The laser points in the rocks ceased firing.

And now new pirate forces appeared, men and women in dark fighting leathers wearing fabulous inconnu masks that gave them heads like living jewels. They came from the hills, from the hidden bunkers, bearing their prized Nagamitsu swords and Matsumoto parrot guns. Moved quickly, these jewel-heads, knowing there was little time before new decisions were made and the yellow kite disregarded. They broke into teams and went from travel platform to travel platform, checking that all were truly crippled. Several explosions broke the silence as jewel-head crews made sure of their earlier work.

Tom turned to Sallander. 'Where is *Almagest*? *Laughing Man*? Where's Ha-Ha's ship?'

'Close, Captain. You'll see them soon.'

Them.

Yes, them. The Restante Lady Say. Who would have thought? Now, like this, ending the Line? But then, all life was the journey made, with or without purpose. Better with, knowing, accepting, choosing to choose or let be. But choosing. Obvious to say, but all life was that, filled with whatever came, whatever was served up. It was how you made sense of it, self from it that mattered.

Tom felt it then like part of his ranging thoughts – ghost footsteps in the mindline, coming near, probing, seeking. At last, here it was! He'd expected it, the Order's Clever Men seeking him out. Part of him had hoped for it, wanting to test it all again, needing to. And here it was, the distinctive prickling, tingling, expanding in that other part of him, other self, something softly stepping in the underline. Footsteps. Voice steps. *Are you there? Are you there?*

Gently, subtly, so subtly done. Nothing forced, nothing sudden, nothing like the mind-shock of facing the Chialis Clever Men on the Air that terrible time, the all-engulfing bludgeoning rush of mind-war. There was a softness to this, a caress, a delicate breeze through an open window at night. Nothing harmful or intrusive. Just an asking. *Are you there? You, is it you?*

But prelude to taking him all the same, Tom knew. Having him, crippling him at least. Shutting him down somehow and emptying him out. Had to be. And something important for them to try this now knowing he'd know. Perhaps to see *if* he'd know. To see how far his talent had developed. His greater knowing.

Tom turned to Sallander at the rail. 'Pat, tell those jewel-heads! Tell Ha-Ha! Incapacitate their Clever Men now! It's urgent! They're trying to get me using the mindline. Tell – '

But the softness, the caress, the gentling breeze was everything in the instant. In one immense snuffing of the candle, he was gone.

He fought in that other place, though they did not want him to. Did not want him conscious. Wanted nothing from him then. Wanted their rogue lulled, sightless, mindless, selfless in limbo, a thing to trade back later for the physical Tom. Or else.

But he fought. The part of him they'd used to bring him and trap him there was made for fighting and he flailed at their fiercely gentling dark. Kept self. Kept something of the same core that he'd found small and hard and so determined in Khoumy, that was so bravely and resolutely there in the haunted, self-haunting mind of Green Glaive, that had risen up as a whispering, stripped nugget of being in the Ship's Eye of *Rynosseros* on that worst of days, that was in the essence of Sajanna Marron Best and the creop Lady Say and others, others. Things of the heart. Things of the dance and the living. Things turning in the light he fought to bring to this enfolding *sleep now* darkness. He spun in the tender grip of their minds, remembering. Became the remembering. Like Khoumy, like Glaive and the rest. Telling what was. Simply yet never simply was.

Rose up to lights running, pouring down, coloured lights flashing and flickering, woke to glinting brass and blue in a different darkness, less blue than he liked or wanted, and sharply edged, framed. But a good dark this. With faces. Faces and lights.

Woke to it, knew it, tried to rise to it, swimming up, plunging forward.

'Steady, Tom,' Tamas Hamm said, cancelling a year or more by being there. Captain Ha-Ha, trickster of Quaelitz, creature of another time. 'We flash-stunned every Clever Man we could find. They had to let you go.'

'Go,' Tom said, marvelling. Tamas Hamm! And the lights! The lights and glinting brass. 'Serenya!'

'Hello, dear Tom,' the antique Lady said, and the lights of her

Israel Board flickered like jewels across the face of the life-support column positioned by his bed.

They were all there. Mylo. Starman Guy. Tom was in a cabin, aboard *Almagest*, that lean lizard of a ship, a true pirate ship. *Laughing Man* itself. That was sky through the ports and these were friends.

'Where . . .?'

'At the engagement point,' Hamm said. 'Still cloaked.'

'You brought down the Kite. Had hangars dug. Underground ambush points – '

'More this time, Tom,' Serenya said. 'Tamas arranged for a decommissioned comsat and some other volatile space junk to collide with the tribal sat tracking this operation.'

'You can do that?'

Hamm smiled. 'My helpers and associates occasionally can. Only once in the greatest while. Contingency, though not just for this. But this was worth it. This is the sort of thing it was for.'

Tom sat up, swung his legs over the side of the bunk and steadied himself.

'Tamas – I'm honoured. All of you.'

'You honour us, Tom. You opened it all up again, you and the other Captains. Things were so fixed. A few of us, myself, others, felt we needed to act. The tribes know so much, do so much, control so much. But they have left openings, weaknesses, chinks in their armour. Forgotten that others were using the old tech as well – *against* them, and *because* of them. They grew complacent with their prescriptions and tribal feuds. Did not see that every other status quo is a going backwards. This will chasten them, sober them.'

'Unite them.'

'If you can believe it. But no toner like adversity.'

'We've been called to the Air.'

'You have. The Princes are gathering. It's Convocation. Djuringa business. They say you face five hundred ships now. Can you imagine it? One from every tribe, every State. A thousand more watching, running perimeter. We dare not risk it. Not there. But here we can. They did not want you reaching the other Captains. They wanted you back, wanted you alive if they could manage it.'

'Tartalen is at Azira.'

'And has things to tell you. Officially. We know. That's what did it. Once back on *Rynosseros*, you can declare official summons and go to him. Make it known. The Order dare not stop you then. But there is so little time and you are here, not with your ship. The Captains are due at the Air in two days. The Order means to delay you. You will never reach Azira.'

'Unless I can learn something here. Find something to trade so I *can* reach *Rynosseros*.'

'The way to play it, I agree. Which is why we are still here. Why we have twenty-three Clever Men and as many ships' officers waiting to be questioned. But it has to be soon. The Madupan, San-Mar and Chansallarangi sats have been commandeered. The Emmened grid has released too on tether. We can't stay hidden long.'

'Show me the Clever Men.'

Hamm turned to his officers. 'Mylo, Guy, take Tom to see our guests.'

It was a dazzling display on the commons of *Almagest*: the Clever Men in their suits of lights seated in three lines, the jewel-heads standing about them in their glittering distortion masks, brandishing their parrot guns. A second group – the ships' officers – sat as quietly close by. *Almagest* had kites lofted, both for shade and in case of a quick departure: photonic parafoils mostly, but with six death-lamps, as many laser-batts salvaged from the stores of the tribal ships, and two stranger kites shaped like trefoils – likely cloaking assists provided by Tosi-Go or one of the other sponsors.

Tom put on desert shades against the glare and crossed to the seated Clever Men and officers. He stood so he could address both groups.

'Fleet commander, please stand and declare.'

An older Ab'O among the officers rose to his feet, a fine imposing figure in unmarked fighting leathers, clearly angry but determined to keep his dignity at all costs. 'Senna Gen Tradu,' he said.

'Mission commander, Senna?'

'Fleet.'

'The mission commander, please.'

A Clever Man stood this time, slightly younger than Tradu, equally controlled, dazzling to look upon. 'Akidy Jan Tullus,' he said.

'Other mission command officers, Akidy, Senna? Think carefully.'

'We all serve the Order,' Akidy Jan Tullus said. 'Everyone here can be activated to command. But Senna and I lead this operation. We assign.'

'Good. Then you are responsible.'

Nothing from the older man. A quick nod from the younger.

'Your mission brief, Akidy, Senna?'

'We will say no more,' the older Ab'O answered.

'Then you will all go with *Almagest*.'

'To what possible end, Captain?' Senna asked.

'None of your concern. You have struck at a Coloured Captain.'

Senna's anger showed at last. 'You are a pirate because of Caerdria! You consort with pirates serving outside enemies! You kidnapped the Lady Dusein. Stole a Gerias Kite. We are the legal response to that.'

Tom saw how they meant to play it. No admissions about retrieving lost life experiments, about incepts and scribed DNA. Perhaps they didn't know more, though Tom found that hard to believe. 'I have a long list too, Senna, and I am the official response to it. I am at the point where twenty-three Clever Men dead are now twenty-three less. *You* have taught me to think like this.'

'You wouldn't dare,' Senna said. 'Why would you?'

'Seven ships against five hundred at the Air in two days. Why would you?'

Senna was silent at that, but Akidy spoke. 'Who knows what may happen in light – of this?'

'Then you will use the mindline, Akidy. You will let me know when the call to the Air has been revoked, when the sats are reassigned and the Princes return home. Until then, your liberty is forfeit. You will remain in the hold.'

'What of our crews?'

'Confined to the hold of *Charkenter*.'

'Captain, for how long? Sats are moving, more ships coming in. You know this.'

'Then your principles count your lives lightly.'

And Tom turned and left the commons. Starman Guy immediately shouted orders. The jewel-heads began escorting the Clever Men below.

When Tom reached the main aft cabin, he found Tamas sitting before Serenya's cylinder, almost exactly as he'd left them.

'Tamas, I need to see what they now do. Those Clever Men are prime mind-fighters, but they are scientists and strategists too. They will use the mindline, will know that I expect them to. They will probably wait for me in case I follow, try again to achieve what they started. They have nothing to lose. But I need to monitor what they say.'

Tamas frowned. 'Can you withstand so many?'

'I have no idea.'

The lights ran on the Israel Board. 'What do you hope to learn, Tom?' Serenya asked.

'Whatever I can. When has the Order ever acted this openly?'

'In exactly twenty minutes, we go,' Tamas said. 'You need to reach *Rynosseros*. Get to Azira and stop this. We need to reach sanctuary.'

'Then give me a comm mote to the hold watch crews, both here and on *Charkenter*. If they strike at me, immediate stunning may be needed again.'

In less than three minutes, Tom lay on his bunk in the darkened cabin again with a comm mote at his throat. Serenya remained close by in her support cradle, lights running softly in the gloom, but Hamm went with Mylo and Starman Guy to plan contingencies. They were stranded halfway through an operation and it worried them.

Tom left them to that. With eyes closed and hands folded on his chest, he began the translation. It was like tipping back into himself, and in moments he was in those familiar roiling corridors of aspect, a willing POV in a shadowland that lacked so much form yet seemed to take whatever was brought with expectation and projection. Who knew what it really was, what it remained when no one was there to require sense of it? But at the very least corridors, yes, highways. Ways through.

Nothing waited for him in that underworld that he could tell, though there were lights and voices ahead, energies twisting, glimmering: the Clever Men ranging, calling. Becoming. Powerful translations there, major vectors. And there was urgency everywhere, incredible presence – especially in contrast to the controlled calm of those men earlier.

Mind war ahead, Tom knew. Fiercest of the Heroes: Ashbiani and Colte, Dos and Imbaro, Challamang, Soonol, Anbas and Marduk, aspects assumed and readied.

Tom needed anything but that. If they came, *when* they came, so be it. No choice then. He would learn as he went. But it was the words he wanted, and so worked to unbraid the strands he discovered suddenly there, fingertouch sampling so as not to alert their makers, found that he could do it, no less than those who had come feather-dancing for him earlier.

Much was idiom and dialect, he found, and therefore useless, but he worked through them all, unpicking, sorting the strands.

'. . . tegana mestu pa sokas, argenna re digan . . .'
    '. . . don't see how they could possibly . . .'
    '. . . enja – enja – enja piatu – enja – enja . . .'
    '. . . within twenty-seven minutes. Delaying them further may . . .'
    '. . . to deal with Ha-Ha once and for all if only . . .'
    '. . . Imbaro – Imbaro – Imbaro – Imbaro . . .'
    '. . . secanta a tenti pos a. Ginas by, ginas by intani mas . . .'

'. . . sometimes, but we will need to ask, and perhaps there . . .'

'. . . Vanu – *ay es* Vanu – Vanu – *ay es* Vanu – Vanu . . .'

'. . . as you say, marsan, we can manage more, but only . . .'

'. . . that title. I have sent to activate Carlyr. Sent to confirm . . .'

'. . . some way to distract these guards while Maku uses . . .'

Tom snatched at that one thread, that key word, marsan, and the reply, found it again and forced location, found it where he'd expected it to be, not on *Almagest* at all, but farther off, in the hold of *Charkenter*, yes! He ranged out, making the path, knowing shapes would come just as the words had, Heroes, deadly protectors, vectors, whatever they were. But needed to risk it, needed that one. Saw the Heroes looming – scraps of Gris and Vanu, rare and powerful, bright Colte as well – and so vocalised to Hamm and the others. Intended to at least.

'Be ready *Charkenter*! Hidden Clever Man. Mission commander. I will shout in their minds. One at least will respond. Stun him!'

Tom said it again in case the words hadn't formed, then yelled down the line, sent the shout of naked force, the word suddenly there, a truer name of power than he had realised.

'Rynemonn!'

Heard the chaos ahead, the shrieked response, fierce and involuntary, heard voices muttering, saw the entoptic spread as mindline phosphenes cohered and delivered the yield.

Biaime, it was! A splendid Imbaro, finest he'd seen since Anna Kemp, the great War Owl rising up there on its own. Never truer. Never more deadly. This hidden one was good.

Tom reached for Soonol, Colte or Challamang, any that would come, but even as he struggled for hold on Colte saw Imbaro vanish, wink out just like that, and knew what had happened in the outer world at this dangerous moment.

The hidden Clever Man had been found and stunned.

Tom plunged back through the quickening night, away from *Charkenter*, snatching at threads in case, reading the new turmoil there.

'. . . did you feel it? That was him. That was . . .'

'. . . has struck at us. Has to be, and I say we lose no . . .'

'. . . anyone? Can anyone tell? I'm not getting . . .'

Then Tom struck up into the day, rose up inside his mind and looked out through his eyes again. Hamm was there, and Starman Guy, and Serenya of course, and the aft cabin of *Almagest*, but *Almagest* moving, he knew it at once. Reeling from his quest, Tom frowned at the sensations of motion, bewildered.

'We have him, Tom,' Hamm said. 'Cleven Nos Peray. The real mission commander. He is safely on *Sycorax* and we are moving in time with her. We'll send you across on a bosun's line.'

'What's happened?'

'Fourteen ships coming in. The Madupan sat began random strikes into the zone we made. An extreme solution, but it shows how determined they are.'

'Risking their own ships?'

'Two gone already. But we're on our way. And now you must be as well.'

'Tamas –'

'Tom, there isn't time.'

Tom accepted that, knew that scattering was the only answer. He made himself stand, turned once to face the creop. 'Serenya –'

'What is ever enough, Tom? There is nothing else for it. You will simply have to return.'

'Aye.' He touched the old brass cylinder once and followed Hamm out of the cabin.

Said more quick farewells, then rode the bosun's line – an expedient as old as ships – across to battered *Sycorax*, already running at 60 k's under borrowed kites, and stood with Sallander and Jell on the poop as *Almagest* swung away under its parafoils at last and left the Road again. Tom saw arms raised in farewell, the flash of jewel-heads, then that lean dark ship powering away to whatever far harbour waited to make it safe.

Cleven Nos Peray was below in Sallander's cabin. Soon, soon they would meet.

But now *Rynosseros* was waiting up ahead, Tartalen was at Azira, and ships were gathering at the Air. Perhaps all safe harbours would prove to be illusions now and it was endgame indeed. Perhaps there was only ever freedom in the choosing. But Sallander chose this, and Jell and the rest. And *Sycorax* ran hard under his hands being what any ship was – at the very least.

Tom grasped the old worn rail of the quarterdeck, gripped it so hard his hands hurt, and smiled. Not *Rynosseros*. Not now. Not yet. But the rest of it, aye. Sometimes you needed to recognise a homecoming when you'd made one.

Sewing Whole Cloth

Carlyr walked the last twenty k's, not just because the tree would sense him coming – no doubt it would, despite the dampeners on his harness – but more to frame the event. He knew the importance of what he was about to do. They had briefed him thoroughly at Cana, had brought in the Order to tell it all again. They had wanted to be sure he understood.

And Carlyr savoured the doing. He had accepted the importance of the mission, but had taken his time, deploying only six photonics on his Kesla skiff when he had fifteen to use, had stopped to talk to nomads and stonemen along the way, wanting to be like any other human out on the land.

The stonemen were mostly good company if you could get them talking – or, alternatively, if you could get a word in. Many were natural talkers if not always gifted storytellers. They walked their Roads, clearing away stones large enough to bother passing charvis, bending, snatching up the hard offending gibbers, fitting them into their slings and spinning them off into the hot terrain, keeping the way reasonably clear. Carlyr saw the satisfaction in that, the endless bending, fitting and slinging, or in using their long iron-tipped crackers to poleaxe the stones into shards. Some preferred the hard jarring necessity of that. Even the most practised, the most economical in their movements, did it with the larger stones.

One stoneman, Rocky Jim, had been a true natural when it

came to slinging, bludgeoning, storytelling, and for a time Carlyr had walked and talked with him just to have the man's company, enjoying his stories, the Kesla following along behind on remote. Of course, Carlyr had his harness on active all the while, had maimed – possibly begun killing – some of the very roadtrees this Rocky Jim seemed to prize so much.

Carlyr had come to see himself as being like a stoneman in many ways. You took what came. You did your job as best you could. He even confessed to much of it.

'I'm a new menage levitive,' he had said. 'A trackmere. A new strain of taskers they're making for the ships.'

Rocky Jim was a storyteller. He had liked that unknown word. 'A trackmere? Is that for "track mother" from *mère* or "track master" from the old words *meier* and *meister*?'

'They never said,' Carlyr had answered, though he liked the master part, liking how names always seemed to go deeper than you first thought. 'But we're for the ships.' No need to make the stoneman feel threatened. 'Experts on the Roads in another way.'

'Well, you're welcome here,' Rocky Jim had said in his rough, resonant voice. 'Anything to bring in more life.'

And there it was. Where their missions were forever at odds.

But they had walked on together for another three hours, most agreeably, sharing a meal, sharing the day, Carlyr's harness set on a never-detectable eight percent, shutting down the life in two more ailing roadposts. Two more of thousands upon thousands, true, but a beginning at least.

Carlyr had smiled, and Rocky Jim had smiled back, never suspecting. It was so good to be in the world.

Sycorax made its hard run along the Quaeda Si towards the Air, keeping a steady 110 k's on that ancient Road under a canopy of thirty borrowed kites, finishing the crossing to Azira that the Gerias Kite had begun, but with this vital detour.

That already seemed an age ago, flying above the land. Now Tom was discovering that being back in the world of ships and kites, of heat and the constant drumming of wheels on desert Roads was far less real somehow.

That need to keep it real, to find something, anything he could cling to, made him decide it was time to question his unwilling guest. The battle was two hours behind them – part of the vivid unreality with Serenya and Tamas Hamm and the pirate fleet involved. Doing the Line there had been days, weeks, when nothing marked one day from another.

Now it was different. Things were happening, accelerating, and he had gone from too little to too much and needed to slough away what remained of the hallucinatory edge.

He had recovered from the effects of mind-fighting. And since the battle, this Cleven – such a name! – had been busy. Tom had felt the stirrings in the mindline, had steadied himself whenever he felt those rangings at the edge of consciousness, trying to lock words and namings, the precise form of the attempt. But there were no direct calls for aid, no giving of a focal surge that others could read and track, just a general 'Are you there?' without focus. Cleven's crews and Clever Men had been released with their com tech destroyed. He wouldn't expect rescue yet. Nothing would be done without clarification and his fleet hadn't reported in. But that he hadn't called for aid also meant that he hoped to learn all he could about Tom and this whole enterprise.

And this Cleven Nos Peray was shrewd, so young for a fleet captain, Hamm had said, though probably kept young-looking as a strategy. He was a trickster like John Coyote.

Yes, now was the time. Too much would be happening in the larger world. Tom felt he had perspective enough, had made the hard decisions without benefit of counsel, without Serenya or Captain Ha-Ha or Starman Guy or John Coyote and the others.

He nodded to Pat Sallander and headed below. Sackritter unlocked the door to the main stateroom and locked it again after him.

The Haldanian officer sat before the large stern ports in the cabin's worn but still impressive conversation bay, gazing out at the tempest of *Sycorax*'s rooster tail as the vessel made its run. Back when *Sycorax* was new, such windows had been meant as a luxury for quiet moorings and soft evenings, not for use in transit like this.

'I wondered how long you'd leave it, Captain,' Cleven said, watching the dust boiling astern, twisting off in skeins and coils to make its peace with the land. He did indeed look young, with a good strong face and just the first touches of grey at the temples.

But Tom had seen his power. He took a seat opposite the Ab'O, taking care that the table was between them. 'I have questions.'

'You were far better organised than we expected.'

'Not my doing.'

'I doubt you will convince me of that.'

'As you wish,' Tom said. 'But it seems I have allies.'

'That will now be factored in. We have not made our scheduled report. We had contingency plans.'

'Like what?'

'Oh, like a thousand ships at the Air instead of five hundred.'

'You have that many?'

'There is a levy on the Princes. We arranged to field that many. Plus support on the shores, and the sats, of course. All that went ahead automatically when you struck at us. You should not have touched our fleet.'

'I'm pleased to say that Captain Ha-Ha has his own agenda. Given my situation, I'm grateful for it.'

'But acting for you.'

'I understand you touched *our* fleet first. Killed Traven.'

'And you gave his ship to Anna Kemp. Hardly good sense.'

'There was a quorum.'

'Not yours to give.'

'Not yours to kill.'

'So now, Captain Tom? We are running for the Air no doubt. Trying for *Rynosseros*.'

'I've made decisions.'

'I'm glad to hear it. I need to contact the Order. It is in your interests to allow it.'

'You haven't given your position. Called for aid.'

Cleven shrugged. 'Part of my brief was to learn what I could. Now, that call?'

'First I'd like to hear about my incept program.'

'Captain, I do need to contact my Order.'

'Or what? You'll field two thousand ships? Look where you are, Cleven.' Tom raised his hands to indicate the old cabin, the mismatched furniture, the sand-scoured glass of the ports.

'You do not begin to understand.'

'Then comments like that automatically become meaningless. So, again, who launched my incept program? Take your time. We are trading here. But consider your answers carefully. I have made hard decisions too.'

The *too* might have done it, taken the edge of melodrama, hinted at the desperation and determination involved.

Cleven hesitated, looked out at the boiling tail beyond the glass, watched it twist away for ten, fifteen seconds before meeting Tom's gaze again.

'That's just it, Captain. We field officers do not know who launched that program.' The Clever Man gave a thin smile. 'In case we are captured, you understand. Tartalen will know, but he belongs to the inner councils. The old biotect colleges.'

'We are discussing the Order, Cleven. Their field officers do not expect to be taken. Your cooperation now will determine a great deal.' Tom pointedly left a few seconds too. 'What of Seren Selie? She was part of the same program. A sister.'

'Hardly, Captain. She was an appropriate strategic response to your inception. *Post initio*. We do not know who scribed your original DNA. The choice was to abort the incept or let it continue, then run tests, model equivalents and potentialities. Everyone suspected that you were created by secret factions, by their own fiercest opponents, whoever they might be, even foreign administrations trying to access the Heroes. No one is certain.'

'I've heard they wanted a National Clever Man! As contingency planning!'

'All after the fact, Captain. Useful disinformation. Always claim special planning behind what you *cannot* control. They sampled your DNA and fast-tracked it to have Seren well before you came to term. She was brilliant, precocious and – well – there were problems.'

'Problems?'

'Behavioural not genetic. She wasn't sufficiently tractable, let's say.'

'But Seren is – '

'One of many. More exotic than most. Tribal and female.'

'Then – '

'The only one left extant – only *other* one.'

Tom saw faces, selves, chances.

Kin.

All denied.

'All killed?'

Cleven's face showed no emotion whatsoever. 'Never lived really. Not really. You must understand. We had to know.'

'But killed.'

'Not my choice.'

'So I was fortunate.'

'No, Captain. You were the original.'

'But I can't know that, can I?'

'I suppose you can't. But then why bother with the pretence? Why not just tell you that you *are* a contingency copy?'

'Because given the incentive, given my resources, I may be able to learn something you can't. A useful strategy either way.'

'True. But far more likely that you were given those resources *because* you are that original.'

They sat looking out the windows, staring into the whirlwind. Tom thought of ID-5982-J then, as he often did, often had doing the Line, the great Iseult-Darrian who had given him Blue, had made *Rynosseros* possible.

'There were machines in the darkness,' he said, remembering. 'Talking to me.'

'Many AIs, Captain. Monitoring, companion AIs. Your precious

•

belltree learned of your existence there. It was already giving Hero Colours and ships, elevating Nationals. It convinced Tartalen.'

'Tricked Tartalen.'

'Possibly. Or came to an understanding. An agreement. Quid pro quo. Far more likely.'

'Rynemonn will speak to me.'

'Rynemonn?'

'My name for ID-5982-J. An old Anglo-Saxon name. It means one skilled in mysteries.'

Cleven's eyes narrowed, the closest thing to emotion this man had so far shown. 'Wait. Let me understand this. That is *your* name for the *tree*?'

'I thought it was time the tree had a name.'

Tom tried to allow the silence that followed, but saw that something was seriously amiss. 'What is it, Cleven?'

'There has been a misunderstanding. Where did you get that name?'

'Rynemonn? From searches. Some old text. It's a very old name, from before the Tribation. What's called a Borrowed Jess. Why?'

The Clever Man hesitated. Tom could see he was calculating, measuring some new development against policy, weighing the repercussions of what he now did or said.

'Cleven, look where we are. You've misunderstood something. Others have as well, it seems. But you are here.'

'It is outside my jurisdiction.'

'But look where you are. You are our guest.'

'Captain, I can say nothing. Accept it.'

'Cleven, we can take this into the mindline.'

Again the Clever Man was genuinely surprised, all there in a narrowing rather than a widening of the eyes. '*You* would challenge *me*?'

'I am not quite what I was, and it is close to all or nothing for both of us. I know you can reach Imbaro. Who knows what Heroes I can reach?'

Cleven made his decision. 'It's a code word. Planted.'

'How do you know?'

'Because it was there – in the Madhouse. More than one companion found it.'

'Found it?'

'Heard it used.'

'So why this? Why now?'

'As you say, you are not quite what you were. We have been mistaken, Captain. The name was in the Madhouse. We thought it was the tree's name for you. The Iseult-Darrian would have found it. Known it. Could have placed it.'

'And now?'

'I wait to see what you will do. There has been a misunderstanding. I cannot say more without consulting my Order. I could use the mindline, but if *you* will let me call them – '

'Explain the misunderstanding. What has happened because of it?'

'Captain . . .' Cleven hesitated, sighed. 'You know what a thanatophon is?'

'I met a thanatis once. Nemwyr. A new menage creation.'

'Well, a new levitive has been sent to murder the tree. A special variant equipped for the task. A trackmere.'

'And you're telling me!'

'Because it's too late. It will have already happened. Or will be happening now. If you let me call my Order – !'

'Your Order would do this? Knowing how much it mattered to us!' Tom made himself stay carefully calm, one of the hardest things he'd ever had to do.

'Factions would. Either way, Captain, the world will not be the same. See it as the pendulum swinging back the other way. Please, let me call them! Perhaps there is time.'

'Factions,' Tom said, and knew then why using the mindline would be a last resort. Tartalen might learn of it. A plan could be uncovered. 'There are always factions to blame. Well, there are no factions here.' His rage was driving him, yet all in a ferocious calm. He reached down and drew his ancient gun. 'This is a C96 Broomhandle Mauser, fitted with homotropically-biased Grunweld sights. It was given to me by the menage high-captain, Ajan Bless Barratin.

It is very old. You say *factions* have sent a trackmere, a living weapon. I have this to use. This makes *me* a living weapon.'

'Captain, such theatrics. Surely you are not one to kill the messenger?'

'Cleven, whatever we do has an emblematic value as well, you agree? So I have learned to take the opposite view, something Machiavelli and Sun Tzu would have appreciated. *Always* kill the messenger! It is a powerful symbol. Then those who scheme and plan and send messengers – sometimes even pose as them – suddenly find they no longer have reliable messengers to send or hide behind. That becomes a message too. No more talk. Simplification.'

'Simplification! But so much is lost! Lives. Things you value –'

'And ignorance is bliss!' The anger and despair would cripple him if he hesitated. 'I remember how it was when I thought I was a born human, imprisoned and mindwiped for some offence to the tribes. I can imagine how Alexander the Great must have felt when he cut the Gordian Knot. No more talk. Emblematic action instead. Simplification.' Tom raised the old gun. 'I think you have just become far more valuable as a symbol, Cleven.'

The Clever Man kept his equanimity, just spread his hands in a mollifying gesture. 'I am expendable. I'll just be replaced.'

'By other individuals who will hide any real powers behind the role of messenger, behind factions, whenever it's convenient. Well, what if they too are eliminated, *before* their messages are delivered? Simplification. What if *I* act as if there are no factions, just the Order? Just you? Simplification.'

Tom levelled the weapon, aimed down the sights. The emotion had him, clenching, tearing –

Cleven's eyes widened. 'This is madness!'

– and ebbed. Purpose came. Time and place. Tom slowed to it again. 'No, this is that fascinating point in human affairs where if things no longer matter, if the things you love and cherish can no longer be protected, then – there is an old gun term I have learned – all safety is off! A death can matter more now than a life. You have helped teach me this. You have brought me this.'

Cleven sensed the danger. 'Captain, perhaps I *can* do something. Give me a chance. We may still save the tree – '

'But for how long, Cleven? Until next time? Till the next threat, the next expedient act? You said it yourself. There are factions. The convenience of factions. You have them. The tribes do. Do you know *Macbeth*?'

'Macbeth? No. What's a macbeth?'

'An old story. From an old drama narrative, like an ode or a sonnet. A character called Macbeth reaches the point of no return in his affairs where he says: "To go back were as tedious as to go o'er." I am at that point, Cleven. Traven is dead. *Rynosseros* has been slain! *Rynosseros*! Things I love are dead or at risk, certainly threatened. I will be like Macbeth, like Alexander. I will simplify now however I can.'

'I can do things. Help you!'

'I doubt you can convince me.'

'Keyword: Sunstar! Cleven OST Sunstar! Enter it now!'

Tom held the gun steady, fascinated at how resolved he was, how truly decided, but there on both sides, yes *and* no. He spoke the activation code.

'Lethe. Cleven OST *Sunstar*.'

The old ship-screen on the table between them darkened, seemed to freeze on a black field.

'There are interdicts to get past!' Cleven said.

'Go on.'

'Madhouse systems.' Cleven saw the look on Tom's face. 'It's the Order, by *Baiame*! You can't just expect – ah!'

The screen cleared. A red wheel sat on the black.

'It will have to be my voice!' Cleven said.

'Very well. Lethe. Single restricted.'

Cleven didn't hesitate. '*Rynemonn*!'

Mostly it was dates that spilled down the screen, but pirated, spoiled, no clear users given. But hundreds of references, thousands. Rynemonn spoken, carrying meaning, unknown meaning, the user or users masked. Just years of dates, days, true nights and false.

Tom lowered his gun. 'As good as nothing.'

'Agreed,' Cleven said. 'Without the payload, without source identity, as good as nothing. May I give another command? There is something else.'

'Lethe. Single restricted.'

Cleven spoke immediately. 'Lock *jacobi 924.*'

The display flashed and held, even as Tom said: '*Jacobi!* The bioform at *Trale!*'

'Correct. It gave you something. Showed you your Star and gave you something.'

'But what?'

'Exactly, but what? A communication, something. Here is our Order, making, building, singularly committed to its tasks. And suddenly this. Our own discards, our cast-offs doing this. One of our own levitives – to use that useful menage term – receiving this communication, giving communication back, we suspect, all *via the mindline*, but responding to a deep programming we believe we did not put there.'

'You *believe*. You are not sure.'

'No,' Cleven said. 'Once we were. No longer.'

Tom couldn't help himself. 'And what about your factions?'

Cleven's smile was wintry. 'Perhaps. That has stayed our hand many times where the Coloured Captains are concerned. But it's more a case of your old AI/AL trap, something else you will appreciate from your days of blissful ignorance, I'm sure. Things you've created acting beyond what you made, what you can control.'

Tom felt himself pulling back, calming now. 'The Order must hate this.'

'Absolutely. It is infuriating in the extreme. Frightening as well.'

'Cleven, what did the *jacobi* give me?'

'Without a deep scan, without hunting you via the mindline, we will never know. Maybe not then. We cannot assume that it even went to your conscious mind at all.'

'But something important?'

'You felt it was. You still do. There was a time when you would have come to us for answers; now we come to you.'

'With nine ships! Hardly a respectful approach, Cleven.'

'We needed to be safe. Old habits die hard. Captain, why haven't you required that I hold a monitor through all this? Verify whether I lie or not?'

'Because that tech comes from what the Order makes available to the tribes. I trust very little these days.'

Cleven was frowning.

'What?' Tom asked.

'The tree. *Rynemonn.* I would have thought that you'd try to send assistance. Called for it. You haven't. You don't believe me?'

'Of course. But why would you mention it if I could do anything in time? That is why I drew my gun.'

'Being a macbeth.'

'And an Alexander. You killed *Anoki.*'

'He broke our laws.'

'Tried to help me.'

'Betrayed a sacred trust.'

'Sacred? There's a word! *Kept* a sacred trust more likely.'

'Not how we see it.'

'Yet *you* betray that same trust. Kill the things you have made.'

'We need to police what we have done. Be responsible enough to be sure that we do.'

'Why do you? Because it's yours? We don't have a monitor. No one can hear. Why do you, Cleven?'

Cleven said nothing, but Tom knew the answer.

Because it's ours! Ours to make. Ours to control. Ours to take.

'Tell me about Tartalen,' Tom said.

'He is at Azira.'

'No, about his part in this. Is he a faction?'

Cleven read the moment, saw the rawness of the emotion held in check and did not smile this time. 'He – has affection for you. He was appointed, made responsible. *Became* responsible. Has remained so. He would prefer that you – be allowed to continue.'

'Though a risk.'

'To fulfil your destiny. Whatever destiny completes this, one way or the other.'

'Do I have his DNA?'

Cleven laughed at the absurdity, a short harsh bark of surprise, then tipped his head to the side, openly marvelling.

'What a thought! You really are seeking a father figure, aren't you?'

'Not possible?'

'Just something *I'd* never considered. Not even as contingency. Others must have no doubt . . .?'

'But it's possible?'

'Of course. He's spoken on your behalf often enough. Urged forbearance.'

'When we meet *Rynosseros*, we will go to Azira.'

'What happens to me?'

'Let's wait till we hear what your factions have done.' Tom sheathed his pistol and stood.

'Then I can assume –'

'Cleven, nothing has changed. The safety is off.' Tom told the computer to shut down and turned to leave the cabin.

He was expecting it when it came and was as ready as he could ever be. It was mind-shock without shape or form, a shout in his mind such as he had used to locate Cleven on *Charkenter*, but far more focused and powerful. Ready as he was, Tom was flung forward, barely raised his hands in time to push clear of the bulkhead. Turned even as Cleven shouted again and stunned him further. Even with his own wall raised and ready, it struck him down.

But Cleven had overreached himself. Even as he struck with such raw force, he sought aspect as well, reached out for *Imbaro* or *Soonol* – such power! – but it divided him, distracted him just enough. It let Tom yell on the physical plane – 'Black dog, Sackritter! Black dog!' – a ship-spiek as old as National charvis, even as he sent a shout back at Cleven in the underline, pure instinct, all he could manage.

It broke the translation. And before Cleven Nos Peray could rally, Sackritter was through the door, borrowed parrot gun already on stun and firing, and Cleven collapsed even as Tom did.

Carlyr could have stayed with Rocky Jim a while longer, braiding in his own larger purpose, sharing more of that special time. But he sailed on in the early afternoon, made two more brief stops, then shared a campfire with the crew of a night-ported National charvi, *Araluen*, out of Port Allure, a ship limited to day runs. He played nomad there just to test whether they'd accept. They did, seemed to anyway, and the next day Carlyr completed the last leg of his journey, parked, set the keep-aways, and began the final twenty k's on foot.

Now the briefing at Cana was vivid again, the careful instructions. The words of the Order too. As if there could be any uncertainty or lack of resolve with something like this.

That stoneman had it right. *Trackmere*. Track master. Carlyr was new in the world, voracious in his thirst for knowledge, and he liked that. As his skiff finally disappeared from sight beyond a rise, he paused to adjust his kill settings. Eighty percent would do it, they had said. But Carlyr set it to maximum, the full hundred. If there were other roadposts on the way, he meant to have them too. Blanket their signals before they could know what was happening, before they could tell others, then rip out their lives. Yes, you did your job as best you could. Carlyr meant to have them all.

In the four hours Tom lay in the after fall-fugue, recovering, rallying, *Sycorax* kept up its run towards the Air, towards the quiet salt and sand beaches where *Rynosseros* waited with the ships of the other Coloured Captains.

With Tom barely conscious, drifting in and out of the fugue, Sallander lofted the final gift from Tamas Hamm – a blue rhino head on ochre – and now that kite sat point beyond the break, beyond Sallander's own faded pinwheel hawk on green.

Twice smaller tribal fleets tried to intercept, were sent to do so; twice Sallander radioed warning that this was a de facto State of Nation *and* tribal Colour ship on mission. Both times those tribal fleet captains moved in regardless, ready to test everything in these uncertain times, only to receive warnings from a *Tosi-Go* comsat. 'Watching and listening, noble captains. We will strike you down for the breach.'

It shocked those captains, more so their listening principals, to know that non-tribal interests were so actively engaged, so intently mindful of tribal law. It reminded them that the world *was* watching something this momentous, that a greater status quo may indeed be at risk.

The Air had always been the official way. The tribes had made it so. It was to be the way still.

So poor battered *Sycorax* plunged on, and Tom rallied in the lazaret as he heard every broadcast and tried not to think of ID-5982-J. *Rynemonn*. Messages came from Cleven Nos Peray to him there. The Clever Man demanded to see him, asked to see him, begged to see him when he was able. Finally sent something worthy of the trade, a few words on a scrap of foil.

I can tell you what it is about your incept that worries us so.

Tom lay in his bunk in the lazaret and knew he would risk it, would expect Cleven to hold back most of the details. Even try to take him again. Who could blame him? The Clever Man was guarding his world, so much that defined him. Cleven hadn't tried to take Tom while he slept. Line of sight was always best, but Cleven could easily have come for him while he drowsed, rested. Or perhaps had only recently recovered himself. The Clever Man would deal with after-fall fugue quickly, but the effects of stunning from a parrot-gun were something else.

More than ever Tom knew he would have to piece everything together himself, as much as he could. Join the parts, stitch the fragments into a whole. Perhaps Tartalen would help, had summoned him to *Azira* for precisely that, it seemed, and so had triggered these desperate measures from others in the Order. Alarming the Princes. It made sense.

Tom believed he knew much of it already – the only thing it could be. The jacobi had reached out, sent a greeting, but it had also found a point of connection, something it could use as one, *could* connect with. Again, it made sense. In trying out its life, in reaching out to more scribed DNA, it had activated something present in that scribing, something dormant, latent, perhaps already accelerating.

The capacity to participate in mind-war. To reach the Heroes, yes, and use a name of power left there long ago. *Rynemonn*.

For that name *had* been there too, it seemed, not just tagged to a Borrowed Jess or a scrap of information casually brought to his attention. A code word left, laden, freighted with purpose, just as Ship and Star had been, but *meant* to remain dormant. Yet when brought out, synonymous with him, something with a natural connection. Something innocently coaxed into life by the jacobi, triggered by the neuraesthenic properties of Seren's poison or her kiss, or something in the fairground sim prepared by *Anoki*; it went on and on. He couldn't know.

But he had fought on the Air as a mind-fighter when he'd first met Sen-Mati, had used mind-war then, some wild form of it, had just now fought the fleet and Clever Men from the Order, had found Cleven Nos Peray and faced him in line of sight and survived.

And, earlier, unknowing, had given that name to ID-5982-J, who must then have acted as that, triggered more things than Tom could possibly know. The death of Traven for one, directly or indirectly! The raising of a thousand ships. Where did it begin and end?

Tom could no longer rest. He swung off the bunk and dressed, then crossed the ship's modest commons to the main cabin. Sackritter and Marcham were both at the door this time, weapons drawn, and this time the door remained open when Tom entered. Once again Cleven was seated before the aft windows, the ship's tail boiling beyond. He stood this time, respectfully, sat only when Tom was seated.

'You understand that I had to try,' he said, without further apology.

'I expected it, Cleven. I expect you to keep trying.'

The Clever Man gave the ghost of a smile and nodded. 'It is my world.'

'And you are held to account, I suspect. But now the guns are set to kill.'

'Partly why I tried what I did. Your anger. Your talk about your gun.'

'I mean *their* guns this time, Cleven.' He gestured back at the open door, at the crewmen waiting there. 'And there are cameras running. We have you on scan. Not how any of us wish it to be, but if you will not – cannot – bend . . .' Tom shrugged. 'You have something to tell me about my incept.'

'You have a sensor implanted in your forehead.'

'A what?'

'A bio-organic sensor mote near the pineal gland, highly sophisticated. No ferric components, no nano rejection factor. Integrated. It has been there from the time of your incept and we have no idea who put it there or, alternatively, why your DNA was scribed so it would be there.'

Don't believe you! You're lying! Who put it there? Who did?

Both strands of thought rushed through his mind, though Tom spoke none of it.

'You're afraid the Order has been compromised. Infiltrated. You attacked me to provoke a response in extremis.'

Cleven seemed glad to have it said so bluntly, so openly. 'Mostly that, yes. And haven't continued to strike you down because I am now inclined to accept that you have not been aware of it. You are more than a sensitive, more than a National Clever Man.'

The jacobi linked to it!

Tom's suspicions had been correct. 'Med scans have never showed it.'

'Which tells us something else. That your nano spread is tailored to shield its existence. We know about it because it was discovered in the Madhouse while your nano was still adapting to do that additional task. It flagged extraordinary functions, highlighted the modification. Tartalen knew.'

'Then Seren could have –'

'She did not. She knows nothing of it. We verified that –'

'Cleven – !'

' – long before you met her, Captain. She is safe at Tarpial. Despite Tartalen's demands, we persevere.'

'I must speak with Tartalen. For all our sakes.'

'I might agree, but many others do not. But you are on your way to do so, though it means your fellow Captains face the Air challenge without you.'

'I could use com. Speak to him now. You have the connection.'

'Captain, such a call would never get through. Too many interested parties would see to that.'

'You relish this, don't you?'

'For all sorts of reasons, yes, but not as much as I did. Most of all I want it ended. The Captains. This mystery. I want to know what *Rynemonn* is, why you named a rogue belltree that, why you shouted it as a mind-war integer when you struck at me.'

'I don't know.'

'I think I believe you. But you have had it all your days. While wearing surveillance tech for others, other motes and tech assists at other times, you have had that too. Reading all the while.'

'Recording?'

'Who knows? Perhaps not. Activated only when needed perhaps. Simply there.'

'You aren't sure of any of this.'

'Not at all.'

'It's not . . .?' Tom hesitated.

'A coterminous personality? No.'

'You're so sure.'

'One of the first things they checked in the Madhouse. This is wholly and solely you.'

'Power readings?'

'Bio-organic, as I said. It is indistinguishable from the power of the brain or central nervous system, the electromagnetic fields of the body's organs. You power it. It *is* you.'

Tom felt enormous relief. 'You say. Not implanted?'

'Seems not. Though that's how we're conditioned to see it. How many still see it.'

'Then it's in your interests – the Order's best interests surely – to let me reach Tartalen.'

'Again, I might agree. Many others do not. Tartalen has always had too much influence. Too much power. Too many secrets.'

'Which is why the Air challenge eventuated.'

'Partly. Most would say that the elevation of Anna caused that.'

'Very convenient though, wouldn't you say? Cleven, what more can you tell me? What more can you do for all of us?'

The Ab'O watched the dust boiling beyond the port. 'My concern now is what you will do with me. I would like to live.'

'We will release you when we reach *Rynosseros.*'

'Can I believe that?' It clearly surprised him.

'Unless you strike at me again, yes.'

'What of your hard decisions? The killing of the tree?'

'I try to tell myself that you are a patriot. I am ashamed of you. As a human you are lacking, but you think you are doing the right thing.'

'You are ashamed of me!' Surprise and anger flashed in the dark eyes.

'Of course. Something is missing. I am sorry for you.'

And Tom stood and left the cabin and went out to be in the day.

Charvolants still used this secondary Road, so Carlyr was only a little surprised to see a stoneman up ahead, tiny with distance but recognisable by the long cracker athwart his back. The distinctive walk-rhythm confirmed it, the bending, fitting and slinging.

Another time, another day, Carlyr would have quickened his pace to join him, but this wasn't something he wanted now – a travelling companion, a witness to what had to be done.

Carlyr slowed his pace. Then, bending to the exigencies of the situation, he finally moved to the side of the Road, found some rocks that gave a little shade and settled against them, pulling the wide brim of his traveller's hat low over his eyes against the harsh light. Even as he rested, he heard – probably imagined – the far-off strike of the stoneman's cracker against the gibbers, even the thrum and whoosh of the sling as a stone was flung aside. He found those things comforting. Reaffirming. It was good to know that the world went on in the little things people did. In what he did too. What he was doing now. He drowsed, knowing it would be soon.

It was ironic that Cleven's presence made possible the night-run, allowed *Sycorax* to reach the great fighting ground of the Air at dawn and without further incident. Ironic too that four tribal charvolants provided escort for the last thirty k's, so that *Sycorax* was allowed to use the old trail of the Gaenea – the McCubbin in old National naming – and so reached the salt beach at Toley with three hours to spare. There on the old salt and sand shore in the early light stood Afervarro's *Songwing*, Lucas's *Serventy*, Glaive's *Quicksilver*, Massen's *Evelyn*, with Doloroso's *Albatross* and Anna's recently inherited *Manticore* beyond them. *Rynosseros* stood further out still, closest to where the Gaenea rejoined the Quaeda Si and continued on to Azira.

Sallander had called ahead, and the long tables on the commons of *Songwing* were set up again and already crowded, the Captains and their crews waiting under awnings as *Sycorax* rolled in.

They made a splendid sight, the seven Coloured ships drawn up like this. In all likelihood, it was the last time they would be together this way, the last time their crews would share talk and time and braid their lives. In three scant hours, they would enter the vast salt lake, go out among the old wrecks left from centuries of tribal war, and face their destiny.

Now *Sycorax* was here, bringing their missing Captain at last, and such a reunion followed – as heartfelt, riotous and bittersweet as circumstances allowed – and it went in stages. Even as Cleven was sent on his way on an old four-kite skiff, with nothing more said than farewell, Tom crossed to *Rynosseros*.

They were all watching as he approached: Scarbo, Shannon,

Strengi, Rimmon and Hammon, not yet at the long tables on *Songwing*, not when there was this to do. *The* homecoming.

Smiles first and the joking.

'See what happens when you go off on your own!' Scarbo called when Tom finally reached the ladder.

'Flying yet!' called Rim, when he was on the travel platform. 'An aviator. You make it hard to keep up!'

And from Shannon, when Tom was on the rungs and climbing: 'You came in for that Tarpial junket and didn't stop by!' Playing moody, miffed, disgruntled.

A Catalan blessing, curse or both from Strengi when Tom first reached the commons (always playing one of the Spanish Exiles), followed by: 'Another fine mess!', key line from one of the ancient entertainments they plundered for their deck-spieks.

A simple 'Welcome home, Tom!' from Hammon, youngest, still not easy with the ragging and jokes. Tom was his first captain ever. Possibly first and last with what was coming. All there in what didn't need to be said by any of them, not yet.

Easy words then, quick replies, treasured spieks to span the days and make it right. Embraces, longer than the usual, more edged on such a day, then the sitting around. But all measured with the deadline approaching.

Harder words then.

'We've discussed it,' Scarbo said. 'Need you to have this. Wouldn't be right any other way. The others agree. You may be able to bring back help. Get us a reprieve. It has to come from the Order. It happens.'

Tom sat among them, let them see he was listening, turning to face whoever spoke. They all did.

Then it was across to *Songwing* and the whole thing over, and seeing Anna there with the others, belonging so well. It put a new edge on the desperation, and touching her, too, was urgent and strange.

No self-recrimination in her, no blaming herself now, but Tom sensed the ghost of where it had been. How could it not? But how could it stay? They had known what they were doing at Balin, all of them.

'We get our chance,' she said, as bluff and torn as the rest, because words couldn't cover this now. 'The world watches more than ever.' All true. So true among the truths.

No time to take it further, no time for anything with them finally down to an hour but renewed strategy talk, renewed urgings with the refrain: 'Let us give you this.'

The six Captains had had their countless genome/DNA printings done well before, had sat through proliferation recordings that would haunt the airwaves for as long as the foreign sats could carry them. Taunting ghosts to remind the world: this time must not pass easily, must not slip away. State of Nation had done its best, too, filed their protests, called in the official observers, though these remained confined to the coastal cities and could only watch what the friendly sats gave.

Then, when half an hour remained and still nothing had been finally decided, they went to their separate ships, and left it to the Gold Captain, first among them, as Tom knew they would.

Aftervarro judged the time, crossed to *Rynosseros* and found Tom at the quarterdeck rail, staring to port out across the vast fighting ground. There were no new words, not really, just this final saying of them.

'Nothing on the tree?' Tom asked.

'Not yet. Corven's *Demeter* is close. May reach it in time. We'll know soon.'

'But not answering?'

'It never has. Always suited itself, you know that.' Afervarro left a ten count. 'Tom, Tartalen is at Azira. Whatever has happened has made him think it's important you know things. He's probably defying the Order, may be putting himself at risk. It has to be important.'

Tom had no new words either. 'Hasn't before. Years of nothing, now he can tell. Why, Phaon?'

'Can't know. Can't know Cleven's place in this either. Just that it's playing out. That you surprised him. But a summons is what it is, an official benefice. There would be outside scrutiny all the way, a monitored official escort. You would likely be safe there and back.'

'While this is happening,' Tom said, regarding the great sweep of the land, dazzling white under blue, flecked with tips of black when you really looked, the wrecks of ships that had fought and died over the years. 'While you go out there.'

'It was always borrowed time, Tom. Since Traven, more clearly so. See us as buying time now. You may get back. We can divide the fleet. Break rules, see what they do. Try some strategies we've been putting together.'

'What, Phaon? What? Divide yourselves? Splay formation? Wedge? Single arrow, what? You think there will be time? This isn't Caerdria? Most definitely isn't.'

'We will call the tribal ships to us. Officially call them. Some may change sides. It's possible. We have Anna – '

'Against how many Clever Men?'

'Tom, who knows what will happen?'

Tom smiled grimly but didn't speak.

Afervarro leant on the rail. 'Against a thousand, what can it matter if we're six or seven? Let us give you this.'

'It's important we're together. That we're seen – '

'And it matters that you want that, Tom. But the outcome won't change. There is no right time. No perfect time for any of us. But this way something continues. This way you have questions answered, answers we've all had in our lives but you haven't. Please let us give you this. Go to Azira. Hear what Tartalen has to say. Come back if you can.'

'Three hours each way, Phaon – '

'Less knowing you and your crew. You can still come back. Early or late, what does it matter? They'll allow it. They want you here. It's the only gift we have, Tom. We dearly need to give it.'

'Phaon – '

'Barely eight years! Take the gift! Honour us! It's all that makes it worth it, don't you see?'

They watched the salt lake together as if there was time.

'Delay them, Phaon,' Tom said then. 'Do anything to waste the day. Hide in the wrecks. Run up to Madiganna, anything. Promise you'll delay them.'

'Aye. We'll do that.' He squeezed Tom's arm once then went to join his ship.

Carlyr saw the tree ahead, this powerful, meddlesome ID-5982-J, which had caused such trouble, proved so durable. A sky-strike could have put an end to it, Carlyr knew, or ship-tech from passing charvis. But more than tribal sats watched this place now. There was Chandrasar and Tosi-Go, Mikel and Sesta, clients, allies, interested parties. Those sats could see the smallest laser strikes if they cared to, could see men with cutters and torches, hammers and blades for that matter, given allocations and alignments. The world knew the story of this tree and what it had done.

So Carlyr played an innocent nomad who just happened to be wandering this back-Road and chanced upon the famous construct. It's what nomads did. No sat could read his kill-tech. He would wander past, focus direction for twenty, thirty seconds, then vanish into the land. Later he would call his skiff to him and sail back to Cana. Later. Now there was this to do.

At 0900 the advance order came through com. The thousand had entered the lake at Cresa and were approaching, a spectacle like none ever seen on the Air, so many ships here for this particular kill. At Toley the six had already lofted battle canopies, signatures deployed among death-lamps and parafoils, everything trimmed for speed and minimum fire damage. Now *Songwing* began moving down the Toley strand, followed by *Serventy*, then *Quicksilver* and *Evelyn*, finally *Albatross* and *Manticore*. That was how they entered the lake, with Afervarro leading, but then – clear message to all – Anna's *Manticore* advanced to point, with Afervarro at her left and Lucas to her right. *Evelyn* took port flank, *Albatross* moved to starboard beyond *Quicksilver*. The ships of the seven Captains had always tended to stay apart, meeting in twos and threes. They had never moved like this, not six together, but they managed it skilfully considering and it, too, was something to see.

Such a hard leave-taking, though little was said, and better for all once it was happening at last. Harder for *Rynosseros* turning away, angling off along the Gaenea to rejoin the Quaeda Si, to seek miracles and answers another world away.

Learning that the ship-core of *Rynosseros* had died had been hard. Knowing ID-5982-J had fallen. That Traven had, and Anoki and aerotropts and so much else. This was the hardest.

Scarbo did what he could to make business, found real tasks to distract them all, all but Tom, who was left to the never-enough of his dilemma. The crew worked quickly and well, took *Rynosseros* to a 100 k's in record time, put speed and ever more distance between them and the Air, getting beyond the beginnings and into the doing. This ship. This deck. This time. Hardest for them, too, in all the different ways, none of it spoken. Only the doing mattered now.

Carlyr saw the tree on its rise, standing back from the Road where it turned by some old rocks. He glanced once at his harness settings, unnecessary, habit and instinct playing out, just what you did. Nothing could be left to chance.

Soon now. Not even five minutes. The Road had followed the old watercourse for the last five k's. Now it made the gentle rise to the tree. All easy.

The stoneman appearing atop the rise surprised him, but was hardly an issue. The rocks had been hiding him was all. He hadn't moved on.

Carlyr had his weapons, his readiness, his training. It was the recognition that did it, made him hesitate. How could it be – *that* stoneman, *that* smile, the hand raised in greeting?

By the land! Rocky Jim! It was! But *here*. Here!

How could it be? He had been, what? – ninety k's away at least! Would have needed time, more time than he'd had, would have –

He had been brought!

Even as Carlyr reacted, the man's sling was there, spinning in the hot air, making its blur, its lightning flash.

Not now! Not like this! Carlyr thought. Not before –

But the lightning was there, small, hard and shockingly real, and all that Carlyr had hoped and dreamed and ever sought to be snapped back into night.

They were running hard when Strengi called up from com. 'Lucas is hit!'

Tom gripped the rail. 'Down?'

'Burning. Still running. A distance strike. But they're closing. Committed.'

Lucas.

Scarbo laid a hand on his friend's shoulder. 'They understand, Tom. They're giving this. You deserve answers too.'

Tom's hands never left the rail. 'Aye. But Lucas.'

Words so simple that again there was silence of a fashion, accepting, caring silence set in the flow of wind, the roar of wheels on sand, other ship-sounds, ineffably dear.

'Forget the three hours!' Shannon said, dealing with the moment. 'I figure two and a half if we push it; two and a half getting back!'

Tom looked about him, saw the talk for what it was, that they truly and keenly understood, knew this too was right. That more than one thing could be. More than one. Accepted that it wasn't the choosing now, just the working through.

But there was the deck, and the wind in the lines, and the sun drawing the kites – that kite! – into the empyrean, and the new drumming thunder of the wheels. Sunlight flash off mica and gypsum. Red gibber. Life and light. Choosing after all.

There is no right time. No perfect time for any of us.

And behind, when he did look back through scan, there were the closing lines of ships, battle canopies flung like toys, startlements, deadly gardens upon the blue, with twisting, spinning death-lamps, so many diamonds in the fiery white gold of the day.

The only moment.

It took him back, forward, completed itself.

As human does.

'Hard about, Ben! Bring us round!'

'But Tom!' Scarbo cried. 'This is –'

'Hard about!' Tom was grinning, laughing. 'It doesn't matter!'

'But we understand. We all do!' Shannon cried, even as Scarbo worked the helm and the ship slowed and began the turn.

'I know you do. I know.' He brought up his hand, open palm. 'See what I have, Rob. See what I already have!'

There were frowns, smiles, nods, acceptance, all in moments as the ship completed its one-eighty and plunged back along the Gaenea. Simple. All simple now. The clear, simple words of a lonely tree in another time.

> *What is in the empty hand but the universe entire,*
> *What is in the eye but all there is.*
> *What is for the heart but the only fire,*
> *And for the soul? The only moment. This.*

Now *Rynosseros* ran, sending out proclaimed intent – this is what we do! – so that all could hear. The Gaenea still flanked the Air; a thirty degree adjustment was all it took.

The crew plundered the kite lockers, something else they *could* lay their hands to. The ship ran under a blossoming mantle, two score kites and more as Scarbo, Rim and Hammon sent them aloft: parafoils, Haikkokus, bright Sodes and Demis, Chinese Hawks, Jacob's Ladders climbing on the sky in tiers, one, then another, with angels, wind-thieves, suncatchers and racing footmen and, highest of all so the tribes and sats could see, the rhino head, blue on ochre. Colour ship here!

They were at 120 k's, heading for 130. Boiling behind was a rooster tail, bloody red becoming white as they entered the Air at last, ran on, on, towards the converging battle lines. The wheels roared, the lines thrummed their own travel song. Deep down the ship cores, the nested, borrowed lives, sang and sang.

The other Captains and crews read her approach soon enough, read choices, more than one, allowed not just closure but slowed their advance so *Rynosseros* would reach them in time. They did more, trimmed their battle canopies, sent up their own signatures and brights as well, their best and finest in tiers and blossoming geometries, so the six ships – the seven! – were like crowns, birds, brilliant flowers, confections of light and colour.

And while – late to the dance – Tom would have kept to the left of the line, two words from Afervarro at centre, first Colour, Gold, flashed on com: *Take point*, and led *Rynosseros* to the middle of the chevron. It was a beautiful manoeuvre, done perfectly this once (such is the irony of desperation!), saw the chevron extend and *Rynosseros* plunging in tandem with Anna on *Manticore*, then ahead, needfully ahead, taking point.

Oh, if you could see them as they ran, the seven against the dazzling thunder of the thousand, a few bright stars before the crackling storm, six kilometres becoming five, four, steadily falling to nothing in the beat, beat, beat of the dance. Oh, if you knew how all across the land we sang in our thousands, not unison, no, fervent discord, sang and sang, all of us that lived, the greatest and the least, startling nomads, travellers, vagrant stonemen, delighting so many who had forgotten to remember we were always there.

And if we could show you how it was at that moment. Our Captain knew with all his heart, how it was at the last, before the fleets met and the sky, yet again, rained fire and ruin, and the chevron plunged into the fire *we* made – the belltrees – how the tribes, the humans in their pride and disregard, had forgotten that, having tasted life, we too would strive, learn, borrow, use everything we had, would rise up and protect our own, what *we* had made.

Our Tom Rynosseros. Ours.

Stone Gift

●

Robert N. Stephenson

Myulli gazed awestruck at the distant Kyjihm mountain range. Her young eyes were wide and glistening as she stared at the craggy peaks. The great, black walls frowned under the weight of the billowing dark sky. 'It brings Gallerra,' whispered Myulli.

'It will bring nothing but much needed rain,' growled Fiali, Myulli's uncle. He wore orange robes, was tall, lean and cantankerous.

'But the message on the stone of coming? Gallerra prophesied . . .'

'You know nothing about the stone, child,' growled her uncle. 'Every storm brings with it the prophecy of Gallerra and the Waiters' usual claims to have seen it foretold in the stone.' Fiali looked down on the girl. 'The Waiters are fools, Myulli, and the sooner you see them for what they are the better.'

The storm clouds embraced the mountains, cutting off their tops. They swallowed the sky like a growing, angry mouth. The range was shrouded with dread. A vibrant contrast against the black and grey cliffs were the Pellin tree forests, their brilliant red foliage spread out like a fluorescing fan at the foot of the ranges. It was through this forest that Gallerra had fled during the Great Expulsion.

Fiali turned to look down into the girl's face. 'Not since the Great Storm sixty years ago has anything come from such prophecies.' The memory of the time eased back like a drop of water over parched

311

earth. He knew these clouds. He shook his head and looked down at the girl. 'All the sky has ever brought is rain.' He offered a faint smile. 'Today will be a wet day, let us go inside and throw some bones to pass the hours.'

'No!' Myulli stamped her bare foot. 'Jashm showed me what to look for, Uncle. She knows things about Gallerra.' Myulli's eyes sparkled with wonder and excitement at the mere mention of the ancient oracle. 'As a Waiter, she knows the signs, she knows . . .'

'Enough of this foolishness, child. Your sister has filled your head with her misty truths and bleary-eyed visions. If this is Gallerra's return where is she? Where is your all-knowing sister?' Myulli looks more like her father each day, he thought. The tightness of the girl's square face and the liveliness of her green eyes, even the subtle wave in her shoulder-length hair resembled her father's dark locks.

'Jashm knows!' Myulli stamped her foot again. She winced as her bare foot scraped against the raised edge of a paving stone. 'You'll see it is so, Uncle. You will see.'

Fiali turned from the girl, shrugging off her childish indignation and started back towards the house. He knew the truth about the Great Storm, he knew the truth behind Gallerra and he also knew it was best kept secret.

The family dwelling stood barren amongst the orchard of blood fruit trees, its windowless walls of ochre stone and mud mortar deepened in colour and texture under the fading light. Fiali watched as the matted leaves of the thatched roof shivered under the caress of the increasing bluster. 'Come now, child, before it rains.'

'But . . .'

'I said enough!' Fiali stood, his back towards Myulli, facing the heavy slatted wood door. He waited for the following steps of his niece, but all he heard was the strengthening breeze brushing against the wide leaves of the blood fruit trees. Foolish child, he thought to himself as he headed to the door.

Beneath the dim light of an oil lamp, Jashm wove the thick strands of spun balla ox hair. A small loom, held deftly in her slight hands, held a good day's work. Jashm hoped to finish the hat before the next harvest gathering so that her father would not suffer under the parching heat of the sun. From beyond the door she heard her Uncle's voice bellowing. What has Myulli done now? she wondered. With haste she stowed the half-finished hat under her thick woollen clothing. Maybe her father's early return from the fields had hastened Uncle Fiali's coming inside. Jashm turned on her stool to face the door.

'Jaja,' called Fiali, opening the door and pulling back the draft curtain.

'Yes Uncle,' she answered. Her voice was soft, so as not to disturb the peacefulness of the room. Jashm's bald head shone under the flickering yellow lamplight and her blue eyes sparkled, reflecting the small flame.

'What have you filled that girl's head with?' Fiali growled, crashing through what she had tried in vain to preserve. 'She's standing waiting for the rain again.'

'I don't know what you mean, Uncle. I have told her nothing other than truths.'

'Truths! Do you call the prophecy of Gallerra truth? Myulli is at this moment standing out in the courtyard waiting for the approaching storm to bring a legend to life.' Fiali rubbed his arms with vigour. 'It grows colder by the moment,' he huffed. 'That girl will catch the sniffing death if she does not come inside.'

Jashm stood from her stool and handed her uncle a blanket.

'What storm?' she asked. Jashm fought her excitement. Can it be? 'Why didn't you tell me a storm was coming. You know the signs, you know . . .'

'I know nothing, Jaja.' Fiali snatched the blanket from her and wrapped it around his shoulders. The old man sagged and his aged grey eyes closed. 'There is a storm approaching from over the mountains,' he said. He opened his eyes and stared into Jashm's face. 'It is just a seasonal rain storm, nothing more.'

'Is it as black as the night?' Jashm asked, as she pulled a small cloth sack from inside her vest. 'Do the clouds swallow the sky?'

'Yes, as do all storm clouds,' he sighed. 'Why do you Waiters persist in your quest?' Fiali scowled. 'Gallerra will not return.'

Jashm stiffened in defence. 'You forget, Uncle, that Gallerra was a great teacher, a diviner. He brought us prosperity from out of the fires of despair.'

'He was a fraud who stole the village's wealth,' Fiali scoffed.

'He is the promise of the future,' Jashm cried. 'When he left he gave us his promise and left a stone engraved with the scene of his return.'

'Gallerra was a thief and the stone is loot he could not carry,' grunted Fiali. 'It is only coincidence that his leaving saw the arrival of the rains again.'

'And the rains still come on time each year,' Jashm felt angry with her uncle. He would never believe in the prophecy and this saddened her.

'You worship a thief!'

'Lies!' Jashm felt her face reddened with rage. 'You disbelievers spread lies about Gallerra and have failed to stop us Waiters. Gallerra will come back to us and he will bring with him great wealth to share with his people, as he has promised.' She clenched her fists. 'He will come and the stone does not lie.'

Fiali looked long and hard into her eyes before he broke contact. 'Go,' he breathed, 'Myulli waits for you.'

Jashm nodded once at her uncle, stepped around him, pulled back the curtain and slipped out the door. The stiffening wind that swept down the courtyard to the house halted her. A smile spread across her face. The sky overhead was a rich blue but the coming darkness was consuming its colour with its rolling, thick clouds. Leaves, dancing together, filled the air with hissing. It was the singing of nature's song, as was prophesied.

'Is it the sign?' called Myulli standing at the edge of the court-yard, one hand holding a branch of an old blood fruit tree.

'Can you see the path?' Jashm called, as she braced herself against one of the stone pots that dotted the courtyard. She leaned forward against the wind, her slight body trembling with the bracing cold.

The Waiters had taught her the signs over the last five years and they were now clear in the heavens and the earth. She patted the offering she'd collected from the secret place – the place in the mountains the Waiters said couldn't be found. 'Faith,' Jashm laughed softly to herself. Her faith in the secret place had driven her to search, and the voice of Gallerra from the sky made it possible. The voice guided her through the mountain forests to a white-stoned clearing barely three paces across. Here she found her offering, and now she would be the one to greet Gallerra.

'Yes, I see it.' Myulli's small voice, picked up by the wind, was thrust into Jashm's ears. She was facing the shadows at the base of the mountains. Myulli shielded her eyes from the dust-filled air with her hand.

Jashm pushed against the wind to stand beside her sister. Both took shelter behind the thick trunk of the tree. They looked towards the base of the mountain. Jashm recalled her return from the mountain forest only yesterday and she was disappointed at not being there now. The crooked line of a path lay out in the distant tight foliage of the pellin trees. It glowed white within the shadows. Jashm dropped to her knees and began chanting the song of welcome, casting out each word like a ship on a rolling sea.

From beyond the walls
of yesterday's promise
You bring to us a new dawn.
From beyond the walls
that imprison our hearts
You bring freshness to our lands.
Gallerra we wait.
For the spirit of rebirth.
Gallerra we chant.
For we are the Waiters.
The keepers of your stone.

'Is it Gallerra?' Myulli called.

'Yes, little sister, it is.' Embracing her, Jashm's eyes filled with tears of joy.

Fiali scooped another ladle of soup into his bowl and sat on one of the stools arranged around the central stone table. The walls of the room were cluttered with shelves, filled with pots, bowls, boxes, furs, clothing, everything that its four occupants owned – it pressed against him with the warmth of memory. This place, of all places, always calmed his heart, eased his mind's wanderings into the past. The only other place he gained comfort from was the other room, the place where they all slept. During the bitterly cold nights they would all huddle around its central pit furnace. Dank smoke rose through an iron flue in the middle of the ceiling to stain the crisp night sky. It was in this room that they would whisper secrets to each other until sleep claimed them. Fiali longed for the return of those nights. Perhaps today's weather will bring a shard of it back this evening, he pondered as he sipped his soup.

On the second mouthful of the rich spicy soup Fiali felt a tingling in his mind. The storm was awakening something deep within his guts, the familiarity of the clouds. The secret he was forced to keep by his father and the curse promised by his grandfather. He remembered the night his father had come down from the Kyjihm Mountains. His face bright with the excitement of discovery, and Grandfather – yes! – Grandfather had cried and cursed father for his foolishness. He remembered the truth behind the Great Storm. Fiali could see the scene as if it had happened this morning.

It was the day of the Great Storm. Grandfather thought he was sleeping, but he heard his tale of the ancient mountaintop clearing, of Basstel and the mysteries of the past. He spoke of the secrets of the Kyjihm Mountains. He admonished his father. Fiali paused. His spoon hovered above the bowl. The thick brown soup trickled over its edge to fall on the table in soft splashes. He could see Grandfather snatch a cloth bag from his father's hand and shake a gnarled fist in his face.

'You fool! May the bells of the night riders steal your dreams.'

He shook the bag in front of father's face. 'These are Basstel's chattels. A sacrifice must now be paid and, damn it, I'll let it be you.' Grandfather stormed from the room. Father fell to his knees.

Fiali thought about the long forgotten legend of Basstel, the butcher priest of the virgin sacrifice. He was so evil that all banished even the thought of him from their minds. He was the bringer of the darkness, the infertility of the land. His temple now lay in ruins, hidden somewhere in the mountains, but his curse still haunted the people.

'Move one stone and I will seek sacrifice.' It was his father who brought the Great Storm on the land and it was his grandfather who paid the sacrifice to Basstel.

The Temple of Basstel! Fiali recalled. Jashm's journey yesterday. Her triumphant return from the mountains. Her wide eyes smile. His mind grasped the meaning like a callused hand on a hot fire poker. The storm?

Fiali leapt up from the table, tore the curtain from the doorway and rushed out into the courtyard screaming.

'Jashm, No!' he screamed into the fierce wind.

Jashm held up the small bag to the blackening sky. 'My gift, Gallerra, my offering to your return.'

'Jashm! Myulli! It is not a storm. Quick children, get inside. It is not a storm!' Fiali pushed against the wind. He faltered under its strength.

'It is Gallerra,' Myulli smiled.

Fiali had almost reached Jashm when the wind turned into a gale and blew him from his feet. Myulli, standing a few paces from the tree, stumbled and slid several arm lengths to be caught by Fiali who had managed to grab hold of one of the heavy flowerpots. Jashm stood facing into the wind, one arm tightly embracing the tree's trunk, the other holding up her gift. Her wet clothes slapped about her, as the light rain began to fall harder.

'Myulli!' yelled Fiali into the girl's face. 'Get inside, this is not a storm, it is Basstel coming for his sacrifice.'

'It is Gallerra,' Myulli cried, her eyes still wild with excitement.

'Get inside, girl! Gallerra is a lie,' Fiali cried out. 'Watch through the cracks in the door if you must but get inside.' Fiali released the girl and pushed her hard in the back towards the house, the gale tumbled her until she connected with its hard stone walls. Myulli pushed against the wind and crawled inside. Fiali watched the girl struggle to close the door. Once it was closed Fiali turned to Jashm.

The rain fell heavily, sleeting into his eyes. The clear blue of the sky was now night black, it was hard to see in the deepening gloom. Jashm stood less than five arm lengths from him but the wind was too strong. He saw with horror the bag Jashm held up to the sky.

'Jashm!' His words were snatched from his lips by the wind. 'What ... is ... in the ... bag?' He could feel his grandfather's fear growing deep in his own belly.

Jashm turned her cold face towards her uncle, a smile fixed in place and her eyes crazed with wild expectation.

'The bag, Jashm, what is in the bag?' He yelled again, trying to make signs she could understand.

She looked at the bag and smiled wider. 'Stones, Uncle. I found the secret place.' Her words flew past him like wet leaves flapping against a rock.

'NO!' Fiali bellowed in terror. 'Throw the bag away,' he cried, tears competing with the rain in his eyes. 'It is Basstel, the bringer of death.' The wind was now a howl and he struggled to hear his own voice.

'They are a gift to Gallerra,' Jashm continued, not hearing her uncle's warning.

'They are the remains of the Temple of Basstel,' he yelled again. 'Throw away the bag.' Jashm heard nothing over the howl of the wind. Fiali was frantic; his heart ached with despair. Calling on his deeper strength he forced himself from the ground and began to crawl towards his niece, gripping the raised edges of the stone paving to pull himself forward.

A great flash of light lit up the valley and mountain face as the heavens exploded in thunder. The sky roared its anger down upon them, as the lashes of Basstel struck out for their victim. Great cloud fingers appeared through the billowing blackness. They clawed at the earth sending trees and soil into the air. The screaming wind and rain assaulted the land.

'Jashm!' sobbed Fiali, touching the heel of her bare foot with his outstretched hand. 'Give me the bag. Please Jashm, give me the bag.'

The clouds erupted again with light and bellowing. Rain dropped like ponds, threatening to drown Fiali as he lay gripping the edge of a stone. Another flash and the pot Fiali had been holding onto just moments before exploded and his ears rang with the clapping percussion that filled the air. A great finger from the sky struck the ground and rent through the courtyard between him and the house. Stone paving danced into the wind like leaves. Fiali clawed his way to his knees, finding minimal shelter from the tree, and pulled at Jashm's wet, flapping dress.

Jashm turned her head, anger erupting from her eyes. 'Let go, Uncle. Gallerra comes, I must receive him.' She was screaming at him.

In turning, Jashm dropped her arm to within reach of Fiali. Releasing his grip on her he grabbed at the bag, his thick fingers gripped hard against the coarse cloth. Fiali, no longer holding on, was picked up by the wind like a child's cloth doll and flung into the hard stone walls of the house. Jashm, feeling her uncle's hand rip the bag from her grasp, turned her back to the wind in time to see his body smash into the house and see the thatched roof rip from its walls to join the wind in its destructive dance.

'Uncle!' she screamed, as another flash of light flung him into the air and into the teeth of the wind. The cloth bag was swept up into the sky with him; both disappearing into enveloping blackness. Jashm wailed and fell to her knees. The wind dropped, then died. Tears flowed from her eyes. Despair sucked her anguish out into the leaving storm. The storm had left. Nothing remained but the cold slap of silence and the trickle of water over stone.

Standing beside the stripped tree, Jashm felt weak, drained of energy. The storm had ended, as if the sky had run out of tears and the wind out of breath. Silence fell like the ash from a funeral pyre, a cold, eerie silence. The darkness lifted, a brilliant sun burnt high in the blue sky. She heard the whimper of a child. Feeling the weight of foreboding grace her shoulders, Jashm cried.

Myulli emerged from the ruins of the house, shaken and scared. She scampered over the deep rent in the earth to fall into the arms of her sister, wet and crying. 'Jashm,' she whispered, fearful of the quiet. 'Jashm, what happened?'

Jashm looked at her sister and touched her smooth cheeks with a trembling hand and cried again. 'Gallerra was displeased.'

The wind was cold, the sky darkening. Jashm murmured praise to Gallerra while Myulli walked around the small clearing collecting smooth, white stones. It had been a hard walk to the mountain for Myulli but she had wanted to come.

'Will Gallerra be pleased with our offering?' Myulli said, interrupting Jashm's prayers.

She looked up at her little sister and saw the wonder in her eyes. 'Yes, Gallerra will be pleased, and so, too, will Uncle Fiali.' Jashm eased herself from the ground and checked in Myulli's cloth bag. 'I see you have gathered fine stones.'

'They should look pretty around Uncle Fiali's grave,' Myulli smiled as she took back the bag. 'I still need some more.'

'Save some for Gallerra,' Jashm laughed. 'Uncle isn't the only one we are doing this for.'

The voice from the sky that had led them to the clearing had stopped when the cool wind had arrived but, like before, Jashm could remember her way back. The Waiters wouldn't believe her when she told them Gallerra spoke to her on the mountain, but now she didn't care. Gallerra would come again and she would be ready.

'Come now, Myulli,' she called. 'We must get to Uncle's grave before the rains come and make the path muddy.'

Myulli ran to stand beside her bigger, wiser sister, the bag held tight to her breast. 'He will be pleased.' Her eyes glittered with childish glee.

A Room
for Improvement

●

Trudi Canavan

Saturday 23rd July

Right now I'm sitting on my bed, in the middle of a million unpacked boxes, all by myself in this big old house. I swear I'll never move house again! Even though Mum and Dad and many of my friends helped, I'm exhausted. But now that I've had time to sit down, I'm all excited again. This house is mine! I can paint the walls any colours I want, and soon. No brown and orange wallpaper can be allowed to exist in my house. Well, it's not my house, really. It's the bank's, for now.

Sunday 24th July

I discovered a strange little room today. I don't think the estate agent even knew about it. I decided to move an old bookcase in the cellar so I could fit more junk in there. It was covering a door. A strange door made of metal.

Beyond it is a small room, bigger than a toilet, but not by much. There's a bookcase in there, and a table and chair – old fashioned but in really good condition. The bookcase contains about fifty leather-bound books and a few ornaments: an ebony elephant, some of those bird cards you can still get in packets of tea, and a little silver flute. There's also a vase of sunflowers that reminded me of Vincent Van Gogh paintings. They seem very real, but they can't be. The bookcase I moved was covered in dust, so the room must have been shut off for years. No flowers would have stayed fresh that long.

The walls and ceiling appear to be made of white stone, polished smooth. It's very strange. I couldn't find any cracks where the walls met. It's like the whole room was carved out of one big slab of flawless marble.

There were three floor lamps in the room, all lit. I tried to turn them off when I left the room, but couldn't find the switches. What a nuisance. They're probably burning away down there now. I'm not looking forward to my first electricity bill.

Monday 25th July

I was still really tired today. I should have taken the day off. Will called and wanted to have dinner. I told him I was too tired, but that wasn't the only reason. I really don't feel like seeing him. It would be nice if we could stay friends, but he reminds me too much of my old life. I want to be here, in my new life, even if I am too tired to do much more than watch television.

Sunday 20th August

My hands are covered in paint and the whole house stinks of it. Dad and I got the bedroom done this weekend. I put the stereo on in the hall and played classical CDs all day. He's such a dag, pretending to conduct an orchestra with his paint brush.

Every now and then I'd look at the brush in my hand and think: I want more time to paint, but this isn't exactly what I have in mind.

Saturday 24th September

It doesn't seem like two months since I moved in. I feel like I know every corner of this place. If I ignore the boxes still left in the cellar I can almost convince myself I've been here for years. I have decided to take a rest from painting the house this weekend. Perhaps I will do some real painting instead.

I just discovered the most incredible thing. I hardly know where to begin. My canvasses were in one of the boxes in the cellar. While I was there, I decided to visit that strange little room again. I had a look at a few of the books. Most were about science, and they were so technical that they may as well have been written in another language. There were a few botanical and zoological books, however, and I spent some time admiring the illustrations.

After an hour had passed, I put the books away and went to the kitchen. Mum had called to say she was coming over at noon, and I wanted to make scones. The kitchen clock said it was ten to eleven, and my watch said it was quarter to twelve, so I changed the batteries in the kitchen clock and fixed the time.

Mum was an hour late, which mean the scones went cold. She told me my clock was wrong. My watch said it was one o'clock while hers said it was noon. I turned the radio on and she was right. I had fixed the kitchen clock when I should have fixed my watch.

This was too strange. I had definitely been in that room for an hour, yet the television and the kitchen clock were telling me I'd been there for only a few minutes. Either I was going mad, or there was something stranger about that room downstairs than stone walls and the absence of light switches.

So I decided to do a little test. I took my alarm clock down to the cellar and set it on a box outside. Then I made sure my watch was set at the same time and took it into the room. Turning around, I looked at the alarm clock.

It had stopped. I waited for ten minutes, then walked out of the room. At once the second hand on the alarm clock began turning again. I did this several times, each time waiting longer before coming out. I can only come to one conclusion. Unless I've dreamed this entire day, I've got a time machine under my house.

Sunday 25th September
I can't stop thinking about that room. I tested it again this morning, and had the same result. It's real.

I wanted to ring Will and get him to have a look. He reads

Scientific American and books about hyperspace, and might have a better idea of what is going on. But I don't want to tell Will about this. I don't want to tell anyone. For a start, what if more people found out about it. They'd want to use it, too. They'd tell other people. Eventually the media would find out. And then the army would take my house from me.

I want to use it myself!

I am a bit scared, though. What if the room is dangerous? What if it's a failed experiment, and there's a good reason it was covered by that old bookcase? What if I come out and find that centuries have passed instead of hours? I should be cautious.

But at the same time I'm excited. This room could be the answer to my dreams. With work and everything else, I just don't have enough time to paint. Oh, I have my evening lessons, but two hours a week isn't enough time to get good at something. This room would give me that time. A few extra hours a day might be all I need. In a year I might have enough paintings for an exhibition.

Monday 26th September

Caution be damned! I had a rotten day at work today. Everyone who worked on this toothpaste campaign wants to blame someone for something. All I could think about was getting home so I could try out my time room. I figure it can't be dangerous. I've been in there a couple of times now, so if there was anything wrong with it I would have found out by now.

Now, at last, I'm home. I've had an early dinner, and thought about what I want to paint, and I'm ready to go inside.

The worst thing just happened. Nothing life-threatening, but something any artist would feel awful about. I just spent four hours painting, and all my effort was wasted. I'm a bit tired (it's only eight o'clock but I've been up much longer), but I'll try to explain clearly.

I took some paints and a board into the room and started working. I decided to do a small painting of the sunflowers. (They're real, by the way. I cut up one of the flowers to confirm it.)

•

Everything was going really well, and I lost all sense of time. I'm not sure if that is an effect of the room, or not. It's probably just because I became so engrossed.

When I was finished, I decided to step out of the room to get a fine brush to do my signature. I looked back and saw the most amazing thing. Everything was moving backwards, like a film in reverse! It was as if there was an invisible artist un-painting all my canvases – and it was happening so fast most was a blur. The brushes I'd used dabbed at the board and, bit by bit, put paint back on the palette. Colours I'd mixed un-mixed themselves. Tubes sucked paint inside themselves again. Then the boards and paints flew through the air toward the doorway. When they reached it, they fell to the floor.

All my work undone, and so quickly I don't think I had taken a breath and let it out again by the time it was over. I feel awful, like someone has played a cruel trick on me.

I had thought this room was the answer to all my dreams, but if this happens every time then it is useless to me.

Tuesday 27th September
I think I'm suffering from jet lag. It's five in the morning and I'm wide awake. I've been lying here in bed thinking about what happened last night. Everything I took into that room went back to the way it was when I entered. Everything, except me. My shirt is hanging over the back of my chair, and I can see that it's stained with paint. Perhaps if I carry the paintings out with me they'll stay painted, too.

That's it. I'm going to get up and try it now.

It works!
I've got it all planned now. I'm going to set up the cellar as a studio. Then, if anyone wants to see where I paint I'll pretend I do it in there. The time room is my little secret now. When people ask how I get the time to do so much, I'll just smile mysteriously.

Tuesday 18th October
I've been thinking about the time room today, and I've come up with a theory. The room is a kind of time bubble. When I go inside time stretches, like an inflating bubble. When I leave it the bubble deflates. There is no paradox because I'm not actually travelling through time, just stretching the moment.

I'm no scientist. This is the only theory I've come up with that makes sense. I wish I could ask Will, or Dad. Or Einstein.

I forgot to take the turps out today. I remembered at the last moment, just after I had stepped out of the room. I turned around and a jar of turps hit me in the chest. I couldn't stop laughing, even though it hurt like hell.

Wednesday 30th November
I fell asleep in the time room last night. It's so easy to lose track of time in there. I was tired, but I wanted to finish a painting. I rested my head in the crook of my arm for a moment, and the next thing I knew I was waking up.

I must have slept for hours. Now my body clock is out again, and I've woken up early. It's given me an idea, through. What if I stayed in there for twenty-four hours, and slept for eight hours of it? I could take food and a little camping bed with me. It would be like having an extra weekend day each week.

Sunday 5th February
So much time has passed, and I haven't written in this diary for months. The time room has made such a difference to my life! Spending twenty-four hours in it at a time has worked very well. I get a few extra days each week in which to paint.

All the practice is paying off. My teacher says I'm improving in leaps and bounds. I'm trying to spend time learning about art, too. The staff at the local library think I'm a very fast reader.

I spilled turps all over one of the library books last week. All I had to do was leave it in the room, step out, and watch the turps leap off the book back into the jar. A few times I've let paintings un-paint, when I wasn't happy with the way they were progressing. And once I changed the positions of all the books on the shelves so I could watch them shuffle back into their places. (I can't take them out, though. They won't go past the doorway.)

There's another, unexpected blessing with this room. I never have to clean it up!

It's easy to lose track, however. I forget things people told me because more time has passed for me than they know. Referring to 'yesterday' can be confusing. Every day I check my computer to make sure I know which day of the week it is.

Thursday 18th May
Good news!

The paintings I took to Impressions Gallery last week have sold. The manager rang today. She wanted more so I brought another five down after work. I took some of my surreal ones as well, just to test the waters. She said she didn't know if they would sell, but that she'd show them to a few people who liked that sort of art.

It's nearly a year since I moved in. It seems much longer. When I was looking through my paintings to see which ones to take to the gallery I was amazed at how much I've improved. I'm quite ashamed of those early attempts from June – and tempted to throw them away.

Monday 10th July
Michelle from Impressions rang again today. She wants more surreal paintings! She suggested an exhibition, and says the gallery has had a cancellation for a week's hanging time for the second week of August. I asked how many paintings I'd need. She said at least thirty. Thirty! I told her I would only need to do a few more, but in truth I'll have to do over twenty paintings in four weeks!

I just worked out how much time I'd need to make up thirty paintings. I can probably have them done if I spend one day in the time room for every day outside. I'd also like to try a few ideas for larger paintings. I'd never dared to do them before, but now that I know people are interested . . .

Saturday 22nd July
Two weeks have passed and I've only finished five paintings, including one big one. At this rate I won't have thirty done before the exhibition, but I'm not worried. I have all the time in the world.

Sunday 6th August
The exhibition was a success! You would not believe the number of people who were there. I owe it all to my new agent, Michelle, who must have sent invitations to the whole world. I was even interviewed by a man from the *Age*!

Half the paintings sold on the opening night. I hadn't paid any attention to the prices Michelle had placed on them. Suddenly I have ten thousand dollars to play with. Michelle said the rest of the paintings will sell in the next few weeks when word gets around about this 'dynamic new artist'.

At last all the hard work is paying off! People like my paintings. I'm going to be famous!

Sunday 23rd July
Has it really been five years since I moved into this house? It seems far longer. It is longer.

People have been telling me I look tired and pale for weeks now. I thought it was from spending so much time indoors. I certainly don't get as much exercise or sunlight as I used to. I've put on a little weight and I'm not as fit as I used to be, but I feel fine. It wasn't until Mum said I had matured very fast in the last few years that I realised what might be happening. So I had a good look at myself in the mirror today.

I'm ageing. I don't feel any older than thirty, but I look it. My skin is drier and creased. My cheekbones are more prominent. My eyelids are different, too. Saggy. There are a few strands of white in my hair.

•

I tried to estimate how much time I have spent in the room. More than a day for a day. More than two, sometimes. Weekends might have stretched to a week. During times of inspiration, I came out only to go to the toilet. I've often wished that whoever had created the room had included one. Often I went into the time room so laden down with food that I could barely carry my painting materials as well.

If I've spent a day inside for every day outside, then I must be thirty-five years old!

Monday 24th July

I haven't entered the room since Sunday. I'm worried that I'm addicted to it. The side-effect of this addiction is premature ageing. I have to think about what I might miss if I continue living this way.

Like a boyfriend or husband. It sounds terrible, but I've been single for ten years. Oh, I've had a few brief relationships, but I was afraid to get too close in case they found out about the room. And children. But I've never felt any great desire to have any, really. I assumed that a day would come when I'd know it was time to do the husband-and-kids thing, but that day hasn't come yet. Perhaps it never would have, whether I'd found the time room or not.

I think I should spend some time away from the room and try to sort out what I want from life.

Sunday 27th August

I've started a new series of paintings. It sounds corny, but they are of clocks and time pieces. They're realistic and intricate, and take many weeks to complete. The first one I did was of women lying in a circle with their feet touching. The woman at one o'clock is young. The woman at six is middle-aged. The woman at twelve is old. I painted the hour-hand at four and the minute-hand at twelve. All the woman have their arms around each other's shoulders.

After this one I did the same thing, but developed it further. The young woman is larger, brighter and a little blurred and faded. The middle-aged woman is in focus, but smaller. The old woman is smaller still, and in shadow. The effect is of a flat cod slowly retreating into the distance.

I see time symbols in everything. I was inspired when I looked down at my tools and saw that a paint tube with a pear-shaped spurt of paint below it, looked like an hourglass. I did a picture of this, too.

The hourglass shape is in everything. I paint thousands of them, in miniature, to make up large, ordinary objects. I paint enormous hourglasses with thousands of ordinary objects inside them. My favourite is of a giant hourglass with a crowd of women standing inside the top half. One is diving gracefully through the aperture. Below her is a mound of sleeping, contented women.

Tuesday 5th March

Michelle gave me yet another cheque today. I didn't know what to do with it. I have all the paints I need, and the house is full of nice furniture. She suggested I buy a sports car, or a home entertainment system, or go on a holiday, and I nearly took her advice.

But then I thought: why bother? I don't drive much any more, and I wouldn't use the home entertainment system. I don't want to leave my house to go anywhere. I have everything I've ever wanted. I told her to send the money to a charity.

Since I gave up work I don't see people very often. I don't want to leave my house. I'm afraid people will discover my room while I'm gone, or that people will wonder why someone in their mid-thirties, who doesn't drink or smoke and didn't spend their youth trying to get a good tan, looks like someone in their sixties.

There's only so much that creams and powders will hide.

Friday 19th May

I've become quite morbid lately. I've started wondering what would happen if I died in the time room. If I had been taken in there by someone else, would I come alive again if they left the room without me? I guess I'll never know. I've never shown anyone else the room, and I don't intend to.

No one can enter after I do, however. Time does not pass in the outside world while I'm in it, so there is no way someone can happen upon the room and open it, thus discovering my body.

But if I died in there, and the room remained 'activated', time would keep stretching out. Would that moment keep expanding forever, or would there come a point when the 'bubble' of time would burst?

Or is the room set to expel its contents if the person who activated it died in there?

Wednesday 12th November

I haven't written in this diary for a long time. As always, I was afraid my family would find it if I took it to hospital with me. They might read it in the hope of finding a reason for my mysterious 'disease'.

I wish I didn't have to put up with these tests, but I can't pretend that there isn't anything wrong with me. The doctors have decided I have a rare ageing disease. Accelerated ageing syndrome, they call it. The same disease suffered by those sad little children I've seen on television. It's something they're born with. The doctors are really puzzled about me, since I appear to have manifested the syndrome in my forties. And what really has them perplexed is that I should have something wrong with my genes, but I don't.

They've finally decided they can't do anything about it. So they sent me home and encouraged me to make the most of my life, doing the things I enjoy. Like painting. Mum and Dad come around every day or so. I wish I could tell them the truth, but I can't risk it.

Though the room won't be of use to me for much longer, I don't want it to fall into the wrong hands after I'm gone.

I'm enjoying spending more time with my parents, though. I haven't seen as much of them as I might have if I hadn't discovered the time room. And we have more in common now that we're almost the same physical age.

Friday 14th July

Michelle visited me here in hospital today and brought me my diaries, as I had asked. She told me that I had won an award. The hospital staff made a big fuss, which was nice. Michelle told them that my paintings are hanging on walls all over the globe. I like the thought that my art has travelled to far-off places. Nobody will ever know how much work and sacrifice was behind my success, but I don't think anyone, except perhaps another artist, can really understand that anyway.

My house was sold yesterday, which is why I risked having my diaries brought to me. They will be sent to the new owner. I had Michelle search for talented creative people who needed a big break. I insisted on being able to interview them myself. I had their entire lives investigated, just to be sure. I don't want my gift to end up in the wrong hands.

Today a shy, young man with a great talent for music will be exploring his new home. I wish I could be there to see him discover the time room. In my mind, I see him skimming over the books and trying the bone flute. It is winter, but it is strangely warm and he can't find the switches to turn off the lights. He'll find his watch is running too fast, or that something he has taken into the room with him flies out of the door when he leaves. Or he'll try to take a book out, and find it won't move past an invisible barrier at the entrance. I see him returning with one of his many instruments, and making beautiful music in that quiet place.

And I see the sunflowers there on the shelves, beautiful forever.

Waste

●

Michael Pryor

'The Brigade isn't for you, lad,' said Captain Dar. 'Leave now, go home, raise children.' He glared with red-rimmed eyes, stubble on his face. 'Are you going to finish that drink?'

Tilden Lambholder looked down at the glass that Captain Dar had thrust towards him. 'No sir.'

'Good.' The captain reached across the desk and swooped on the glass. He threw the brandy down his throat as if it were medicine. 'I mean it, lad. Go home. Don't make the same mistake I did.'

'But sir! I've always wanted to be in the Brigade! It's been my dream!'

Captain Dar smiled a little at that, but it was a wintry smile. 'Forty-two years ago I said the same thing, lad, on my first day in the Brigade. I wish someone told me then what I'm telling you now.'

Lambholder sat back in his chair. Captain Dar's office was small. It looked as if it was trying to work its way up from dilapidated to shabby, but was losing the struggle. Piles of papers stood on the desk and most of the floor. Some had toppled over but the dust that lay on them seemed to indicate that this event happened a long time ago.

Only two features of this room looked at all cared for. One was a calendar, with dates conscientiously marked off. The other was a shelf that stretched along one wall. On it were earthenware and metal crucibles. Most were old and battered, some were badly cracked. They ranged in size from one the size of a teacup to one made of rusty iron, a hand-span tall.

Dates had been scratched into these crucibles, or splashed on with paint. 'Argan Heights, 876', 'Tanniput, 879', 'Outskirts of Shandler'.

Lambholder noticed, with some interest, that a few of these pots still glimmered from the magic they had once held safely.

A single grimy window gave a view of the gates to the depot. A collection of buildings stood around sheepishly. They looked as if they'd been painted in the past, but these days didn't have anything to do with fancy muck like that. A haze hovered over this depressing scene, and seemed to come from several pillars of smoke or vapour behind the buildings.

'You don't mean it, sir,' Lambholder said stoutly. 'You don't really mean I should go home and not join up.'

'Oh yes I do,' Captain Dar said softly. 'The Brigade is a laughing stock. The lowest foot soldier in the army looks down on us. The swabbies on our war galleys lord it over us. Even the low life in the city watch think they're a cut above us. You don't want to be part of that. Get yourself a respectable job. Take up cobbling. Cobbling's always good.'

This wasn't what Tilden Lambholder had been expecting when he'd farewelled his white-haired mother and ten white-haired aunts days ago. After all, tales of the Brigade had been his bedtime stories since he was small. 'No sir. It's the Brigade for me.'

Captain Dar put down his glass, placed both elbows on the desk, cradled his chin in his hands and studied Lambholder with pity. 'And why, lad? Why this demented dream to join the Brigade?'

Lambholder's huge frame squirmed a little in his seat before he caught himself and sat up straight. 'It's honourable, sir, the Brigade is. Doing something for people, helping others.'

'Oh yes. It does that.'

'And . . .' Lambholder hesitated.

'And?'

'And it's in the family, sir. My da was in the service.'

334

Captain Dar closed his eyes and bowed his head. 'I should have known. Thirteen months to retirement and this happens,' he mumbled. He looked up and studied the ceiling. 'Your father was Felden Lambholder, wasn't he?'

'Yes sir! The bravest, most reliable, most hardworking corpsman ever!'

Captain Dar nodded slowly. 'Your ma told you that, did she?'

'Yes sir! And my ten aunts. I never knew my da, of course, but I've heard all about him.'

'And did they tell you how he bought the farm?'

'The farm? We had a farm long before Da joined the Brigade.'

'Cashed it in, lad. Have his number come up. Bit the big one.'

'Sir?'

'Died, lad. Did they tell you how he died?'

'Well, they said it was heroically defending his friends, giving his life so that others –'

'Short on detail, were they?'

'In a manner of speaking,' Lambholder said stiffly. His father's demise had always been spoken of in hushed whispers. In the great store of stories about Felden Lambholder that his mother and his ten aunts would tell throughout the long frigid nights of Upper Harkbut, Felden Lambholder's last stand was the least repeated.

'So they didn't tell you about how he was caught in a wave of waste magic that turned him into what looked like a puddle of gently simmering vegetable soup?'

Lambholder's mouth hung open and he had some difficulty in closing it. 'Ah?' he finally managed.

'I was there,' Commander Dar went on, his gaze distant. 'It was a nasty situation we were called out for. Grade nine, at least. Felden didn't see it coming, at least he had that mercy. But I saw the wave roll down the hill. Raw, untamed magic, it was. It hit a boulder, diverted, but a splash caught Felden in the middle of the back. He was soup in the blink of an eye.' He sighed. 'But that's life in the Waste Brigade. When your sole job is to take care of magic overflow, waste and build-up, what do you expect?'

At that moment, a short, red-faced man bustled into the office and saluted. 'Chief, Private Tremen wants to see you.'

Captain Dar sucked his cheek for a while and stared at the bottle of brandy. 'Take care of it, will you Crully?' he said to the red-faced man. 'I've had enough of that social climbing leech.'

Crully saluted again. He seemed to enjoy it. 'Like to sir, but can't. Tremen has a man with him, and the man specifically asked to see you. He was very persistent.'

'Give me a moment,' Dar sighed, 'then send him in.'

'Righto, Chief.' Crully turned to go, but something leapt to his mind with enough force to make him topple a few steps backwards. 'Oh, and Private Wambley's gone. Meant to mention it earlier.'

'Gone?'

'Left to join the army. He said he was wasted here. He said it like it was a joke, sir.'

'It probably was, Crully. It probably was.'

'Ah. I'll see to Tremen and the man, then, Chief.'

At that moment, Lambholder felt the floor under his feet shake a little, and a dull explosion sounded nearby. Captain Dar glanced out of the window. 'And take a squad out to see about that, will you Crully? It sounds like Leaching Pond 3 is playing up again.'

'Righto, Chief.'

Captain Dar turned his attention to Lambholder. 'You see what sort of outfit this is? We clean up waste magic, which is dangerous and nerve-wracking and no one wants to do it. We're necessary – everyone admits that – but we're not on anyone's "must invite" list when it comes to royal balls, gallery openings or gala hooplas.'

'Sir, I wouldn't know what to do with a gala hoopla if one came along. I just want to join the Brigade.'

Commander Dar sighed, rubbed his face with both hands, swept the bottle of brandy into the top drawer, stood and sighed again. 'Don't say I didn't warn you.'

A minute later and Private (Probationary) Tilden Lambholder had been sworn in as the newest member of the Waste Brigade.

'Right,' Captain Dar said. 'You stand against that wall and try to look threatening. It might help get rid of this visitor.'

Lambholder did his best. With his height and the muscles he'd developed working on the farm, he had the physical attributes to look threatening. However, the mildness of his demeanour and naturally sunny expression made it a difficult task.

But a new corpsman had to try. Shoulders back, chest out, he attempted a scowl and a menacing posture, even though he'd never been much good at it. Ma and Aunt Mona said he was just a big cuddly fella and they would never let him deal with the sheep thieves that infested Upper Harkbut.

Lambholder wondered, guiltily, how they were managing without him.

Captain Dar sat and stared at the door, drumming his fingers.

Lambholder wasn't often the doubting type. His life – until this point – had been one of utter certainty. The weather in Upper Harkbut was certain (cold). The sheep were certain (woolly). His future was certain (joining the Waste Brigade). But a flicker of a shadow of a hint of a doubt was beginning to touch the outermost fringes of his mind.

Lambholder was beginning to suspect that Captain Dar wasn't the paragon of perfection that he expected the leader of the Waste Brigade to be. Lambholder had imagined a rugged individual, hard bitten but dedicated to the common good. Brave, enduring, idealistic, but with a tough practical core. Instead, he saw a man with liquor on his breath and stubble on his chin, one who tried to dissuade Lambholder from joining the Brigade. Lambholder was mildly hurt at this. He hadn't thought he'd get a ceremonial welcome, but he was disappointed that the son of the great Felden Lambholder wasn't accorded some sort of recognition.

A knock came from the door. Before Captain Dar could answer, it swung open and a corpsman sidled in. He was small and neat, in contrast to Crully. His hair was clean and perfectly parted in the middle, his face was well shaven, and his uniform looked altogether made from better material than the standard issue. He paused in the doorway and ushered in a lean, smiling civilian. The civilian was dressed in the neat jacket and leggings of a small-time merchant. He was carrying a compact trunk, and he slapped it on the desk with a grin.

Captain Dar looked at both men. His expression indicated that he was definitely thinking of retirement, or perhaps the bottle in his third drawer. 'Tremen,' he said to the corpsman, 'what is it this time? Who's this?'

The corpsman saluted lazily. 'Someone I think you'd like to meet, Captain.'

'Another one of your friends?'

'Not all of them are in high places,' Tremen said, smirking a little. 'Just most of them.'

'I see. And this is?'

'Chindler Sheeze,' the civilian said. 'Thanks for agreeing to meet me, Captain Dar. This could be your lucky day.'

Sheeze leaned across the desk and stuck out his hand. Dar eyed it sourly, then stood and took it. 'What do you want?'

'I have something a man in your position may be very interested in.' Sheeze stopped and looked over both shoulders. 'Is this room secure?'

Dar lifted an eyebrow. 'It's well attached to the rest of the building, if that's what you mean.'

'What about him? Can he be trusted?'

'That's Private Lambholder. He's one of the Brigade. Of course he can be trusted.'

He's one of the Brigade. Lambholder beamed until he remembered his role, and after that the scowl fought with a grin for possession of his face.

Sheeze threw a worried glance at Lambholder before turning back to Captain Dar and smiling. Lambholder decided he didn't like that smile. It reminded him of the man who'd once come to the farm selling sheepdogs. He smiled a lot. He smiled when he told about his clever dogs. He smiled when he said what a nice house the Lambholders had. He smiled when he accepted the ludicrously

•

low price Aunt Crendula paid for the dogs. He smiled as he waved and left. And, that night, when his dogs ran away from the Lambholders and joined him, he probably smiled a lot, too.

Tremen cut in smoothly. 'Sheeze here has come into possession of a remarkable item.'

'That's right,' Sheeze hurried on. 'And it's something only a professional would appreciate, Captain. A man like yourself, experienced in the area of disposal and confinement of magical waste.'

'And you want me to give you money, is that it? I can sense these things, you know.'

Sheeze blinked. 'I don't see investing in our enterprise as *giving* us money. In fact, we'll be giving your money back a thousandfold in a very short period of time.'

Captain Dar sighed and looked at the calendar on the wall. 'And what is it this time? Magic proof gloves? Enchantment resistant goggles? I warn you, I've seen them all.'

While this had been going on, something had been unsettling Lambholder. Up on the farm, the Lambholders didn't have many visitors, so the sound of a horse or a wagon was something to be aware of – for better or for worse. He'd grown used to hearing the rattle of a wagon long before it came into sight. It was a useful skill, as it allowed the Lambholders to prepare for visitors, of all sorts.

And so, without really realising it, he'd been tracking the progress of a wagon. A single wagon, and from the sounds it seemed as if it was racing towards the Waste Brigade depot.

It was only when the screaming started that he started to pay more attention to it.

'Sir,' Lambholder said, interrupting Sheeze before he could answer the captain. 'There's something happening outside.'

'It's not Crully, is it? He hasn't fallen into a holding pond and got turned into a frog or anything?'

'No sir. There's a wagon coming our way, very fast. And someone in it is screaming.'

Dar found a ring of water on the desk where his glass had been. He dipped a finger in it and traced an elaborate doodle. 'A novice wizard. That's all I need.' He stood. 'Tremen, wait here with your friend. Sheeze, don't move until I get back. Lambholder, you come with me.'

Lambholder followed Captain Dar. They hurried along a short, dark corridor and into the large room through which Lambholder had first entered the building. A bare wooden counter – unattended – divided the room in half. Captain Dar vaulted over it and ran to the racks of equipment by the door.

'Here, get this on,' Captain Dar said. 'We've got a situation on our hands.'

He grabbed a heavy leather coat from the row of coats hanging on hooks. Then he struggled into one himself. 'Gloves, too,' he snapped, 'and mask.'

Captain Dar was dressed well before Lambholder had finished fastening the ankle length coat. He was almost completely covered in stained and battered leather, featureless in the mask. 'Hurry,' he said, voice muffled. With a clumsy-looking swaying gait, he was gone.

Lambholder seized the leather helmet and gauntlets and stumbled outside.

The wooden fence surrounding the depot had seen better days. Lambholder decided it would make poor farming country. He couldn't see any grass or plants growing inside the fence, and the trees closest on the other side looked as if they were sorry they'd chosen the neighbourhood. The buildings were weather-worn bare wood, long and low, barracks and store rooms mostly, he thought. The grey, bare earth beneath his feet was dusty and tired looking. Behind the buildings, he could see fumes and vapours drifting upwards.

When Lambholder joined Captain Dar, he was standing at the head of a mob of villains, thieves and cut throats. Lambholder immediately rushed to the captain's side to defend him from them. To a man, they were unshaven and poorly groomed. Clothes hung on them with a hint of desperation, as if covering up the ill-made bodies was a civic responsibility. They were all muttering, spitting and scratching various parts that – if everyone was lucky – were private. All this immediately proved Lambholder wrong when he had, at first, assumed them incapable of doing two things at once.

The stench that came from this assembly was enough to make Lambholder long for the dung pit back home on the farm.

Captain Dar, however, wasn't fazed by this evil gang. He marched right up to them and pulled his helmet off.

'Get back to work, you lot!' he shouted. 'Haven't you heard a novice wizard before?'

The sound of screaming was very close now, and Lambholder could catch glimpses of a wagon hurtling along the dusty road leading to the depot. But over that noise, and the increased muttering, spitting and foot shuffling, Lambholder could hear one sound rising clearly over them all. It was the sound of his dreams slowly deflating.

The motley bunch in front of him weren't assassins, bullies or out of work henchmen. They were the members of the Waste Brigade.

Lambholder had been brought up to believe that the members of the Waste Brigade were the elite. The highest standards of physical, moral and intellectual rectitude were the norm. Strong of arm, keen of eye, firm of heart, these were the qualities of the average corpsman. On the long winter nights, with only a pitiful peat fire for warmth – and several hundred sheep crammed into the living area – Lambholder had been entranced by tales of the shining examples of selflessness set by the Waste Brigade, risking their lives to clean up magic waste, pitting their strength against rough and wild enchantments, cleaning up where no one had cleaned up before, and all with a song in their hearts a smile on their lips and a sense of justice over all.

The reality, it appeared, was somewhat different.

'Sounded like a good un on the way, Chief,' a voice came from the ranks. One of the ranker ranks, Lambholder thought. 'Looks like it'll be a bit of fun.'

'Haven't you got work to do?' Captain Dar snarled.

'We're off duty,' came the chorus from the grimy assembly.

Captain Dar jabbed a finger at them. 'There's no off duty when it comes to emergencies. You know that. Now fall back and wait for your orders.'

He motioned to Lambholder, and the new recruit stumbled back. As he did, the mysterious wagon bolted from the last of the trees, and raced through the gates.

The horse was wild-eyed and a-lather. The driver was standing on the seat, robes billowing, one hand holding the reins, the other slapping wildly at his waist and midriff. He was screaming like a boiled wildcat.

The corpsman started cheering and whistling at this performance. Some even stopped spitting to do so.

'Enough!' Captain Dar bellowed as he seized the horse's bridle. 'Atch! Parjee! He's hot! Get a Number 15 barrel. Stat! Where's Stat? Stat, you find Corporal Crully. The rest of you, bring buckets of water from the pump. Move!'

The cheering stopped and the corpsman shuffled, stumbled and staggered into action.

Lambholder felt in a daze. This was the Waste Brigade in action? He turned his attention to the screaming wizard.

The wizard was only half Lambholder's height, and painfully thin. His screaming was rising and falling, but even though the horses had come to a halt, he still stood on the seat of the cart. He plucked at his belt, but kept his gaze rigidly on the horizon. Light rippled and bloomed from him in waves.

'Lambholder! We have to get him down!'

Manhandling the screaming wizard was like hoisting a very loud bundle of sticks, but he was much heavier than Lambholder had guessed. Once the Captain and Lambholder touched him, he became completely rigid, arms by his side. This close, Lambholder could see that the glowing and pulsing came from under the wizard's clothes. Slowly, the light changed colour, but sickly yellows and browns were the main theme. And even through the heavy leather, Lambholder could feel how hot the wizard was.

'Where's that barrel?' Captain Dar snarled, but then saw the barrel was near, propelled by two of the shaggiest of the corpsman. 'Upright!' Captain Dar snapped.

The buckets began arriving at that moment, and soon the barrel was full. Distantly, Lambholder noticed his gauntlets were beginning to smoke. 'Easy, now,' Dar said over the screaming. 'Lift him up. Feet first, into the barrel.'

The other corpsmen stood well back at this stage. Lambholder wasn't reassured by this at all. To add to his discomfort, he was sweating under the heavy leather gear, and he had an excruciating itch under his left armpit.

When the wizard's feet hit the water, they hissed. Steam billowed upwards. 'More water!' Dar called. Soon, a bucket brigade had formed, the corpsmen passing buckets between the water pump and the barrel.

'Slowly now,' Captain Dar said. 'Slowly.'

As the reluctant corpsmen topped up the barrel, Captain Dar and Lambholder eased the wizard into the water little by little. Soon the water had risen over the wizard's feet and up to his knees. When it reached his waist, a cloud of steam billowed from the barrel and the water started to boil violently. 'Hold him!' Dar shouted to Lambholder over the wizard's keening. 'More water! More water!' he called to the corpsmen.

Then the wizard sagged a little and the screaming stopped. His eyes focused for a moment, then he sighed and closed them. Lambholder put an arm around the wizard's shoulders to steady him.

Soon, the water was up to his chest, and he bobbed gently in the barrel, either asleep or unconscious. His head rested on his chest.

Lambholder straightened, ready to clap the captain on the back. At last, a real Waste Brigade adventure! Then he noticed that the corpsmen had all backed off again. His sweat grew chill.

'Don't move,' Captain Dar said.

'Yes sir.'

'Crully!'

'Yes Chief?' Crully called from a distance.

'Get one of the big storage crucibles. The Invincible.'

'The Invincible?'

'You'd better take a few of the lads to help you.' Captain Dar looked at Lambholder through the lenses of his leather mask. 'I have to get the storage vials from him. He's overloaded.'

'Ah. Oh. Storage vials?'

A small twitch of the helmet may have indicated that Captain Dar was smiling. 'Didn't your ma tell you about this part of the job either?'

'Well, no, not really. I realise now that most of the stories were a bit short on detail.'

'Most stories are, lad.'

Lambholder struggled with this. 'What do we do now?'

'This wizard is obviously a novice. He hasn't paid much attention to the basic rule of magic.'

Lambholder knew this part. It was the whole reason for the existence of the Waste Brigade. 'Action and reaction,' he said smartly. 'Every time a magician expends magical force externally, an equal amount of magical force rebounds on the magician.'

'Good lad. Gradually, of course, this builds up. Big magic, big build-up. In the old days, magicians simply used to slough this waste magic off. The great pools of raw magical waste were unusable, toxic, and that's when the Waste Brigade was founded. It was our job to go around and siphon this stuff into tarred barrels and store them where they wouldn't do any harm. Dangerous work, that. Nowadays, of course, things are a bit more civilised, thanks to the storage vials.'

Captain Dar motioned Lambholder closer to the barrel containing the magician. The magic-user was still unconscious, but the waves of heat had subsided. 'See?' Captain Dar said as he reached into the water and eased the magician's robes apart. Bands of metal circled the magician's waist, and they were glowing fitfully. Strapped to the metal bands were six jars each the size of Lambholder's hand. They radiated light and heat.

'Copper wire,' Captain Dar explained. 'All magicians have

lengths of it strapped around their waist. It channels the excess magic into the storage vials. When the storage vials are full, the magician brings them to a waste depot like this one. We drain the waste into barrels or holding ponds, then the magician is set to go again. This one obviously wasn't paying attention to the levels of his vials. They were probably nearly full when he tried something extravagant like raising the dead, or turning lead into gold. Still, it could've been worse. I've seen life-sized charcoal statues shaped exactly like wizards, you know.'

Lambholder swallowed. 'He's all right now?'

'Not nearly,' Captain Dar said. 'We've cooled him down a bit, but it's only temporary. He could go off any second. We still have to drain the vials. Where's Crully?'

'Right here, Chief!' Crully had taken time to don the protective gear, and he was waddling alongside two husky corpsmen. They were carrying an earthenware receptacle nearly as tall as Crully himself. 'Just put old Invincible next to Captain Dar, boys. Right-hand side. I'll just stand back so I won't get in your way.'

'Lambholder,' Captain Dar said. 'You hold the magician steady. Very steady.'

Lambholder tried to imagine he was back on the farm, dealing with old Cornelius, a particularly testy ram. Old Cornelius had been known to have territorial disputes with wild dogs, wolves, cows, trees and large rocks. He usually won these battles, and handling this cantankerous old ram was an exercise in tact and not moving too quickly.

Captain Dar lifted an eyebrow. 'What do we have here?' he muttered. He lifted his head a little. 'Crully, is the lid off the Invincible?'

'Yes Chief!' Crully's voice came from some distance away.

Lambholder had a better view than he really wanted, but he was helpless not to watch. Captain Dar moved slowly, gently unhooking wires from the stoppers in each vial. His hands were sure as they eased the first vial off the wire belt. 'One,' he said and he held it up for scrutiny. Water dripped from the vial as he studied it.

'New design,' he grunted, and turned and lowered it gently into the crucible.

The second vial was more troublesome, but Captain Dar worked at it until it came free. 'Two.'

Three, four and five went easily, but number six wouldn't budge. 'Anything I can do?' Lambholder whispered.

'No,' Captain Dar said tersely, then he swore under his breath. 'I've nearly got it.'

At that moment, the wizard's eyes flew open. Lambholder didn't like the look of those eyes. Slightly glassy, with a fever bright sheen. 'Of course I can do it,' he said earnestly. 'Just leave a deposit and I'll get back to you.'

'Ignore him,' Captain Dar said. 'It'll be a while before he's himself again. There.'

Captain Dar straightened, holding the last vial. 'Crully! Ready with the lid!'

'You men there!' came Crully's far-away voice. 'Ready with the lid!'

Captain Dar deposited the vial and stood back as the lid was slid on.

Lambholder's ears popped with a sudden pressure change as the assembled corpsmen all let out the breath they were holding.

'Well, take him to the infirmary, Lambholder,' Captain Dar ordered. He stripped off his gauntlets and removed his helmet. He stood there, stretching and massaging his neck. 'Crully, you help him.'

Lambholder followed Captain Dar's example and took off his gauntlets and helmet. Then, as the wizard looked around brightly, Lambholder and Crully dragged him out of the barrel. The wizard's body remained limp and he began a stream of formless chatter. 'Of course, sir, I'm an experienced wizard,' he said to no one that Lambholder could see. 'I'll take care of all your enchantment needs.'

'You take his top half, sonny,' Crully said, ignoring the wizard's jabber. 'I'll manage his legs.'

'This way,' Captain Dar said, and he marched off.

'You want a levitating house, just like the Vizier's?' the wizard went on. 'Not a problem. By tomorrow? Of course!'

'They always promise more than they can deliver,' Crully said as they shuffled towards the infirmary. 'Next thing they know, they're up to their neck in magical overload. It's inexperience what does it, of course.'

The magician continued his unfocused babble. 'And Mr Sheeze, you're sure these new vials can handle twice the usual amount of waste? And that your waste processing facility will take all my waste for a fraction of the cost of the Waste Brigade depot? Sign me up!'

Lambholder stopped short. 'What is it?' Crully asked.

'Sheeze. Captain Dar, wasn't Chindler Sheeze the man who wanted to see you?'

Captain Dar rubbed his chin. 'Tremen's friend. Very interesting.'

'The one with Tremen?' Crully put in. 'Well, doesn't that beat all! I saw them both riding out of here a while ago, just after this feller appeared. Seemed to be in a hurry, they did. And, come to think of it, that's the same feller I saw with Tremen a couple of weeks ago, nosing around some of the oldest holding ponds. The ones right out the back.'

Captain Dar's face creased in a small smile as he looked towards the gate. 'Well, Mr Tremen. Important friends or no, you might just be in serious trouble.' He noticed Lambholder. 'Waste dumping, lad, is highly illegal. Not to mention dangerous. From what our hapless friend here has had to say, Chindler Sheeze isn't just peddling second rate storage vials, he's offering to store waste for wizards, too.'

'But isn't that what we do? Store waste?'

'And we're the only ones who do it properly, lad. Plenty of fly by night outfits offer to store magical waste, but they know how dangerous it is. They simply find some out of the way gully or hole in the ground, and dump it. Untended, there's no telling what the magic'll get up to. It can even get into the water system, and then there's hell to pay.'

'Like on Soogli Bay, right Chief?' Crully put in.

'Soogli Bay?' Lambholder's head was spinning. The sordid side of the magical waste business had never entered his childhood stories.

'The fishing industry there was ruined when some illegally dumped waste flowed into it,' Captain Dar said.

'All the fish were killed?'

'Not exactly. The raw magic changed the fish into tentacled monsters. The entire fishing fleet went out one morning and never came back.'

'Oh.'

The wizard had just been bedded down in the infirmary when the floor shook again. Immediately after the tremor came a sound like very high-pitched thunder. It went on and on, and as it did, Captain Dar's face blanched.

Crully looked out the window. 'Oh, glory be,' he whispered. 'Glory, glory be.'

Crully's face was green when he turned back to Captain Dar and Lambholder. Then it turned red, and when it changed to a ghostly blue Lambholder realised that Crully's face was being lit by light coming from outside.

Captain Dar sighed. 'Ever had one of those days?' he asked the ceiling. He bowed his head, pinched the bridge of his nose and rubbed it a little. Then he looked at the tips of his fingers for a moment, thinking.

His mind made up, Captain Dar strode to the door. 'Lambholder, you're with me. Crully, round up the men. Get all the crash wagons, the pumps, all the crucibles we've got. Full protective gear all round.'

Lambholder made his way to the window. Not far away, a huge fountain of sickly light was blasting skywards. An indigo dark cloud was collecting at its head, and Lambholder could see ugly, half-formed shapes in it. His childhood nightmare monster, the Midnight Sheepeater, seemed rather jolly compared to these. He found his voice. 'What's happening?'

'I think we've found where Tremen and Sheeze have been dumping their waste.'

●

The horses pulling Captain Dar's wagon were stolid creatures. They had to be, Lambholder decided, if they had to attend many magical waste spills. But even they had sensed the urgency of the situation. Draped in leather protective gear, the horses rumbled along at a bone-shaking pace, and Lambholder's nervousness grew.

As they drew closer, the fountain of fire swelled, distended and grew. Hideous things were flapping in the cloud that was expanding like a leech the size of a thunderhead. It rippled, too. It reminded Lambholder, unfortunately, of the sheep carcass he had found after searching for the lost animal for two days. As he'd approached, its sides had moved and he was sure it was alive. But as he came closer he saw that the motion was that of thousands of maggots writhing on and just under the skin of the dead sheep.

Lambholder shuddered and turned away from the cloud.

Captain Dar drove the horses in silence. Lambholder had tried to talk to him as they wound through the gently glowing holding ponds, past the pits full of tarred barrels, around the mounds of cracked storage vials and crucibles. It was no use.

Lambholder was worried. The bottle that Captain Dar had clamped between his legs hadn't been opened, but Lambholder thought it was only a matter of time. He looked over his shoulder. The rest of the brigade was strung out behind them, carts and wagons piled high with barrels, sweepers, booms, scrapers, hoses and other paraphernalia Lambholder couldn't even guess at. The final wagon at the rear was some distance behind, and Lambholder thought he could make out the tubby leather-swathed figure of Corporal Crully.

In the rear of Lambholder's wagon was the largest crucible he'd seen. Brown with age, it was three times the size of the Invincible. Two large corpsmen were needed to wrestle the lid alone into place.

The wagon rounded a slide of fallen rock and Lambholder finally saw where the fountain began. It was a jumble of boulders and shards of rock right at the far end of the expanse of leaching and holding ponds. The fountain blasted from the rocks like a pillar of fire. It swayed and pulsed, its colour a ghastly mixture of brown and dark purple that would make an interior decorator blanch.

'I think you'd better stay here, Lambholder. This is no place for you.'

Lambholder tore his gaze away from the horrible sight. 'But sir! I'm here to help.'

'Thanks, lad, but there's not much you can do.' He pointed at the fountain. 'That's coming from one of the old underground cess pits.'

The other wagons drew up. After some arguing, swearing and spitting from the men, Captain Dar stood. For a long moment, he stared at the bottle in his hands. He lifted it, weighed it in one hand then the other, then shook his head and passed it to Lambholder.

Straightening, Captain Dar took off his helmet and addressed the corpsmen. 'Men, we're facing possibly the most dangerous situation in my time with the Waste Brigade.' He paused, took a deep breath and went on. 'Tremen and his friend thought they were onto a good thing, obviously. The old underground cess pits haven't been used for a long, long time, and they thought they could dump waste in there for years before anyone found out.' He jabbed a finger at the fountain. 'But we stopped using the cess pits for a good reason. When enough high level waste accumulates in a confined space, this sort of thing happens. And that's not the end of it. If we can't plug this, it's going to blow.'

A mutter of concern ran through the corpsmen. 'That's right. It could set off all the waste held here, in ponds, pits and barrels. The country for a day's ride hereabouts would simply cease to exist. Then raw magic waste would rain down on the rest of the kingdom for a week.' He drew a deep breath. 'Nothing would be unaffected. The familiar would become the monstrous. Horror would become commonplace. Nightmares would walk the earth.' He narrowed his eyes. 'Men, it's up to us to stop it.'

Corporal Crully stepped forwards. 'This'll be overtime, then?'

Captain Dar snorted. 'Call it triple time if you like, Crully. If we stop this I'll personally see to it.'

Lambholder thought that if the cheer that went up were any more ragged, beggars would refuse to wear it.

'Crully,' Captain Dar said. 'I want you to stay here.'

'Righto, Chief!'

'Once we've capped this bruiser there'll be plenty of mopping up to do. I want you to take half the men and take care of it.'

'I'm on it.'

'Squads 2, 4 and 6 will come with me.'

'Sir!' Lambholder said urgently. 'Sir!'

'No, lad. You stay with Crully.' He slapped Lambholder on the shoulder. 'You'll make a corpsman, lad. Felden Lambholder would be proud of you.'

'But that's the point, sir! I have to go with you! I want to be part of a story, too!'

Captain Dar paused. He studied Lambholder. 'All right, lad. Stick close by me.'

'I'll still stay here, Chief?' Crully asked in a way that admitted only one answer.

'Do that, Crully.'

Lambholder took up his seat alongside Captain Dar. The captain silently drove the horses, and the unlucky corpsmen plodded along behind.

Soon, they were forced to abandon the wagon as the road petered out. Lambholder helped the men lift the huge crucible off the wagon. It took a dozen of them.

'Right lads,' Captain Dar said and he led the way. They tottered towards the magical blast. Lambholder found it hard to look closely at the pillar of magic. It shifted colours and *squirmed* in his sight, making his stomach churn. He decided to keep his head down, concentrating on placing his feet carefully and shouldering his part of the weight of the massive crucible.

Glittering flakes began to drop through the air. The men cursed as the going quickly became slippery underfoot. Several of the corpsmen fell, and one couldn't get up again. He lay there, flopping loosely. Another crawled away, butting his head against rocks as he went.

The crucible started to slip. 'Hands!' gasped Lambholder, and together they eased the crucible to the ground. The glittering flakes continued to fall all around.

'Fairy dust!' Captain Dar called over the roar of the magical blast. 'It's from the blast! Don't let it touch your bare skin!'

Lambholder nodded, then gritted his teeth and lifted his side of the huge crucible.

They staggered on. Lambholder found he had to lean forward, as if struggling against a gale.

The weight of the crucible increased, and Lambholder looked up to see that one of the men had let go and wandered off while another was crouching and appeared to be earnestly talking to a rock. The rest were skipping off, hand in hand.

'It's just you and me, lad!' Captain Dar shouted. He took hold of the crucible and steadied the weight. His helmet jerked in the buffeting waves of magic thrown off by the blast.

Lambholder gritted his teeth and staggered forward, holding on desperately to the crucible. Despite the helmet, strange smells were creeping into his nostrils – coal, wintergreen and dry paper. His eyes itched.

'Here! Put it down!' Captain Dar shouted over the roaring. Lambholder looked up to see they were only a few paces away from the mighty jet as it threw itself skywards. Overhead, the inky cloud was writhing and boiling. Lambholder shuddered, but eased the crucible to the rocky ground.

Just as he was steadying it, the ground underfoot heaved and lifted. Lambholder was thrown off his feet. He hit the ground, hard, and then frantically tried to scramble to his feet. Large rocks were being tossed around like marbles as the blast belched and doubled in vigour.

Lambholder squinted and shaded his eyes. All the rocks had rolled aside, and the magical blast was now erupting from a bare hole in the ground. Captain Dar had somehow managed to move the crucible right onto the lip of the hole. He held one arm over his eyes.

Overhead, booming laughter rolled across the sky.

Lambholder lay on his stomach and lifted his head. He thought of his ma and his ten aunts. He smiled at the memory of the farm and the frosty beauty of Upper Harkbut. He wondered what the sheep would do without him.

But something inside Tilden Lambholder had changed. He knew you could take the boy out of Upper Harkbut, but you could never take Upper Harkbut out of the boy, but for a long, long time his heart had belonged to the Waste Brigade. True, his dreams weren't exactly matched by the reality, but wasn't that why dreams were dreams and reality was reality? Here he was, a real-life down-to-earth corpsman in the Waste Brigade. If his life was about to end, at least he had achieved what he'd wanted to do, what he'd left home and all he'd ever known for.

Tilden Lambholder looked out at an out of control magical eruption of the highest magnitude, knowing that it might be the last out of control magical eruption of the highest magnitude he'd ever see, with a strange sort of contentment.

He saw Captain Dar, labouring to keep his feet in the face of the blast, hugging the crucible and using it as a shield. But even the great crucible was rocking backwards and forwards as the blast jetted upwards, magic bursting forth in all directions.

At the last moment, Lambholder saw what Captain Dar was trying to do.

'Captain!' he cried.

Captain Dar, with one last effort, tilted the great crucible and tipped it into the spouting maw of the magical eruption. He teetered a little, but then flung himself backwards.

In an instant, the blast was shut off as the great crucible jammed tight in the mouth of the cesspit. The fiery pillar stuttered, faded, then disappeared.

Lambholder ripped off his helmet and cheered. But before he could go to the weary looking figure of Captain Dar, something plopped next to him.

It was a sticky sound, like thick custard falling on a floor.

Lambholder blinked. Gently at first, drops were falling to earth all around. Sticky, multi-coloured drops. Some of them writhed when they hit the ground. Some grew wings and flew off, buzzing. Others simply hissed and dissolved the earth.

The sound of feet came from behind. Lambholder slowly climbed to his feet in time to greet Corporal Crully and the rest of the brigade.

'I'd keep that helmet on, if I were you!' Crully said to him. Then he rubbed his hands together. 'Righto, men! We've got work to do!'

The next day, Lambholder was in Captain Dar's office again.

Captain Dar's eyebrows were singed and the tip of one ear had turned to silver, but apart from that he seemed unaffected by his ordeal.

The only significant change that Lambholder had noticed was that the wastepaper basket was full of bottles. Most of them weren't empty.

Captain Dar speared Lambholder with a look. 'So, you still want to be part of the Waste Brigade?'

From outside came the sounds of the brigade at work – whooping and calling as they rounded up lively sproutings from the magical fallout, swearing as stuff proved harder to scrape into a crucible than it looked, spitting and then cursing as they realised for the thousandth time that spitting inside a helmet wasn't a good idea.

'Yes sir. More than anything.' Lambholder felt a twinge at thus declaring his future and leaving his ma and ten aunts to run the farm all by themselves. They'd been brave when he'd set off, but he knew that things were going to be hard for them without him.

'I see.'

Captain Dar sat back in his chair. He eyed the calendar for a moment, then turned away from it. 'Tough job, the Waste Brigade.'

'Believe me, sir, I understand that.'

Captain Dar snorted. 'I'd say you would. Not your ordinary day, yesterday. You picked a good one as your first.' He drummed his fingers on the table. 'Well, I'm actually glad you've decided to stay. We're one short since Tremen disappeared.'

'No sign of him, sir?'

'Nor his friend. Don't worry, we'll catch up with them.'

A knock came at the door. 'Yes?' Dar called.

The door swung open and the novice wizard appeared. He was pale, his eyes had dark circles underneath, and his beard was matted and straggly. All in all, he looked much better than yesterday.

'Never again,' he said clearly.

Captain Dar glanced at Lambholder. 'Take him back to the infirmary. He's still not well.'

The wizard sniffed and drew himself up. 'I'm perfectly fine, thank you. I was just telling you that I was never going to touch magic again.'

'Wise decision,' Captain Dar said. 'Looking for some other trade, then?'

'Indeed. Something as far away from magic as I can get.'

Lambholder brightened. 'How do you feel about farming?'

Afterword

•

John Foyster

'The market – oh God, how I hate that word.'

'The market', of course, is for us a market for some sort of writing. When we think about this past decade, we might also think back to a different decade: a decade at the end, not of the twentieth century, but of the nineteenth century.

At the end of that decade, we can find a remarkable work of fiction which has had substantial impact on writing in the twentieth century. And this is, of course, *The Time Machine* (1895). H. G. Wells' novel was impressive for many readers, and not just any reader: for example, Henry James, when *The Time Machine* was published, was immediately impressed by that work, and indicated that he would himself hope at some stage to imitate H. G. Wells' *The Time Machine*. Eventually, in about 1912, he did begin working on what was to have been a novel about time travel. Unfortunately, he wasn't able to finish that novel.

But there were at around that time many other works of a similar nature. For example, only a few years after *The Time Machine* was published, there was another work, in 1903, by Harriet Prescott Spofford: *The Ray of Displacement*, about another sort of travel. This was about developing a Y-ray that increased the space between matter so that solid bodies could pass through one another. Of course, something like that had to be included in *The Time Machine* if you were to travel through time to the future or the past.

So the thought of writing that kind of fiction was popular in those years amongst many writers and, one assumes, therefore, also very popular with many readers. But it wasn't just fiction that was like that. Physics, at this time, was also particularly concerned about time and space. Although we identify Albert Einstein as someone who worked out how to connect time and space in physics, we could go back much earlier. For example, in music, over twenty years earlier, in the early 1880s Richard Wagner was composing *Parsifal* (1882). Here, Wagner's mythological libretto indicates his interest in the connection between time and space, which was very important to him.

If you go forward instead of backwards in time and identify a change, you find that in the first decade of the twentieth century the composer Gustav Mahler was dealing with compositions handling time in a fundamentally very similar and 'old-fashioned' way. Then, from the teens of the twentieth century onward, you find Arnold Schoenberg and many other composers getting on to more complex time structures. So, around the transition from the nineteenth to the twentieth century, there was a lot of interest in the way in which time and space are linked in music. And, of course, if you look at art works, again from about 1912 onwards, through Marinetti and the Futurists, in paintings and sculpture, you can see a change in the way of thinking. If you want a representative work, Marcel Duchamp's *The Bride Stripped Bare by Her Bachelors, Even* is a good example of somebody trying to do in art what was done by Wells or Spofford a little bit earlier, with respect to time and how it should be managed.

To take another example from writing, it is not hard to establish that Marcel Proust, in *In Search of Lost Time*, is largely concerned about the movement of time and how we recollect the past, how we anticipate the future, how all these are put together: how we handle these complex relationships between what we believe to be very fundamental aspects of our perception of the universe in which we live.

The key element of these works of fiction is that they try to explain to us how the world really exists. Wells in *The Time Machine* is trying to explain to us what the world is like in a universal sense. In that particular case, he goes and imagines the far past and the far future, but there is a continuum and that is, I suggest, the real world. When you come to a case like *Parsifal*, and music, perhaps it's not quite so true that we're talking about the real world. What Wagner is dealing with in the case of *Parsifal* is the Christian myth and the mythological notion of how time and space might be put together.

Interestingly enough, during the decade of the 1890s, William Morris was writing quite a few novels which were, in a sense, mythological. His approach was not to describe the world as it physically 'really' is, but rather to try to describe how the world might be. And he and a number of other writers at the same time tried to do exactly this. So one has writers such as Wells, Proust and a number of others trying to describe how the world really was, and occasionally having to deal with issues such as time, and then one also has other writers who thought it was useful to describe the world, not as it really was, but as it might be in some mythological sense.

An interesting development followed, from 1910 to the 1930s, when writers began to have the opportunity to demonstrate what they meant by the nature of the world. A very early example was Hugo Gernsback's *Ralph 124C 41+* (1911–12), in which Ralph, a future scientist, is able to describe to us what the world might be like in the future. Later, Gernsback realised that there was a substantial (though not a huge) market for this kind of description: that is, let us try to imagine what the world really might be, in more detail. Gernsback started to publish fiction of that kind, which eventually led to the first science fiction magazine in 1926. But, before that, other writers were able to enjoy approval by writing more stories of a mythological kind, so that *Weird Tales* began to be published from 1923 onwards.

But there was something different about the fiction that was published in these two magazines. It might have been about the old mythology. It might have been about the future. But, rather than being novels, this fiction was, to a substantial extent, short stories. From 1923, with *Weird Tales*, and 1926, with *Amazing Stories*, the magazine publishers gave writers an opportunity to publish short stories about ideas, not about people, and therefore they could use substantially different approaches to what they were wanting to examine.

Earlier, there had already been short stories and novels that we now might call 'science fiction' and 'fantasy'. The new magazines from the 1920s dealt basically in short stories. One other change also needs to be noted. By the time we come to the end of the twentieth century, when we consider the kind of fiction that we could describe as a genre, we have fiction which is set in the future or the past or an alternative past, and we have mythological fiction, but we also have examples of short fictions which don't require the world that the writer has invented to be completely described. This is a kind of fiction that many people write. In fact, it is sometimes identified as being a fiction for a particular market.

'The market – oh God, how I hate that word.' That sentence appears in Tony Ramsay's twenty-first-century radio adaptation of a novel written by George Gissing in 1891: *New Grub Street*. One consequence of the existence of a market for science fiction, or for fantasy, or for mythological fiction, is that works are published not because they have an idea or a structure that the author wants but, rather, because the author has had to contribute to a market that a publisher or an editor really wants. So it is important not to get confused between the kind of fiction that writers develop according to their own belief in what they need to express, and the kind of fiction that Gissing's character Edwin Reardon remarks upon: 'The market – oh God, how I hate that word.' Alternatively, Gissing also give us an account of marketable skills, and let's hope that writers in these stories do not match Gissing's character Jasper Milvain: 'My talent flourishes at 500 words' – their talent flourishes at a greater length.

Contributors

•

Carmel Bird was born in Swan Hill, but is more easily recognised as a Melbourne-based contemporary fiction writer whose stories are frequently found in literary journals. However, she often pushes the envelope into science fiction, fantasy and horror, where some of her most intriguing work can be found. Bird also conducts workshops and masterclasses in writing, and is one of those rare few who can support herself from her literary output.

Russell Blackford is a Melbourne-based author, editor and critic. 'The Sword of God' won Best Fantasy Short Story in the 1996 Aurealis Awards, and several other stories, most notably 'Lucent Carbon', have been short-listed in the SF and Fantasy Divisions in other years. While Russell's fiction is usually published within Australia, his critical essays appear internationally, particularly in the *New York Review of Science Fiction*. His background in the Law has given rise to a number of articles on industrial relations and constitutional theory, and he has co-authored a critical history of Australian science fiction with Van Ikin and Sean McMullen.

Damien Broderick is a Melbourne-based author, editor and critic, widely regarded as the grand old man of Australian genre fiction. He has had a major impact as an Australian SF writer since 1964, and is undoubtedly the country's leading theorist of the genre. He has three times won Aurealis Awards for his fiction – both at short story and novel length. His non-fiction books rank with those of Paul Davies in their breadth and under-standing of their subject matter, and his critical essays can often be found in the *New York Review of Science Fiction*. Broderick is also the science book reviewer for the *Australian* newspaper.

Edward Burger is a Melbourne-based writer of short stories, experimental prose, poetry, performance scripts, and a novel. He has been published in numerous literary journals and on CD, and has appeared on radio and TV. He frequently performs his work at spoken word events around Melbourne, and in 1999 he was winner of the Melbourne Fringe Festival Spoken-Word Award. Whilst only some of his work falls into the fantasy/sci-fi genre, much of it is fantastical, bizarre or surreal. Burger is inspired by the absurdity, diversity and complexity of life. His work is intended to be a tribute to the boundlessness of the imagination and the freedom this inspires.

Trudi Canavan lives in Melbourne, where she runs an illustration and graphic design business called The Telltale Art. In her spare time she is the designer and art editor for *Aurealis Magazine*, and has managed the Aurealis Online website. She has recently sold a fantasy trilogy to a leading local publisher.

Isobelle Carmody was born in northern Victoria, and raised in the Geelong area. She completed a BA majoring in Literature, before working in public relations and journalism. She became a full-time writer in 1988, and quickly became one of Australia's leading young adult writers. Her work often straddles the boundaries of science fiction, fantasy and horror. Carmody believes that the short story is the most perfect form of literature.

Terry Dowling is a Sydney-based and internationally acclaimed writer of science fiction, fantasy and horror: his stories often appear in US collections. He is the author of a number of books, including *Rynosseros, Blue Tyson, Twilight Beach* (in the *Rynosseros* cycle), *Wormwood, The Man Who Lost Red*, and two horror collections, *An Intimate Knowledge of the Night* and *Blackwater Days*. His fiction has won him numerous awards, including ten Ditmars, two Readercons, A Prix Wolkenstein – and two Aurealis Awards in the horror division. Dowling is also a reviewer for the *Australian* newspaper.

Leanne Frahm was born and raised in northern Queensland. She was notable in the early 1980s for being the most successful writer to come out of the workshops of the 1970s, building an international career with her short stories. In 1996, a limited-edition collection of some of her work, featuring a new SF novella, *Borderline*, appeared from MirrorDanse Books. *Borderline* went on to take out the Aurealis Award in the science fiction division

John Foyster died recently, struck down by an irreversible condition in that part of his being that had, until then, served him so well. John was best known for his awesome intellect, the speed by which he would read and absorb complex documents (he was a statistician by vocation) and his critical analysis of a wide range of literature, especially his favourite genre, science fiction. Personal integrity was his hallmark, and carried over into all aspects of his work and personal life. Thinking 'outside the square' was a constant in his life, and many of his colleagues found themselves swept along in his wake. Much of his work was located overseas, particularly in Malaysia and South Africa. On the negative side, he suffered from polio as a boy, and was revisited by consequences of the disease during the last decade of his life. He left the certainty of permanent employment and its superannuation benefits, and became an independent consultant. His registered company was called Foyster Fact and Fiction. With this, as with every other part of his life, he never looked back.

Alexander James was born and raised in Adelaide. He has a background in advertising, but more recently has pursued his creative side with work on various novels, feature films and television projects – including the revival of a classic BBC science fiction series. 'A Spell at the End of the World' is an introduction to the universe of Barker Moon (which includes a series of short stories, several novels and a television series . . . which, if all goes well, should present themselves some time this millennium).

Margo Lanagan was born in Newcastle, and is a writer, poet and editor. Her early novels are distinctly for young adults, but she has also written teen romance novels under various pseudonyms. Her latest collection, *White Time*, represents her best work to date, and the collection itself ranks with the finest of the past decade.

Rosaleen Love is a Melbourne-based writer of science fiction, contemporary fiction, and fantasy. She lectures at the Swinburne Institute of Technology in the history and philosophy of science. Love is strongly connected to the feminist movement, although her work is usually light-hearted and/or clever, with a touch of wry self-deprecation, rather than being politically confrontational. Unsurprisingly, given her leaning to mainstream, she began her writing career with a series of short stories in contemporary literary journals and by 1989 had published her first collection: *The Total Devotion Machine and Other Stories*, which she followed in 1993 with *Evolution Annie and Other Stories*. These latter stories best describe the niche Love has taken upon herself – a fashioner of scientific fables.

Ben Peek is a Sydney-based author. He is the creator of the Urban Sprawl Project, a pamphlet that mixed photography and prose about the Sydney suburbs. He co-wrote the short novel *The Enigma Variant* with Chris Mowbray, which was published by MirrorDanse Press. His short fiction and poetry have appeared in a number of magazines and anthologies around the world, and most recently he has appeared in the magazine *Voiceworks*, and the anthologies *Passing Strange*, edited by Bill Congreve, and *Agog! Fantastic Fiction*, edited by Cat Sparks. He has a bimonthly column on the website www.popmatters.com titled 'Sydney Before 2 am'. He is currently doing a PhD in fiction at the University of New South Wales.

Marianne de Pierres is a Brisbane-based author and co-founder of the Vision writers' group. She is published in children's and adult fiction and reviews books for the literary supplement of the *Courier Mail*. Her short fiction has appeared in *Eidolon*, *Agog!* and *Fables and Reflections*. She has also sold a three-book series, featuring her fatal femme, *Parrish Plessis*, to Orbit books in the United Kingdom.

Michael Pryor was born in Swan Hill, but was educated and grew up in Geelong. Pryor is a secondary school English teacher. He is best known as a children's writer, with his stories appearing in a variety of magazines. Most of his adult fiction has appeared in *Aurealis* magazine. He has also produced four novels in the young adult genre. At all levels, his work is witty and humorous, his story 'Waste' (which appears here) being typical of his approach.

Tim Richards was born, raised and is currently living in the small Victorian town of Hampton. Richards is an author with a propensity for abstract ideas, for the abstruse and the unusual. He is a self-professed 'obsessive-compulsive diarist' with an intriguing relationship with time and memory. More plainly, he is reguarded as a writer of contemporary fiction, with a strong leaning to fantasy. His latest novel, *The Prince*, has placed him firmly in the path of the critics. Many consider him persona non grata, but he is beginning to create a quiet cult following with his unusual bent towards philosophic irony and his affinity with the obscure nature of post-modernist writing.

Robert N. Stephenson is an Adelaide-based writer, editor and a literary agent. He divides his time between writing short fiction, his own occasional unpublished novels, and editing the works of other novelists who, like him, are trying to break into the mainstream book market. He has sold short stories to *Interzone, Aurealis, Nowa Fantastyka* and even had two appear in his own, short-lived magazine, *Altair.* The story in this anthology is his most rejected story and also the one he had the most belief in despite the opinions of others. In 2003 Robert will take up the tutoring position in creative writing at the Australian College of Journalism, where he hopes to share his experiences. With 40 stories now in print he feels the future may be just that bit brighter than the hard slog it took to get there. Persistence, he has found, is the key in the writing business.

Lucy Sussex was born in New Zealand, and moved to Australia at an early age. Her work ranges over science fiction and fantasy into her own form of surrealist mainstream, and often mixes all three areas with great success. Her short story, 'Merlusine', falls into this category and took out the Aurealis Awards Fantasy category in 1997, while being short-listed for science fiction at the same time. Sussex has co-edited three anthologies of mostly original stories, has published a mainstream children's book, *The Peace Garden,* and three fantasy novels, the best known of which are the young-adult novels *Deersnake* and *Black Ice.* Her short work is collected in the fine *My Lady Tongue And Other Tales.*

Also from Wakefield Press

All This is So
A future history

by John F. Roe

A girl stepped out on to the lane, a small figure carrying a bunch of flowers. As if the path were a stage, two men climbed out of the bushes. One pursued her and, as he caught her, flung her down and his boot slammed into her back and her head. Martin and Red ignored a lifetime of advice to stay out of the Daylight People's affairs and ran forward.

Orr has lost his memory and an eye. The land he finds himself in is a divided one. The twisters have been driven from the villages and the Matrix rule Westermain with a velvet glove. When Orr comes upon two soldiers attacking a young girl he is determined to exact revenge. Where he travels, who he meets and what he discovers in his quest will change this strange world forever.

In the world of *All This is So*, people fish, picnic, plant trees, pick flowers, watch plays, laugh at Punch and Judy, perform music and own dogs; they fall in love, fear death, cherish their children, make mistakes and commit crimes. So is it our world?

Not quite, or not quite yet. The air is pure, the seas are crystal, but the horses are dead. Our great aspiration is theirs but writ larger – freedom. They chafe at power, and know that the intoxication of controlling others' lives must always be subdued. To find the equation that balances power, freedom and responsibility is no easy task, but they try.

From beneath the story emerges the will to survive, seeking always and only the future. When Macbeth asks the witches whether the vision they have shown him is indeed the future they reply; 'All this is so.' He will not believe them – and then goes on to make that future.

For more information visit www.wakefieldpress.com.au

Wakefield Press is an independent publishing and
distribution company based in Adelaide, South Australia.
We love good stories and publish beautiful books.
To see our full range of titles, please visit our website at
www.wakefieldpress.com.au.

Wakefield Press thanks Fox Creek Wines
and Arts South Australia for their support.